The Vista

S. A. Hoag

The Vista: Book One of The Wildblood
Copyright © 2015, 2025 by S. A. Hoag
Wildblood Ventures Books

All rights reserved. No part of this publication may be reproduced, stored in a retrieval system or transmitted in any form or by any means electronic, mechanical, photocopying, recording or otherwise, without the prior written permission of the author. No part of this book may be used for the training of any artificial intelligence systems.

This is a work of fiction. Names, characters, businesses, places, events, locales, and incidents are either the products of the author's imagination or used in a fictitious manner. Any resemblance to actual persons, living or dead, or actual events is purely coincidental. Not everything depicted is accurate in the real world.

This is Revised from the original edition.
AI free zone. This book is 100% written by a human – me.
Cover designed by GetCovers.com
Formatting by Other Worlds Ink
ISBN: 978-1-966538-01-1

Contents

Chapter 1	1
Chapter 2	23
Chapter 3	38
Chapter 4	56
Chapter 5	69
Chapter 6	91
Chapter 7	103
Chapter 8	134
Chapter 9	150
Chapter 10	157
Chapter 11	173
Chapter 12	194
Chapter 13	208
Chapter 14	217
Chapter 15	226
Chapter 16	238
Chapter 17	251
Chapter 18	275
Chapter 19	284
Chapter 20	309
Chapter 21	317
Chapter 22	334
Chapter 23	356
Chapter 24	361
For More	369
Also by S. A. Hoag	373
About the Author	375

Reader Reviews of 'The Vista'

"First time reading this genre and a longer story than my recent reads. Having said that, I'm hooked."

"As a huge fan of the Fallout franchise and post-apocalyptic fiction and media in general, The Vista series feels like it has fallen from the sky into my grasp!"

"This is dystopian fiction at its best. Looking forward to the sequel."

"There are only a few books that make me want to immediately re-read the second I finish reading. This is one of those books."

"As a fan of post-apocalyptic fiction, I was curious to see what new ground this story would cover. Not disappointed! The post-nuclear world is a bit different from the stories Generation X was told."

To Jim, for putting up with it. <3

Chapter One

near The Vista April 11 4am

Cities were no place for people. World War Last, a generation earlier, had seen to that.

Shan didn't fear the dangers that lurked in the desolate landscape she watched over, but even in a world gone dark, it was too quiet. With a weather front approaching, she gave in to the uneasiness she felt and headed for home.

As she crossed the Continental Divide, sometime closer to daybreak than midnight, the sleet turned to snow, huge white flakes splattering on the windshield of her car, dotting the highway with icy spots. The radio crackled with static, but minutes later, two words came through clear in the noise.

Code Seven. An active aggressive incident, outside the outer perimeter. Away from The Vista, but close enough to cause concern. It was her job to stop problems before they got there. She shifted the car into overdrive and came down the mountain full tilt, pushing her luck on a road known to devour Scouts.

Then the outer marker went 'blip' as she passed. If there had been an alert, proximity warnings should have gone off in Dispatch, the stations, and her car. She stared at the radio for a moment, realizing what she had stumbled in to.

War games. The call-out wasn't real.

"Car Ten, this is a radio check. Alert status," she said on the air, dead calm. She'd been a Scout for three years. In the outlands, calm was a relative thing.

"Alert Six, Car Ten," Dispatch acknowledged. No alert. Things happened when she stayed on the far side of the divide for most of a day. This time, she missed war games. Too late to pretend she had known, Shan decided to try for a timed run, the reason everyone was out on the roads tonight. The adrenaline in her system wouldn't let her slow down anyway.

In the dark, a flicker of tail lights ahead warned her she wasn't alone. It would be someone aware of the situation. As Shan caught up to them, she recognized the car. Team One, a Guardian team from her station, rotated back to her schedule. Yesterday. They hadn't even been to a debriefing together yet. She flashed her high-beams at them to clear the lane. No response.

They were supposed to be in radio-silence too, but hell, no one bothered to tell her about the war games. "Move it over, Lt. Hunter," Shan warned on the air, annoyed at everyone from herself right up the chain-of-command. She shared some expletives with the junior officer, knowing who was driving by mere reputation. Rookie.

Team One did indeed move. Shannon passed them like they were parked, turning on her emergency lights to illuminate the rusted skeleton of a semi trailer not quite off the road. She drove past the wreckage a dozen times a week. Team One was likely unaware of it. Guardians tended to not pay attention to the maps Scouts detailed for them.

"She'll do what?" Hunter asked his partner, Dallas, amused at her tirade and understanding exactly what she meant.

"You heard her." Dallas knew better than to think it was funny. He knew Shannon.

"Fuck up my life forever," the younger man repeated, still grinning to himself. "Does she get that from Wade?"

"Cmdr. Wade rarely swears. She gets that from Maj. MacKenzie, and most everyone involved in Security." Dallas emphasized the rank of her Guardian team to make a point.

Hunter shrugged. He wasn't worried. Senior officers were an eccentric bunch and kept to themselves for the most part. It would be twenty minutes before they caught up with her, but only because she stopped.

Dallas saw Shan cutting through the crowd and knew better than to be in her line of fire. Hunter was about to learn that the hard way.

"Lieutenant." Her tone was ice cold, but her eyes smoldered with some wild emotion. She got right in front of him to make her complaint. "Who taught you to drive?"

"Dallas," he answered, hitching a thumb at his partner. Hunter, tall, blond, and lean, was well-aware the southern accent that never completely faded from his voice had an amazing effect on women.

Most women, anyway. "You didn't pay enough attention," Shannon told him point-blank.

Now he understood the stories he'd heard since joining Security. What they failed to mention, how easy on the eyes she was. The joke was on him. A rookie mistake, Dallas would say.

"Yes, ma'am," he answered, wondering what else he'd missed.

"When I tell you to move, lieutenant, you better be doing it so fast I don't get the sentence finished. Code Calls out here have a body count." Shannon had never been shy, and chewing up a rookie was nothing new. There was always a point.

He was out of his element. Scouts bumped rank on anyone under command status when they were beyond The Vista. Guardians protected populated areas and kept the peace. Scouts roamed the lands beyond the perimeters, as recon and first defense, the reason most of them went full-on military style.

She wore tactical gear, winter camos, a heavy scarf for head cover, a hunting knife on her belt, and was armed with two fair-sized handguns. Long dark hair, piercing eyes that looked gray in the false light of snow and headlights; in short, nothing like what he'd imagined.

"You weren't at the Station briefing, Captain. We didn't know you timed the run." Hunter had a legitimate excuse.

"Neither did I." She was still ready for a fight that wasn't there.

Dallas understood. "I'm serious, Capt. Allen, Shan," he said. "You should have warned Dispatch."

"Major Dallas," she acknowledged, rubbing her eyes, the adrenaline slowly burning off to fatigue. She'd been out on her regular run for most of three days. "I crossed the divide after the call-out went on the air. For the record."

"I didn't know."

"Neither did I," she repeated. It was over.

"Are we on report?" Dallas asked, hoping Hunter would have the good sense not to let his mouth talk them into any real trouble with her.

"For what?" she wondered out loud. "Being a rookie?"

"You never can tell." Dallas changed the subject. "Team Three missed the call-out, too." Her team, and she wasn't surprised.

"They're parked on the road." She turned to gaze into the dark as if she could see them. "They both drive like..." Shan glanced back at Hunter. "Well, like Guardians. Rookies. Civilians, sometimes."

Dallas damned sure would move, the first time she said it, out there on the interstate, in the dark, at seventy miles an hour. Not that Hunter blamed him, as tight teams were. Wade had developed an instant dislike of Hunter, and Wade was their Section Commander.

Shan became distracted by Maj. MacKenzie joining them from the tangle of cars on the blacktop. "When did you decide to join the party?" she asked, smug that she'd beat them.

"They stopped registering at twenty minutes," Mac pretended to whisper to her. The mud didn't bother him, neither did the snow or the cold. He'd dressed for the occasion in jeans and a flack jacket.

"So, when did you clock in?"

"Oh, about twenty-five minutes, I suppose," he grinned.

"You should have stayed home," Dallas and Shan said together. All three of them laughed, the issue of bad driving forgotten.

"That's what I said," Mac confirmed, offering her an arm and escorting Shan towards the hastily thrown together tents. The oldest of Team Three at almost twenty-four, four years older than Shan but only a couple months Wade's senior, Mac was tall and lanky. What most people didn't realize, he was solid muscle, strong, and fast.

"What was that?" Hunter asked Dallas as they made their way to the debriefing.

"She came in hot," Dallas said. It wouldn't be a big secret by daybreak. Stations were the best place to hear current gossip.

"You're kidding. Did she have her radio off?"

"Not likely. Other side of the pass. Sometimes Scouts wander through the cities, especially when the weather breaks. My advice is to steer clear of her for a few days, give her time to forget about it. It wasn't us that pissed her off to begin with."

"Forget? I doubt it. And thanks for spending the past year insinuating she wasn't anything to look at. Damn," Hunter shook his head.

"She won't hold a grudge. Shan's a good kid," Dallas told him. Out of necessity, close to twenty years earlier, founders of The Vista trained those once considered too young, to be protectors of the city. The first generation post-war were taking over those duties now, with Team Three being at the forefront of the movement.

Hunter watched her walking away.

"Do you want Team Three to catch you leering at her?"

"That's no kid," Hunter pointed out.

"All right, she's spoken for." Dallas made it easy for him.

He shrugged.

"Where you see one of them, the other two are close by. You should remember that."

"How did I miss her for the past year, then?" Hunter asked.

"Not by accident."

Wade had shown. Time for a lecture on what they'd done wrong, but he wouldn't miss what they'd done right, either. In Security, he was known to be difficult and hard to get next to.

"Half of you made the allotted time, half of you did not. We all did good, with this being the first live practice of the year. Expect it to happen again, soon. In the meantime..." he gestured. Rain, snow, and ice were falling out of the sky, a storm setting in to the valley. The weather was nothing unusual, but a concern with so many officers away from their regular posts. "If anyone wants to read the stats, they'll be posted at the station tomorrow. In case you missed it, there were two callouts in this drill, one a few minutes after the first. Fewer car wrecks than we anticipated also, so a good job there. As soon as Cmdr. Duncan is finished, all cars and all officers are on recall."

"Short rotation?" Shan asked, waiting for the rest of the speech they'd get again in a few hours.

"Sweeps start in weeks," Mac said. "Believe it or not. It's that time again, boys and girls." Every spring, Security sent teams out to survey areas beyond where they watched, in search of other people. This year would be no exception.

"Girls?" Shan was the only female currently on a team. Her mother never let her forget that point, especially when one of them landed in the Emergency Room. Dr. Deirdre Allen had higher ambitions for her only child.

Shannon wasn't interested in whatever those aspirations were.

"We've had three feet of snow in April. We should get this show on the road," Hunter said to no one in particular. All their vehicles were four-wheel drive capable. The weather brought them to a standstill inside The Vista frequently, despite that. Guardians relied on snow-cats, snowmobiles, and horses most of the year.

"Have they picked teams?" Dallas asked, glad Hunter had chosen some place to stand other than next to Shannon. Of course, that would've put him close to Wade or MacKenzie.

"Too soon," Mac said. "Command waits until the last minute for details." The past three years with Shan as Team Three's Scout, they drew two Sweeps runs. They'd lost the chance last year, with both men on medical waivers. Shan had opted out rather than go with a different team.

"You haven't stayed at home in weeks," Wade said as several other officers joined the growing crowd. He glanced at Hunter.

"Someone has tattled on me," Shan said. At nineteen, she expected a certain amount of freedom. Now and then, it happened.

"Make a point, especially with Sweeps so close," Wade said. Their yearly trek outside the confines of the valley was more than a little strenuous for their families, not to mention the wear and tear on the teams.

Noel and Taylor, both Scouts, joined the conversation. "Short rotation is a miserable job," Taylor said, having enough time on the job to know it for a fact.

"Most ranking Scouts are doing two runs a week anyway," Mac said, adjusting his sidearm and messing Shan's pony-tailed hair. She slapped his hand away, feigning annoyance. "Short rotation cuts you back to one so you can rest up for Sweeps." He grinned at that, the perfect amount of sarcasm for the middle of the night in the middle of a Montana blizzard.

"Teams get reservists, rookies, and screwed up rotations," Noel added. "It's all fun and games until someone rolls a car."

"Too bad senior teams don't decide who goes," Dallas said.

"That would include Team Three," Shan pointed out.

"No, not years in Security," Taylor said. "Just years." He laughed. So did most of them. He was three days younger than her.

"Was that aimed at us?" Hunter asked Dallas. Being the rookie, he took everything personal.

"Don't worry about it," Dallas told him. "They're just blowing off steam." He'd made it to fifty-something while Hunter was pushing thirty. It didn't bother him that a bunch of younger officers outranked him, either. They had trained for it all their lives.

"Who do you have to bribe?" Hunter asked, to stir things up.

"His father," Taylor said, nodding to Wade.

"Ouch," Noel grimaced.

"Step-father, and that's not funny," Wade said. Richard Cameron wasn't popular in Security circles. As a Council Member, they only dealt with him when they had no other choice. The rift between the two governing bodies, Security and Council, was clear.

"Capt. Allen," Cmdr. Duncan called from the front of the tent. "Car Eight is down. When you head for home, I need you for transport back to The Vista."

"Not a problem."

"Taylor's with Wade, I'm with you," Mac volunteered. "We should get a game started soon."

"Baseball or hockey?" Taylor asked.

"Yeah," Mac said. "One of those."

"I suppose it depends on how cold it is."

"Listen up so we can do this and go home," Cmdr. Duncan said, loud enough for everyone to hear. He called out the lead teams who made the predetermined times, letting them discuss it for a few moments. "Again, good job. We have some Guardians making progress. Thank our Scouts for that. They're giving up their free days to ride around and show you the finer points of driving in the conditions we get."

"Car Ten?" Hunter asked Dallas, hearing it listed as having made the allotted time. He knew it was her car. He'd made comment as she passed them, about the smiley face drawn in the 'o' of the '10' stenciled on the rear quarter panel.

"It's her job. Scouts spend more time out here than in The Vista," Dallas said. He'd tried the position. It wasn't for him, even a decade ago.

Wade took over again. "Mechanical failure is still our biggest problem." Someone made a snide comment to Taylor, and a murmur of laughter passed through the crowd. He'd made good time on both runs, and broke his steering column while moving off the road.

"What we need to concentrate on for the next few months is keeping the outer perimeter patrolled and the inner perimeter clear. We have a couple of trouble spots that persist year after year." Wade paced as he talked. It wasn't a nervous habit. He bordered on hyperactive.

"The Junction, Highways 141 and 12, is less than twenty miles from The Vista, the closest point on the inner perimeter. That's mere minutes for those of us that don't drive so much. Minutes from downtown." Wade let them think about it. "In the past three years, we've had eight call-outs. Everyone in Security is aware we've lost officers there, not including the Nomad attack in September of '54. That's a lecture for another day."

Duncan spoke up. "We've activated motion detectors along those roads to cover times when personnel can't. They aren't as reliable as we'd like. Keep that in mind when you get the assignment. Trust your instincts."

"In the summer, at least two officers will drive The Junction every day," Wade told them. "Same thing for our hot spot in Butte, all season long." Tall, with dark hair, brilliant blue eyes and a well-maintained physique, Wade had a reputation for pursuing many females of no particular type. He hadn't settled in with any one companion and his personal life made for a lot of gossip at the stations. Monogamy was the standard, not the rule, in The Vista, although the survivors of the war were far more prone to it than their children. The post-war generation abandoned many traditions started by a dead civilization.

"Recall at dawn to Station Two for new assignments," Duncan announced, signaling the end of the debriefing. "Scouts are free to go. The rest of you wait for daylight."

"Watch your backs," Wade said. "Capt. Allen, help me clear Car Eight so we can head for home," he motioned to her.

"I'll wait," Mac said. He'd been out all night, and wasn't as nocturnal as his partners.

"You came in hot from Butte on that second call-out," Wade started the conversation. He took the driver's seat and began logging inventory on a clipboard. That was about as high tech as it got in The Vista.

"I didn't realize it was the second alert, either." Shan shook her head, still annoyed she hadn't known. She should have. Wade didn't have to say so.

"Why do you do that to yourself?" Mac asked, knowing she didn't like this city, or any city.

"I learn more wandering the streets there than I ever will here, while we're sitting, waiting for nothing to happen."

Ghosts. Not those in the paranormal stories they heard as kids, but the kind they knew.

"You look tired," Wade said.

"Yeah. I was heading in for the end of the run. I'd be curled up in my bed at Station Two if I had sense enough to figure it out." She leaned forward, digging loose shotgun shells from under the seat.

"Go to my place and get some rest before you see your parents. Deirdre would take great joy in slapping a medical on us again this year." Station Two was a madhouse before Sweeps. Her room was likely being used by rookies, or worse, trainees that didn't know better than to not touch her few belongings. Wade's home was one of the larger ones in The Vista, with several living areas, fortified, hidden, on the outskirts of the city. Private.

"I won't find any of your girlfriends waiting?"

"You might. Throw them out."

"Them?"

"Her, them, whatever," Wade grinned, knowing Shan was aware of what was mere rumor.

Shan shook her head. "Not a problem." She didn't get along with either of his current companions.

"Don't let Mac keep you awake."

"He'll be out before I get a mile down the road."

"No, I mean later. Don't let him keep you awake," he repeated slower.

"Stop worrying," Shan told him.

"Shouldn't I?"

"Not so much as you'd imagine. Rumors of our sex life are exaggerated, and I'm the careful one."

"Let him drive in," Wade suggested, not wanting to get into that discussion. He had no place to lecture her, but his concerns were valid.

"With ice falling out of the sky? No, not happening. We'll be lucky to get everyone in without a wreck as it is."

"Good point. Your mother, she's still trying to talk you out of Security." It wasn't a question, or a subtle change-of-subject.

"Of course."

"What do you tell her?"

"Nothing. Why do you think I haven't stayed at home in so long? All we do is fight, and she's right and I'm stupid." Shan took a breath.

"It's good that you recognize she's right and you're stupid," he said, keeping a straight face, knowing Deirdre never called her stupid. He'd seen their arguments. It wasn't as bad as Shan imagined, but then, the issues with his step-father were comparable. "You've had the job five years. Sooner or later, she'll see how futile it is."

"It's like they don't know us. How did we all grow up in the same house and no one knew?"

If Mac was still awake in the backseat, he was pretending to be asleep to keep out of the conversation.

"Do you really think that's true?"

"None of the adults ever said a thing. We were different, even then. Nine or ten parents, always close, and we were pretty obvious."

"I was, and showed you how to disguise the little things that stood out. They were dealing with trying to keep us alive, and keep The Vista hidden."

"Yeah," Shan said, unconvinced it was that simple.

"If you want to talk about it, we'll have time later. What did you see today that brought this on?"

"Nothing in particular. There's a lot of time to think, and some things make no sense."

"Uh-huh. We'll talk tonight."

Shan nodded. "Clear. I'm sorry. It's because I'm sleep-deprived."

He leaned over and kissed her on the forehead. They were far closer to being siblings than anything else. "Sure. Get some rest. That's an order."

"Of course it is. Watch your back."

"Always. It's going to be a long season," Wade said.

She believed him.

Downtown–a city renamed and rebuilt, it held little semblance to the place it used to be. Station Two was one of the tallest buildings in The Vista, with three stories above ground and two sub-basements. The lowest level, Evac Center One; the next Depot One, where work on Security vehicles took place. Ground floor held Dispatch, a small cafeteria, several offices, and emergency stockpiles including a vaulted armory. The second floor was officer quarters and large dayroom, the third floor various work spaces, plus more storage.

Connected by a concrete tunnel that ran under the parking lot, an odd, bricked-in building sat behind the station. A jail, a place no one wanted, but it was there, the tunnel its single access point. The Vista housed a few permanent prisoners. They sentenced repeat offenders more often than not to exile. Harsher rulings existed.

East of the station, City Hall, an impressive two story library that housed the information left by the twentieth century. Books, many books, and other formats; computer drives, DVDs, microfiche, film, even newspapers, magazines, and audiotapes. Adults reliving the past frequented it as much as their children trying to understand their history. Upstairs housed the Council Chambers and a trio of courtrooms.

Like most of the city, a natural gas run steam plant provided electricity downtown, with solar and wind turbine backups across the valley. Many areas had separate sources. The city powered down at dusk, leaving on only the essentials. In the beginning, to hide from marauders and conserve precious fuel. They'd kept the practice.

Security drove in from the south, parking in front of the station. Early in the day, a swarm of older students emerged from the Secondary School Annex moments after the sound of engines filled the morning air. Half of them expected to train for Security. A handful would last their first season beyond Dispatch. The cars fascinated them. Security, the Caravans and emergency vehicles were the only ones used in The Vista; Security provided a shuttle service in town when the need arose. Parts were too difficult to manufacture for everyone to have a car. Fuel was sparse, even with most vehicles adapted to use methane and solar power.

"Power's out in the 'D' Section," Wade told Shan over a handset. That meant the hospital. Her mother was on-duty there because of it, being Chief of Staff.

"The whole thing?"

"Just downtown. Is Mac asleep?"

"Put him in the back seat and he sleeps like a baby."

"You've never been around an irritable baby," Wade told her. He had two of his own and considered himself lucky they lived with their respective mothers. No doubt he loved them, but he didn't have a clue about their upkeep. Bryan was almost four, and Jessie sixteen months, but when they demanded attention, there was no ignoring it.

"Ah, that's a negative unless we count yours." Shan grinned, knowing Taylor's wife was expecting their first. He'd heard quite a few stories from other officers at the stations, and he hadn't run away yet. "I'm out, Cmdr. Wade."

"Home?" Mac asked from the backseat as they rolled to a stop.

"Downtown for a few," Shan told him. She stood and stretched, yawning. As an afterthought, she put a blue tag under her windshield wiper. The mechanics would haul it to the shop, and with any luck, she'd have it back by her next run.

"What's on the schedule?"

"Breakfast?"

"No, thanks." Mac came around and leaned against the car, trying to wake up.

"Let's get another car and get gone before they put us to work. I can have a shower at Wade's and catch some sleep. So can you."

"Outstanding," Mac winked at her.

"Sleep," she repeated.

"What's wrong with your car?" Michael Allen asked as he crossed the street to greet his daughter. Shannon got her eyes from him, green, animated. He wasn't yet forty, an electrical engineer, and founding member of The Vista. He'd been her age when civilization ended itself.

"I have a list," Shan said, throwing her arms around him for a brief hug. "The exhaust is rattling like it's ready to fall off and it starts hard. New spark plugs, maybe."

"I believe you," Michael said, shaking Mac's hand. "How are things at the Ranches?" Mac's father supervised several ranches at the southern end of the valley while helping rebuild the electrical grid in that area.

"Pretty quiet right now." The twins, his fifteen-year-old siblings, had been working there, but it looked like Colin would make the move to Security in the autumn. Mac wasn't certain how he felt about that. Carri loved working with animals and wanted to stay on.

"Can I borrow my daughter for a minute?" Michael excused himself.

"Always," Mac pointed, indicating he was headed for the station.

"What's going on?" Shan asked. A group of teenagers had gathered to look at the cars, the reason Security parked them out front.

"You're taking a new group out soon?"

"In the next couple of days, we'll put the rookies on the road."

Winter left Guardians on call and short patrols, Scouts working Dispatch and rotation with their team. Springtime brought a crazy rush of activity, with increased movement from Nomads, and the looming Sweeps. Scavengers were another problem.

"This is a great bunch of kids," Michael told her. Many adults in The Vista tried to pass on what they had learned to survive. Besides regular classes, Michael taught winter and wilderness survival. He'd learned them firsthand. The weather was colder and harsher than before. Nuclear Winter might have been an unproven theory, but the weather was skewed. Someone, and a short time later several some-ones, two decades earlier, had opted to use nuclear weapons to make their point.

"Mac thinks Colin is going to move to Security. He's not overjoyed," Shan said.

"Colin's sharp, they all are."

"But what?"

"They're kids," he said. "If they haven't seen it, it didn't happen. They can't know what we went through to get here, no matter how many stories we tell. You barely remember the bomb on the Missouri Breaks. How could they?"

A lie she told, and hated. Most of the rookies he was talking about were older than her.

"They don't remember what it was like," he repeated.

"You think they aren't taking their training serious?"

"They're serious, they just..." Even after all this time, he couldn't think of the war and put it to words. He shook his head. "You have initiations. Show them, scare them."

A few weeks in Security would start weeding out the ones that weren't serious. "We can do that. Did you have something specific in mind?" She wouldn't discuss initiations with him. Although some of them were for fun, some were dangerous.

"Show them the helicopters."

"I don't know..." she started.

"Denial," Michael said, shaking his head.

"Not just a river in Egypt," Shan finished the saying for him. She'd admit to nothing, officially.

"The pair of military helicopters they brought down at Dillon. You remember the Blackout, when they kept you in quarantine at Station Three, so your mother didn't see you. When we buried six officers."

"I remember." She held up a hand, not wanting to hear more. The nightmares plagued her still. "Who tells you these things?"

"Annie Cameron." Wade's half-sister.

She'd have guessed as much. "The helicopters were near Sheridan. They still are. I was in quarantine for good reasons."

"You got shot," Michael stated.

"Please don't say that to anyone else."

"Meaning your mother?"

"Meaning Command could take it out on me if they heard rumors coming from civilians. Anyone, Dad, because there's no point in scaring people over something that happened three years ago. It was an isolated incident. And yeah, don't tell Deirdre. She wants me out of Security."

"I want you to do what you want," Michael told her.

"Even if it's so damned dangerous?" She instantly wished she hadn't cussed in front of him.

"Even then."

"The outlands aren't as bad as people claim."

"Does Security execute exiles that come back here?"

Shannon cringed. She'd only known of that happening once. "That's not my field, and if I knew about it, I couldn't tell you." Mac was about to rejoin them and she didn't need him hearing this.

"The point is, these kids have never seen someone die from radiation poisoning. They've never watched marauders burn the city. The Flu is only a tale that makes their parents have nightmares," Michael summed it up. "They need to know, before they go out there, what it could be like."

Shan agreed, "We can do something."

"What are we doing?" Mac asked.

"Teaching the rookies a rough lesson," Michael answered.

"We won't mention this to Deirdre." Shan was adamant.

"No," Michael agreed. "Take care of each other," he told Mac, going to rounding up his students.

"We will," Mac said. Then, "What was that?"

"He wants us to throw a scare into the rookies. Sounds like they are a bit too cocky."

"We should consult with Officers Lambert and Bennett on this," Mac decided, thinking of ideas for them.

"If we get in trouble, that makes you responsible," Shan pointed out.

"There won't be any trouble. It's training."

"No trouble," Shan repeated. "I've heard that before."

Team Three gathered in the tiny park behind City Hall as they went off duty, a routine for them during the slow season. Wade wondered who might show up later. He'd spent the afternoon in a grueling Council meeting. Due back at Station One by daybreak, he figured it was the penance he paid for getting put in charge. Being hours past dark, at the moment, they had nowhere else to be.

It surprised Shan to find Wade alone. Their nights on call included Wade and his current woman, Mac, Taylor, Lambert, their girlfriends, and whoever else from the 'Conda that had free time. Team Two, Ballentyne and Green, were conspicuously absent. Sometimes there were a dozen people or more. Tonight, it was Team Three. She suspected it was by design. They sat on the picnic table, enjoying the break.

"They were testing us," Wade finally said. The first thing brought up in Council was to offer him the next open position. If he accepted, it would mean his resignation from Security.

They wanted Mac in charge of the new outpost. After Sweeps

mapped a suitable location, with Command approval, of course. Now he was having a beer, his third of the night, thinking about that. They had no say over the outpost. Pretending they did pissed him off.

Shannon walked out of the meeting before they could make her an offer. "I failed then, because they weren't even subtle," she said. As an afterthought, she reached over and snatched the bottle of Mac's beer, chugging it. "You're done for tonight," she told him.

"So are you," Wade said. "We're on call. I might need you to drive later." He had declined Council's offers for the entire team, telling Council Chair Haines they would stay together until they decided otherwise or Command made it an order. Haines had nothing to say on the matter, being a Security matter.

"What do we do?" she asked.

"Nothing. They didn't expect any of us to take the offers."

Mac shrugged. "Why even bother?"

"To see how serious we are about the outpost, about staying together as a team." Wade said. "I guess they have their answer. It's putting the idea out there for us. If we get into a disagreement, they hope we'll remember this and consider changing the team."

"They won't screw with Command, they just won't," Mac decided, still fuming.

"No," Wade agreed, "They don't have any authority to." He'd formed the 'Conda, the Anaconda Central Security Corps, named for Station One, as a backup to regular Security. Everyone in The Vista had at least an idea what their true purpose was. Most of them were wrong. "You should remember, these are our friends and family. When they do something, anything, they're doing it to protect us. Like they always have and like we're trying to do for them."

"We're adults now," Shan said.

"Not to them," Wade disagreed. "We have reasons to stay together. Reasons far and away beyond Security, but it's the excuse we use. We can't tell them why we distance ourselves from people. It would be counterproductive to everything we do."

She sighed, nodding.

"I don't want to involve the 'Conda in this bickering with Council," he said. "None of us need the distraction." The group had a dual purpose, and only one involved Team Three. The other was for the safety of all.

Mac agreed. "With Sweeps, we push for the Cody base. They've kept us isolated here too long."

"Cody is the most compatible we've found?" Shan asked. She hadn't gone with them on Sweeps four years earlier. She'd been a rookie working in Dispatch.

"The inhabitants fortified and isolated the city," Wade said. He didn't have to mention it hadn't helped them. Cody had no human population when they made the cursory survey. "It's got the best potential of any place we've seen. The others are too small, too big, flooded or burned. Cities attract Scavengers. Too small or damaged, and we'd need a lot of construction for a working base."

"Then it's Cody." Shan trusted his judgment. "Are we going to rename it?"

Wade smiled to himself. Their parents renamed everything right after the war. He figured it made it easier for them to cope.

"We want Council to think it's their idea," Mac said.

"It's Command's idea," Wade said. "And Council will be thrilled to agree with them. They'll both believe they got what they wanted, and they'll both be right."

"All this time, we keep pretending," Shan said. The three had shared a mild psychic link from the time they were small. The occurrences were usually confined to their sleep, but could happen any time. At least with Wade and Shan. Mac had difficulties. Other shared abilities were more complicated. They had no answers, only conjecture, and their parents seemed oblivious.

"You'll give yourself a headache," Wade warned, knowing she was trying to find some sort of reason to what they were. He'd taken to calling it Gen En, genetically enhanced, from the information he found in pre-war media stored in The Vista's extensive library system. It seemed to him the files had been censored. What little he discovered made him cautious about telling others. A great deal of controversy surrounded the possibility of humans carrying engineered genetics.

"Yeah. Already there."

"So we do nothing," Mac said.

"For now, we keep Council happy and let Command tell us what to do. When Sweeps finishes, we have a draft in order and submit it to them. We insist, we persist." Wade always had plans, and more plans, hating the idea of leaving anything to chance.

"What if they still say no?" Mac asked. "Like the past nine years." He wasn't exaggerating. The base hadn't been their idea.

"We aren't prisoners here," Shan said. "We get people from the 'Conda and go to Cody."

"You don't think they'd try to stop us?" Mac asked the obvious. As much as Shannon and Wade could finish each other's ideas, he was on the outside. Wade knew things, Shan knew things, and Mac had to figure it out for himself. It didn't bother him, because he was far from clueless, having a different viewpoint. There were times he felt guilty over letting them assume he didn't understand.

"Sure they would. They'd use our jobs, and friends, our families to make us stay," Wade said. "For now, we will."

"We'll have the outpost," Shan added. "Sooner now, because later isn't an option. We aren't children. It's time."

"Two years max," Wade said. "We take who we can and what we can. As much as they'll threaten and complain, they won't let us go empty-handed."

"With reservists ready to move in to our positions," Mac said. "Like we do now. We keep the numbers up for a reason. Don't think Council hasn't noticed the upswing in the number of new recruits."

"Command agrees with the 'Conda on that subject," Shan said. While Wade had them as his backup, Mac had a specialized group of civilians at his disposal. Their positions were all organized with a purpose. She worked with Command. All were coordinated with their objectives in mind.

"You're right. It's time." After a few moments, Wade asked her, "Did you get near Portland?" He'd been born there and had vague memories of a city teeming with so many people. He knew Scouts were making trips authorized by Command but kept from Council.

"No." Shan was quick to answer, then had to amend it. "In the area south, not the city. I didn't get close," she skipped details.

"Why?"

"I didn't think it was safe."

"Specify?" Wade persisted.

Shan looked to Mac for some sort of support.

"So why didn't you go in?" Mac asked, being no help at all. "We hear about how you love driving the big cities."

"Nomads, Scavengers, giant cockroaches, zombies, tidal wave, radiation, rogue comet." Wade made her a list to pick from.

"Helluva list there," Mac pointed out.

"Radiation," she answered. "Higher than I wanted to deal with. The place was enormous, a lot larger than Butte."

"Was the radiation higher or lower than out by the Missouri Breaks?"

"Higher."

"I'm glad you stayed away. Good call." No emotion.

"I'm sorry," she said.

"You didn't drop the warheads." Wade put an end to the conversation. His biological father had died trying to get them out of the city.

They fell silent, Shan wondering why he asked.

"The Council, our parents, everyone that lived through it, they want us to believe our lives are so much more dangerous now," Mac said. "It's a lie. We have different issues, not more. The world is different, we're different."

"Everyone is," Shan said. "The biggest problem we have is coping with our parents and the other survivors, because of their fears."

"Yes," Wade said. "If our parents know nothing about us, it's because everything fell apart and they tried to put it back together.

Of course children were different than before. It was more obvious in a few of us. That's all they might see. But this is the world we know. It's not their world, not anymore. We've taken on the duty of protecting them, and that's what we're going to do."

"What do we do now?" Mac asked, putting an arm around his shivering partner. The female one. "As in tonight."

"Go to the station and find a nice warm bed," Shan suggested.

"This is a bust," Wade said.

"Too cold to party," Mac agreed. "Or anything else."

"Cody is cold," Wade reminded them.

"Plan B for next week, if the weather is still like this," Mac said. "Let's get to Space 123 and at least make it an evening out."

"Sounds good," Shan said. They hadn't been to the club to relax in a month.

"It's a date," Wade told them. "I'll have Taylor tell the 'Conda. Remember to reserve it for us. It's the last chance we'll get before Sweeps. Last chance before we have a foot of snow on the ground."

"Springtime in the Rockies," she recited an old saying.

"And it's forty below," Mac finished. It wasn't a joke anymore.

Chapter Two

April 14 9am

Wade drove the Junction run, with Mac riding shotgun. They didn't bother leaving Station Two until full daylight, appropriating Car Ten first and deeming it clean. Their own car, caught in an ambush during the Blackout, stayed parked. Not that Security was superstitious. They were, everyone knew they were. No officer would take a car involved in a previous attack out for The Junction or Butte runs. Bad karma. If someone died in a car, they scrapped it.

"Too early for this," he said, being a man of few words. "Or too late."

Mac glanced up from the book he'd been reading to see what was so fascinating outside, doing a double-take. "Dispatch," he called in to relay the news.

"Central Dispatch, Team Three. Go ahead." Shan worked well there, good at handling orders, calm, efficient. It was her first job during training and she preferred it in the winter to being stuck out at Station Three for weeks at a time. Besides that, she didn't have a car and wanted to keep track of them herself.

"Trace snow falling six miles east," Mac told her. They could have snow, a lot of snow, any month of the year. April held no surprises, but with Sweeps on the calendar, everyone held their collective breath for a heartbeat. Planning was not only time-consuming, it caused more friction between Council and Security and there was enough of that already.

"Noted. When it's sticking to the ground, tell me."

"How are you this morning, Captain?" Wade asked her. "Who's working with you?"

"I'm outstanding, and Cmdr. Niles is here running the show. Noel is observing."

"Just Niles," he corrected. "I'm retired now." He'd survived seventeen years in Security, from its inception, in the first years when they were far less organized and far more vulnerable.

"If anything is out of place," Shan went on. "Don't stop to wonder why." Rolling hills and a variety of abandoned buildings, too many perfect places for an ambush, surrounded the Junction. "Call it out and come home."

"Subtle," Wade said, not to her.

"We'll be home by noon," Mac replied, checking the shotgun. Loaded and secured. If Shan had a specific concern, they'd be aware by now. "Council meeting again next week?"

"Tuesday. We're putting pressure on for the outpost. It's not up to them, but we need those civilian contractors. Go if you can. Taylor will, and Shan is going to watch from the sidelines and see who jumps."

"Picking a fight with Council is one thing, but Haines isn't someone we want to make an enemy of."

"Haines isn't the problem," Wade said. "If he approves anything, Council tables it. Three people disagree, and that's what happens. So we're stuck in this vicious circle."

"What's next?"

"Make a protest about their inactivity. Threaten a recall, threaten a confidence vote." Wade was tired of playing their games.

"Is Cameron on that list?"

"If he wants to be," Sometimes his step-father voted for Security issues, sometimes he didn't, and it wasn't discussed outside the meetings. Lydia Cameron had made it clear she wouldn't tolerate such arguments in her home. "We have to show them the outpost is a good idea. Prove it on paper, make it obvious."

"It's obvious now. An outpost would add to their defenses, and maybe provide resources we don't have access to here. They aren't considering all the possibilities, they never do until something forces them to look at options. Remember the Blackout?" Mac had some ideas of his own.

"Don't keep all your eggs in one basket." Someone famous had said it first, a long time ago.

"Call a closed session. Pull the files on the Blackout and show them how the station at Anaconda cut our losses. It's pretty damned clear." Mac understood, a dangerous move, and one they needed approval to commit to.

"Pacifica will find out, and claim we're hiding more than helicopters." Wade envisioned that train wreck. They might not avoid this one. The group was well-organized, and as their name belied, dedicated to pacifism. They didn't approve of certain Security methods. Council Chambers provided a solid sounding board for their concerns.

"What's true is true. Does it matter what they think?"

"Now, yes, at least until we get approval. We don't give Pacifica an inch, or Council details of the Blackout. Command can figure that out later." Shan was working with them on several issues. She could handle another.

"We need to get a green light this year. Just once, it'd be nice for things to go easy."

"You don't have to convince me." Wade was familiar with their methods. A game, push and shove. Naturally, they wanted something in return.

"That's the plan," Mac said.

"Gotcha," Shan told them, a blip on a motion detector in Dispatch pinpointing their position. "Are you making the circle?"

"Yeah, get it over with." Wade wanted to be done. The roads, broken pavement in places, those places Scouts memorized and Guardians watched for on paper maps that weren't always accurate. He proceeded with caution.

"I've got nothing here. You should be clear," Shan confirmed. "If you stop lolly-gagging around out there, we can get a game in before the change of shift at Station One. Unless you bring snow back with you."

"Even with snow. Find us a team," Wade told her.

"Already have."

"That means Team One," Mac told Wade.

"Yeah, they switched off with Team Two a week ago. It makes it easier on Taylor, with his wife due pretty soon." Wade knew his teams, their families and their friends. The Vista had a little over four thousand people. It wasn't too difficult.

"That's going to be quite a change in the Taylor home," Mac said. Besides the twins, he had an eight-year-old sister. He knew all about having a baby in the house.

Wade didn't share a house with anyone. It was less complicated to have his own place. Despite all their precautions, he was aware his team's abilities likely weren't as secret as he wanted. A move to Cody might ease his concerns.

As an only child, Shannon had her parents to put blinders on. Them, and a full shift of officers she'd grown up around. "Tell me when you're headed back," she said on the air.

"We're turning around right now. Meet you in an hour," Wade said.

Shannon sat out of the game, waiting for shift replacements to show up from The Vista. They weren't late yet, but if it happened, they'd make it up sometime soon. It wasn't a good idea to get in debt to other officers, especially those on teams, payback being long hours in Dispatch or Station Three during the worst of winter.

Green, one of the Guardians on Team Two, was keeping her company. Noel joined them, bringing a portable radio from the com room.

"Let's go," she called, clapping. Taylor was at bat, with no one on base. They were losing to third shift by two runs at the bottom of the inning. They didn't keep track of innings much. When they got tired or there was a shift change, that signaled the end of the game. Springtime or not, it was cold. It made the game more interesting, with patches of snow and ice on the field.

Cassie Elliott pitched. At the station four days a week as a maintenance worker, she repaired things they broke, and cooked a late meal for second shift. She traveled with short-distance caravans in the summer as well. Most residents had a variety of duties. It kept the city running; no one was homeless, no one went hungry.

Taylor hit the edge of the ball, sending it high over third base. Cassie's brother Mitch backpedaled, catching it with little effort despite all the catcalls from first shift. Mitch was a Guardian, third year, so not a rookie anymore. He waved back at them.

Station One had been a ski resort, back when. Repurposed, it was fortified, complete with all the amenities plus a depot, stable, armory, and a supply cache for those weeks when the snow isolated them. A dozen new houses lined the hillside, running northwest towards the abandoned village, more like subterranean yurts than conventional pre-war homes. It was also the 'Conda base of operations, away from the prying eyes they couldn't avoid in The Vista.

"Well, that was pointless," Taylor summed up his turn at bat, taking a seat on the low stone wall next to Shan. She handed him his sidearm.

Hunter was up next. Dallas had gone off to re-supply their car, saying he was too old to be running circles in the mud. Hunter had taken that as a challenge.

"Could be worse," Shan told Taylor.

"How's that?" he wondered, taking a long drink from his canteen.

"Chris could've been pitching," Shan grinned. His younger brother often tagged along and was showing his own skills. He'd start training as a Scout when summer rolled around.

"He's taller than me now."

"When did that happen?"

Taylor shook his head. "Hell if I know, but it can't be good. Kids. They grow up way too fast."

Shan laughed with him. "Next game should be hockey."

"You can bat for me anytime," he volunteered. She played goalie when they switched off to hockey, street or ice, it didn't matter. For baseball, she was a standby.

"So you're aware, all Station One teams are going out on Sweeps this year."

"Did I miss something?" He'd grown up in the same house with her for almost a decade, right along with the Camerons and Mackenzies. For a time, before they began moving in to separate homes, there had been eleven kids in the house.

"The 'Conda wants the outpost, now. Security too. We're nagging them day and night." She wasn't joking. On her own, she'd spoken with a dozen Council members over the past week.

"So they, what? Punish us by sending us out across the dotted line?" Noel asked. The dotted lines being the old boundaries from old maps that meant nothing. He'd been a rookie Scout with Shan and they remained friends despite different affiliations.

"Not exactly. They'll ask for details. You remember how they are about details."

"Just like some other group?" Green added his comment. He meant the 'Conda.

"We need to get those details, even if we've done it before. We collect so much information on the cities we're looking at, they give us one just to clear the paperwork out of City Hall," she said.

Chapter Two

Taylor shook his head.

"Laugh now," Shan said. "This can work. If they make us wait another year," she shrugged, knowing Wade was out of patience. "We'll pack up and go when he gets the urge." She didn't have to say who she meant.

"He's said that," Taylor agreed with her. "Would you go?"

"Of course," she told him. Shan considered it. "Two years ago, the baby stopped him."

"Does he think Courtney got pregnant on purpose?"

"I do," Shan said. "Tia did the same thing. She thought she'd have Wade all tied up in a big red ribbon for herself because she had a baby. That didn't turn out quite like she planned, either. The reasons don't matter."

"Maybe not to you. What did Wade say?"

"He said he's done with excuses, done with the waiting. What are you planning for the summer?"

"If I told you, I'd have to kill you," Taylor laughed again. So did Green and Noel. A favorite pass time, old movies and video games, occupied a lot of hours when the weather turned. Shan rarely joined in, and didn't know what they were talking about.

Hunter was on third base now, within earshot of where they sat, so the conversation was over.

"Great. I'm going to catch a couple hours sleep," she stifled a yawn. "I have to be back at Station Two tomorrow at a reasonable hour."

"What's 'reasonable'?" Taylor asked.

"Damned if I know. Whenever Mac or Wade head in that direction. They keep stealing my car." She hopped down off the wall and meandered towards the station.

"So I should hide my keys?"

"You all better."

"They have the doors off the rooms on the third floor. You should grab one downstairs before the rest of the first shift gets them," Green warned. A Blackfoot, a Siksika, his home was the sovereign nation of The Ranchlands, north of The Vista.

"I already have one," she smiled. "An advantage of working the com room."

"You still sleep naked?" Green asked for the benefit of the rookie, putting on his best innocent face. Hunter on third and Reid at shortstop both lost their attention on whoever was at bat.

"Except during Sweeps." She didn't miss a beat.

"Are they kidding?" Hunter asked Reid.

"Oh, hell if I know." Reid didn't want to get involved. "Go ask someone on Team Three."

It always started the same. Shan could hear the helicopters, feel the beat of their blades against the frigid morning air, somewhere far in the distance. It only sounded like one, but she knew there were two. The UH-60s, Black Hawks, painted in winter camo. One was armed with a pair of M60 machine guns, the other carried missiles. Louder and faster than anything she'd ever seen, she wanted to hide, no clue where might be safe. She tried to call for help, but couldn't move. Where they came from, or who they were, she didn't know. After a few moments, she realized they weren't at Depot South. Security didn't get the chance to lure them away. She was in The Vista. The helicopters had found them.

Thrashing around, she sat up, going for her gun, holstered and hanging from the bedpost, and then stopped, awake, aware it was only a nightmare. The cold and the memory left her shivering, sometime long past dark, certain Wade sensed her distress. She waited, wrapping the blanket around herself. Moments later, Mac was there. He didn't bother to knock.

"Are you all right?"

"I am now. I'll be fine," she whispered.

"Same dream?" He meant the one that plagued her since the Blackout. Every officer involved, including himself, had a version of that nightmare.

"Always." She didn't have to give details. "I woke Wade this time."

"He's at home. Rock Creek inspection in the morning." Wearing hastily pulled on blue jeans, he ushered her over, crawling into bed. She didn't sleep naked except during the warmest part of the summer. "Are you sure you're okay?"

She'd stopped shivering, at least. It was freezing outside, but no new snow had fallen. "I'm just cold now."

"Helicopters," he said. "For me, the Missouri Breaks brings on bad dreams." He'd wondered if it was something else for a few moments. She had dreams that might or might not be memories of things that happened when she was a child. Wade did as well.

"Oh, hell yes." At nine, she'd seen the lazy mushroom cloud rising to the north, after the detonation. As far as she could figure, the nightmares about the helicopters were worse because they'd been up close and personal.

He wrapped an arm around her shoulders. "Remind me to show you what we've been doing at Depot South someday. After Sweeps."

"What are you doing out there?" she murmured. The depot had burned during the Blackout, and only a supply cache and small check point remained.

"After Sweeps," he repeated. "Imagine something nice and go to sleep."

"Sleep is over-rated." She curled up against him.

"Yes, but we don't have time for anything else."

"True thing," she whispered back, smiling.

"Remember when five or six of us slept in one bed and our parents said how cute we looked?"

"I do." It hadn't been that long ago. "There's your nice thought."

They both slept until daybreak.

The Vista City Council Chambers 12:30pm April 16

"Chair recognizes Lt. Taylor." Haines didn't need a microphone to get their attention. Dark-skinned and taller than most, he'd been an air traffic controller in the Dallas-Fort Worth metroplex before the war, military prior to being a civilian. After a short time in Security more than a decade ago, he'd left to help organize the caravans into a coherent operation. His position grew from that, and he was known as a peacemaker.

"I move that Council approves plans for an outpost during the first meeting after this Sweep is complete." Taylor put it out there, knowing he was in for a fight.

"That could give us days to go over results from the Sweep," Haines said.

"Security has resubmitted yearly, with no progress because of Council inactivity. We respectfully ask to skip that step this time."

"Council needs to catch up with new information, Lt. Taylor."

"We're willing to offer a week for Council to review what we bring you, if you agree to call a special session. Otherwise, this is a Security outpost. Command can move the project forward on their own."

"No," Markie Bennett spoke from the audience seating section. She was fifteen and had a brother in Security but was herself a vocal member of Pacifica. "We don't need a military base. We want a village for normal, peace-loving people."

"You aren't normal," Chris Taylor said to his brother, standing next to him at the podium.

"Tell that to the Scavengers," someone shouted.

"You're not recognized," Haines told Markie. "Go ahead, Lt. Taylor."

"Security will determine the status of the area for at least a year after we establish the base. If it's a reasonable risk, then civilians could be assigned as support groups."

"Your satellite village would be under direct supervision from Command?" Haines confirmed.

"Yes," Taylor said, without giving details.

"Do you have a written proposal?" Haines knew the answer. The 'Conda and Security were too close for them to not have something well-prepared.

Taylor held up the hard copy file, over three hundred pages, mostly hand-written, by a dozen officers. "This is a copy for Council's use. The main proposal is followed by a breakdown of our top three sites. Council can contact any member of Command for further details." He was aware Command would direct questions to Team Two or Three officers.

"How many people are required for this initial phase?"

"Fifty." Taylor had argued for more. Wade didn't expect they could get approval, and he was worried about stretching officers too thin for The Vista.

"Do you have fifty people in mind?"

"There is a pool we'd pick from."

"'We' being whom?"

"Security Command." Taylor had answers all lined up. The pool of volunteers was less than fifty, but it would grow once they announced tentative plans.

"Under-aged citizens can't take part in this," an older adult spoke out. "Must be eighteen."

"Sixteen is the age of consent. It has been since The Vista's inception," Haines reminded everyone.

"Who's in charge of it, then?" Markie asked without waiting to be recognized.

"That is Command's decision." Haines was unwavering and a loud teenager didn't intimidate him. "The list is brief and all the candidates are senior officers. Young lady, if you are going to attend my council meetings, please learn to follow policies and procedures."

"They'll never give up a community they establish," she made a last-ditch protest.

"If I recall correctly," David MacKenzie stood, paused and waited to be recognized. Haines motioned for him to continue. "Security is asking for permission and they've been more than patient. We need the expansion. They don't need our approval."

"In case anyone has forgotten," Haines added. "Security works for us, for all the citizens of The Vista. They're here for our protection. We've seen repeated accounts of the lawlessness encountered with the Nomad bands and Scavengers. I think we can all agree, we need our Guardian teams and Scout support in their present capacity."

"But do we want them to be our contact with other cities?" the girl persisted.

Taylor got a few words in. "Officers are the first contact for The Vista now. Until we occupy the area for at least a couple of years, we can only guess at the issues facing us. We want to do this the safest way possible, for us and any people we might cross paths with."

"We wouldn't support a Security-based outpost," Markie added.

"No one was asking you to," Chris told her.

"Pointless to argue, that's what she wants," Taylor spoke to his brother.

"Pacifica hasn't set a policy concerning this outpost or its citizens," Annie Cameron clarified, being their representative for the day. "Or the officers known as the 'Conda. We don't have sufficient information to do so."

"You're welcome to attend any function of the 'Conda. We allow non-members full access," Taylor added.

"Council determines nothing for Security," Haines folded his hands on the desk. "This is a courtesy to us. Security has asked permission so at a later date, we can come to a civil compromise on the issue of civilians moving to the new base. That's how we work together. They have permission to submit their proposal."

"And to accept additional candidates for the command of any such outpost," Richard Cameron amended, finally having something to say.

Taylor didn't like that, and he knew Wade would like it even less.

Haines ignored the comment, but someone seconded him. "Did you have someone in mind, Richard?"

"We should keep options open. One of those options being a civilian command position. We've discussed in previous meetings as well. If the Council has candidates, Command should at least consider them."

"Yeah, he's taking a free shot at Cmdr. Wade," Chris leaned over to speak to his brother. "Pacifica wants to nominate civilians, to throw a wrench into the 'Conda. There's no way that is happening."

"Nice try, though," Taylor admitted. He doubted the move would trouble, or even surprise Team Three. If he thought too much, it would piss him off.

"This is a Command project, and they have the final say. When it comes down to it, we're all free to go where we want, in The Vista and points beyond," Haines said. "We should remember that fact."

It took Wade a few moments to sense her, being not quite awake and not quite asleep himself. Shan, staying at Station Two and him at Station One. Mac was at his apartment in Station Two, right down the hall from her, asleep. If they needed to, Shan could draw him into their communication.

~I hear Bennett's little sister tried to throw a wrench into the Council meeting,~ Wade said.

~She did,~ Shan answered. ~Loud, pointless, and annoying. It's what Pacifica always does when they have nothing to say but want everyone to hear them.~

~Did Haines set things straight?~

~Oh, yes. Guess who was the most offended by her outburst?~ She could sense he didn't. ~Chris.~

~Taylor?~ Wade answered, amused. ~That's outstanding. We

need to get him out on a Sweeps. It won't be this year, but the sooner the better.~

~We've got trouble from Cameron,~ she told him.

~I'm aware of his plans.~

~Were you aware he was going to ask for civilian nominations for command of the Cody base? Because he did and Council accepted.~

~Did anyone mention the position is only available to officers?~

~No. They don't read the proposal, tough for them,~ she figured. ~You aren't worried about it?~

~Elections are coming up at the end of the year. Everyone will be out to make an impression. Richard's getting a head start. Don't over-think it. He's spouting the same things he always does. More Council say in Security matters. It's just talk. That's why we have Command. They'd need to approve a civilian in the post, and they won't.~

~And you want to be on the Council? On purpose?~ Shan didn't understand that, not even a little.

~Some day,~ Wade confessed. ~Not now, not right away. There are a lot of other ideas I'd like to explore, and that's at the bottom of my list. The Cody Base is first. All three of us need to get there and start figuring out the things they've hidden from us here.~

~They've taken a swipe at the team twice this week. What in the hell did we do to piss them off?~

~They don't like that we're spurring on the push to move outside this cozy little valley. They're afraid.~ It was a simple explanation with a lot of complicated facts, and he knew they didn't have all the facts.

~Afraid of what?~

~Take your pick.~

~Of what we are? Or of what might be out there?~

~Both.~ Wade said. ~Someone purged information from the library. Almost everything about humans being genetically engineered. They don't want us to know what we are. So yes, I think they're afraid of us. Then there's the statistical improbability that The Vista is the center of the world. It's not. We need to find out what else, who else, lives out in the world. Stagnating here, that's not for us. If Command hasn't figured it out, they will soon.~

Chapter Three

Station One, Anaconda April 17 daybreak

Taylor didn't expect anyone awake and about so early, even with the rush of activity leading up to Sweeps. Still, Wade had come in overnight, because he was in the loft apartment, watching out over the lobby as he repacked his gear. He'd spent more than a few nights there since they'd put him in charge of the shift, a year ago. The place was home to thirty-odd people at any time, but he was the only commander that was a regular.

"You're getting a lot of hours on the road this week," Taylor made small talk, joining him.

"It's now or never," Wade said. "This autumn, we need to be in Cody, and I'd like to think we'll be there to stay." If the plan went the way he wanted, they'd make the move in two parts. The first, with Team Three and their inner circle. The next was of less consequence. "If you aren't ready to commit to a full year, with the baby coming soon, say so. I understand, and it won't affect a future transfer."

"We're doing this, all of this, to protect our families. We make hard choices. It goes with the job."

"As long as everyone is aware of the commitment."

"Where's Mac this morning?" Taylor asked, done talking about his family.

Wade caught his unease. "Station Two. He did a split shift in Dispatch yesterday, another today, and probably the rest of the week."

"Shan?"

"At Station Two. She starts a run in about five minutes. Why?" Privacy was a rare and coveted commodity. Wade appreciated his and didn't enjoy interfering with theirs.

"What are we going to do about Mac?"

"Did something happen I haven't heard?" He was wary. Taylor had said 'Mac', not 'Mac and Shan', and he knew where the conversation was going. The underlying tension between the men was odd because he couldn't see a reason.

"No, but it will." Taylor sounded certain. He disagreed with Mac often enough. They weren't friends, and with team matters, he had no problem going over his head to Wade, causing more than a little friction between them. This was no different, even if it was personal.

"Sweeps won't be a problem, it never has," Wade said. No room for extra supplies, and Mac knew better than to sneak contraband along. "It's under control."

"Shan will be out on a run and you'll be somewhere else and Mac will slip up."

"He'd never come on duty after a binge. He'd call off." Wade didn't want to discuss it, even with Taylor. It was something they couldn't keep ignoring. Talking had helped, for a time. He turned to Shannon next.

"The Vista is a small world. Someone will figure it out, if it isn't obvious already. What do you think Command will do? How far are you willing to go to cover for him?" He was fresh out of ideas. Shan would deny all if he even attempted to broach the subject with her.

"Whatever it takes. The summer is easier because we're busy. After this summer," he shrugged, "Things will be better."

"Cody."

"I'll be in charge of Cody."

"What are you going to do?" Taylor asked. "Declare Prohibition? Let him keep doing this to himself?"

"No." He didn't have a fast answer, and it bothered him more than he'd admit.

"If it happens here, they'll fire him. He won't be the first cop in The Vista to be moved out of his position because he drinks too much, too often."

"We deal, if it happens. Shan..." he began.

"Not 'if', Wade, 'when'," Taylor corrected.

"She knows the warning signs. We've got it."

"For now," Taylor said. His job was to bring up potential problems. One of his jobs. "We can't leave her alone with this. All hell will break loose, and it will end the team."

"She's stronger than you give her credit for."

"She is, but this is Mac. You understand how it is with those two. If something is going to cause problems, my money would be on that."

"Do you imagine I haven't considered this?"

"No. The only weaknesses the three of you have out in the world are each other. And Shannon," he didn't have to finish. "Some day, she's going to find out the truth about a lot of things. Who do you think she's going to be pissed at? It won't be Mac."

"Once we get to Cody would be a good time to delve into some of our issues."

Taylor nodded. "As good as any time, better than most." He didn't think Wade had an actual plan other than letting things fall apart and picking up the pieces as best he could. "You're still going to make him second in command of Cody."

"Yes, I am. Who do you want me to put in charge–Shannon? You? Ballentyne?"

"Oh, hell, I don't want the job."

"If Mac goes to Cody, he'll be second in command, end-of-story. If he doesn't go, there's a fifty-fifty chance Shan won't go and then the things we've been working towards the past five plus years were a waste of time. We want Cody for specific reasons. It doesn't matter if you like Mac or not. He's Team Three, just like I am, just like she is." This wasn't the first time Wade had words with him over Cody, or Mac.

"He's not like you," Taylor said.

"Splitting hairs. Don't. I'm not breaking the team up because of your personal feelings. Team Three is Team Three."

"Your call, your responsibility. He could go as a civilian. You should be aware, I'll back you either way."

Wade read into his statement. Taylor would back him. Not Mac, and not Shannon if it came to that. "You said we all make choices."

"We do."

"Good enough. Right now, Shan has a partner for the day. She's taking your brother out on a run," Wade told him, satisfied with what they said, and left unspoken. Taylor knew better, and yet, here they were.

"Outstanding," Taylor added. "God help us all."

Depot North 7:50 am

Bella was the oldest person Shannon knew. Born in Hall, now Depot North, no one could dispute that. He also claimed to be seventy-six years old, although she recalled he'd been seventy-five when she met him years ago. With his thick Greek accent and one-sided smile, he assured her she was confused. Of course, he couldn't recall what year he'd been born, because, he said, he was young at the time. Along with his son Nikolas, he operated Depot North during the summer.

Shan had been skipping around the countryside on her run with Chris Taylor, spending the nights at Station One rather than out in the field. The younger Taylor was smart and paid attention, so they had an easy couple of days.

"When you resupply, keep it simple or you'll be sorry later," she said. "They prep quick, hot meals here at the depot. Learn a pace, eat light, stay hydrated. Don't get extras today. We're heading in soon." Shan waited in the car while gas trickled into the dual tanks. Chris wandered back to the depot with Bella, in the middle of one of his many colorful stories. Close to shift change, Team Six was across the lot refueling. Parr acknowledged her, waving, waiting for his partner to return.

Shan fidgeted, adjusting her sidearm, then the mirrors, opening her door to let fresh air in. Distracted, for no apparent reason. Overreacting, she reasoned. In the spring, when the snow melted, and the Nomads started moving, everyone got skittish. Besides, Wade was minutes behind her, and Team One sitting on the interstate a few miles away.

"Car Ten, radio check." She heard the tension in her voice. If Wade talked to her, she'd be able to shake the sensation.

"Car Ten," Dispatch replied. "You're clear."

It wasn't the response she wanted and suppressed the urge to call Wade, seeing Quinlen emerge from the depot. Shan waved him down, opening her door. "Hold up a few minutes."

"What's going on?" he asked.

"I'm not sure," she said. "I'll tell you as soon as I figure it out." They were both 'Conda, they'd wait.

"Keep us here too long and you owe us breakfast."

As she glanced up to see where her rookie had gone off to, Shan caught a movement, something in her rear-view mirror. A faint cloud of dust from the east, towards The Vista. It was gone before she could decide what it was.

Not dust, but smoke. One of the south outbuildings erupted with a deafening roar, sending debris in all directions. The force rocked her car and slammed her forward into the steering wheel, vision darkening for a few long moments. Her rear window crackled in a spiderweb pattern. It held.

Training and instinct kicking in, Shan swiped blood off her face, away from her eyes. It didn't hurt, so it wasn't an immediate worry. Smoke made it impossible to see beyond the burning structure. "Code Nine," she radioed in. "Code Nine, Depot North. We're under large arms fire. They're east of us."

The airway screamed to life, Dispatch issuing orders to all on-duty personnel. Inside the depot, someone activated its defense system, a series of reinforced steel plates tilting up from the ground. They provided a minimum of protection when the hydraulics worked. Today, they did, throwing even more dust into the air.

If the intruders knew how to use what they had, Shan realized she never would've heard the explosion. They were too far away for a shotgun to be of any use. She was a close-quarters shooter, not a sniper. Blood running into her eyes, she lurched out of the car and fell to her hands and knees, wanting to vomit the rations she'd eaten for breakfast. The ground spun. She waited for it to stop.

Parr was yelling at her, the ringing in her ears making it a futile attempt on his part. Shan felt heat from the fire and realized it was close, spreading in all directions fast.

"Back it up, back it up, dammit," Parr went on the air. He knew she was sitting on forty gallons of gasoline, not to mention the underground storage tanks. They'd hear that explosion clear to The Vista.

Nausea forgotten, she groped for the steering wheel and pulled herself back into the driver's seat. Then she threw it in reverse and floored it. The car swung backwards, tires spinning in the gravel. She sideswiped a canopy support, metal shrieking agony against metal. The car stalled as she hit the retaining wall, but the canopy didn't come down. The pump hose snapped off, dry. Someone inside had turned them off.

Snatching an Uzi from the back seat, Shan folded out the stock and took a defensive position at the wall, needing to steady herself. Vertigo. Another explosion hit the base of the barricade on the southeast corner, ripping part of it free and spinning it into the air. She crouched down, covering her head with one hand as a shower of dirt and rock fell. The sound of a heavy dull thud got her attention as the metal landed flat, somewhere in the weeds, past the parking lot.

She sprang up and aimed, firing a quick burst. Out of range. It didn't matter. She ducked, waiting, hoping the return fire would discourage the intruders from moving closer. "Team Three, part one. Six Scavengers, two hundred yards east," Shan reported on her collar mic.

Reinforcements made the barrier, with headlights flashing in another cloud of dust. She swung around to see the car, to confirm it was Security, then coughed until she couldn't.

Shan got a 9mm in hand, ready to pass off the Uzi, wanting to be sick again. Dizzy, too. Concussion, she figured, swearing to herself.

"Let's see how long it takes for them to run." The voice was unmistakable, with his faded southern drawl. Hunter carried an AK-47. "You're hurt," he noted the blood on her jacket.

"Steering wheel attacked me," Shan said. He was in no hurry, taking aim and firing. She decided she was comfortable, watching their backs, sitting in the dirt. "Wade was right behind me."

"This is the only place hit," he told her. "He was on the air. You should've taken cover."

"I got recon. Now you know where they are."

"We'd have found them."

"Sure," Shan scoffed. "We don't want them to run, we want to keep them from telling anyone else we're here." There were sirens, close now.

"Here comes the cavalry." He grinned, firing, aware of protocol.

"What cavalry?" she asked.

"Never mind," Hunter told her. It would take too long to explain. "They're running south," he reported on his headset. "I picked one off way out in the field."

"I hit nothing but dirt," Shan said, annoyed, standing, unsteady. "Are we clear?"

"Not even close. You know better than that, Capt. Allen. Just because I don't see anyone doesn't mean they aren't out there."

"I'm going to my car, ten feet away. Cover me, would you pretty please, if you're not too busy?" she scoffed.

"Yes, ma'am."

"I am not your mother, don't call me 'ma'am', ever, Lt." Shan tried to walk away and discovered she couldn't. She wondered if a concussion would keep her out of Sweeps. Two weeks away, but Deirdre might not care. Team Three wouldn't go without her, and it would cancel their plans for the summer, their plans for Cody.

"I'll be resting right here for a bit first," she said.

Chris came over with a towel in hand and concern on his face. "They called for an ambulance."

"They always do on a Code Nine. Hold this," he directed Shan, towel to forehead. "Stay with her," Hunter told Chris. "We are not clear. Keep your eyes open." Then he went off in search of his partner.

"Is Bella okay?" Shan asked, handing him the Uzi.

"That's one tough old man," Chris said.

"Remember it." She wanted to close her eyes, to catch a few moments of rest, and tried to get moving again. Not the best idea she'd had. Standing was tentative. "Find out what's going on. Find out where Wade is."

"Why?"

She got to her car. "He's in charge. I need a medic," Shan said, attempting to sound casual about it. Lying down on the hood, her first thought was how warm it felt and how nice it would be to sleep for a bit. "Don't ask, just do."

That scared him. "Who's medical?" Chris asked out loud. The place was a noisy disaster area, with more people showing up by the minute.

Mac, Shannon knew, but he was thirty miles away. Hunter, then. She'd seen it in his files and that was about all it said, which was weird. Later, she'd have to find out why.

"What's up?" Hunter asked, making his way back.

Pleased when she was right, Shan told him, "Getting shaky and cold. Tired. Loopy."

"Loopy?" He took her pulse against her neck, moving the towel to look at the cut over her eye. "This isn't from glass?"

"I told you, steering wheel, first blast."

A worry line creased his forehead. "Officer Taylor, tell Capt. Quinlen to have the ambulance come on in." He rummaged around in the first aid kit from her car for a moment.

"Shit," Shan said as he leaned over and looked into her eyes.

"Relax Captain, it's a precaution." He stared, close for a few moments, flashing a penlight on. "Mild, even if you have a concussion. Wade would kill me if I didn't send you in. Literally." Hunter swabbed and taped a square of gauze on her forehead. Infection was a thing in a world with few antibiotics.

"Bit of an exaggeration," Shan said, knowing Wade would send her in if he didn't.

"Sniper," someone called.

"Damned, but I'm popular today," Hunter drawled, pretending to be bored. "We'll have to dance later." Parr was there too. "Keep her awake, keep her talking to you," he told them. "Capt. Allen, as a medic, I'm ordering you not to fall asleep."

"Wouldn't dream of it, and miss all this excitement." It had to be making him pleased, to be giving her orders.

"If she goes out, make her walk. If she can't walk, drag her around the lot until the ambulance gets here," he said, serious.

~Wade,~ she thought, reaching out.

Something burning close by smelled acidic, sharp.

A cool breeze started, dragging the smoke away, replacing it with the high mountain scent of forest, pine and moss and damp leaves.

She swore she could hear the creek, two miles away, bubbling along during the spring thaw, her ears still ringing.

"Shannon," Wade spoke. "Stay here." He turned and stalked away, leaving Chris there with her.

"Are we under fire?" she asked her rookie.

"No."

"How long was I out?"

"You weren't. Hunter called for a transport and Wade got here."

A residual effect of abilities she had little control over. They called it 'ghosts', seeing glimpses of past events. She'd stopped it before it started, being in the middle of an active incident.

Shan wondered how she might talk herself out of an overnight at the hospital. As a child, she had to stay there with her mother when her parents were both working. Back then, if you went to the hospital, you were dying.

From the corner of her eye, she spotted Hunter and Wade engaged in an intense conversation. An argument. She recognized anger boiling up in Wade. A moment later, Wade lunged at him and the two were in a free-for-all.

It was far from her first brawl, just the first one on duty. Jumping right in, she ended up with a handful of Hunter's parka rather than her partner, jerked off her feet as he spun to defend himself.

The fight was forgotten when he saw who he'd almost hit. "Damn it," he growled, backing away.

Ballentyne had a hold on Wade, getting the situation under control before it really started. Green was there, too.

"Stop it," Shan told Wade, tone sharp. "Listen to me." She got right in front of him, up close. "We don't need this, not now, not you. Too close to Sweeps."

He stopped struggling and waved them off. Everyone stepped away.

"What's the problem?" Cmdr. Duncan asked, already having a good idea. Fights among officers weren't uncommon. He had a depot in chaos, at least three teams out of commission for the day, dead Scavengers, and a pile of paperwork to deal with, his mood rapidly tipping towards foul. He was in charge because, technically, it was in his section. Station Two.

"A difference of opinion," Ballentyne said. Council Chair Haines' nephew, he could get away with a lot of things. He wouldn't step into Wades' line of fire for anything. Or Duncan's, if at all avoidable.

"We don't settle differences of opinions in a street brawl, in the middle of an incident," Duncan reprimanded everyone in earshot. "Are we in kindergarten or are we Security Officers?" He didn't wait for an answer. "We're clear now, in case anyone is interested. Officer Wade, Officer Hunter, I expect detailed written reports on your 'difference of opinion' on my desk by the end of my shift. Wade, get your Scout to the hospital."

They scattered before he changed his mind and put them on report. "What happened?" Ballentyne asked Shan.

"I don't know."

Wade motioned at her to head for his car.

"What in the hell was that?" Shan repeated for the curious among them.

"Nothing."

"Bullshit."

Wade was furious, but not at her. "Stay away from him, Shan. He's trouble."

"Hunter? I've never gotten into trouble with you, right? I mean, just now, for example."

"Not like this. I've seen how he watches you."

"I met him four days ago."

"He's on the prowl."

Telling him it was none of his business would be a lie. It was his business. Everything one of them did affected all three, including their private lives. "I can handle Hunter," Shan assured him.

"Has he said anything to you?"

"I haven't seen him since the callout except about three seconds at the station yesterday. He won't be the first guy in Security I've turned down."

"Are you sure you're going to turn him down?"

"Are you sure he's interested?"

"I am."

Shan's head ached. It was seeping blood through the bandage and she didn't want to discuss this with him, here. "I'll figure it out when it happens," she said, trying to be flippant and failing.

"He's going to be trouble, Shan. I can see it already."

"I believe you," she said. "Duncan won't forget this either."

"No," Wade agreed. "He won't. At least I wasn't there alone. He'll count this as a Team Three incident. We should warn Mac."

"I don't want to go to the hospital in the ambulance. Deirdre will jump all over that and I'll miss Sweeps again." Shan knew her mother.

"Good point. You have to go."

"I'll drive in," she started.

"That's not happening. I'm here for the rest of the morning. Ask if you can ride in with Team One," he smirked, over his anger as fast as it started.

"I could do that, or there's Team Six." Shan had an alternative.

Wade nodded. "Quinlen," he called. "I need to report on this mess before tomorrow. Shan needs to go to the hospital now."

Quinlen joined them. "Is the ambulance out of service?"

"Dr. Allen is on duty," Wade said.

"Ah," he understood. "Let's go. Parr can bring Car Ten back, provided it's still running. It looks like someone forgot how to drive."

"Shut up," Shan said, knowing the torment she'd get for months to come about wrecking her car in a parking lot.

"The road is clear," Wade confirmed with Dispatch for them. "Go."

Fourteen ultra-fine stitches lined the cut over Shan's left eyebrow. It matched the curve of her steering wheel and itched already, purely in her imagination and she knew it.

Dr. DeCino taped a bandage in place after she finished staring in the mirror. "It won't be an obvious scar. Your vitals are fine, but I'd still prefer if you stayed overnight."

"No," she shook her head and wished she hadn't. "I am not comfortable here. Not ever. You understand why."

He did. "Are you staying with your parents?"

"I'm staying at Station Two." Despite all her fevered independence, or maybe because of it, Shan never found time to move. She'd have to petition the Housing Committee for a single occupancy and if none were available, look for a roommate she could tolerate. Or worse yet, find herself stuck with someone she didn't know and didn't care to.

Her other choice was to move in with Wade. That would bring on a whole new level of issues. Few understood they saw each other as siblings. Plus, she didn't want to deal with his many admirers.

Mac also still lived with his parents. Technically, like her.

"I can release you to one of your partners if you are going to be staying there."

Team Three was on duty and DeCino would check. They were working out of Station One for the rest of the week. It had been eleven months since she stayed with her parents. "Home then?" she asked.

"That or here."

Either way, Deirdre would approve.

Like most houses in The Vista, the Allen home was brick, half buried in the landscape, and rebuilt for defense. An impressive fireplace on the north wall, again, the same as most. Undistinguished on the outside and fortified on the inside. Much of the east side of the city burned the second winter after the war, the reason behind brick housing. Marauders were the reason for other features.

Shannon remembered moving after the detonation on the Missouri Breaks. Before that, things were more difficult. Families had grouped together for convenience and out of necessity. With fewer houses, they needed fewer supplies to heat them, fewer people to defend them, less places to conceal.

There had always been someone to play with, though. With blackout curtains down, the adults speaking in hushed, tense voices, children oblivious to why. By the time Shan turned four, the boys taught her to play poker, checkers and a game they called chess but wasn't; and about books. Someone insisted books were important. People of The Vista hoarded many books of all types.

She remembered standing out in the yard after dark, watching the stars. She remembered the adults, scanning the airways for some sign of life beyond the valley, calling to anyone that might be out there. They never got an answer to their pleas. When she was six, they stopped transmitting.

The adults expected their children would be different. How could they not? Wade, not yet four, saw the riots, the city burning as they fled Portland. His father hadn't made it out.

The MacKenzies, three hundred miles east of Los Angeles, somewhere in the Arizona desert, seeing the fireballs rise over the coast. Six warheads, with radiation that would come straight at them, carried in weather patterns.

The Allens, running from the plague that gripped the Cheyenne/Denver metroplex. By October of War Year, they converged in west-central Montana, along with four hundred others. The Vista was founded in November, and by the end of the year, had grown to a thousand. In twelve months, they numbered twenty-two hundred, but only a handful of babies born that year lived. Shannon was one, Kyle Taylor another.

The adults never spoke much about their lives before the war, or how they came to Montana. They put it down to the fact every aspect of life was different when they realized some of their children didn't act like children had before. If anyone thought otherwise, they kept it to themselves.

Their house had some new furniture, Shan noted, hanging her

parka in the entryway. As an afterthought, she put her sidearm with it, leaving the Tanto blade Wade got for her last birthday strapped in her left boot. She didn't expect a brawl to the death in her parents' living room, but she was there to visit Deirdre. No guns at dinner. Shan went nowhere unarmed. That included bathing and sleeping.

The fireplace warded off the late afternoon chill. Wood was by far the easiest commodity to come by, and Michael loved to build a roaring fire. Half the time, he nearly roasted them out of the house, but by early morning, a perfect temperature happened.

"Hey Mom, what's for supper?" she called, not wanting to sneak up on anyone. Deirdre knew how to defend herself. She chose not to carry a weapon. She was a doctor, to help, not harm. Michael carried a handgun most of the time and a knife always. Shan picked up a lot of habits from him.

"I understand there was a fight at Depot North," Deirdre said as they finished dinner. The vegetables, grown in the garden Michael kept out back, plus a roasted duck stuffed with grain and rice. The fresh bread from a neighbor, traded for another commodity.

Shan had been expecting it all afternoon. They'd made small talk. Deirdre would work her way around to that. She wouldn't be aware someone lobbed RPGs at them, however. Only a certain amount of information leaked back to The Vista, to the civilian population. If the raw truth be told, they didn't know, and they didn't want to know. Security existed for a reason.

"It's not like Geoffrey to hit a junior officer," Michael said about Wade. He helped raise that houseful of kids, he still called them by their given names. All the parents did. At least they refrained from doing it in public.

"That's not what happened." Shannon wondered if they would notice her sneaking out the back door. Talk, not fight, she reminded herself.

"What happened to you?" her mother asked, having held that question as long as she could.

Shan resisted the urge to scratch her forehead. "I can't say."

"I'm your mother." Deirdre could check on medical files at any time. She never had.

"I know. The steering wheel hit my head. Or I bounced my head off the steering wheel, depending on your perspective." If she got lucky, they'd suspect a game of demolition derby going on at the depot again. "Besides, Wade wasn't on duty." Shan realized how weak that sounded. "And Hunter's a jerk." Getting worse and worse, she shut up and concentrated on finishing her vegetables. She loved zucchini and disliked peas a lot. Dinner included both, mixed.

"Hunter's fault, then." Deirdre said. "He must be new. I can't put a face to the name."

"Year and a half in, still a rookie. He worked with the caravans for quite a few years. Wade hasn't forgotten he called out Security all the time. It wasn't anyone's fault." Shan gave up on the vegetables.

"So they did fight?" Michael repeated.

"No, a..." Pissing contest, she almost said. "They were scuffling around in the dirt like a couple of kids," she recalled Duncan's words.

"What started it?"

"Me, getting this," Shan rubbed at the bandage on her forehead. "We had a callout, a car wreck by the depot, and Wade got stuck in the middle. We haven't worked with Team One and rookies take getting used to."

"Where was Alex?" Deirdre offered her more coffee, what they called coffee, and she accepted.

"Mac? At Station Two, asleep, waiting for Wade to get back. I need his job, I swear. One shift in Dispatch and he gets two days off." She rolled her eyes. "Oh, and I'm supposed to remind you, Sweeps starts at the end of the month."

"Are you scheduled to go out?" At five foot two, her golden hair turning silver at the temples, Deirdre was the Chief of Staff at the only hospital in The Vista. It wasn't a title she wanted. Someone had to do it.

"No idea, but I'd say yes," Shan confessed. She recognized they were ganging up on her.

"I hate Sweeps," Deirdre said.

"It isn't any worse than regular summer assignments."

"My point." Her opinion wasn't a new one.

Here comes the lecture, Shan thought.

"Isn't there something you'd rather be doing? Something here in The Vista that keeps you home and keeps you safe?"

"Like what?" Shan shook her head. "I am safe, even out on a run." Nothing she might say would convince her mother.

"You forget, I patch up officers all the time."

"I never forget," Shan told her. "That's why I do this. I like the people I work with, and I like my job."

Michael cut in. "Is Chris Taylor going to be your permanent partner?"

"After Sweeps, if I want a partner and take another position. So, I doubt it." The whole move to Cody was still privileged information. She'd tell them when the official announcement happened, or when one of them brought it up.

"What other position?" Michael hadn't heard of promotions yet. Everything was on standby until the Sweeps teams were home.

"Nothing in particular. There are always positions at Station One and it would save me a lot of driving time, but I enjoy being out there. It all depends on what Mac decides." If they made him a commander, Team Three wouldn't be Allen, Wade, and MacKenzie anymore. It was another idea Council put out. They'd get new assignments and Shan, she didn't have a clue where she'd go. Dispatch seemed a natural progression. All being contingent on the move south, and she like to keep her options open.

"I think there's a female Guardian team getting ready to go on the road," Michael said.

"Not me," Shan said. "Unless I got demoted, and no one told me." The rivalry between Guardians and Scouts was longstanding, but harmless.

"Women served on police forces and in the military before." The war, he meant.

The melancholy in his voice scared the hell out of her. Watching the world collapse around them traumatized them all in varying degrees. Most of them moved on. Some, like Lydia Cameron, were more damaged. Wade's mother was one of the worst cases. She'd worked for the government, earning college degrees as a teenager. Now she taught elementary school, the youngest classes, and sometimes she had trouble with that, he'd confided.

The 'Conda kept close tabs on everyone born before the war. Meltdown wasn't a problem. On paper, they could see where it might be in the future. There was no way to predict the outcome. So, they watched for issues. It was the other reason the group existed.

"What are you doing until Sweeps?" Deirdre asked.

"I'm going to Dispatch tomorrow. Wherever I get sent for now."

"I feel better when you're with Geoffrey and Alex," Michael said.

"Me too," Shan smiled. She didn't think she'd be in Security without them, but she couldn't imagine doing anything else. "It's what I want."

"Then that's what's important," Deirdre said, unconvinced the discussion was over. "Just be careful. You don't know what to expect out there."

Shan couldn't argue about that.

Chapter Four

Station Three White Sulphur Springs 8am April 21

Station Three, heavily staffed and often isolated because of the weather, it had a specialized purpose. More than a hundred miles from The Vista, it was the quarantine point for incoming travelers. Two days before Sweeps departure, the station was a scene of chaos, the good kind. Dozens of people involved in getting them on their way choked the main hall, making the ground floor standing room only. Everyone, from commanders to caravan runners, maintenance workers to wranglers, gathered to await the final assignments that would put things in motion.

Duncan had been a law enforcement officer, before. His uneventful two years of service in some flyspeck town in Nebraska hadn't prepared him for this. He'd been in Vista Security before they called it that, before they made a solid plan to defend themselves.

"If everyone would pay attention for a few more minutes," he announced over the buzz of a dozen people talking at once. "I can finish with most of you and get with team leaders for the ugly details."

Shan stood in her usual place during these functions, between Mac and Wade. "We drew," she said, pretending she didn't know days ago.

Wade was a lot more enthusiastic. "You bet we did. We always draw. In fact, we'd have to get special permission from Command to not go on Sweeps." He flashed a grin, pleased with himself. His usual demeanor was gone, replaced with all the intrigue and adventure they were in for. The boredom was easy to forget, a welcomed break from the routine.

Mac shook his head, catching her arm, and whispered something in her ear as she leaned in under the edge of the dilapidated cowboy hat he wore today. Shan clamped a hand over her mouth, knowing Duncan would throw them out if they didn't quiet down.

"Listen," Wade urged, eager to get on with it.

"Station One 'A' group, first shift, has prevailed again this year and drawn three Sweeps positions." Duncan was proud of his people. It showed during Sweeps.

"That's everyone," Mac commentated for them, pointing out the obvious.

"Damn," Wade exhaled. Both his partners stared. He rarely swore.

"What brought that on?" Shan asked.

"Just hide and watch."

"Despite previous inactivity in the matter of outpost expansions, we will survey sites on Command request, some more completely than others." He waited for the wave of cheers to subside. They were quick to quiet down this time. Duncan didn't pace like Wade tended to, he lectured, planted in one spot unless he had a reason to move. "Team leaders will have details, and that's what I expect–details. Many details; photographs, video, blue-prints, topographical maps, anything pertinent you can carry back. Pack it up and bring it home for further consideration."

"Are we getting any real say in where we establish this base?"

someone in the crowd asked, a civilian in a support position, no doubt. They had discussed it half to death.

"Wade?" Duncan asked.

"Yes, we will," was all he offered.

"Take him at his word," Duncan continued. "We have eleven routes this year, six for Station One, two for Two and three for Three. Reserve officers are already running short rotations. We expect them to go to a regular schedule tomorrow." He glanced up at them as he spoke. "One note I'll pass along is that we have two young women following in Capt. Allen's footsteps, as our first female Guardian Team."

"Do I have time to talk them out of it?" Shan asked.

"No."

Everyone laughed, especially the handful of them that knew she might be serious.

"I've set team leaders." Duncan looked at his written notes, shuffling through them. Paperwork was a necessary evil. Also, a pain in the ass as far as the people getting stuck with it were concerned.

Wade kept his comments to himself.

"What?" Shan asked again.

"He doesn't forget, and I can guess what's next. So can you. I knew when he gave me our assignment last night."

"You didn't read it?" Mac asked. "Why?"

"I'm not supposed to. This is payback."

"Damn," Shan repeated for him, half-amused. The amusement would fade, she suspected, considering Sweeps lasted weeks, depending on a lot of things. The weather, the team, Nomads, Scavengers, and areas of radiation all played a part. They'd lost no one in previous years, though. A few minor injuries were a win, considering the circumstances.

"Are you going to let me in on your private joke?" Mac asked.

"You weren't there," Wade said.

"And?"

"Maj. MacKenzie," Duncan interrupted their conversation. "Give me five more minutes?"

"Not a problem." They were all anxious.

"As usual, Sweeps Team Three is Security Team Four and Five." Nothing new. Duncan had paired them several times over the past decade despite personnel changes.

"Sweeps Team Two is Team Six and Two." That left one possibility. "Sweeps Team One, Team One and Three." Duncan told them. "Make any arrangements you haven't. Get with your people. Supplies are being distributed from now until departure, but try to do an early pickup. Some of our larger equipment is being rationed."

"Ouch," Mac offered his condolences, pushing his hat back. "That's interesting."

"Team One," Shan repeated. "What happened to being paired with Team Two?" They ran together on purpose. While Wade had Taylor as back-up, his second, Green was Shannon's. Another safety for Team Three, as much for protecting the others as for them.

"He gave us Team One, like it or not, Capt. Allen," Wade said.

"Oh, don't blame this on me."

"This is because of what happened at Depot North and you know it." The meeting was over, groups forming to lament their fates, or at least discuss Sweeps possibilities.

"I didn't hit Hunter," Shan said.

No, but you would have, Wade thought. "We're going to spend five or six weeks in a tent with Dallas, Noel, and Hunter. Get used to it."

"He did it on purpose. Duncan." Mac was playing catch-up on their issues.

"Yes," Wade said.

"I'm going to get over this a lot faster than you. Are you going to behave?" Shan straightened Wade's collar and brushed imaginary dust from his sleeve.

"You bet I will."

"Are you going to tell me what I'm missing?" Shan was persistent.

Wade wasn't budging. "We had a personal dispute, nothing more."

"Is that your story?"

"And I'm sticking with it."

"Okay," she gave up. "This is his first Sweeps." She meant Hunter. It was her second on record.

"Wonderful," Mac piped up. "A virgin."

Shannon couldn't suppress her grin. "You're on a roll today."

"Laugh it up now," Wade warned.

"Do you know something we don't?" Mac asked.

Wade smiled. "I'm sure I do–but not about what you mean."

"We've lost our seconds," Shan said. "How do we compensate?"

"When we're out," Wade looked south, "Past the dotted line, it's not so important. We need them in The Vista, for obvious reasons."

"I don't like our private lives being in full view of a rookie," Shan said. "Nothing personal, but he's still the rookie."

"You've said that," Wade said. "There's nothing to do unless you want to opt out of Sweeps."

She shook her head. "Not happening."

"Then here we are."

"Where are we going? I need to tell my parents something."

"Yeah, me too," Mac agreed.

Wade had a secret. "Tell them Cody. We're going farther than Cody. That will be our return rendezvous point."

"Farther. Nebraska?" Shan guessed. She couldn't imagine what was in Nebraska they'd want to look at.

"South."

"Colorado," Mac figured.

"Colorado," Wade confirmed. "NORAD."

April 22 The Vista

Sometime after four in the morning, Shannon found Wade again. He'd sequestered himself out at the airport, using a hangar to go over his gear and test his weapons. There was an assortment of them to pack. One hundred rounds through the sniper rifle, a Barrett 50 cal, cleaned, loaded and strapped into its leather case. The Glock .45 had thirty rounds fired, cleaned, reloaded, and holstered. He did the same for his .25 boot gun, and he was working on its twin.

"Did you get any sleep?" Shan dropped her pack on the floor, tying her long dark hair back into a ponytail.

"This afternoon, after I drove in." He dry-fired, not liking the sound. "You?"

"Yeah. A couple of hours, earlier."

"Packed yet?"

"I did this yesterday."

"Good." Wade had a tendency to isolate himself before Sweeps. The quiet helped him to relax, to concentrate. "What are you taking?"

"The usual. A pair of Sig 9mms, a .380 boot gun, and a .22 pump action. I was hoping to bring a bow this year, but I'm not accurate enough to bother."

He handed her the .25. "Close-quarters, rapid fire."

Shan dropped to one knee and fired down the range at a paper target twenty-five feet away. She centered, pulling to the left and putting all six rounds in an inch wide grouping. Then she handed it back to Wade. "I think the firing pin is damaged. It clicks funny."

"I love it when you talk technical to me." He took the gun and put it in its case. "I thought so too. How is Mac?"

"He can sleep the night before Sweeps start."

"That's one thing we don't have to be concerned with for a few weeks," Wade mused. He didn't mean Mac's sleep patterns.

"And a dozen different things we do need to worry about," Shan said. "Besides the fact he says I worry entirely too much about him."

"Someone has to do it. I doubt he'd have it any other way, either, but I have some concerns. We should talk."

"About?"

"When did you see Bryan last?" Wade started on a tangent about his oldest child.

It caught her off-guard. "Two days ago. Courtney had him at the clinic when she was helping my mom. Why?"

"Because he has my genes, and I still believe genetic tampering is why you and I and Mac are the way we are. I've uncovered some media at the main library. A dozen countries and over a hundred corporations were experimenting with human genetic manipulation. A few of them had been doing it since World War Two."

Shan nodded. She'd heard this before. Wade's concerns had caused her and Mac to be more cautious with their physical relationship. Neither wanted children now, and that they both likely carried engineered genetics scared them. Fear of what they knew, fear of what they didn't know.

"You remember what I was like at four?" she asked.

"Sure."

"Bryan is a normal four-year-old. He's not like I was."

"I needed a second opinion. I was only eight."

"Of everyone in The Vista, the three of us are aware we're different. There are others and they seem... dormant. I can sense them, for lack of a better word. I get nothing like that from Bryan."

"If you sensed something."

"You'd hear it from me," Shan said.

"Without a doubt." He wanted her to say it.

"I would tell you. There's no sign in your children, your sisters, Mac's siblings. Nothing."

He nodded, satisfied.

"Weren't we here to talk about Alex?"

"Oh, we still are." He drew a circle in the dust with the toe of his boot. "This is me, and what I know." Making a second circle that intersected the first, he continued, "And this is you and your knowledge."

"We are Venn diagrams."

"For this conversation, we are. Which means you understand where I'm going." Wade drew a third circle, intersecting each of the other two, a smaller section. "This is Mac, and what he knows."

She nodded, careful as always to listen to his advice. "About the Gen En."

"Well, concerning everything, but yes, the Gen En. You and I, we share some abilities. Mac may not be aligned with us. That doesn't mean his abilities are lesser."

"Different."

"Exactly."

"It always seems like we're leaving him behind."

Wade went back to packing his weaponry. "What's the first rule of Team Three?"

"You didn't say we were having a test." Getting a side-eye glance, she took the hint. It was hours from Sweeps, and he was being one hundred percent serious. "No one knows everything."

"No one knows everything," he said. "That's true for us, even more than the 'Conda."

"Okay," she said. "Fair enough. I can agree with the idea, and still not like it."

"Has he been drinking?"

"Not when I've been around. My informants have seen nothing suspicious, either." She wasn't joking about having informants.

"Don't kid yourself that he won't," Wade warned her.

"Never. I tell him he's going to lose his job, and he tells me he'll go to the Caravans."

Wade rubbed his eyes. He needed to get some sleep. "Be there when he needs you." Things suppressed from them were causing damage, and he didn't know how to stop it. He didn't even understand where to start.

"And for you," Shan told him.

"Are you going to be good without Team Two?"

"We'll have to be careful about what we say, that's all."

Wade agreed, "Like every day."

April 23 before daybreak West End Stables

"Let me," Noel stepped up next to Shan and pushed his knee against the horse's ribs carefully until the animal exhaled. He pulled the cinch strap down tight, fastening it. "There you go, Captain. He knows you're afraid of him. Don't let him bully you."

The West End Stables was the staging area for Station One Sweeps Teams. They were preparing to depart inside the hour, under the cover of night. It was an idea implemented because of long-standing concerns about being discovered. Later, after nightfall, Station Two teams would depart. Scrambling the schedule every year also kept curious civilians away.

Shan shook her head, annoyed she'd needed help. "Thanks." Then she muttered, "I'm not afraid of horses. I prefer other transportation."

"Too bad we can't drive where we're going," he said, laughing at the idea.

"You know," Hunter pointed out. "If you were nicer to him, he'd be nicer to you." He slung his pack on, ready to go, horse saddled five minutes ago.

"This better be a nice horse," she warned. "Or I'll trade it for a pack mule."

"Milo is a 'he'. Milo's a good horse." Noel patted him on the neck, scratching behind his ear.

"Milo?"

He nodded.

"Does everyone's horse have a name?" Shan asked.

The rest of Sweeps Team One told her their animal's name.

"Now that we've all been introduced," Wade spoke quietly and carried a big gun. "Assignments. In case we split up, rank determines command. Dallas is second in charge, Mac gets point, Shannon flank. Hunter, you are my designated sniper. Noel is in charge of supplies. Simple enough. Everyone gets a say. The final decision is mine. Questions?"

"I write up the daily reports?" Dallas wanted to confirm.

"Yes. Night sentry will run in four-hour shifts on rotation. I'll assign other duties as needed. I left our rendezvous points off your maps for a reason, so remember where they are. Big Timber is a cache that has intermittent communications with The Vista. Cody, of course. Further south, we haven't established yet." Wade was memorizing details, their mannerisms and attitudes.

"Shouldn't we?" Hunter came forward. "I mean, there's over four hundred rough miles between Cody and NORAD.

"We should. Your first assignment is to find a place in southern Wyoming and one in central Colorado," Wade said. "Watch those red lines. They can vary with the weather." Radiation hot spots. There were few, but they existed. "Get them picked out by tomorrow at nightfall. You've worked in the caravans, you know what to look for."

"Does anyone need clips or ammo?" Noel asked. They didn't. "Good. Everyone gets an Uzi and three clips," he indicated the weapons stacked on a nearby bench.

"I have a large arms weapon," Mac said. He meant a grenade launcher. "I've passed out shotguns. Share them if you need to. Knives–carry at least two. Shan, how many do you have?"

"Six knives of varying use. Two fixed blades; one combat, one hunting. A lock blade, a multi-tool, and two that are your preference. For me, that's a smaller fixed blade, and a boning knife. I also recommend a crossbow if you've qualified. Thirty bolts."

"Good number. If anyone wants more, stock up now out front. They come in damned handy. So do compound bows."

"We'll use standard Sweeps protocol until we cross into Colorado or until I say otherwise," Wade continued. "No outside fires after dark, no one does anything alone, weapons discharge of single rounds only unless we're under fire. Everyone will wear their body armor when we're on the move." He stopped and looked at his team. "That means you, too, Mac and Shannon. No exceptions."

"We go in fifteen," Dallas said, thinking he was too old for this. Once Hunter got past rookie status, he figured he could bow out of Sweeps and leave it to people half his age. "If we've forgotten something, speak up." Again, silence.

"Take care of any business you need to," Wade said, dismissing them.

While Mac went to find a set of body armor, Shan was in search of Team Two. They were easy to find in the next row of stables and doing the same thing. "Where are you going?" she pried.

Green gave her a smile. "I'm not supposed to tell you."

"I wasn't aware you were afraid of Council."

"Council and Command spend months arguing over routes before Command approves it. Hell, they've started planning for next year already. I'd like to go."

"That's not an answer," she grinned, shaking her head. "Idaho again?"

"Utah, along I-15."

She hadn't known they traveled there, not for Sweeps or anything else. "Be careful," she said. "That's a lot of gateway cities to wander through."

"I don't like it any better than you."

"No, I mean it. Be careful in Utah."

He caught her intentions. "What's in Utah?"

"No idea. Utah, Nevada and the California desert all have red zones. Don't take chances." Shan wasn't sure, but it bothered her.

"We're taking Geiger counters," Green said. "Other than that, we can take care of whatever we run across. Maybe later this summer, Command will send someone for a closer inspection. One of those clandestine things some of us do."

"Watch your back." She hugged him. "All of you."

"We look like we're going to start a war," Hunter told Dallas, having to rearrange his weaponry.

"Don't let Pacifica catch you say things like that." During the last war, Dallas had fled west with the eleven-year-old Hunter, out of the city, through the firestorms in the eastern plains, the barricades along the Front Range. Sometimes they were on foot, more often they used motorcycles taken from places where the previous owners no longer needed them. They'd found a group of survivors gathering in the mountains of Montana and stayed.

"They'll try to get me fired. No big deal." He wasn't fond of the group, but he understood their motives. Hunter didn't associate with any clique other than Security and that was as close to a normal social life as he got. "Is it that bad out there? Are hoards of Nomads and mutants waiting for us across the dotted line?"

"No," Dallas pulled himself astride the big bay gelding. "I've been on six Sweeps. Twice we've come under fire. It's a game of hide-and-seek."

"Hide-and-seek, with guns," Hunter said.

Dallas raised his eyebrows. "Now you see the score. There aren't that many people out there, but they're well-armed and aggressive." The timid didn't have good odds of survival.

"Everything all right?" Mac asked while Wade double check the grenade launcher he'd carry in a backpack for the next several weeks.

"It's clean and ready. We're as ready as we're going to get. The weather looks bad, but that's the time of year."

"I have six grenades. Command is rationing them," Mac said.

"If the blast doors at Cheyenne Mountain are closed, six grenades won't help," Shan observed for them. She had on body armor and a raincoat, already mounted up and waiting for them.

"Where do you hear things like that?" Hunter asked.

Wade was certain Hunter was talking to Shan to irk him. He ignored the conversation.

"If I told you, I'd have to kill you," she said with a straight face.

Mac laughed out loud. Wade shook his head. She stopped her horse beside him. "It was a joke," Shan leaned close enough to discuss it privately.

"I don't find it funny."

"You're being Commander Wade. Geoffrey thinks it's hilarious."

"Don't call me Geoffrey. From now on, until we're here again in a few weeks, we're on duty," he said. "Team One is nowhere as uninformed as you imagine they are."

"Problematic beyond Sweeps?"

"No," Wade was sure. Maybe Dallas, or even Hunter. One of them knew something and both of them had secrets. "Let's move," he spoke up. "It's a long way there and a long way back."

The weather didn't get better. A cold, constant deluge of rain fell the first three days. On the morning of their fourth day out of The Vista, the team could see blue sky. They crossed into The Park, into Yellowstone, and spent two days winding through. Then over the Continental Divide, and the team set their sights on Laramie. Laramie was a gateway city, a gateway into the mountains or beyond. Gateway cities were hot zones, to be accessed with caution. They considered the entire Front Range of the Rockies hot, for a variety of reasons. Once they found NORAD, it would be time to break out carefully packed equipment.

In August twenty years earlier, three or perhaps four warheads had fallen on Denver. Every one of them memorized the radioactive hot spots, two right next to each other. Rocky Flats was the other. Nothing normal lived there, nothing would for centuries.

Chapter Five

May 14 daybreak near Colorado Springs

"What was it?" Noel stared at the ruins scattered up the hillside. He'd seen a lot of abandoned places, but this wasn't the same. "Because this is all kind of spooky."

"No, it's not." Shan was fascinated.

"What sort of pervert would put a zoo on top of a nuclear weapons storage facility?" Hunter asked, catching up with the Scouts, an Uzi slung over his shoulder. They were walking uphill, with just enough snow on the ground to make it slushy and treacherous.

"A zoo?" Noel was aghast. "Which was here first?"

"NORAD. This is so vivid, I can practically see the animals." The enclosures had twenty years of weather.

"Home Base, this is the Outfield," Noel let the others know they were in position. "We're in a zoo."

"That would be the Cheyenne Mountain Zoo," Dallas answered, somewhere in the valley south of the city. "You've got an hour."

"Cheyenne is in Wyoming," Noel said, brushing a plaque clean with a gloved hand, reading them.

"True, but this is Cheyenne Mountain. Big difference," she said. Even with Noel being in Pacifica, they were friends. It was her recommendation that got him an auxiliary position in the 'Conda. "Interesting, though."

"What?" Hunter asked, serious.

"The animals didn't die in their cages."

"Oh, that's not funny," Noel said, fidgeting to be moving on. The nameplate said 'Siberian Tiger', the next one 'Northern Snow Leopard'.

"The doors are open with the locks locked. No remains. Someone turned all the animals loose." Her reasoning was solid, and she knew it was true.

"Could be," Hunter said.

"You mean there are tigers running around here? Could they survive in this climate?" Noel wasn't casual in his discomfort.

"Maybe, and yes," Hunter answered.

"Why are we here?" Noel wanted to know.

"Recon," Shan said. "Having a look around. Also, they didn't start storing big bombs here until the twenty-first century. It was an archive or something, before."

"Can't we recon somewhere else? Somewhere there aren't tigers wandering around?"

"Any movement out there?" Shan asked Home Base, Dallas, for Noel's peace of mind.

"Just you."

"Be on the lookout for non-indigenous wildlife."

There were a few moments of silence. "Lions, tigers, or bears?"

"Oh my," Hunter added.

"All the above."

"Are you clear?" Wade asked.

"We're clear."

"Get the video we need and get back here. Your position is compromised if anyone is listening."

"Oh shit," Noel said. "Am I in trouble?"

"No," Shan told him. "He's impatient with me.

It took them an hour to go around the zoo and longer to get back to their team. Hunter took video, while the Scouts kept eyes out for anything that might need further attention. There weren't any tigers, or at least, none they saw.

Wade pulled Team Three aside. "We have daylight. Do we go today or wait and recon tomorrow?"

"The farther we get from The Vista, the closer to this place we've gotten, the more consumed by it both of you are," Mac said. "Why?"

"It makes no sense, to use one of the most secure places on the planet just to hide nukes. Everyone had weapons, and if they didn't, it wasn't that difficult to get them," Shan answered first.

"So technically, you might have been here before." Wade didn't have to fill in the details for her.

"There's a bio lab here?" Mac asked.

"Maybe," both his partners answered.

"I didn't know."

"They didn't advertise where, I could be wrong," Wade said. "It's conjecture, but we need to go see. Are we clear?"

"Yes," Mac said.

Shan didn't answer.

"Are we clear?" he repeated. "Or are we being watched?"

"No, not now. I've not had that sensation since we started this way."

"The moment anything happens, say so," Wade told her. "I don't care who hears."

"It's not my imagination getting away from me," Mac said.

"No," Shan said.

"No," Wade agreed. "It's not one thing in particular. It's Sweeps, this place, a lot of factors."

"Right now, we're clear," Shan said. "Tomorrow, who knows? I'll be glad when we put miles between us and here."

"You say go?" Wade asked.

They both nodded.

"Three for three then."

"We're six right now," Mac said, a reminder they shared decisions today.

"I'm aware." He spoke to all of them. "Unless we have a serious issue, we're going to do this and get it finished. There's a safe camp waiting for us a few days north of here."

"Let's do it," Dallas said.

"A change in roster," Wade added. "I want Noel with Team Three, Shan with Team One." He needed eyes on the outside. "If there's trouble, and it's always possible in a gateway city, let's not give up our Scouts. They've never been to Cody from the southern route. Lost is not what we want to be out here."

Near dusk, the Sweeps Team gathered outside the long concrete tunnel that led into Cheyenne Mountain. "Report," Wade said to Dallas, both tired from the excursion, fatigue showing on their faces.

"I swear, it doesn't seem like anyone has been here for twenty years. Some streets were clear, less than I expected. Fires in most areas. It's a ghost town." Dallas had seen enough abandoned cities. "The usual for cities near military installations."

"The military didn't have time to act or react," Mac said. "But no unusual radiation. The facility inside the mountain is locked down. There's no way in. We still shouldn't discount the problem of silos dotted across the countryside, like the ones near the Missouri Breaks. Half of them were active at the time of the war. We don't know how many launched, or if any."

"Great," Hunter muttered. "Nukes for everyone."

Chapter Five   73

"Do you want to see it?" Wade asked Shan. "They sealed the blast doors, but there's a small operations base. Nothing interesting."

"No, thanks. I'll have to pass." She absolutely didn't. The reasons were many, and personal.

"Then we're done here. The plan for now – we're finding a camping spot up in the trees. Tomorrow at daybreak, we're going around the mountain and making for Cripple Creek." Wade believed they were prepared for any scenario, including the possibility of crossing other humans, hostile or not. "It's forty-five or fifty miles. They'll be rough miles. Expect to stay there overnight. Don't get comfortable."

The first morning out of Cripple Creek, they lost a pack mule in a landslide, and almost lost Noel, too. Since the war, there was no such thing as typical or average weather. The South Platte River was in the midst of spring thaw, flooding large swathes throughout the valley. Travel was treacherous at best, and slow, clearly not the first time the river had flooded, from the sheer amount of debris. It was hours after dark before they got to Lake George, and the team found no improvement in conditions. Halfway up a hillside towards the north, they found a hotel as intact as they could expect for a building unmaintained twenty years.

Stabling the horses in the lobby, Wade and Dallas took first watch while the rest set up on the second floor to crash for the night. Or four hours, for whoever drew the duty next. A few pieces of dilapidated furniture cleared out of the way gave everybody dry, livable space, although rest was the biggest motivation.

"I can't move," Mac announced, staring at the ceiling from his sleeping bag.

"I'll take the shift," Shan offered, working up the effort to peer over at him. They all carried various bumps and bruises from their brush with Mother Nature.

He groaned, an answer that might have been a yes or no.

"I'm awake, anyway."

"The watch is with Hunter."

Silence. "Okay, forget I offered," she told him.

"Thanks anyway."

It seemed like she had just fallen asleep when Mac was there again, shaking her. "Quiet, quick," he whispered, crouching next to her with his 10mm in hand. She was moving, dressed, tactical gear on, pack rolled, ready to go. Noel and Hunter too, stowing their supplies.

"Wade and Dallas are downstairs," Mac motioned, letting them know. "We're going to split and run. We've been over the contingencies for this dozens of times. I hope you were paying attention."

"Nomads," Hunter said. "A dozen or more, carrying serious firepower. They might not be looking for us, but they're looking for someone."

"Get your headsets," Mac ordered. "We're going to be too busy to be screwing around with hand held ones."

"Three groups," Wade got on the air and told them. "Major, get them moving." Gunfire erupted, close enough they could hear without the headsets.

"We need to break up our Scouts." Mac said.

"Do it."

Mac didn't like changing their plans, but neither of them had made the trip to Cody. Traveling blind was dangerous enough without the threat of Nomads, and it was a different route than the one they'd followed south. Their rookie had been to the area with his previous job in the caravans. "All right, Shan, you're with Hunter."

"Alex," Shan said. Mac stopped, a warning when they used given names while in the field. "This is the sort of trouble Wade thought we might cross."

"Get out, use any force necessary. Primary rendezvous point." Mac didn't have time to worry about other details. They were being overrun.

Chapter Five

"The north side is clear. Go," Wade said.

"We're on the second floor," Shan said, as if they needed a reminder.

"No shit," Hunter offered, pushing the window open and having a careful look outside. The hill sloped enough the drop wasn't dangerous, but they would need to circle half the building to get at their horses. "You jump, I'll cover," he said.

"Watch your back," she said, gripping her pack with both hands. She jumped. The ground was wet rather than frozen and Shan rolled before she came up on her feet. Hunter dropped rifles to her and hit the ground a moment later. They ran, trying to be quiet, trying to spot intruders.

Dallas met them with horses. "Don't wait around for us," he said. Nomads opened fire, muzzle flashes giving away their positions. Hunter's horse squealed once and thudded to the ground, twitching. Shannon returned fire with her Uzi, spraying the entire corner of the building. Hunter pulled himself astride one of the remaining horses.

"Hand up, Captain," he called.

She grabbed his arm as he cut a close circle, getting a foot in the stirrup. "Go," she shouted, seeing Noel and Dallas were moving. She didn't need to encourage him.

"We'll be on foot if we aren't careful in this mud," Hunter said. She turned to fire, and seeing it was pointless, didn't, saving her ammo.

The dark didn't make it easier to evade their pursuers. They doubled back half a dozen times before going over the ridge and heading south. They both understood, wrong direction, but there was little choice in the matter.

Hunter pulled the horse up as they cleared the first stand of trees, intending to fight rather than flee. Shan flung herself off the animal and got positioned behind a truck-sized boulder, Uzi aimed down slope. Hunter didn't wait for an order, firing from horseback as the first Nomads found them. Shan popped another rider. Then they waited, cold, wet, and not having a clue how many more Nomads were coming for them.

Wade was shouting orders in her headset.

"Are we clear?" Hunter asked. He'd lost his.

"No, they're tracking all of us."

"Sonofabitch," he breathed. "Come on, then," he challenged.

"They are." Shan stepped back into cover, raising the gun and waiting. "I've got the left. You take the right." Two more Nomads crested the hill and were dead a moment later. "Check their gear, grab anything we can use because we have no supplies," she said. "Make it fast."

A quick search came up with sparse ammo and no weapons worth taking. No supplies. "We should ride double. Easier to hide," Hunter said. They cut the cinch straps on the other horses, a warning Security had picked up from years of dealing with Nomads. It meant if they kept following, they wouldn't need their horses anymore.

"Hunter and Allen," she called on her headset, hearing a lot of static. They were moving away from each other. Hunter mounted up and offered her a hand.

"Report." Wade sounded distant.

"We're clear," she told him.

"They're looking for us," Wade told her. "Don't trust that you're clear. We'll be out of range soon. You know the routine. Make for home base."

"Understood. Let's go," she told Hunter, pulling herself up behind him.

They headed south again, following the range. In most places, the snowdrifts less than a foot deep, but enough to slow them down. It was dawn before they stopped. Wrong direction, true, but on purpose this time.

"Damn," Hunter said, reining the horse up to see if anyone followed them. "That was too close." He swung a leg over the horse's neck and jumped down, ready to go again.

Shan dismounted, looking back the way they'd come. "We might not be finished yet."

"We need to decide what in the hell to do now."

"Inventory first." It didn't take long to count the few items from the saddlebag.

"If we get into a fight, we better hope they're armed with sticks and stones," he said. Their weapons were low on ammunition. "We've got no supplies. Someone had to notice. Where are we going?" He figured if she was in charge, she should have the answers. "Will they look for us? The rest of the team, I mean."

"Our rendezvous point is Cody," Shan confirmed. "Mac and Wade both said it. We're supposed to handle this on our own. That's what all those days and nights of training were for. All we have to do now is get there alive." She was stuck with a rookie, alone, in the middle of Nowhere, Colorado.

"Let's go to Cody," Hunter said, like they had another choice. It started to snow.

May 20

"Your opinion." Shan handed the binoculars to Hunter.

He peered across the valley floor at the farmhouse nestled against the hillside. Two out-buildings sat to its left, the farthest back on the tree line. Each had a corral and nothing looked like anyone had used it in years. The fences were standing, buildings with doors and windows intact, however.

"Perfect spot for an ambush," he said.

"That's what I thought."

"We've been out here three days. Unless you want to head west, we have to go north. And that's north," he nodded. "Everyone else is halfway to Cody by now."

She scooted backwards down the slope, and then stood, trying to consider a better option. If the weather held, their winter camos would be blatant against the landscape in a couple more days. That was the most minor of her concerns.

Hunter followed her. "Your call, Captain."

"We'll see what it looks like towards nightfall."

"It'll look the same as at daybreak, and the same as it does now."

She hated to admit he was right, so she didn't. "We're not going down there now. We might go when the light starts to fade. Not in full daylight, not in the dark. It all depends on how I feel about it."

Hunter didn't like the idea that what they were going to do depended on how a teenage girl felt. He hoped to hell her rank was the real thing. So far, she'd held her own. Dallas told him she'd earned her way in Security, and if he was wrong, they'd probably both be dead by daybreak.

Dusk, or as close to it as the overcast afternoon was going to give before dark. Two-thirds of the way across the valley, in the fading gray light, Hunter slipped off the horse to sneak into the trees and cover her. If anyone was there, they wouldn't realize she was female, or armed, until they were close. If they were that close, she could take care of it.

A 9mm in her lap, Shan stopped in front of the house at a discreet distance. She dismounted, holding the weapon against her leg, and moved towards the porch. It was quiet out, even the steady wind having died down like it did every evening. Not wanting to get out of Hunter's line-of-sight, she stopped at the door, knowing they weren't alone, waiting for someone else to move first.

Hunter opened fired the moment after Scavengers broke cover and converged on the house. So did two or three of the Scavengers, although several turned and ran at the first sign of resistance. He didn't bother picking off those running. Ammunition was getting scarce.

She barely got the 9mm raised as she fired at the tall, scrawny one lunging towards her. He caught her across the legs as he went down and sent her sprawling across the porch. "Milo," she whistled, the horse side-stepping away from a pair of the marauders. There was more fire. Wood chips shattered from the windowsill above her and she rolled off the porch, coming up against the front of it, returning fire.

Hunter covered ground fast once the gun play started, despite the snow. He popped two men sneaking up the east side of the house and a lone Scavenger sniping at him from the corral. Doubling back and dodging between the barns, he heard Shannon whistle, then more gunfire. He found himself face-to-face with an AK-47 wielded by an angry camo-clad man. Hunter flinched as he fired, no time to do anything else.

The bullets spattered harmlessly in the dirt. A startled look covered the Scavenger's face as he collapsed forward onto the ground, bleeding out. The handle of a good-sized butcher knife protruded from his spine - no blade, just a handle. Actual Scavengers were feral. From appearances, being clean shaven, and wearing well-kept clothes, the man wielding the knife was no Scavenger. He nodded, smiling. Collecting the AK, he motioning for Hunter to be silent and follow him. Hunter decided it was a good idea.

By the time they got around the house, what had been happening was over. There was a dead Scavenger lying in front of the door, another ten yards out. "Shan," he called after a few moments. She had a way of disappearing into the scenery when she wanted to.

"Hunter," she answered from the roof, the .22 pointed in their general direction.

"It's all right, he's not one of them," Hunter told her. "Are we clear?"

She shook her head, "No. Catch." Shan dropped the rifle to him. On the lowest overhang, she hopped down next to Milo. The horse looked bored. "We need to clear the house," she said. "And see where we stand."

"My sons are taking care of the rest of the raiders," Hunter's savior spoke.

"How many sons?" Hunter asked, throwing Shan a look. They weren't out of the fire yet.

He held up three fingers.

"Three?" Hunter asked.

"Three," he agreed.

"Where are they?"

He gestured towards the outbuildings. "There, waiting for me. I'm Jacob Lowry. I've lived here sixty-six years." He could have been any age. Salt-and-pepper hair cut but not buzzed, with a matching full beard and mustache that covered a weathered face. He was taller than Hunter even though he stooped a bit and seemed to have a limp. In faded denims and a once blue shirt, he looked as strong as a horse.

"I'm Hunter, this is Shannon," he introduced, if she was a senior officer or not. "We're traveling together. Are there more Scavengers here?"

"Scavengers. Raiders, yes. There are more, but they'll run. We're too many and we have guns now." Shan tried not to start for a weapon as two more men appeared from inside the house. "Simon and Oliver, my sons. Mason is watching out back. He's the youngest. He was born after the war, like you," he told Shannon.

Jacob talked to his sons out of earshot. Shan sighed, not liking how dark it had gotten or how vulnerable they were. These people weren't hostile, at least not towards her and Hunter. They harbored a hatred of the raiders. There was something else, too.

"Meltdown?" Hunter whispered.

"No, isolation."

"Of course the 'Conda – isn't that what you call yourselves? They claim everyone over twenty-five has meltdown. That would include me, wouldn't it?"

"Do you have meltdown, Lt.?"

"Define meltdown. Do I have scars of what happened during the war, of what I saw? Yes, I do. So I suppose that's your answer."

"For them, isolation is the issue. As far as meltdown, anyone who can remember the war qualifies," she stated, so he would understand.

"That sure as hell includes me."

She tried not to notice how hollow his voice sounded. "Meltdown isn't my biggest concern right now. First, how secure are we here?"

"Our hosts, are they allies or enemy?"

"They aren't hostile towards us, as long as they don't think we're raiders."

"If they thought that, we'd already know," he scoffed, remembering how quickly Jacob had dispatched that raider.

"I agree."

"Now what?" Hunter accepted her instinct about their predicament because Wade trusted her judgment and he was a fucking Commander.

"We see if we can barter for some supplies. Maybe they can tell us the best route north. I don't know." She rubbed her eyes, so far beyond tired. "It's high time to get out of Colorado."

He pushed loose hair back from her forehead. "Hurt?"

"No. I have this fantasy about a hot shower and a bed with a pad instead of the frozen ground."

"Proper food," Hunter said. They'd been picking off small game with the .22 since they left Lake George, but the rain had driven most creatures with any sense into cover.

"Oh yeah, that's at the bottom of the wishing well."

Jacob returned. "You should stay. Nighttime is dangerous to travel. There's plenty of supper, and we have a room upstairs where it's warm. The roof doesn't leak. Spend some time and talk. There aren't many visitors out this way anymore."

"We'll stay," Hunter said, taking the lead. It seemed safer that way. "See," he told her. "Sometimes wishes come true."

Someone once told her to be careful what she wished for. They hadn't said why.

May 21

The stew was rabbit, with carrots, garlic, green peppers, onions, and potatoes, and it had been delicious. Well past midnight by the time they got to eat, they made small talk with their host, Hunter doing most of the talking. Shan excused herself after a while to use the bathtub next to their room. A quick bath, but it was a bath. The bed was a real down-filled feather mattress, so soft she imagined she might sink in completely. She fell asleep in moments.

When she woke, it wasn't because of anything in particular. Right then, she didn't have the impression of someone watching her. Sometimes, she could almost see a face to go with the sensation. As she slipped back towards sleep, the idea came to her. There wasn't one face beyond her sight. There were several. Shan pulled herself awake, sitting up.

"What?" Hunter, having isolated himself on the far edge of the mattress, asked, only a little awake himself. He'd stayed downstairs with their host most of the night.

"Nothing," she whispered. "What's the time?"

"Just before daybreak."

Shan moved closer. "You're warm."

He could feel her breathing on his neck. It tickled, among other sensations. "And you're spoken for." She stifled a laugh, and he remembered how young she was.

"Who tells you these things?"

"Dallas."

"I'm not married, not engaged, and any relationship I have you'd call open. Right now I'm cold. Unless you had something else in mind."

"No," Hunter said, wondering if he lost his mind over the past few days. He silently cursed at Dallas, then Wade. In a few moments, he sat up, pulling his boots on.

"Where did you get clean clothes?" He'd given her a set of thermals to sleep in.

"Jacob." He pointed to a dresser in the corner. "There are some that should fit you, or at least come close."

She recalled a discussion in the middle of the night. They'd used horses to drag the dead Scavengers over to the next field to burn them. Hunter had collected her clothes and taken them downstairs. She didn't remember him returning. They'd been sharing a sleeping bag, so she was used to him being close.

He stopped beside her. "He said, if these don't suit you, we can go to town and get some that do."

"Town?"

Hunter shook his head, smiling, and exited downstairs.

Shan followed a couple of minutes later and the first thing he noticed was the conspicuous absence of her sidearms. She'd adapted the too-large clothes to fit her using his belt and rolling the sleeves. With her hair tied up, she didn't look dangerous. Hunter knew better now. He owed Dallas a drink.

No one else was around.

"They have things to do," Hunter said.

"So do we. Like figuring out how long it's going to take us to get to Cody, and how late we are." If Wade didn't send teams from Cody out looking for them, she figured Mac would talk him in to it. Then she'd raise hell with both of them. She wasn't a child, she could find her way.

"Four and a half days since we got jumped in Lake George," he said, leaning against a counter, contemplating how good a cup of coffee would be.

"Is that all?" Shan wasn't hungry. "Perishable food would be in an icebox of some sort since they don't have working electricity." The stove was cast iron and powered by wood.

"Rabbit stew?"

"No, thanks."

"Should we make a side trip to Jacob's town?"

"Even if it's close, more of a delay."

"You're worried about Wade. If we come dragging into Cody a week after everyone else, he's liable to fire me and be done." He didn't like Wade, but he'd developed a certain amount of respect.

"When you get on his bad side, it's a long road back." She wasn't aware of the details of their fist fight, but she knew why. "At least you don't think he's going to kill you anymore," she teased, then fell right back to being Capt. Allen. "This is important. As in, the most important thing we've uncovered during Sweeps. We found what could be an actual town out here. And I'm not worried about Wade, I'm worried about being treated like a rookie."

"Ouch. But you're right. The Vista can't be the center of the universe."

"How many people live in this town?"

"Six hundred and some," Jacob answered, wandering into the kitchen. He was quiet for someone so large. "The state, this part of it, has farms all over. We provide food and livestock, the town protects us as best they can."

"Do the raiders live near town?" Hunter asked.

"Oh, no," Jacob's face lit up with amusement. "Vance ran them out a long time ago," he recalled. "Ten years or more."

"Vance?" Shan asked.

"He'd be the governor of Colorado, if we still had elections, or governors," Jacob confirmed. "He keeps the raiders away most of the time. Sometimes strays come in, from the south or the east."

"How did he run them out?" Hunter asked.

"He took over. Killed the raiders who refused to leave."

"Sounds reasonable to me," Shan said. "Where is this town?"

"That direction," Jacob pointed to the south. "A summer day's ride. If you leave right after breakfast, you get there before the sun sets."

"Tell us about the raiders Vance chased off."

"Before they came to Colorado, Vance was one of them." Jacob told the story he'd heard. "They raided here too, but Vance, he wanted to stop, to settle here and have a quiet life. Some of them sided with Vance, and some didn't. They fought." Jacob didn't enjoy remembering. He fidgeted as he spoke, shifting from one foot to the other.

"Did you help Vance?" Hunter asked.

Jacob nodded again. "I lost a son in the fight. The raiders stayed in town. There weren't so many people then, and when they got to fighting, many of us helped. Vance and his people killed most of the others. Some ran and Vance hunted them. Now there are safe places and some laws."

"Like before the war," Hunter said.

"Nothing is like before the war," Jacob said. "Not even people. Are you going to town today?"

"No," Hunter told him. Shannon looked skeptical.

"Talk with her," Jacob told them, off again, about his business.

"What do you want to do?" Hunter asked, following Shan to the porch. She sat on the edge, deep in thought.

"I want to go to Jacob's town. We need to get to Cody and report this."

He sat next to her. "If the weather holds, there could be a team out here before winter. It's the end of May. We might be home by mid-June, send a team out, and they'd get here by the end of July."

"If the weather holds, and if Command agrees. That's a big 'if' because we have a stalemate going with Council, in case you hadn't heard." Shan had to decide. Input from her team would make it easier, but they weren't co-dependent like that.

"So?"

"We go to Cody," she told him.

"What is it that makes Council put a roadblock up with everything we do?" Hunter had never gotten the entire story, or even a clear picture of what the story was. It was something intriguing and mysterious. Security seemed to lean that way.

"Six years ago, when Carl Dewitt died, several Council members and civilians opted for the Chair position." Shan remembered, although she'd still been in school and the situation hadn't meant a lot to her. "When it came down to a final vote, Security pushed for Haines. Guess who came in second?"

"Richard Cameron?"

"Indeed. Mary Dona Delgado found out she was pregnant, and quit the next week. Since the vote was less than thirty days old, that's how Richard got to be a Council member without even being elected. It's split Council ever since. Richard has a grudge. He figured with Wade being an officer, he was a shoo-in."

"Wade chose Security over his step-father."

"Not that simple," Shan said. "He'd only been in a few months. He was a rookie, but he'd known Richard for twelve years. I missed the details, being a kid and not caring about things like politics."

"I bet that makes for some interesting family dinners."

"You better believe it does," Shan told him. She'd experienced a few of those. "That's why I don't crack jokes about Cameron."

He smiled, catching the reference. "When should we go?"

"Soon. Let's say tomorrow morning. I want to sleep in that bed again tonight."

"I'll tell Jacob."

"We'll leave early. He seems to talk easier to you. Barter for some supplies, an extra horse. The only guns I've seen here besides what we picked off the Scavengers yesterday are an old twelve gauge in sorry shape and a .22 long rifle in worse. Offer him my .22 and ammo. Give him the box of shotgun shells to sweeten the deal even if he doesn't want to trade. It might sway him."

"We can spare it."

"Whoever was following us, isn't now. We can try to go straight-shot, use the highways, and make Cody in a few days," she said. "Less if we get lucky and the weather doesn't open the skies up on us again. Get another horse, everything will be easier. Or it might take weeks. Any way, we can sneak north, like we have been. I'm not going to worry about it for a few hours."

"This reminds me of the ranch a little," Hunter reminisced,

watching the dogs playing along the dirt path. Wildflowers were in bloom past the stables and it was... peaceful.

"You had a ranch?"

"My family had three homes. The big house in the city, a ranch out in the country, and a place near Taos, for vacations. The ranch had dogs, and chickens, horses. I remember some cows, a few llamas." He smiled at the memory.

"They had a bit of money, did they?" she smiled back, enjoying a few moments of quiet.

"I suppose. We spent long weekends at the ranch."

"Taos?"

"Northern New Mexico, way off the beaten path up in the mountains. We'd fly into Taos and take the back roads. Used to be a big ski resort."

"Was that a bit terrifying?"

"Skiing or flying?"

"I ski just fine," Shan said.

"Flying. It was something we always did. I never even thought to be afraid."

"You see it in movies, but no. I don't think I could pull that one off. I'd cry like a little girl."

He nudged her with an elbow. "You are a girl."

"You noticed."

Hunter didn't answer.

"Is that why you and Wade fight? Because I'm a girl?" She'd heard every rumor, and they didn't bother her. If Wade was pissed, there was something more.

"I'd rather not discuss it."

"That's what I figured you'd say. Whatever you've heard, it's probably not be true," Shan offered a truce. "Wade has his harem of women and I'm not part of that. He's my best friend, my partner, and I'd do damned near anything he asked me to."

"Understood," Hunter said.

"I don't care what happened between the two of you because it was the heat of the moment. Play with Security, get some bumps and bruises. Wade knows what he's doing. If you don't trust him, look for another line of work."

"I've had my fill of running with the caravans."

"Kicked out?"

"Quit. Moved on."

"Why?" Shan asked.

"Seems to me we weren't much different from Scavengers. We didn't kill people because they were there, but picking through empty cities, it's rough. Some days are worse than others. I wanted something better."

"Security?" She found it amusing, having wondered more than once if she should move to the caravans. A lot of officers did.

"Here I am," he figured. "I guess we'll see how that works out when we get to Cody."

"Stop worrying," she told him.

"As soon as you do."

Something worked around the edges of his thoughts, distracting him, and it was before breakfast. The sensation became a little clearer, then it was gone, happening twice more in rapid succession. Vance gave up the idea of sleep, heading to the City Center on a day he'd hoped to get away. Summer issues were far more urgent than winter ones. This was exponentially worse.

"Tell Caulder and Cooper I'm here and send them in as soon as they arrive," he told his sentry. Then he sat down for a cup of tea. Chamomile. Appropriate, considering. He'd need more than tea to calm things down if what he'd sensed was accurate, and the more he thought about it, the more certain he was.

A soft rap on the door a short time later, and both men appeared. "What's today's plans?" Caulder, preferring to be called JT, asked for both of them.

"No, nothing so organized as that," Vance said. "It's my day off." A nice day, too, high clouds against the deep blue Rocky Mountain sky, warm too, for so early in the year. A wasted day now.

Cooper understood. "That means something unexpected has reared its ugly head and we get to go clean it up."

They were damned near half his age. Going out for weeks at a time didn't bother them. Getting into a fight didn't either. True, JT was a temporary resident, but he did the job he was there for. "Do you remember that recurring problem we had up north?" Vance asked.

"Up north," Cooper repeated, crossing his arms.

"Up north."

"Do you mean that little enclave with a batch of active Altered?"

"I do."

"How many are a 'batch'?" JT asked. He had faint memories of the big war, but the smaller ones, hell, he'd been involved in a lot of those. This didn't sound good.

"I don't know. After civilization left us, we've avoided prolonged contact with each other as much as possible. The part that concerns me is the active part." Vance had no illusions that this wouldn't become a problem. "At the very least, there are two."

"Two?" JT repeated. "Are two a concern?"

"These two are," Cooper said.

JT put together conversations he'd overheard. "Are these the ones in Montana?"

Cooper and Vance nodded. "Except sometimes they aren't in Montana," Vance continued. "Sometimes they wander about to see the sights. We try to keep tabs on them, but it's not a simple thing to do because of a lot of reasons, not the least being distance, weather and the fact they are active."

"That's why we're here," JT said.

"Where are they now?" Cooper asked.

"If the weather stays good, you could have lunch with them tomorrow."

"Ah, hell, tell me they aren't snooping around NORAD."

"I could tell you that," Vance said. "Or I might tell you they were there yesterday."

"What do we do about it?" JT asked.

"Nothing," Vance said. "For now. Nothing may come of this. It all depends on Rafe."

"He took up residence damned close to NORAD a few years ago."

"A few," Cooper agreed. "He won't react well to this."

"If he even knows," JT said.

"He knows," Vance said.

"So we wait for Rafe to make a move?" JT had met him, but all he knew was what they'd told him, and that wasn't much.

"We stay the hell out of his way," Cooper said. "We'll live longer."

"If Rafe does anything about this, we'll hear. I will. What comes next is up to him," Vance said.

"Of course. So we get to spend the summer waiting for a psychopath to decide what town he wants to burn out next."

"He's not indiscriminate. We wait, we watch. When the opportunity arises, we go sift through the ashes to find out what he's done."

"Should we warn them?" JT asked.

"Montana is none of our business," Vance said. "Until Rafe makes it our business."

Chapter Six

May 26 Cody 8am

Wade knew the rumors, and in fact, it wasn't unexpected or even much of a surprise. One of his people got a message relayed to Cody to confirm with him. He was still pissed, to imagine Cameron waited until Sweeps, until they were on Alert One, to pull a stunt like this. Richard had gotten himself a majority of Council votes and closed some of the long distance caches. He was always sneaking up on Security with something. Wade would have to wait to deal with the issue until he got back to The Vista, not sitting in a makeshift com room hundreds of miles away.

"What are you going to do now?" Dallas asked. He didn't approve of all his methods, but it was called a generation gap. He understood why Wade was cautious of his step-father.

"Richard is predictable, and the 'Conda is in no real danger. The caches are a minor problem." They could only order the official ones closed, after all.

Dallas nodded.

"Are we off the record?"

Again, a nod. "If we need to be," Dallas told him.

"We do. Other officers are aware, but don't repeat this. The caches on paper aren't the only ones. They never have been, and now you see the reason."

"Why are you telling me? I don't fit the profile of your circle of friends."

Wade pushed back in his chair. "I trust you; you're neutral in this, and the welfare of The Vista is your priority."

"Is that their priority?"

"Of course."

"Would you care to elaborate?" Dallas asked.

Wade considered it for a few moments. "You've got to understand, The Vista isn't the only city left in North America. If we're alive, there are other survivors. Statistically, the numbers are there. Allies made are better than enemies unknown."

"What if they aren't allies?"

"Would you rather be blind, or know what's out there? Who is out there? Council believes it would be better to wait for first contact to be made by them rather than us."

"I can't think waiting for outlanders to find us is a good idea. It goes against standard protocols, for one. Attracting Nomads or worse towards The Vista, not so good, either."

"We're not going to hand them a map of Montana with a big 'We Are Here' sign," Wade said.

"True enough. What about Hunter?" The animosity between them was obvious.

"He has nothing to do with this."

"Right now, he's out here somewhere as part of your Sweeps Team, so I beg to differ. He could be an asset to the 'Conda," Dallas said.

"I don't see that happening." Wade shifted, crossing his arms. "Why are his files sealed?"

"For his safety."

An instant, a thought Wade had that startled him. What if

Hunter was like them? Wouldn't Shannon have known? Or was he something they'd never run across, like them, but that she couldn't sense? Fatigue, Wade decided, putting stray thoughts in his mind. He shook it off. "Safety from what?" he asked, anyway.

"From things long dead."

No help. "You can't be more specific?"

"No more specific than you can be about the 'Conda. It would defeat the purpose of sealed files."

"If it compromised the safety of my team, I want to warn them."

"Your team is in no danger from Hunter's past," Dallas assured him.

"Convince me," Wade said. "How would telling me be a danger to him?"

"You have a point. The quick version. His family was a prominent one. When war became imminent, they sent me to bring him home, but too late. Communications went down first, then everything was gone. We ended up in The Vista after a few months. The rest of his family, we lost contact early on. We wouldn't even know where to look for them."

"There are dozens, maybe hundreds, of stories similar to that in our archives," Wade said, getting no hint of a lie.

"I adopted him. I consider him my son, as much a part of my family as my biological children. He's an adult now. If he screws up, that's not my problem. It's his responsibility."

"Is he an oldest child?"

An odd question, Dallas thought. "No."

Wade nodded, relieved. The Gen Ens, the aware ones, were firstborn. It might not hold true, but it was his observation. "Hunter doesn't need to be told about this. Neither does Shannon. This doesn't concern their jobs."

"It does, but I understand. You should still consider he might be an asset to you."

"If things go as planned," Wade continued, "we'll man the outpost here in Cody by the end of the summer. Command will recognize the 'Conda as being in charge. He can apply to transfer out here, like any other officer."

"Are you taking over Station One?" he asked, only half-joking. They already had.

"The village, too, for accommodations. A separate security force is an added layer of protection, and being outside the confines of The Vista leaves us free to deal with imminent threats and not have to ask permission first." The 'Conda wouldn't approve of Dallas being told such information, but it was Wade's decision. Even in private, few would question him.

"You're asking for trouble from Council, not like those arguments in chambers. Real trouble."

"I'm a member of Command. Council concerns aren't my concerns."

"Shannon disappearing in Colorado with Hunter is?"

"No." Mac had sent her off with Hunter, not him. It wasn't a bad call. That didn't change the fact it bothered him.

"Is there anything I can help you with?" Dallas asked.

"Not unless you can tell me about the Nomads we ran across in Colorado. They might be the same group that set off the warhead on the Missouri Breaks ten years ago."

May 27 outskirts of Cody midday

"Where in Cody are we going?" Hunter asked.

"As our navigator, you're supposed to know these things," Shan said, itching to be done with their little adventure. "Did they set up camp close to the highway or somewhere less obvious?"

"Virgin, remember, my first Sweeps?" he teased, having heard it from her a few times.

"Then we're officially lost."

"After bailing out of Colorado like we did? Maybe not so much.

You're lucky and I'm good. Plus, I traveled here with a caravan not long ago. We staged near the highway, up in the west end, at an old school complex." He peered through his binoculars for a few moments. "That's an airport right in front of us, if it helps."

Shan tried her handset. "Sweeps Team One, Team Base, are you on the air?" Static. "They should've been here for days already." She didn't dare try to contact her partners in their unconventional way, not with Hunter so close. He wasn't stupid, and he might just think she was crazy.

"Just because they're not talking to you doesn't mean they're not here."

"Well, that makes me feel better." She sighed, knowing it wouldn't get easier. "They're here, but Cody is bigger than The Vista. We might spend a long time tracking them down."

"Especially if they don't want to be found."

"Team Base, over?" The sun was as high as it was going to be for the day. They had time to look.

"West," Hunter repeated.

Shan let him lead. Cody looked like every other city she'd seen, as if humans had simply stopped existing. It was damned close to the truth.

Close to an hour later, noise crackled on the radio. Then, "Sweeps Team One, go ahead." She recognized Kyle Taylor, even through a garbled reply. She was relieved his team was out of Utah.

"Call word?" Hunter cautioned.

She knew that. "What's your call word?"

"Orion. And yours?"

"Rodeo. Is this Lt. Taylor?"

"Yes it is, Capt. Allen. Good to hear from you. Did you decide to vacation in Bora Bora? Because if that's the case, we all want an invitation."

"Is everyone in Security a smart ass?" Shan asked, but not on the air. She wasn't even certain where Bora Bora was.

"As far as I can tell," Hunter said.

"Is Cmdr. Wade in?"

"Not at the moment. Wade and MacKenzie are out surveying for something or another, due back before dark, or when they get bored."

"What's happening around town?"

There were a few moments of silence. "I was going to ask you the same thing."

"Nothing unusual that I'm aware of," Shan proceeded with caution. Team Three needed to figure out what in the hell had happened.

"No tailgaters following you out of Colorado?"

"No." She didn't have to elaborate.

"Where are you now?" Taylor asked.

"We're in the west section. We crossed a double set of railroad tracks and there's a water tower about a mile east of us," Hunter relayed.

"Gotcha," Taylor said. "The city is clear for now. I'll send Green and Ballentyne around to bring you in."

"Perfect," Shan said. "Out."

Hunter dismounted. "This place has a good defensive position, better than The Vista. The valley is narrower, less access."

"They had to block seven roads to close off The Vista, twenty years ago," Shan told him. "This place has a lot more."

"They fortified it, maybe before the war. Everyone died or left. A lot of communities, especially out west, tried to isolate themselves when the flu started killing people."

"Did the governments even try to stem the spread?"

"The way things were, you could fly anywhere in hours. With the outbreak in Eastern Europe, they never had containment. They developed a vaccine for the first one, it was a seasonal thing. Two doses ten days apart, hurt like hell."

"The ones we have now are pretty basic." According to her mother, rudimentary but necessary.

"Speculation was, radiation mutated the virus. It moved too fast. And here we are." Hunter was remembering, not reciting.

"The war and what came before is ancient history to me, a thing they teach us about in school."

"I spent my eleventh birthday somewhere in Iowa, running from the firestorms... The entire state must have burned." He remembered, crystal clear. "Fire fell out of the sky like rain. I got sick, maybe it was the flu, maybe it wasn't. Scared the hell out of Dallas and that was when he decided to travel north rather than west. Less traffic."

"I saw the bomb on the Missouri Breaks," Shan said, sharing confessions. "I still have nightmares. That, and the helicopters."

"They never thought anyone would use the nukes."

"When have people ever had a weapon they didn't use?"

"You don't have a clue about life before, so don't pretend you do. It doesn't matter how many books you've read or movies you've seen. It doesn't matter what your parents remember. You didn't live it." He stopped, anger misplaced.

"That's what separates us, and it's a rift we can't span. Command keeps trying, we know better." Shan was the calm one for a change.

"The 'Conda is making excuses," he started.

"No, don't." She slid from her horse to exercise her legs. "Don't tell me things I'll have to repeat to them later."

"I wasn't aware they cared what I thought."

"Do you think they're playing house out at Station One? They brought down the helicopters after Vista Security took so many casualties."

"You say it like you're not a part."

"I advise them on matters," Shan told him.

"You're not a member?"

She started walking. "No, I'm not."

"Any reason?"

"That, Lt., is none of your business." As a founder of the group, she wasn't a member. None of Team Three were, to keep them out of Council's cross-hairs. A technicality, but it worked.

"You have a reason for everything you do, or don't do," he stated a simple fact. "Are Wade and Mac members?"

Shan glanced over. "I'm not at liberty to divulge such information."

"You enjoy having that hint of mystery."

She smiled at him and kept walking.

"Home Base, this is Team Three."

Busy place today, Taylor decided as he crossed the hall to get to the radio. "Team Three, go ahead."

"Team Three."

"Call word Echo," Taylor answered.

"What's a word that begins with 'H'?" Wade asked Mac. They were weary of gathering information, knowing the chances anyone would read it were slim. East of Cody, looking down on the city they'd soon be calling home, it was time to call it a day.

Mac raised his eyebrows. "Happy. Horny."

"You want me to use 'horny' as a call word on the air?"

"No," he said. "I couldn't think of anything else. At least Pacifica isn't listening in here to report us." They laughed at the idea, knowing if they were home, it might happen.

Leaning forward to adjust himself in the saddle, Wade said, "Home Base, this is Team Three."

"Go ahead."

When they stopped laughing again, Wade answered with, "Horizon, Home Base."

"Good enough," Taylor said. By then Shannon had joined him in the temporary com room to see what the issue was.

"They couldn't think of a call word," she told him.

"We'll be there in an hour, give or take ten. Minutes, I mean. What's our status?"

"We're all clear."

"Have our wayward officers shown?" Wade asked.

"In fact, Senior Wayward Officer is right here. They've been at the base long enough to eat and hit the showers, in that order."

"Damn, I'm glad that's done." Mac breathed a sigh of relief for both of them.

"Let me talk to her," Wade said.

"Don't pin designations on me like that because it will stick," she scolded Taylor.

"SWO," Taylor repeated. "Senior Wayward Officer."

"You, shut up."

"Did you run into trouble?" Wade asked her.

"We had Scavenger trouble, not Nomad trouble. Not the trouble we saw at Lake George. We took care of it."

"Are you all right?"

"We both are. They didn't follow us out of Colorado. And you?"

"Collecting that information Command wants. It's time to head north." They were both aware of the routine, but Wade was the one responsible for all of them. "Team Three needs to meet today. I don't care how late we get there."

"We do," she agreed. "I need to talk to you about things I only talk to you about." Not-so-subtle double talk, because of Taylor.

"I want radio silence."

"Copy," Taylor noted.

"Out."

"The past couple of days, he's been quiet," Taylor told Shan. "Too quiet. You see how he gets."

Wade was always quiet. "I know," she said. It could be what he worried the most about, whoever was watching them, and why. To her, it didn't feel that way.

"I mean, damn, Shannon. You scared the hell out of him."

"Didn't do me much good either. Would it have bothered him if it was you or Mac out there?" She suspected the Nomads were of far more a concern than her lost in Colorado with the rookie.

"You know the answer. Your safety is more important to him than his own. It's always been that way."

She didn't respond, a discussion between Dallas and Hunter coming into earshot.

"Wade was concerned about team members wandering the Rockies with no backup, too," Taylor clarified.

"It's his job to be concerned."

"And my job is to cover him."

"Stick with that story," Shan said. "Did they know we didn't have any supplies?"

"They said you lost your horse."

"Milo is alive and well and resting in the stable."

"That was my horse," Hunter said, joining them. "With all the supplies I grabbed when we ran."

"How did that happen?" Taylor asked Shan.

"I was just tagging along for the hell of it," she scoffed, getting annoyed at the unnecessary questions. "I left everything but my guns and backpack in the hotel when I jumped out the window. There were other concerns."

"A scenario for the rookies. Drop them off somewhere with no supplies." Taylor thought it was a great idea, knowing full well Hunter was a rookie.

"We had a couple of guns, a canteen, a sleeping bag, and not much else," Hunter added.

"Just one?" Taylor chuckled.

"I'm glad this amuses you," Shan said. "It wasn't funny then, it's not funny now."

"Thanks." Hunter pretended to be hurt.

She scowled at Hunter, then Taylor. "I outrank both of you, right?" Without waiting for an answer, she stalked off to go wait for Team Three.

"Now she's pissed at me." Hunter didn't like the idea.

"If she was, she wouldn't have left," Taylor told him. "She'd be here thinking up new ways of torture. For us. Trust me."

"You better hope so," Dallas said. "You're due for a promotion. Guess who's on the Senior Security Board this year?"

"Team Three?" Hunter asked.

Dallas smiled. "Bingo."

"How does a teenager get to be a senior officer?"

"There's a story. All three of them fit that description. She started in Dispatch at fourteen, and they put her on the road a year and a half later with Ballentyne. She's been driving circles around The Vista by herself for four years," Taylor said. "Wade's been an officer two years longer than her, Mac a few months more. Ask one of them about the Blackout sometime, in private, and you'll find out why they're. Or more to the point, Command," Taylor amended. Seniority was by team designations and nothing official.

"She said the 'Conda brought down the helicopters," Hunter remembered.

Taylor snorted. "Yeah, they get credit for the first one. The second one, Team Three took out, and two of them got shot. Nothing you read about the firefight is accurate, but again, ask them, not me. Make it off the record if you want to hear the actual story, if they decide to share."

"So I should catch Wade in a good mood."

"Without a doubt," Taylor said. "Or if you're smart, ask anyone but him."

"Wade doesn't like talking business."

"About his team, no. If you're not part of his inner circle and you want to make a career of Security, some things are better left alone. Team Three is at the top of that list."

June 5 before daybreak

"How is Milo this morning?" Hunter scratched behind his ear and patted him on the nose. The horse was disinterested, chewing on his bit.

"Milo is fine." Shannon said, busy adjusting her gear. They'd be home before dark. It felt good to see the familiar valley, the mountains she knew by heart.

"How is Capt. Allen?" he asked, having accomplished what he set out to do. Any animosity lingering between them was forgotten.

"I'm fine."

"Sure, everyone's fine now." Not perfect timing, but he went for it, anyway. "Capt. Allen?" he repeated. "There's something I want you to be aware of, before we get home and get lost in our routines." When she looked up, he caught the collar of her parka, pulled her close, kissed her, and she let him. It wasn't a delicate little thing either.

Shannon stepped back. He was expecting to get slapped, and she obliged him.

"Next time, ask first," she growled, emphasizing the last word. Grabbing Milo's reins, she flung herself into the saddle and started down the trail.

Next time, he thought. She could have hurt him a lot worse than a half-hearted smack, too. He wore a grin the rest of the way to The Vista.

Chapter Seven

June 7 after dark Station One

The 'Conda had monthly get-togethers, weather permitting. In the summer, the meetings might happen every week, and in the winter, they often had to move to the dayroom in Station Two. It was a time to catch up on the best gossip, have a cookout, a sleepover, play video games or baseball, set plans for the next meeting, enjoy some time off. Stress relief, in short. This one wasn't on the calendar, as Sweeps finished late.

The crowd grew restless. Wade made them wait anyway, patience being a good thing to learn. As it got dark, people wandered in from The Vista. Most jobs didn't require a third shift and few had strict schedules. The Stations were an exception, having four, with a rotation shift between second and third to keep a saturation of officers.

Today, they were expecting something different from the usual. It was a rare thing that Team Three attended en force.

"There is one item I'd like to propose tonight, to you as the

'Conda, as the Anaconda Central Security Corps," Wade announced after a few more minutes of letting them settle in.

Thirty-one 'Conda members and advisors turned their attention to him. All he had to say was 'listen' and they did. Sequestered away in the west wing of Station One, they'd found the privacy here they longed for. It held the depot, and an armory comparable to the one in The Vista. Several new houses nearly complete on the near side of the village would be ready for occupants by winter.

"I propose to appoint Denny Lambert as the official First Officer of the 'Conda for the next year," Wade put to them. Lambert was Team Five's Scout. He'd helped Wade establish the group and later find somewhere to make their base.

"I concede the position," Taylor said on cue.

"Are there any objections?" Wade asked. This handful of people didn't comprise a majority of the group, but what he wanted, he got. There were no objections. "Accept it or not," he told Lambert.

"I accept." The announcement didn't surprise him.

"You're aware of the 'Conda statutes. Will you abide by them as you do your Security oath?" Wade asked.

"I will."

Just like that, they had a new leader. The rest of Team Three wondered what in the hell they'd missed. Shan went to find out. She found Mac first.

"Why the sudden change?" she asked.

"Not even a clue. Are you on a run?"

"I'm heading to Station Two tonight, Dispatch tomorrow, a run with Chris soon. He's going to be out on his own in a couple more weeks. I need to get him some hours on the road." Dressed in civilian clothes, cowboy boots, blue jeans and a black tee shirt, she wore a single 9mm on her right hip. The team looked like they'd coordinated their wardrobe for the casual look. They hadn't.

"Try not to get him shot at," he teased.

"Too late, already did that." She kissed him. "You're terrible."

"That's not what all the ladies tell me."

Chapter Seven 105

Shan smiled. "I'm going to find Wade and see what we've missed."

"Fill me in later. I have company to entertain," Mac winked.

"Have fun." If she should be jealous, she didn't know. Mac's female companions were temporary, and of no concern to her.

By the time Shan tracked him down, he'd found a corner spot to settle in, and Courtney Noel sat with him. "I need to borrow Cmdr. Wade," she said, monotone.

Courtney wasn't pleased about the intrusion. "Security secrets, I suppose."

"Hmm," Shan contemplated. "I'm afraid that is classified." She'd never liked Courtney, and nothing would to change her mind. It didn't bother her that the other woman was aware.

Wade interrupted, jumping up to escort Shan a few steps away. "We are pregnant again," he told her when they were out of earshot.

"You know what causes that, yes?"

He shook his head. "Perfect timing too, don't you think?"

"Do you care what I think?" In her mind, another roadblock, another delay.

Wade didn't like the sound of that. He caught her gaze.

"This feels calculated," Shan told him. "It's not my concern, though, it's yours. Why did you replace Taylor? You could have warned us."

"I wasn't certain until a few minutes ago. Lambert needs the experience. It's only for a year. We'll see how he works out."

"Is this related to the Council offering you a position?" She hadn't heard of anyone retiring, but she hadn't known Wade was working on kid number three a few minutes earlier, either. He always had a plan within a plan and Shannon had given up a long time ago trying to see all of them. One step ahead of her, again, as sure as the sun would come up in the morning.

"They might make an offer. I'm not taking it. We want the Cody station clear of Council interference."

"If you were on the Council, you could push an outpost through their red tape a lot faster."

"They'll ask for a minimum two-year commitment. I'm not willing to wait that long."

"The two years clause is news to me," she confessed. "Still an option. We could have the place up and running and waiting for you in two years."

"They started that when Haines became Chair. It's not a viable option for me right now," he went on, not disclosing details, not yet. "Are you staying here tonight?" He wouldn't even venture into prying, not with the news he'd gotten.

"No, prior commitments."

"Take a walk with me," Wade said. Outside, the night was clear and cold, a thick pattern of stars across the sky. "I'm worried about the Nomads in Colorado."

"So am I." They walked the long gravel driveway around the station, a firebreak as well. No one else was out. Nights had been quite planet wide, going on twenty years.

"Contingencies, Shan. Remember those contingencies." To the rest of Security outside his closest friends, Wade was methodical and often distant. There was a reason for that.

Shan knew his dark side, she'd seen firsthand. When she claimed to be his bodyguard, it wasn't a joke.

"I remember."

"We're going to deal with the Nomads. It'll be sooner than later. All I can hope right now is that we can take this problem to Cody. If it gets to The Vista…"

"You have contingencies for that too," Shan said. Some they'd made together, others he'd planned with Mac. She suspected some were his alone.

"Yes."

"Do I get a clue?"

"When you need to, you will."

She sighed. "Of course."

"You have backup. No names, not now, but they're here. No, they aren't all in Security." He paused, turning to head back. "Can I ask you a personal question?" Fair warning, he figured.

"You can ask."

"Is there going to be trouble between Hunter and Mac?"

"I remember there being trouble between you and Hunter."

"Not the same sort of thing. Are you seeing him?"

"Like you're seeing Courtney, no," she scowled. "I'm on heavy rotation with Team One, so I'm practically living with them." She skipped the detail that Dallas stayed home most nights with his family rather than Station Two. He would be aware.

"Just curious."

"Do you think I'd let them fight over me? I can deal with two men the same way you have half a dozen women."

"Two?" he questioned. "Which two?"

Shan gave him a crusty look, a warning that the conversation wasn't going there.

"Even if one of those men is Alex?" Wade pressed her.

"Especially if one of those men is Alex," she said. "It changes nothing between him and I, because someday we may decide that concern doesn't matter."

"I'm sorry," he offered, knowing what she meant.

"It's not your fault, and you're right. I hate that you're right, by the way." She wasn't angry at him, not about this. She also wasn't willing to challenge the idea that their genetics were the reason they were different. "What did Hunter say to you at Depot North?"

A conversation he'd rather not have. "You're working with him now. Do you want me to repeat a snide comment he made months ago, before he knew you?"

"I've heard it all before."

"He asked if I was that lucky or if you were on my team for a reason."

Shan digested that for a few moments. Not as bad as she'd

expected, even if Wade had cleaned it up for her. "I guess after Sweeps he has his answer."

"He meant the swipe at me, not you."

"He has a problem with authority, just like you. The problem is, you're that authority figure now."

"Ouch," Wade grimaced. They stopped back at the depot, and he had a slate of activities for the next few days. "I don't have a problem with you seeing him, Shan. I don't want you to get hurt."

"That's part of life. Stop worrying about me, because eventually, we all get hurt by someone."

He nodded. Sometimes, she was far more philosophical than he could manage.

"Do you need me here for anything?" she asked.

"I can't think of a thing. If you don't want to drive alone, find someone to ride shotgun. Otherwise, radio in when you get there."

June 16 Station Two 6pm

It started out as a typical evening. Mac, having dinner in the second floor cafeteria with the Taylors, discussing how tense things were since Sweeps. A hockey game was in the works at any rate. Unlike baseball, they played hockey in summer or winter, the only difference being in the winter, they flooded a street or vacant lot, waited for it to freeze, and put on ice skates.

Cmdr. Duncan, heading for the parking garage, was going off duty after half a shift besides his own. This time of year, the weather was almost perfect, and he was looking forward to a long weekend at home.

Team One was going on duty, waiting for their Scout to show up. Dallas and Hunter stopped in the main lobby to talk to Duncan for a few minutes. He invited both over for an evening of cards. Dallas accepted, Hunter hadn't made plans.

Shannon, bored with waiting in David MacKenzie's office, listening to him banter with Wade about the ill effects of isolation such as The Vista had. It wasn't a real argument, but it was obvious where each man stood, a generation gap created by a world war. She understood David's reasons; she agreed with Wade.

They all heard the main security doors unlatch and slide open in Detention, on the other side of the tunnel, because it echoed. The metallic clang was unmistakable.

"What in the hell was that?" David MacKenzie lost his train of thought. Wrong time, he understood. Security never opened that set of doors when civilians were in the building. They didn't move prisoners during the day.

"They'll seal the building," Shannon said, rising to her feet. Even as she spoke, the lights flickered off for a moment, the automated system signaling something had triggered it. The monitors lining the west wall, scanning the jail side, went to black, then static.

A hard reset didn't work, the screens returning to static. "They're down," David said, nothing more he could do without going to the source.

"What ever happens, stay in your office," Wade said to the elder MacKenzie. "No matter what, don't leave this area," he repeated. "Dispatch is inaccessible. We're on our own for now. Do you have a weapon?"

David nodded, "Of course."

"Get it. Defend yourself if you need to," Wade told him. "Let's go," he motioned for Shannon to join him. Moments later, they ran into Hunter. He'd already drawn his sidearm, pretty certain of what happened.

"Shift change," Wade said. "There are civilians in the building."

"Damn sure," Hunter said. "Do we have any ears on?" He was trying to raise someone on his headset.

Wade shook his head. "No. How many prisoners?"

"Eleven, as of last night," Shan told them. All three had weapons drawn as Green and Ballentyne emerged from the stairwell.

"Join the party," Wade invited them. "We know the layout of the jail. We have to consider if there are prisoners loose, they have hostages and guns." When he needed a shooter and Shan was out on a run, he called Green.

"Mac and both Taylors are on the second floor," Hunter reported. "Armed and waiting for orders."

"Dallas and Duncan?"

"In the depot." They'd gone so Dallas could smoke a cigarette, and might as well have been on another planet. The power failure had also locked out the depot.

"Standby," Wade said. "We need to get over there and assess the situation. Hunter can report it to whoever is running things outside. We want to keep this contained. There are civilians here, and there's the armory to consider."

"It's closed," Ballentyne said. "Anything they need to blast it open is across town."

"That's not an absolute," Green pointed out. "After the Blackout, they ran a series of tests. Short story, when the power to Station Two gets cut, the armory vault stays locked most of the time. Sometimes it resets, like the jail doors did just now. They've never been able to figure out a way to fix it. You didn't think we open and close it manually for the fun of it?"

"So the door might be wide open," Wade said. "With eleven hostiles roaming the station. Someone has to go to the armory. Can we secure the door?" He looked at Shannon because she'd worked Dispatch the longest and Dispatch officers often manned Station One. Whoever had seniority was responsible for the armory during those times.

Shan shook her head. "I'm not a tech, so maybe."

"No, but you're my close quarters shooter," Wade said. "Bennett and Lambert are too, and they're both likely on the jail side." They all knew Ballentyne was a large arms expert, having watched him launch grenades out at the airport two days earlier.

"What now?" she asked.

"First, you and Mick," Wade meant Ballentyne, "are going to secure the armory, get all the civilians in one place and clear this floor. Green is going to watch the tunnel to make sure no one crosses." He gestured to Hunter. "We're going to go upstairs to collect some reinforcements. Then we'll show Council how we take care of problems."

Security used the offices in the west half of the building for emergency supplies and overflow inventory from the caravan centers. Anyone could get what they needed on Saturdays. At the end of the corridor, the vaulted armory. Shannon waited, taking the left side while Ballentyne took the right. He cleared a room and motioned for her to check the next. In the dark, with an unknown number of civilians, they worked slower than usual. They inspected each stack of boxes, pushed open unlocked doors, and tried to be quiet.

The next door Ballentyne tried wouldn't budge. Locked. It was an antique thing, the lock with a key that someone somewhere in The Vista had. He looked back at Shannon, and then waved her on. Unlocked, she moved through the room. Stacks of boxes, labeled and dated, lined all four walls. Someone had bricked the windows in long ago. Other than that, no human occupants, and she moved on.

As soon as he opened the next door, they both saw movement. Shan was behind him, going low as he went high. "Clear," he called out after a quick sweep.

"Civilians," Shan announced, holstering her gun. Two of the five were children. She held a finger up in front of her lips. "Vista Security," she told them. "We have to be quiet now."

"In a few minutes, we're going to move you to one of the east wing offices. Stay there, stay quiet and try not to move around a lot until we can get them to open the doors," Ballentyne said.

"Why did they lock them?" a boy of about eight asked.

Shan crouched down next to him so she could look at him at eye level. "The power is out and the doors in the jail might have opened. So, they locked all the doors until we can make sure it's safe."

"Are you armed?" Ballentyne asked.

One of the two men nodded.

"There are several civilians here," he told them. "Once we move, David MacKenzie will have you standing guard until you aren't. Until this is over. He used to be in Security, he knows what to do."

The adults agreed, nodding.

"What's your name?" Shan asked the boy.

"Aaron Maestas," he whispered. "Are you really in Security?"

"Yes, I am. I'm a Scout."

"I saw you at the hospital."

"Why were you at the hospital?" she asked, keeping him occupied for a few minutes while Ballentyne briefed the adults.

"I got hit with a stick and needed stitches."

"Ouch," Shan smiled. "I hate getting stitches."

"Me too," Aaron said.

"What doctor helped you?"

"Dr. Allen," he said after a few seconds.

"I was there to visit her, too. She's my Mom."

His hand slipped up to hold his mother's hand. "I didn't know that."

"Yep," Shan told him. "I'll tell her I saw you today."

Aaron nodded. "We'll be okay, won't we?"

"Yes, you will. That's why we're here. But you have to stay quiet and help your brother be quiet. Okay?"

Another nod.

"Stay with your mom and do what she tells you. We're going down the hall." Shan stood, waiting.

"Let's do this," Ballentyne said. "Take point."

They left their civilians in David MacKenzie's office and cleared the last three rooms outside the armory. The vault door was standing open. Shan went first this time, but it was empty, the red emergency light on. She peered at the array of weaponry and the Uzis caught her eye. Impractical, in this circumstance. She helped herself to four extra clips for her 9mm, stuffing two of them in each vest pocket because three wouldn't fit.

"Mick," she called. Ballentyne appeared in the doorway.

"Not a bad idea," he agreed, choosing the same as she had. "Are you armed enough now? Got enough guns? Got enough ammo?"

Shan grinned. "I hope so. You can never have too much ammo unless it's the wrong size. I'd like the firepower of an Uzi, but in these close quarters, it's pointless."

They both exited and stared at the digital magnetic lock on the door, a thing left over from early in the century. It had three color coded lights, and the green one kept flashing.

"It's electronically operated with a battery backup." Shan thought.

"Can you lock it?"

"It's been years. I watched them fiddling with it because I got bored, but it was pretty boring too." Shan tried to recall what the tech had been doing. Finally, she pushed the door shut. It clicked, and the green turned steady.

"What does that mean?" he asked. Shan looked skeptical. He pulled the door open. "Okay, that means it's unlocked."

"Yeah."

Ballentyne closed the door. "We need the code."

"Would David know?"

"No reason for him to. Duncan or Wade, but we don't have a working radio."

Shan had a thought and pressed the '8' button several times until it beeped at her and the light turned red. She tried the door. It wouldn't budge. Then she tried the 'clear' button. Nothing. "Some old doors at the hospital work the same."

"You either locked it or broke it."

"I don't care which right now," Shan told him.

"Me either. Let's go sit with the civilians until we get told otherwise."

Ballentyne stood in the doorway, watching, backing up Green, getting stir crazy fast. Shan paced, messing with the headset David MacKenzie had found. "We're safe here," Ballentyne told the group. "There's no reason to leave this office until the building is secure."

"How long will it be?" Aaron asked.

Shannon looked at Ballentyne. "We're not sure," she said.

"The officers will get this over with as quick as they can," he said for all their benefit.

Excusing herself to the hall, Shan tried the headset. It seemed to function. "Sweeps Team One, Sweeps Team Two, this is Team Three, part one. Alert status." It was as subtle as she could get and not tell any unfriendly ears information they didn't need to know.

"Code Six, Alert Two," Kyle Taylor came back, terse. The alert meant nearby areas were being evacuated. "No floor is clear. Keep to radio silence."

That was the end of the conversation. Shan relayed the information to Ballentyne. "Can we hear gunfire from the jail here?"

"As much as they've reinforced this place? I doubt it," he told her.

"Fantastic," she muttered.

Hunter took the lead, with Wade right behind him. They were on the second floor mere moments before Kyle Taylor and Mac met them.

"Where's your brother?" Wade asked.

"We have a couple of civilians. Chris is with them in the dayroom."

"Anyone on three would be Security," Wade said. "There's no other way in except the fire escape, and that's locked out. Let's clear three and head to the jail to sort this mess."

"Shan's downstairs?" Mac asked. They were only two-thirds of a team without her.

"Armory."

"That's where I'd have sent her."

"Don't worry," Wade said. "We'll pick her up on the way back."

"This should be quick," Taylor said. "I think everyone was still out for the day." He was right. They headed downstairs, as quietly as the old wooden staircase would let them.

"We need a plan, a simple and quick one," Wade told the group of officers, out of ear-shot of civilians. Mac and Shan, Taylor and Taylor, Green and Ballentyne, Hunter and Wade were the sum of their forces.

"We're outnumbered," Green said. "Two rookies and six officers."

"Unless you consider the officers already in the jail," Ballentyne disagreed. They'd been partners for years, they could argue. "We should count them in. According to the schedule, Bennett and Lambert are there."

"Noel, too, since he checked in and he's not here," Dallas said.

"Good point," Wade said. "We aren't playing games either. I'm issuing shoot-to-kill orders. We will meet any resistance with deadly force. Am I clear?"

Everyone acknowledged.

"Are you in on this, Hunter? And I mean all the way. Command and Council will review everything we do in the next few minutes and then they'll review it again, especially since civilians are involved." Wade asked, having to know if he was going to back him or not.

"I'm in," Hunter said.

"Chris?" he asked the younger Taylor.

"One hundred percent," he said.

"Body armor," Wade said. "I've got mine."

Taylor stripped off his vest and gave it to Hunter.

Neither Mac nor Shan was wearing theirs. "We were off duty," Mac said. "In a pack, in my room."

"Mine too," Shan chimed in.

"Fantastic," Wade said. "Anyone else wearing theirs?"

They weren't.

"I'm not a rookie, I'll be fine," Mac assured them. Shan.

"Right," she said, not at all agreeing, and ignoring the fact she was without as well.

"You know the protocol—no talking to anyone about this until Command clears you. I'm leaving Taylor and Taylor here to keep the civilians company. Yes, because you're a rookie. That leaves us with one intact kill team." He indicated his team. It wasn't a term he enjoyed using, or would ever repeat, in public. Sometimes it was true. "Mac and Hunter are going in first. Find cover, hold your fire until it's time not to. I'm next to do the talking. Green and Allen are our shooters. They won't miss, so don't second guess them by thinking they might. Try not to stand in their line-of-sight. If we get a chance, we take it. If not, they will."

"What if they surrender?" Green asked.

"If they give up, they get a pass. Ballentyne will be back-up. Put them on the floor, wait for us. If I don't give the word, shoot anyone coming through that door who isn't Security," Wade told him.

"Not a problem."

"Keep it clean. Let's do this," Wade said. "Hunter, you still have point."

Shattered glass covered the entryway floor in the jail. Someone had shot out the half-wall partitions and the cameras. "Stay alert," Wade whispered, motioning for Mac to move. He did, keeping below the solid wall until he reached the first set of offices. There were only two, one on each side of the hall. After that, the metal doors everyone heard open.

Mac motioned for them to keep low and move to the office on the right. They did, single file and as quietly as possible.

Bennett had been waiting for back-up and it seemed like hours. "We've got problems," he told them. "They have Lambert and Noel. I tried to shut the doors, and nothing. Electricity is still out and we're on generator power."

Hunter swore under his breath. He'd thought of that when their Scout wasn't in the station. "What do they want?"

"The usual. More guns and a car," Bennett said. "Supplies. A way out."

"What a surprise," Wade said. "They aren't going anywhere. Bennett, you're back-up with Ballentyne. Same plan. Mac, you go first. Hunter will cover you, then you'll cover him. No hostiles get out of the jail. I'll follow you in and try talking first. The idea is to get them where we can see them." He pointed down the hallway. "If anyone has to change position, shout it out so our shooters know."

"Be careful," Shan told them. Sometimes she couldn't stop herself. It didn't affect the way she worked.

Mac drew fire and rolled into the foyer, up against a filing cabinet, grimacing. Hunter returned fire, then dropped and followed him, pivoting to the opposite side of the room. His cover was at least a solid wall.

Wade moved in, not rushed as he fired an entire clip, dropped it and slapped another into place without missing a beat. He stopped beside Hunter, motioning for them to wait. The Scavengers didn't enjoy waiting and began shouting demands as soon as the gunfire stopped.

Wade motioned to Mac. He nodded. Wade pointed to the left. There was a cubicle desk for cover just inside the bars. Then he held up three fingers. Two. One.

Mac dodged into the room, the first eyes in, knowing there were hostages. Hunter went low, hoping for a shot. The Scavengers had people as shields. Mac didn't have a shot. Neither did Hunter.

"Two cars," one Scavenger yelled. "You have cars. We want two, loaded with food and water." They kept to the back of the hall and the light was out.

"What if I tell you no?" Wade asked, standing in the open, hands visible, gun tucked into the small of his back.

"We kill them and you," the second shouted back.

"That won't get you anywhere," Wade told him. "We need to have a truce to figure this out, so no one gets hurt. Not us, not you." He could see Denny Lambert and he didn't look good.

"You better understand I've got no problem killing you."

"I get that," Wade said. "You should understand, if something happens to any of us, the people waiting at the other end of the tunnel won't let you out of here. They have no problem with killing, either."

"So it's a standoff," the Scavenger decided. "You want your friends alive? We want to leave."

"What do you propose?" Wade asked.

"I want a car and my friend wants a car. Food. Water. Ammo for these guns. No one follows us and after we drive for a few hours, we let our hostages go." He had it all figured out.

Wade shifted from one foot to the other, signaling which target was primary and to give the Scavenger the illusion he was nervous. "How do I know you won't kill them, anyway?"

"You're going to have to trust me," the Scavenger leered. "Life will be easier."

From the corner of his eye, Wade saw a 'no go' nod from Hunter. Mac too. "I'm not authorized to let you go with cars and hostages."

"You better get someone in here that is," he said, getting impatient.

"Fine, fine, we're waiting for a commander. The power is out. It'll take a few minutes." Wade made an excuse. "Don't do anything crazy."

"I can be crazy," the Scavenger said.

Wade scratched his neck, fidgeting. "Give us a few minutes."

"That's it, the one on the right. Get ready," Shan whispered to Green. "Switch sides with me." The way was clear, and now she could see Mac. The back of his shirt was spotted dark with blood from his roll through the glass.

"How about when the boss gets here, you take me as a hostage instead?" Wade offered.

The Scavenger leaned to peer at Wade. "I think we'll keep your friend," he said.

It was enough. Everyone moved, a scenario they'd practiced countless times. Wade snatched his gun and took the shot. Lambert went down with the Scavenger, knowing it was safer there.

As the first Scavenger swung around to aim at Wade, Green and Shan both fired. Noel didn't even have time to blink, and it was over. "Out," Mac ordered, gun trained on the foyer, Hunter following his lead. Noel dragged Lambert down the hall. Ballentyne had them under cover fast.

"Two dead," Wade called, loud enough for everyone, including the remaining inmates, to hear. "How many left?"

"Nine," Ballentyne said, taking the cue. "Shoot-to-kill orders still stand."

"Understood." Wade waited a few strategic moments. "In the jail. This is your one chance to come out. Otherwise, we're coming in."

Several loud conversations broke out in the jail section. After some bickering, one voice said, "Wait, wait." A short, gray-haired man of indeterminate age appeared, holding up his hands. "There are four of us still in cells. Two more dead."

That left three on the loose, counting the one speaking. Wade motioned for the man to step out. "Search him," he told Hunter. Mac had a shoulder full of glass shards.

"Who's next?" Wade said after they sent the first one out. They filed out, got searched, and sent down the hall. "It's not set in stone that there are two dead and four locked up. We think we've cleared all the weapons, but let's pretend we're not sure," he instructed. "You good for a few more, Mac?"

"I'm fine," he said. "Let's finish up."

"After this, you go to the hospital," Wade said, not a suggestion. Infections were serious. "All right, Hunter, you take the lead."

Like the short man had said, two Scavengers were dead in their cells and four others still locked up. Wade had Mac keep a weapon on the live ones as they searched each man and locked them together in a clean cell.

"We're clear," Wade said, satisfied. The incident had taken a good portion of the evening. "Hunter, contact Dispatch, tell them the jail is secure and have them open it up. I have three injured officers in here." To Mac, "I want you with Lambert and Noel. Go to the hospital and get checked out. Allen and Green, escort them to the main floor."

Mac nodded, not up to arguing. His shoulder was on fire and he wasn't above looking for sympathy later. Shan followed the walking wounded down the corridor. They were already discussing how long it would take to get out of the building.

"Someone is getting the power online now. That turned out pretty well, considering," Hunter thought out loud as they made their way back.

"Considering what?" Bennett asked.

"You had that little girl come in here as your shooter," Hunter told Wade, uncertain why that irked him. He understood it was her job, he'd seen her in action. They stopped in the foyer at the open set of doors.

Wade knew why. Hunter might realize it and he might not, but he was trying to protect her. And pick a fight with him. "That little girl," Wade repeated. "I would've been worried about us shooting each other if 'that little girl' wasn't here."

Hunter made a sound of disgust.

"Shannon has been on my incursion team since she was sixteen," Wade said. "Once, when she was seventeen, I sent her out as bait to draw a helicopter from cover because I was in charge and it was the right thing to do under the circumstances." Wade didn't like telling stories about the team. There was always a chance someone would see through them. "That call got her hurt. When you almost get a team member killed, you stop and wonder why you picked this job."

I'm certain I picked right. That's why my team doesn't question me and that's why Command doesn't question me, rookie."

"So you've never made a mistake," Hunter said. "Damn."

"I never said that. Look at what happened out at Sheridan. When I tell her to do something, there's a good reason."

"Are you two going to argue every time you work together?" Bennett asked. This was round two.

"It's a possibility," Wade confessed. "It won't be an issue." He was more annoyed than angry. Annoyed that Hunter didn't know his place. He was a Lt., and he'd learned about half of what he needed to survive long enough to be a Captain.

"What he said," Hunter agreed with Wade.

"Outstanding. Not for the record," Ballentyne chimed in. "When Shannon finds out you called her a little girl, she's liable to beat you with a stick, and I don't mean figuratively."

"You don't need to repeat any part of the conversation to her," Wade said.

"If you two are going to fight over her, tell her." Ballentyne smiled at them.

Both Wade and Hunter made rude comments under their breath.

"That's what I thought," he said, pleased.

"Let's finish cleaning up this mess," Wade said. "We're on Alert Two, and half the city is out of their beds for the night, including us. After Command is done with your debriefing, Council will call for a hearing. Don't volunteer information. Answer their questions as briefly as possible. Everyone involved will have to speak with a counselor soon. Do it."

"Are we in trouble for any of this?" Bennett asked.

"No. We went by procedure." Despite his confidence, Wade was shaken. Nothing had been this close, this personal, in quite a few years.

June 17 daybreak

A surprise to no one, Council called for an emergency meeting at 6pm. The only topic would be the Station Two incident. Everybody in The Vista was aware prisoners had died and officers were hospitalized, with the most disturbing fact being that it happened in the center of The Vista. Not some long-abandoned city or forgotten highway, right there close to their homes.

With the city in Blackout, Duncan kept the teams at the station and everyone on call. No sleep for Security. Later, Wade got his people rounded up in the dayroom on the second floor, for convenience and to keep questions from other officers at a minimum. Ironic, he thought, Team One was now part of his people. Inevitable, too, he figured, after Sweeps and now this.

Taylor and Shan had taken up opposite ends of a sofa, trying to sleep, buried under blankets, still wearing their side arms. Mac checked himself out of the hospital and was occupying Shan's regular room. Painkillers helped, but he knew what was on his teammate's minds. How did it happen?

A dozen other officers Wade called in found whatever space they could. In the next few hours, before they went to Council, they had some serious things to discuss. Things not all of them would agree with, and they'd hoped to avoid. Team Three hadn't talked with the 'Conda about Sweeps, about what happened. Now they had to.

Council was in committee red tape over what to do concerning Jacob's town, and Command was waiting for their response. There would be no compromises in the near future.

Knowing she was awake anyway, Wade crouched next to Shan. "We have a crew coming in soon to make breakfast for everyone," he told her.

"Mac's got my room, that's why I'm out here," she shielded her eyes with a hand, trying to block out the faint light starting in the east windows.

"I'm sending you upstairs, too. He's drugged, and when did you sleep last?"

She shrugged. "Two nights ago? Three?"

"Don't ask me. Go to your room. I can let you get three or four hours before I call everyone in."

"There's no way I'm bothering him," she said, dropping her hand. "I'll have breakfast and catch a few somewhere between the 'Conda meeting and the Council meeting."

"There might not be time and I need you sharp. You won't wake Mac. I'll even save you some breakfast," Wade offered.

"Promises, promises." She thought about it and knew it was the best offer she'd get today. "What about him?" she nodded at Taylor.

"He can stretch out here once you're out of the way."

"Fair enough, I'm gone." Shan gave in, too tired to fight it.

"Take off your gun or you'll be sorry later," Wade warned, giving her a hand up. "I'll see you in four hours."

She gave a thumbs up and meandered towards her room. Mac was asleep, and she dug out a spare bedroll, getting as comfortable as possible on the hardwood floor, wondering why she bothered to move. After a few minutes, she sat up to take off her gun and shoved it under her pillow. She hoped she remembered where it was later.

June 17 6pm City Hall

The crowd began gathering early, then overflowed from the hearing room to the hallways, and out onto the street. An officer on duty got a technician to set up a video display for those stuck outside. The Vista was still on Alert One, and it would be dark soon enough. As civilized as they claimed to be, the night still brought fear. People weren't certain what to do or to think. They wanted to know what happened and if it could happen again.

"This is an informal meeting for the benefit of the citizens, to set their minds at ease," Haines began. "Formal hearings will be held at a later date. That isn't our concern tonight. I'd like to introduce Cmdr. Duncan of Station Two, and let him make his statement now."

Duncan stood up from his seat in the front row and nodded an acknowledgment. "We stayed on Alert One today to keep officers visible and moving around The Vista. Pending any overnight call-outs, my recommendation is to drop the alert at daybreak tomorrow so my officers can return to regular shifts. We expect no further threat to The Vista, and are considering this an isolated event. As Chairperson Haines stated, this is an informal meeting rather than an inquest. I won't be taking questions from the audience."

"Commander, can you give us an overview of what happened in Station Two yesterday afternoon?" Haines continued.

"Of course. Approximately twenty-four hours ago, at shift change, a glitch in the electrical grid at Station Two caused the power to fail. We haven't determined the cause yet. This resulted in the doors resetting and several remained open, including those in the detention area and the armory doors on the ground floor. Because the power was off, the building went in to lockdown. No one gets in or out until we open it from the outside at a separate power source. This is a fail-safe installed over ten years ago."

Haines nodded. "How many people were inside?"

"Sixteen civilians, eight Security Officers, and eleven inmates with three additional officers as hostages," Duncan recited.

"The understanding is, four inmates died in the incident," Haines read from the report.

"My officers are responsible for the two holding hostages." He wouldn't name names. If they wanted to know, they might try to get them from other sources. "We discovered two more deceased in their cells. We haven't determined the circumstances, other than it was not Vista Security."

"How many injured?" Haines already had the answers.

"No injuries among the civilians. We took three Security Officers and one prisoner to the hospital. They released two officers this morning." Again, Duncan wouldn't reveal names. Privacy was scarce enough. They seldom had as much as they wished.

"Was the armory compromised?" A question many people wondered, so Haines made it a point.

"Under orders from Cmdr. Wade, the armory was secured first, each floor of the station cleared by officers before they moved into detention. At no time did any prisoner escape to the station side. Security accounted for everyone and then requested the station be released from lockdown." Standard protocol.

"Have there been any further incidents in the last twenty-four hours?" Haines finished with his questions.

"The power was out in the 'A' section for half an hour at midnight. A relay switch tripped because of Station Two being reset. There was a chimney fire on South Garfield Street, but the resident had it put out before we got there. The fire department is currently trying to recruit him." Duncan smiled at the ripple of laughter that ran through the crowd. He saw no point in scaring people, not until they identified a problem. This problem hadn't been, not yet. "Other than that, no calls."

"Please make your officers aware there could be a formal public hearing after we receive the official report. We'll contact you with details later. As you said, Security goes back to its regular schedule at daybreak when the alert expires. Unless someone in Council objects, we need to let everyone go home and get some rest." Haines knew he needed at least eight hours.

No one objected. Security breathed a collective sigh of relief. Any of the Council members could have made it another long night.

Mac caught up with Shan as she was coming out of her room. The floor was empty and dark, quiet, lit by a single light at the top of the stairs. "Did you get any rest?"

"A couple hours, sure. Is the Council thing over?" She'd sat in Dispatch all day, as requested.

"It took about five minutes. They'll have an inquiry soon."

She wasn't worried. "Did you get to eat?"

Mac shook his head. "I had something this morning."

"Have you had anything to drink?" Shan asked, catching his hand. It wasn't the first time she'd asked, it wouldn't be the last.

"Other than water, no." Mac took notice she wasn't wearing body armor. He could tell things like that.

"Prove it," she challenged, getting up close. Then she kissed him, slow and long. He didn't taste like alcohol. "When is dinner?" she said against his ear, unbuttoning his shirt.

"In about an hour," he whispered, because his voice wouldn't work right while she kept nipping at his earlobe. He slid his arms around her and moved back towards her room. "Are you taking advantage of me because I'm on painkillers?" An old joke he'd heard in a movie.

"Yes." She'd seen it, too.

"Are you safe?" Not a joke.

"I wouldn't be doing this otherwise," she said. Once they were in her room, he slammed the door, locking it, his shoulder forgotten.

"This once in a while thing isn't healthy for either of us, Shan."

"I know."

"This has to stop. We have to stop," he whispered.

"I know, Alex," she repeated.

"Good." Then he forgot why for a while.

A hot meal lightened their moods - baked chicken with rice, fresh bread and snap peas. Of course, Shan thought, peas. Not too many vegetables grew well in the cold climate, but they'd been developing hardier ones in the greenhouses. Mac sat next to her, looking bored, tired, or both. He smiled at her and fidgeted in his chair, painkiller wearing off.

After they had a chance to eat and relax, Wade would summon his inner circle and discuss those things. Still in Blackout, the quiet was a good sign. So was the dark, giving everyone time to regroup.

Green and Ballentyne, Lambert, Parr, Quinlen, Bennett, and, of course, Taylor, were the inner circle Team Three relied on. Lambert was still in the hospital. The rest of them gathered downstairs, in front of the offices where they'd hidden civilians not too long ago, and waited for Wade and Taylor.

"The 'Conda is always looking for new people. You should ask Hunter," Ballentyne told Shan, making small talk. "He's smart, he's serious about his job."

"Wade doesn't want to be in the same room as Hunter," Shan pointed out the obvious. "I'd rather not cause another brawl."

"Wade knows a capable officer when he works with them. He'd at least consider it."

"I doubt Hunter would be interested. Plus, I'd be pushing that age thing everyone pretends doesn't exist. I already pushed the Pacifica thing with Noel."

"He's not like our parents, and he still wouldn't be the oldest person in the 'Conda. I would. Hunter is four or five years younger than me. You're young 'uns." Of all the cops in The Vista, Ballentyne was one of the most charismatic and persuasive, right there with Wade. He was more diplomatic, and if anyone had as many admiring female fans as Wade, it was Ballentyne. "Besides, who taught you to push those limits? Wade did. Consider it, at least."

Shan smiled. "Why me?"

"You could get Hunter to do about anything. Hell, he'd jump out a window if you asked," he grinned. "Except you already did that." They all had a good laugh.

"I jumped first," Shan pointed out, not minding they thought it was funny. Now it was.

Wade came in from a side door and got right to business. "Command will get to us in a day or two for a formal debriefing. Don't discuss it with anyone, including other officers involved, until you're cleared. As far as our actions, there's nothing to be concerned about."

"But what?" Green asked. "And where have you sent Taylor off to?"

"Taylor is taking care of some business. I have concerns about how this happened."

"I was told seconds ago we aren't supposed to discuss it." Parr said.

"We're not, and if we do, one of us will report it prior to the debriefing. A non-issue. This is about getting into the logistics of our outpost. Taylor is arranging the basics. Then we'll know what we have, and what we need. We're going to Cody."

"We're heading for Cody." Green wanted clarification. "When did Council approve the release of our supplies?"

"They didn't," Wade said. "They won't. We're going. We'll use our own caches. This mess in the jail wasn't an accident or an escape attempt."

"What in the hell was it, then?" Bennett asked.

"And here we are, discussing it," Shan chimed in. "I'll report anything relevant to Command."

"It was a test of our defenses," Wade told them.

"A test? By who?" Bennett came back.

"By whom," Shan said. "We don't know who it is, but we crossed their home grounds in Colorado during Sweeps. Unintentional. They were just returning the favor."

"We run to Cody?" Ballentyne didn't like the idea. Too many variables they couldn't cover. "How does that give us an advantage?"

"We take it away from The Vista. After seeing what this group did here yesterday, it's clear they can make problems like when we went to blackout every night," Wade said. "You remember that. Huddled in bricked up houses, listening to our parents plan how to get out alive when the Scavengers came."

Shan shuddered, remembering.

"Command and Council will come at us with questions. We have answers they don't want to hear. They won't listen. They think there are ulterior motives. We take what we can and go now, so we have a working base before the weather changes."

"What about Vista Security?" Bennett had one more question.

"There are enough reserves in place to take over and not leave any gaps. This has been in the planning stages since before I started. We'll have the supplies we need to get a start. The Vista gets to keep the officers it needs, without this added threat of attack."

"They'll throw everything they can at us to stop us from going," Green said.

"If any of you change your mind, neither the 'Conda nor Cody Security will hold it against you," Wade said. "We understand. I understand."

"What do we do in the meantime?" Ballentyne asked.

"We keep to our schedule. Do your jobs, take care of anything you need to. I may have additional assignments for some of you pertaining to Cody. By that, I mean my team members will be busy. Get ready to go." Wade wouldn't lie to them. "It's going to be a hard winter. We'll be living in the same few buildings with each other. The first year will be rough, but nothing like it was here. Keep that in mind."

June 25

"C'mon, Kendrick," Chris shouted across the field. "You play like a girl." He said it, then realized he was standing within a stick-length of Shannon, in the net. "Sorry," he offered, hesitant to put his back to her now. She had a way of hooking opposing players. And maybe people being obnoxious even if they were on her team, Chris thought.

She smiled behind the mask. "You say that like it's a bad thing. Hide and watch." The ball skidded to center court and Kendrick smacked it towards her. Shan slapped it back onto the field with a padded arm. They tried for a rebound, but she sent the ball flying towards the opposite end with a clean stick save as three players collided in front of her and thudded to the ground.

Waving the dust away, she told them, "Go play at the other end." Hunter grinned at her, climbing out of the pile as the whistle blew. The other team was Station Three, second shift. They lined up for a puck drop.

"Any words of encouragement?" he asked, still grinning.

"You don't play like a rookie." Then she hooked her stick around the knee of a player standing too close to her net and dumped him on the ground.

They skated off to grapple at the other goal, making more dust, and Station One scored despite the mist rolling in on them. Rain caused a game delay before they resumed, sending everyone to mill around Bennett's house, waiting for the drizzle to stop.

"That's the end of that," Taylor said, watching as the storm turned to a downpour. "Even if it stops pretty damned soon, Shan won't play in the mud. No goalie, no game, and there's no one to stand in for her."

Hunter shrugged, standing with him at the big bay window that faced west, towards the street and the storm front. "First rain of the summer. It's not that much mud."

"Enough," Taylor said. Shan was in the next room, talking to Chris and drying her hair with a spare tee shirt. "We're going to be stuck here or on recall. This could last all day. All night."

"All week." The weather was unpredictable, at best. "Before Sweeps," Hunter said, "I was pretty sure the 'Conda was a social club using Security as an excuse."

"Now?"

"You're coordinated and have goals. Cody isn't just an idea on paper. It hasn't been for a long time and you're waiting for Command to say go."

"It wasn't our idea or our plans. Security started hoarding supplies for Cody before any of us were old enough to even consider joining. Spreading out our defenses, that is Wade's idea. He could see us, all of us, getting trapped in this valley if a force of any size threatened The Vista."

"Five roads," Hunter remembered from his time with the caravans. Only five roads led in–or out–of The Vista. They'd changed the routes as they reclaimed the valley.

"We need to spread out and find out about these other places," Taylor said.

"You wonder if there are other places, other towns like The Vista?"

"I know there are. You do too. Tiny places, handfuls of survivors. The caravans run across them now and again."

"The 'Conda is worried about what else is out there," Hunter said.

"Tell me you've never wondered," Taylor challenged.

"Sure I have. Not so long ago, I wondered who'd be crazy enough to go find out."

"Now you know."

"It'd be a damned sight easier to send a few people out, let them wander around like Nomads and see what they could see."

"Command has thought about another option," Taylor told him. He got to decide if Hunter was 'Conda material or not. The rookie wasn't stupid, but intent, another issue to be considered.

"Have they already done it?" The idea didn't surprise Hunter.

"I'm not in Command."

"You wouldn't tell me, anyway."

"True enough." A crack of thunder loud enough to rattle the windows rolled across the valley. "Close one."

Hunter nodded. It looked dark out and happened fast. The weather had never been predictable; and now, harsher than before the nukes fell.

"This morning, they opened a lottery for officers beyond their first year to be considered for the Cody Base," Taylor ventured. "Have you thought about it?"

"Are you asking me to go back to Wyoming?" Hunter knew there were a lot of motives at work. He wasn't certain what Taylor's were.

"I'm asking if you're going to apply."

"I have a week to decide," Hunter said.

"Wade will be in charge, in case you wondered. It's one hell of a chance at a quick promotion, if that sort of thing interests you," Taylor baited him.

"I'm interested. Do 'Conda members get preference?"

Taylor waited to answer. Shan wandered into the living room, handing them each a beer. "Dispatch just called a Code Seventeen right along with the Code Twenty-One." Reservists were called up to help prepare for any evacuations that might happen, and a severe weather alert, in case anyone hadn't noticed.

"Are we on recall?" Taylor asked.

She shook her head. "They said to stay put for now. Bennett has a full basement, which includes a bunch of video game systems and beer."

"The weather's not that bad," Hunter reiterated.

"Way worse north of us. Sit here for a few, Lt." Holding up her mug in a toast, she headed for the kitchen. Someone was cooking the steaks they had for the cookout after the game.

"Yes, she'll be going to Cody. Team Three is a given because that's what Command wants," Taylor said, a little too cool. "Command gets a say in who goes. Don't sign up just because of her." Thunder again, louder and closer than before, interrupted him. "And yes, 'Conda membership has preference, because Wade gets the final say."

"I won't uproot my entire life to chase after a girl," Hunter scoffed. A half-truth, but what Taylor wanted to hear. "Why the sudden interest in my plans?"

"Wade wants my opinion."

"About?"

"You. Someone suggested you might ask to join. They also suggested it might be a good idea." Taylor had no qualms telling the junior officer how he felt about him, on a personal or professional level.

"Who suggested this?"

"It wasn't Shannon. Be glad. You need someone to nominate you and someone else to sponsor you. Both those people have to be full members or advisors."

"And you don't think there are two people willing to take a chance with me?"

"It'd be a hell of a lot easier for Wade to take you seriously if you stopped thinking with your dick."

"At least you're honest with me, so I'll be cold fucking honest with you," Hunter said. "I'd apply even if Capt. Allen wasn't going. I'd apply if I'd never met her or Team Three. I have my own motives. One of those is to make this a career. The rest of them are none of your damned business."

"I'll keep that in mind," Taylor told him.

"You do that," Hunter agreed, having a swig of beer. "Come on downstairs when you get tired of watching the rain fall, and I'll beat your ass at any video game you can find."

"That's a challenge," Taylor said. "You're on."

Chapter Eight

July 14 midday

"Hey, Mac," Baker called across the second floor day room. "Team Three up to a run?"

"Maybe," Mac told him. "What's happening?"

"Ah... the motion detectors are down at The Junction. We thought the last storm didn't do any damage out that way, and now, nothing."

"The Junction?" He tried not to be superstitious, but still.

"Yeah, that's the one." Baker had been a Scout for a couple years, he'd understand if Mac said no.

"Council is in session with Command, I don't have a partner." That meant he couldn't do the run, not in the summer, not to The Junction. "If Shan is on the air and doesn't laugh at me for asking, we'll go. Talk some other poor fool into it otherwise." Only one member of Team Three was required to attend Command meetings.

"Hey woman," Mac said on their channel, using Dispatch. If she was home, at her parents, she might be asleep but would have a radio on.

"'Woman'?" Shan asked after a few seconds.

"Last time I checked. The only one monitoring this channel, too."

"I'll give you that. What are you up to this morning?" She sounded like she'd just woke. Good timing.

"It's after noon. Baker wants us to do a run for him. You game?"

"To where?" she asked. If it wasn't something out-of-the-ordinary, he'd show up at the house and ask in person.

"Out to The Junction."

A long silence. Then, "Wade's in Council."

"Affirmative," Mac said. "I traded shifts so he could attend this one."

"Sure, I'll go with you," she decided. "Clock out, pick me up at home. I'll be ready in twenty minutes."

"Outstanding."

"Well?" Mac asked, on-edge. A light breeze was picking up out of the south. Other than that, a clear and cool day. The mountains had shed the last of their snow and shown blue gray against a brilliant sky.

"I don't have the overwhelming urge to run," Shan said. "No worse than usual for this place, anyway." She'd let Mac drive for that reason.

He followed the designated route, slower than she would have, waiting for something to happen. Dispatch still couldn't see them on the monitors. They completed the loop and stopped in the middle of the road.

"Are we clear?" he asked.

"No idea. You want to be here as much as I do. Other than that, damned if I know." Shan wished she was anywhere else because Mac was so wound up. He felt the tension because she did, a vicious cycle that started the moment he asked her to ride shotgun.

Mac nodded, knowing she was right, not wanting to make the

call. "Let's do this," he sighed, resigned to the fact someone had to clear the area, and they were already there.

The relay box was installed in a dilapidated barn half a mile east of the actual interchange. The south wall had been removed years ago, and none of the windows remained. They pulled up and Mac turned the car off. "We could go home," he suggested.

"Take the keys," Shan told him.

Mac knew that look. "Why?"

She shook her head. "Just do it."

He pocketed the keys. "Okay, Captain, let's get this dance done." They put on headsets, checked their side arms, both wishing they'd found an excuse not to go. After a quick survey of the area, it was time to move on to the business at hand.

"This?" Shan peered at a metallic cylinder sticking out of the ground.

"Do I look like a tech to you?" Mac asked, squinting. "That's a monitor, a motion detector. It sends the signal and the one in Dispatch sends it back here. There are a dozen here. It's a network. Or something like that." He tapped it with the toe of his boot.

"Anything?" Shan asked Baker, in Dispatch. She shook her head and kicked it again. "Come on. It doesn't look broke."

Baker was used to conversations between Team Three members being colorful, if not downright bizarre. Open mics during this particular run. "Not even a blip. Check the other ones. They're set up in a diamond pattern."

"I don't think kicking it is going to work," Mac was telling her when something, some sensation, passed through her like a storm cloud over the face of the sun. "What?" he whispered, knowing, as all the color drained from her face.

She swallowed, mouth dry. "I think we should leave."

"Go," Mac told her, hand on his gun.

"Mac, what's wrong?" Baker asked, grabbing a headset. There was no answer, only heavy gunfire.

Chapter Eight

"Go," Mac said, pushing her in front of him, pistol in hand. Scavengers or Nomads, it didn't matter. They were twenty feet from their car, caught in the open.

His intent was to take cover under the car until help could reach them. It would only be minutes. He grabbed Shannon as the firing started. They both slammed into the car hard, and then the ground, cold for July.

Shan never lost consciousness, even when her ribs cracked as she hit the car door sideways. She got a hand on her gun, but the ground came rushing up at her, bright pinpoints of light blocking her vision.

Her gun discharged, and she struggled to keep moving, to stay conscious. Mac was face down, his 10mm a few feet away. The blood was dark, almost black, and there was a lot. Shan didn't realize she'd been hit, too many sensations flooding her mind. It hurt to breathe, but Mac, she didn't think he was breathing at all.

"Code Thirteen," she said in her headset, hearing Baker calling a Code Nine. "Code Thirteen at The Junction," she repeated, staggering to her feet and firing towards the shadows on the far side of the wall. Shan jerked the car door open and got the shotgun.

"Mac," she started talking. "Say something, Mac." She dropped the shotgun next to him, afraid to look. They'd shot him in the back. "Alex," she called out, edging closer to panic. Shan rolled him over and her brain went into shutdown. It wasn't as bad as she thought, it just wasn't real. She pressed the heel of her hand against the hole in his chest. With all the traffic over the air on a Code Thirteen, Shan didn't hear it anymore. She was listening for the crickets. They should chirp, even a little, this time of day. They were quiet. Whoever jumped them was still close.

The shotgun lay next to them and her 9mm had a couple of rounds left, Mac's gun out of reach, and she couldn't release the pressure on his chest, anyway. She knew what would happen. He groaned, trying to move.

"Alex," she said. "Don't you leave me out here alone."

"Go," he managed. "Get to cover."

"Yeah. That's not happening."

"That's an order," he told her.

"I can't understand you, Alex. I'm not going anywhere." She sat up, firing at movement until the slide clicked open, empty. Shan dropped it and grabbed the .380 in her boot holster. Somewhere close, sirens.

"Our Colorado Nomads," he said.

"Don't talk, Alex. Hold on. You have to hold on."

He smiled, eyes flickering open for a moment. "Don't cry," he whispered. "Shannon."

"Alex, don't you leave me," she told him. When Taylor jumped out of his car, she turned on him.

"Shan," he said, hesitating as he looked down the barrel of her sidearm.

She didn't acknowledge him for several long seconds. "I know what you did," she whispered. Then she dropped the gun and turned her attention back to Mac, aware of nothing else.

The Vista July 14 3pm

When Duncan met him in the corridor as he stepped out of Council chambers, Wade knew it meant trouble. Duncan's face was a mask, and Wade wasn't the only one who recognized it.

"In private," Duncan said. Denny Lambert was there, stoic, and Wade felt an icy chill creep up his spine. He followed them into the antechamber, closing the door behind him.

"We had a team hit at The Junction half an hour ago," Duncan told him. "I pulled you in here because Security is still clearing the area and notifying their next of kin."

"Who?" A simple question.

Duncan looked at Lambert. Wade understood, not Lambert's team, not Team Five. "Team Three."

"The motion detectors went down. Dispatch thought the storm knocked them out," Lambert filled in. "Mac is bad off. Taylor says he's real bad."

"Shan?" Wade asked.

"No word."

Wade nodded, a storm brewing. "Are they at the hospital yet?" His voice sounded hollow, as if someone else was speaking.

"On their way in," Duncan said. "I've sent people over, and Dr. Allen isn't on duty. She'll be detained until the situation settles."

"Get Taylor," Wade told Lambert. "As soon as you can."

"He's bringing Shannon in."

"I need to speak to you both as soon as he's here. Get Team Two if they're available or not." Wade had too many things to do. Their time had run out.

"This isn't a 'Conda matter," Duncan said.

"No," Wade agreed. "This has nothing to do with them. I saw it coming, and didn't do enough to protect us."

"You know who did this," Duncan said, the situation out of his hands now. Nothing Command or Council might do would control Wade. There were only two people that could, and he wasn't even certain either had survived the ambush.

"I've got to go to the hospital."

Lambert knew there was no turning back.

Taylor intercepted Wade the moment he strode through the doors leading into Emergency. "Mac just went into surgery, there's no word yet."

Wade didn't slow down and Taylor got in front of him, blocking his path, making him stop. A dangerous thing to do, especially now when he wasn't thinking like himself.

"Listen to me. I know what you're going to do, so you have to listen." Taylor had no intention of getting into an altercation with him.

Wade stopped, staring hard at him, giving a curt nod.

"Mac flat-lined on the way in. Shan sensed it. I could see it on her face when it happened. She killed two Nomads out there and has a slug in her shoulder that would put any of us down."

"Shan's always been the strongest, the most resilient of the three..." His words sounded distant. The three of us. He didn't finish saying it.

"She's unresponsive, Wade. You didn't know what happened until someone told you. Why not? Why in the hell didn't you, if you know when she's had a nightmare?"

It hadn't occurred to him until Taylor asked.

"She didn't recognize me out at The Junction. For a second, I thought she was going to shoot me. Mac told her who I was."

"What are you getting at?"

"What in the hell is wrong with her?"

She was on the other side of the double doors, outside the surgery theater. Leaning against the wall, thoughts stuck in a loop. Other officers with her were wondering the same thing as Taylor.

"Shock," Wade told him. "I can sense her."

"Are you sure?"

"She knows something she doesn't want to." He moved past Taylor. "Get my gear from the station and put it in Car Ten."

"What about Command?"

"What about them?" Wade asked.

Shan leaned against the wall, arms folded, staring at some indeterminate spot on the ceiling. There was blood across her legs and down the front of her jacket. Some was hers, most of it was Mac's.

"Who has her sidearm?" Wade asked. Chris Taylor was from his shift, the only one he recognized without thinking about it. The rest were reservists, or from Station Three. Already on Alert One, he was a heartbeat away from calling an Alert Four, a Blackout.

"I have Mac's," Taylor murmured. "He didn't get a round off."

An officer handed Wade both Shan's weapons. He took them and approached her. She needed a doctor, shoulder still seeping blood through a rough bandage. The others didn't want to tell her again, uncertain about what her reaction might be. Wade motioned for them to go. Taylor ushered them out past the doors into the waiting room.

"Tell me what happened, Shannon," he said as Taylor returned.

No response. He couldn't even see her breathing.

"Report on The Junction run," he tried.

No response.

"Shan, come on back and talk to me."

She blinked and shifted her gaze to another spot on the ceiling.

The two men exchanged glances. "That's the way she's been since I got her in the car," Taylor repeated.

"What happened to Mac?" Wade asked, leaning in close.

She straightened, flinching at the white-hot pain in her shoulder. "They staked out The Junction at daybreak. They knew we'd be there." She met Wade's gaze. "It was supposed to be you."

"Who?"

"The Nomads out of Colorado."

"Are they still here?"

She shook her head. "No. They ran south. You remember where."

He did. More than likely, entrenched in the base at NORAD. "You need to see a doctor."

"I'm waiting to hear about Alex," she said, as if he hadn't known. The breath caught in her throat.

"You took a hit, Shan." Wade didn't think she remembered that detail.

"Shot," she repeated, touching her shoulder. She let him take her good arm.

"Let's go see a doctor."

"Why now?" Taylor had to ask. "Why here?"

"Because we invaded their home first," Wade told him. True, to a point.

Wade met with their next of kin, people he'd known all his life, but they weren't communal parents today, they were civilians. Richard, conspicuously missing, attending an emergency meeting of Council called about the ambush. Command had gone silent. Too many things had happened too close to home. The Vista was in Blackout on his orders.

Michael Allen was also absent. "He's at Caralaros–Ranch Seventeen, the power was out," David MacKenzie said. Holding his wife's hand, they sat with Deirdre, waiting. They'd been told what happened, minus the gory details.

"Mac is in surgery," Wade said. "Dr. Kline and Dr. DeCino are the attending surgeons. I won't lie about this. His injuries are critical and life-threatening. I have no other details." Maggie MacKenzie leaned on Deirdre, silent tears falling.

"Shannon is injured, but she's mobile. I got her with Dr. Roberts a few minutes ago, and she'll be going into surgery. She called in the attack. It will be public soon enough, and you should be aware. She killed at least two Nomads out there." That fact wouldn't be public. "Security has gone to Blackout. I consider the threat to The Vista minimal, for the time being."

"We heard that not even two weeks ago when they rioted at the jail," David pointed out. "Is this related?"

Wade was beyond covering it up. "It is. I think there could be more trouble if we don't take care of it now. I'd appreciate it if that statement doesn't go past this room. It's my opinion."

"She wouldn't see me earlier," Deirdre said, scared.

"I just talked to her. She's going to be fine. I have to deal with Security matters. Someone from the hospital staff will keep you up-to-date on their conditions. I've sent a team for Michael and a car for my mother." Then he was gone.

Taylor and Lambert followed him to Station One.

Hours later, the anesthesia wore off. Shan found herself in a hospital room, taped up and feeling the effects of heavy drugs. It was decorated like any generic bedroom except for the wall lined with specialized equipment. When the room stopped spinning, she had a look around. A pile of clean clothes lay folded on the counter next to the sink. She took the initiative, as soon as she could, to have a shower. It was a slow, cautious event and dressing herself was even slower, considering she wanted to avoid using her left arm. When she returned to her room, Michael was waiting.

He hugged her, careful. "You're supposed to call for a nurse when you wake up."

"Did you hear anything about Mac?" she asked.

"I came right here after I saw your mother."

"Is she okay?"

"She's fine, Shannon, waiting downstairs in case they need her."

Shan drew away and sat on the edge of her bed. "What time is it?"

"After ten, at night. Still the fourteenth. You shouldn't be up."

"I'm all right," she reassured him. Every muscle ached, every fiber was in full rebellion. It hurt to move. Her head throbbed, her shoulder was numb, but that wouldn't last. "Where's Wade?"

He had that look on his face, behind a graying beard and the wrinkles at the corners of his eyes. "We thought he'd gone to Station One... That's where they meet?" he asked.

Shan nodded. "He's not there?"

"Not at either station, not here or at home. Not anywhere in between. Security claims they don't know where he is. Do you?"

She ran her fingers back through damp hair. "I don't." They thought he was somewhere in The Vista. Shan didn't. She knew what he would do, his intent stamped in her thoughts. "Maybe."

"Security is still on Alert Four. Nothing else has happened."

"Are there any officers in the building?"

"I'm not sure," Michael told her. "I came here."

Shan looked around for her gear, her guns, a radio. They were in the closet, arranged as her clothes had been, and Shan doubted her mother had done it. Not the guns, not Deirdre. Green then, or one of the mysterious benefactors Wade told her about. Probably Green. All three of her sidearms were there with an extra pack of clips for the 9mms. She carried a single Sig on duty, and both when she was traveling.

"Who's on the air?" she asked, a frequency specified by Wade for the 'Conda. Not Security and not monitored by them.

"Standby," a youthful male voice told her. "ID please."

"This is Team Three, Part One."

"Shannon," Ballentyne answered, not concerned about names on the air at this point. "You're supposed to be in the hospital."

"I am. Where's Wade?"

"MIA," he said, tension obvious in his voice.

"What about Mac?"

"He made it through surgery, another one scheduled for in the morning. They say the next few days will tell. We've been sending officers up there all evening to donate blood. How are you?" He wouldn't give her details, even if he had them.

"I need to see Lambert and Noel or Taylor. Make that Taylor and anyone else from the 'Conda." She remembered Lambert being left in charge not too long ago.

"Now?"

"In fifteen minutes, in front of the library," she decided. It was less obvious than the station.

"It's done."

"You shouldn't leave the hospital," Michael told her.

"I can't do anything for Mac," she said, hoping her voice held. It did, for the moment. "I have to find Wade before it's too late."

Michael wouldn't dream of stopping her. Deirdre would never forgive him.

"You're not going after him," Taylor announced as soon as he spotted her.

"You don't get to make that call, Lieutenant." Shan shoved a duffel bag in the front seat and popped the trunk open. She was moving a little better, knowing she'd pay later. Painkillers could only do so much.

Green stood by, watching, knowing it would be a fight and knowing better than to get involved unless he had to. Catching up with her as she was sneaking out a side door of the hospital was no accident. He'd been following her around as her second for years.

"What about the 'Conda?" Taylor attempted to reason with her.

"That's not my job, it's Lambert's."

"I can't let you do this," he said, catching her good arm, but she flinched anyway. "Shan, you can't go. Wade told me to not let you leave The Vista."

"He wasn't there, he doesn't understand..."

"What? Everyone knows how you feel about Mac."

"Not that. I saw them waiting for us at The Junction today."

"Like you and Team Three see things," Taylor said.

"Yeah, like that," she agreed. "Wade is running into a trap. Another trap. I think they caused what happened at the Missouri Breaks."

It was worse than he imagined. "I'll go."

"How will you find him?" she asked. "Because you can't."

"Then the two of us."

Shan shook her head. "Be ready to help Lambert run things in case this isn't over. If I'd guess, I'd say it's just starting."

"There's a reason the two of you aren't partners," Green reminded him.

"Why?" Shan caught the inflection, the subterfuge. "Why aren't we partners, Damon?" She went after Green first, with misplaced anger.

"I can't say," he answered, not afraid of her.

"Can't or won't?"

"Won't."

"Kyle," Shan turned on him next.

"You don't need this problem now," he said.

"What fucking problem?" she yelled.

"You already know what fucking problem. Hell, there's a good chance you knew before Wade told me," he yelled right back.

Dead silence. It only took her a moment, but she did. "You're right," she said. "Now isn't the time. I guess I always did, and none of us ever got around to saying it out loud."

"You both know, end of discussion," Green said. "We have more pressing problems than sibling rivalry. Shan, meet your brother. Now both of you get over it."

"Pick someone," Taylor said.

"I can't ask anyone to go out with me. Command won't take this well." She wouldn't make it an order, either.

"No way I'm letting you go after Wade alone, no way in hell." He was about to tell Green it was him, but rank was a problem. Green had a year and a promotion on him, and there were prior commitments, with a Blackout in effect.

"I'm not dragging Green with me," Shan stopped him.

"Pick someone or I will," Taylor warned. "Rank or not. No one goes out alone."

"Wade already has." Shan looked past him, towards Team One, walking over from City Hall. "Great," she sighed. "Company."

"You did check yourself out of the hospital," Dallas said in amazement. "You should go right back." But she wouldn't. "You're going after Wade."

She groaned, no need for an actual answer.

"You can't. The Vista is in Blackout and you, Capt. Allen, are injured." Dallas, Major Dallas, could issue orders where Lt. Taylor and Capt. Green could not. It remained to be seen if she would listen to any of them.

"I don't have time to discuss this again," Shan said. "Which way did he go?"

No answer.

"You think I can't figure that out?" she directed at Taylor. "Really? East, maybe, more likely south. He took the Sweeps route," she decided. Two of them knew she was right and two of them didn't.

"Captain," Dallas held the car door shut as she reached for it. "You should consider an alternative."

"Major, I already have," she said, not giving in. "I'm going. There's no time to stop for a debate."

"I can order you back to the hospital," he told her.

"No, you can't," Shan said. "We're in Blackout and I'm a Scout going to the perimeter."

"But I can, on a medical," Hunter said. "And I will."

"Don't make me do something every single one of us will regret later," Shan told them. "I'll go as a civilian."

Dallas didn't budge. "Civilians don't get vehicles."

"I'll steal it."

"I'll arrest you," Dallas said.

"Fine. I'm in Command," she said, an idea officers on the outside only wondered about, until right at that moment. Shan put an end to all the speculation about who was in charge. Unless an actual commander showed, she was, and the fault was Wade's.

"She is," Green confirmed reluctantly.

"Tell the Judge Advocate in the morning," Dallas didn't back down, either.

"Kyle," she sighed. "Wade's going to get himself killed if I don't find him." Taylor stepped up, not liking this at all. Green was right beside him. It had a foul taste to it, like this was what the Colorado Nomads wanted. Security at each other's throats.

"Ah, no," Dallas said, glancing back over his shoulder. Hunter.

"It's two on three, Major," she said.

"You could no more take on one of us than jump onto a horse and gallop out of the plaza," Dallas returned. "I've seen your ER chart. You've had enough painkillers, I'm surprised you can walk."

"I'm talking about Wade's life. To hell with the hole in my shoulder. I'll heal."

"This is going nowhere," Taylor said. "She's right. We need to back him up."

Dallas had to agree with that. To Shan, "You still need to be in the hospital."

"Why her?" Hunter asked. "Send me and Green. Or anyone not shot full of holes." Earlier, when they'd escorted the ambulance to the ER, Mac had told Hunter he was going with Shannon, after Wade. He hadn't believed him.

Dallas' eyes locked with hers. "Can you find him?"

She nodded, "Of course." It was a blatant lie. Shan wasn't sure she would make it to the inner perimeter marker.

"They've run across Colorado together," Dallas said. After all was said and done, they'd hold her more responsible than him, Blackout or not. "Hunter, you go. If she gets sick, you haul her back home."

"Yeah," Shan scoffed.

"Lock her in the back seat and bring her in if you need to. How far are you going to follow him, Shan?" Taylor said.

"Until I find him."

"You pointed your gun at me, out at The Junction. What did you mean when you said 'I know what you did'?"

"I drew down on you? I don't remember that."

"You did, and I was curious what would make you say that," he said. Shock did weird things.

She shook her head. "I have no idea."

Taylor believed her. "You better figure out what your plan is. You better do it fast. We'll have snow in a few weeks."

"I was aware," she said. To Hunter, "You drive." She didn't know if she could hold the steering wheel steady, and had no intention of admitting it.

Forty miles out of The Vista, not quite to the Inner Perimeter, she got a chill, cold as mid-January, shaking so hard, she thought she'd die before it stopped.

Hunter drove.

Chapter Nine

July 15 middle of the night

Shannon, trapped in the nightmare of the day before, woke, sudden and violent, going for a weapon that wasn't there. Drenched in sweat, shaking, cold... in a car.

Hunter put his hand on her arm, so she'd be aware of him. Then to her forehead. "You've got a low grade fever, Captain. If it gets worse, or if you still have one in twenty-four hours, we're going home."

"Like hell," she managed.

"Oh, Capt. Allen, you're in no condition to stop me. And by the way," Hunter added while he was thinking about it. "What's this throwing 'I'm in Command' at us? They're going to reprimand Dallas. What they'll do to us, I can't imagine. The Caravans look better and better."

She waited for him to finish. "Is that all?"

"No. You need to be in a hospital. This is insane."

"You haven't been over that fence."

"No? That's where you're wrong, Captain."

She gazed at him for a moment. "Same fence, different pasture, I suppose. Where are we?"

"Montana?" he said. "Or northern Wyoming, but I doubt it."

She rubbed her eyes and groaned as they bounced over an uneven section of road. Shan hurt more than she had ever imagined, and, oh god, they had tried to kill Mac. Might have succeeded. She wouldn't try to sense him again.

"Did you drive all night?"

"A little over four hours."

With their speed, she figured where they were, and Hunter's guess was as good as hers. Still, she could follow Wade and that was something. He was traveling south and his fury hadn't diminished. No caution, and only the idea of revenge.

"How long since we lost contact with The Vista?"

"An hour, more than that now." He was tired. Hunter knew where her question was going. "Mac's condition hasn't changed. He's still critical."

She closed her eyes for a long time and he thought she'd gone back to sleep. "We are in what–Car Sixteen?"

"Car Eight. Lt. Taylor's Scout car. It runs on regular gas."

"Wade?"

"Car Ten. They'll scrap Twenty-four after what happened."

Shan didn't need reminding. "He shouldn't have taken Ten. My alternator's going bad."

Hunter sighed. "That's not a bad thing."

"Find a decent pull off. If we can get a couple hours sleep, maybe we can take a straight shot down the Front Range and catch him."

"You just woke up," Hunter pointed out. "What are you going to do if we find him? What if he's as unreasonable as you are?" He was pretty certain Wade would be far less reasonable.

"I can talk to him," she said. "He'll listen to me. He has to."

"Does he listen to anyone?"

She glared at him a moment, then turned her attention to their supplies. Shan had no intention of doing a replay of their Sweeps adventure. There were a couple of caches close by. "You get the back seat." Such as it was and not much more than half a back seat. If she didn't lie down, she was going to throw up or pass out. Her ribs felt crushed and her shoulder ached. What she needed to do to convince Wade to come home, she didn't have a clue. He would listen to her. It might not change his mind.

Hunter found a dirt road to pull off, back in the trees, out of sight from the highway. They had darkness for a few hours. He took advantage of the partial back seat, listening for any movement from Shan. She was restless, hurt, and that made her dangerous to herself and others.

The next thing she knew, the sun was shining, and it was getting uncomfortable in the car. Shan sat up, dizzy for a few moments. She held onto the seat, waiting for the nausea to pass.

"You look like hell," Hunter told her. He figured he'd gotten two hours of sleep.

"I didn't ask for your opinion," she told him. No doubt, she looked as bad as she felt.

"Since you're the senior officer, what's our plan?" He climbed out of the car, needing to stretch.

"Wade's smart enough to figure out he's being baited by now. If we can catch him, I'll insist on going with him. He'll drag me back to the hospital." It sounded as good as anything else she'd been able to come up with.

"You think that'll work?" Hunter drawled, his accent always more evident when he was tired.

"It's all I've got."

"Let's see how the weather holds up. And you," he said, offering her a hand. When she took it and stood, he put the heel of his other hand against her forehead. He had nothing to say.

"I'm in Command. That's not some story I made up. They won't hold Dallas responsible for what I'm doing, or what you're doing out here."

"I hope you're right."

It took them half an hour to get on the road. Shan wasn't hungry.

She felt sure he was making a list of reasons to tell her they had to go back. Today, more parts of her body hurt than yesterday. The painkillers had worked out of her system, but she wasn't quite ready to ask him for more.

"You left Taylor in charge of what – the 'Conda?" Hunter made small talk.

"No, Lambert, with Taylor giving him advice on the sidelines," she told him. "I hope they can work together." It wasn't her first concern. Rain clouds to the south and west. That would mean cold. She remembered how sick Wade had been with pneumonia a couple of winters ago and her immune system was already in overdrive.

"Taylor is tight with you, with Team Three. Wasn't it his brother you were training as a Scout?"

She nodded.

"You are a talkative one today," he said. "Are you seeing him?"

"Chris? No."

"Kyle. You spend a lot of time with him."

"He joined right after I did. Our teams work the same shifts."

"So, are you seeing him?"

"He's married." She wasn't in the mood to delve into her family tree, which had more branches than she'd been aware of a day ago.

"That makes a difference to you?"

She nodded, indignant, "Of course. Doesn't it matter to you?"

"Yeah," he confessed. "I'm just making conversation." A distraction, trying to keep her mind off other things. "What about Green?"

"He's not married," she told him, absolutely meaning to sound suggestive. Shan peered under the edge of the bandage across her shoulder.

"Don't mess with that. I'll take care of it later."

"I don't remember getting shot." Shan went right where he was trying to keep her away from.

"No, I guess sometimes you don't. Tell me something about the 'Conda." He wondered how long she'd hold up before she'd turn back or get too sick to go on. But then, they'd gone across Colorado like a tornado, on one horse and no rations.

"What do you want to know?" she asked instead of the standard 'no'.

"What is their purpose, their real agenda?"

"First, to provide security for The Vista beyond official parameters. Second, to help establish satellite communities, and third, to initiate contact with unknown areas beyond The Vista."

"That was a lovely recital," Hunter told her. "Who wrote it?"

"Wade did," she told him.

"What aren't you telling me?" He wondered if she trusted anyone outside that circle.

She didn't answer, leaning her head back and closing her eyes.

"Fine," he said. "Why don't you trust me?"

"Why are your files sealed?"

"My family had enemies, powerful ones. My parents split us up and sent us away because of the fear they'd try to use us against them." He'd never spoken of it to anyone but Dallas, and he'd been there. "I'm sure they had no clue war would happen the way it did. I couldn't get home once it started."

"Where are you from?"

"We lived in Mountain Brook," he told her. "A suburb of Birmingham, which was in Alabama."

"Hunter isn't your real name," she said in revelation, gazing at him. It hadn't even occurred to her before.

"No, but it's the only one I've used for twenty years. So I guess it is," he said, avoiding details and making the story short. "What's the 'Conda for real?"

"We've made them a separate, self-sufficient entity, established to guard against any lapses that might occur in The Vista government because of repercussions of the war experienced by original survivors." Another recital, but the true one, the one no one spoke of outside a select few.

Hunter took a few seconds to understand, getting caught off-guard. "Repercussions? Security is afraid everyone is getting meltdown?" He didn't know if he should laugh or cry.

"Not Security, the 'Conda, and not everyone," she emphasized. "It isn't speculation anymore. Every year, there are issues and sometimes they're serious. You've seen it." Everyone that lived through the war had mental scars. "No one will admit to it, but everyone over the age of ten knows. It has caused breaches in Security. We want to expand to cover those lapses, and other issues that might arise."

"You have all this documented?"

Shan looked at him and didn't have to answer. Monitoring meltdown was a cover for hiding the Gen En issue, but both were a genuine concern.

"I asked you once if you thought I had meltdown. What does my 'Conda file say?" He wasn't angry yet, but heading that way.

"You are unaffected for a consideration of ninety-five percent." Shan knew she wasn't supposed to reveal information to non-members. She figured Hunter earned the right. If Wade thought differently, he could tell her in person.

He wasn't sure how to react. Ninety-five percent functioning. "What gives you the right to pass judgment on others?" Now he was getting angry, because they were right and no one else had done anything about it before.

"Stop being paranoid. No one gets higher than ninety-five percent. It's just a number. We aren't judging anyone, we're trying to protect The Vista."

"From itself, from meltdown?"

"From groups like the Nomads that came out of Colorado and ran through us like wildfire. It wasn't the first time either. They set off the bomb on the Missouri Breaks..." She clamped her mouth shut, having said too much.

"Where did you hear that?" Hunter asked. Adults told their children stories that would never seem real, because they weren't, not anymore.

"Doesn't matter."

"If you are being lied to, it does."

Shan rubbed her eyes.

"Wade told you," Hunter figured. "Can he prove it?"

"Yes, we can."

"Did we go to Colorado to track these people down?" He couldn't imagine half the team being in the dark, but he put nothing past Wade. There was more happening here, even beyond Shan's confessions.

"We didn't realize it until we were back in Cody."

"Command must be aware."

"No. I mean…," Shan said, getting short with him. "I don't know everything Wade does, and that's between him and Command. All I am is the Scout."

He'd pushed her enough. "It doesn't matter. Try to get some rest. This won't get any easier." He had one more question. "Why are you telling me this now, when I couldn't have pried two words out of you earlier?"

"You're out here with me, and we're as unauthorized as hell. That means we're both in trouble, me more than you, but still trouble. They'll tell you not to do it again. I'm looking at a demotion at least. You should understand why. I'm done keeping secrets because this is where it's gotten us." Shan was aware of what she needed to do. The effort might be for nothing if she didn't find Wade. "I trust you, or you wouldn't be here, Hunter. Remember that."

Chapter Ten

Wyoming/Montana border July 19 morning

"I don't see how we're going anywhere now," Hunter said, pulling himself from underneath the car. Shan sat next to him, leaning against the front tire. He jumped up and gazed off across the valley at nothing in particular.

The drive shaft had snapped. He'd hit a washout in the road before daybreak and the car wasn't going any further. It wasn't one of their spare parts. Even if it was, neither of them was a mechanic. He was damned glad she'd been wearing a seat belt.

Shannon had no reply. He paced around to the other side of the car, digging through their supplies for clean clothes. Then he washed and shaved, certain she was sitting there, crying. That made him almost as certain she was getting sick. She didn't cry. Hunter had never even seen her close to tears. He let her be.

Soon, he broke up her pity party. "Are you all right?" he asked, repacking his gear.

"I'm fine."

"What now, Captain?" he asked, leaning against the bumper. "We're uncertain what's in that direction," he meant south. "But home is back that way."

"What do you want from me?" Pale, eyes red, it could be fever, tears, or both.

"I want you to say 'Let's go home'," Hunter said, running a hand over his face. "Taylor should've just told you no."

"Not his call, and not Dallas' call. It was mine." Shan rubbed her eyes, trying to think, trying to sense Wade.

"You want to take the blame for this when they go after someone," he decided. "I don't need protection from the Council."

"No, when it's time to face Command, have the good sense to let me. I understand how to deal with them. Council doesn't get to say a thing about it."

"How many times have you disobeyed orders? Stolen a car? Not to mention disappearing for god-knows how long we're going to be out here." Hunter knew this was a first, despite all the pushing of the rules Team Three did. He thought she could lose her job, it was that serious. She'd alluded to it earlier.

"Again. Command," she repeated. "I get to do a lot of things. If you weren't a rookie, you'd know this."

"You're out here with me, rookie or not. And you're just the Scout." He was beginning to wonder what hold Team Three had on Command, because it was there.

"Jacob Lowry's town," Shan said, ignoring his previous comment.

"What?" he asked. "Can you even tell me where it is from here?"

She stood up, unsteady, and dusted her backside off. "South."

Hunter cocked his head sideways and looked at her. "Ya think?"

She was unaware that he'd been driving them in wide circles. Wyoming looked like Colorado looked like Montana, as long as he stayed in the mountains and she spent most of the days sleeping. Plus, the pain pills kept her groggy.

"Are we going to walk there?" Hunter asked.

Chapter Ten

"We can walk, or we can lug all these guns with us and trade for a horse or two the next time we run across Nomads that are friendly." She had a way of knowing their intent. A time, not too far in the future, she was going to need to explain that to him. Hunter would think she'd gone bat shit crazy.

"You're still running a fever off and on. We won't make a hell of a lot of progress walking. We need to stay close to the main roads so we can find shelter at night or you're going to get sick, and I mean truly sick," he warned her.

"I'm taking all those drugs you have."

"Those are low grade antibiotics made in The Vista. They won't do a thing if you build fluid in your lungs or get an infection in your shoulder." Hunter pulled no punches. "I'm not a doctor."

"The weather has been good, and this time of year, we should have time." A little time.

"Five weeks, Shan, at the outside. We're in the Rocky Mountains. If we get caught out here when it turns to winter, we're going to be stranded until April."

"I'm aware of that."

"Let me push the car off the road and we'll decide what we can carry," Hunter said. By 'we,' he meant himself. "I want to change that bandage today, too."

She waited until he got the car into cover. Stripping off her shirt, one of Hunter's because it fit over the bulky bandage, she sat in the back seat.

"Lay down," Hunter told her. "This will sting." He thought she might pass out. The past few days, she'd come close a couple of times.

Shan leaned back, throwing her good arm over her face so she wasn't tempted to look. The lace camisole was her last layer of shirts, not that she cared at the moment. She'd been in various states of undress with him over the past few months, and figured he'd seen other women naked before. "What are you going to do?"

"That's pretty sexy," he noted.

"Shut up, Hunter," she mumbled, feeling anything but sexy. Exhausted and alone, dusty, tired, and home-sick. Mostly, she felt numb. She was afraid of anything else.

"I'm going to clean it up, make sure there's no infection, and put on a nice, sterile bandage. If there is any problem, we aren't going south." He leaned over her, peeling the gauze away. "Huh," he mused.

"What?"

"If I didn't know this happened five days ago, I'd say it was a lot longer. You're healing fast."

"You said that yesterday, and the day before," she reminded him.

"This looks weeks healed, not days."

"A good thing," she said, trying to brush it off.

"Yes it is." He went about poking and prodding. "Dr. Roberts did this?"

"Yep."

"I'll be finished in two minutes," he told her. Then he dumped alcohol on it.

"That's cold," she informed him tersely.

"Sorry." Hunter put a fresh bandage across her shoulder and taped it up. "You're ready to go." She sat up and he took the seat next to her. "Are you sure you want to do this, Shan?"

"I have to," she whispered. "If Dallas got in trouble, wouldn't you do anything you could to help him?"

"I would," he confessed with a sigh. "Let's get moving, Captain."

July 20 mid morning

Dressed in forest camos, they sat on the edge of a clearing up-slope from the highway, watching a small band of travelers across the valley floor. If they had more horses, and if fewer of them were on foot, Shan might let Hunter try to approach them to trade. Non-aggressive as far as she sensed. They carried an array of weapons, and the pair remained hidden.

"Tell me about you, something not related to our work," Hunter made conversation, passing time. There was shelter a few miles behind them and if the way didn't clear, they would go back for the night.

"Like what?" She'd grown more at ease, but some subjects were still off-limits. Days were long. They stopped frequently for her to rest, and had little to talk about.

"Your families lived together when you were kids. What was it like?"

She considered it, what she remembered most vividly from her childhood. Until she'd been almost ten, the Allen, Cameron, Taylor, and MacKenzie families shared the same house. True, a big house, fortified and rebuilt for defense, but that wasn't a concern of children.

"Our dads used to take us camping in the summer, up past where the West End Stables are now, by that little lake. The moms would tell them, 'Keep an eye on them, don't let them get hurt, don't let them get dirty.'" She smiled. "We played rough even then. Wade might have been stronger, but Mac and I were faster. Taylor was sneaky. Wade didn't always win. I could out-shoot the boys by the time I was eight. Our dads would whoop it up over that, but Wade would just say 'I can get better.'"

"He's always been competitive."

"We always encouraged each other." She wouldn't think about Mac.

"That sounds competitive to me." Hunter remembered his siblings.

"Encouraged," she repeated. "They talked me into jumping in the pond behind the house, trying to teach me to swim, the summer I was five."

"What happened?"

"David MacKenzie saw me jump. He pulled me out, half-drowned. They got in so much trouble." She smiled again at the memory.

Hunter decided he liked it when she smiled. "Did you learn to swim?"

"No, I never have."

"So Team Three isn't perfect."

"I don't remember any of us claiming to be perfect. Where do you hear these things?"

"That's how the trainees see you. Team Three is what they want to be."

Shan rolled her eyes. "How wrong is that?"

"Tell me one of Wade's flaws. Anything, quick," Hunter challenged her, taking a moment to peer at the highway through his binoculars.

"No," she shook her head.

"See?"

"I mean, I won't tell you."

"You know, I have meltdown, I'll probably forget, anyway." He offered her a rations pack.

She declined. "You don't have meltdown," Shan told him, voice odd. He'd hit a nerve.

For a moment, he was stunned. "Does Wade?"

"No." Cautionary now.

"Does he think he does?"

"The rule is–anyone who can remember the war. Wade can remember the war," Shan said. It wasn't meltdown he feared, but something far darker, something they couldn't name.

"How old was he?"

"Almost four."

"A kid that age doesn't know... He couldn't have meltdown from memories at that age. I understood what was happening," Hunter said. It made little sense.

"He sees his mother, and it scares the hell out of him." Not much scared Wade. "He loses sleep over making plans and rules and contingencies so there are no mistakes. No slip-ups, no one dies because of meltdown." Or other things that haunted him.

"I didn't realize why he felt so adamant," Hunter confessed. It gave him a new perspective.

"You never heard that," Shan said.

"Understood." He looked through the binoculars again. "They'll be out of sight in a few more minutes. We should look for shelter the way they came from."

"Sure. We'll wait a bit. Sometimes there are more tagging along behind."

"What are you afraid of, Shannon?"

She squinted away from the noonday sun, trying to decide how to answer. Trusting someone new was unknown territory for her. "I'm afraid of what's out here."

"Afraid that The Vista isn't the center of the universe?"

"Not the point. You remember the warheads?"

"We were a hundred miles away when St. Louis...." He let it go, the memory still too vivid.

"I'm afraid that someone out here knows how to do that again. I have nightmares about bombs going off, the heat flash, the EMP, the mushroom clouds." A chill ran up her spine and she shuddered. "My mother has videos in her library. Ones they made at the hospital those first years."

He grimaced. Radiation poisoning wasn't a good way to die. They'd gotten lucky, being west of the detonation. They traveled for days without stopping to rest, avoiding people as much as the poison in the air. "I read somewhere that they will fight World War Four with sticks and stones."

Shan smiled, pushing the dark memories away. "I hope they're right. Sticks and stones we can deal with. What about you, Hunter? What keeps you awake at night?"

"I wasn't with my family when I should have been," he said. He didn't need to think about it.

"Your parents thought you'd be safer if they split you up."

"We should've been together. We didn't get that choice." Hunter shrugged it off. "Maybe they were right. It doesn't matter now."

"Yes, it does," she told him.

"Are you ready to head down the hill?"

"As I'll ever be," she said, aware he was done sharing.

"I'll carry your pack until we get to the road."

She slung the rifle over her uninjured shoulder. "We're making camp on the same side as the creek if we get a choice. I want a bath, even a quickie."

"Sounds good," he chuckled, following her.

"I meant a quick bath." Shan cleared that up.

"Do I get to take a lookout while you take a bath?" He already knew he'd be hauling water for her, because the chance of finding a place with plumbing that worked was close to zero.

Shan shook her head, not even turning around. "You bet."

July 22 afternoon

"Three guns for two horses. Did we get a good deal or a bad one?" Hunter asked. The horses, well, they'd seen better days. At least they weren't walking.

Distracted, Shan answered, "They're old, not sick." They'd traded for the animals earlier and put some miles behind them.

Her definition of old sometimes disturbed him. "You've accused me of both."

"Damn," she jumped off the horse and stomped around in the mud a bit, stopping to peer at the horizon as if she couldn't quite see it.

"Shan?" he asked for the second time.

"I thought it was because I've got a head cold. It's not. I'm losing Wade. He's moving away from us again, fast. I don't understand this. Why east instead of south?"

"What in the hell are you talking about?"

"Wade," she threw up her arms in frustration, wishing she hadn't, healing muscles pulling.

He joined her, standing in the ditch off the road, in the weeds. "Okay, pretend I still don't get what you're talking about."

"It's good for a couple hundred miles, as far as I can tell. I'm losing him, its gone way shallow." A pained expression crossed her face. "In an hour, nothing will be there."

Hunter was silent for a few moments. "What sort of tracking device are you using?"

"Me, Hunter, I'm the tracking device."

He wondered how bad of a concussion she'd had. "How do you do that, exactly?"

She turned to look at him. "I can't explain it, but I was born like this. All three of us were."

"Like what?" He didn't have to ask who she meant.

"We have a psychic connection, we have since we were kids. Our best guess is that genetic manipulation caused it. We can sense each other. Right now, I'm losing him." She thought she'd already lost Mac, and now Wade.

"You're not kidding."

"I'm not in the mood for kidding." Shan wouldn't give up, but she was running out of ideas.

"Holy shit," he said, remembering something from a long time ago. His father hadn't approved, and it caused him a great deal of concern. "There were governments experimenting in genetic engineering from the 1940s right until the war."

"Great bit of trivia." Shan didn't have an answer for any of the questions he was about to ask.

"I remember politicians fighting about if it should be legal or not." He recalled rumors from not-so-long ago, too. Rumors in The Vista most people considered urban legends.

"Apparently, it was."

"Not necessarily," Hunter said. He wasn't sure about anything at the moment. "It's not legal or illegal until there are actual laws. I think that's where they were at. Figuring out what to do."

"You told me I have issues with trust. Now you know why, and need to trust me," Shan told him, wishing she had avoided this. "Wade stopped when he crossed the divide and threw the radio out of Car Ten. That's why we couldn't get him to answer. He's traveling at night and sleeping during the day." She shook her head. "I know he thinks Alex died. Now he's ignoring me."

"Shan," he said, lost. So was she.

"This is their real secret," she said. "I can prove it, I just can't prove it right now."

"Who else knows?"

"Taylor, Lambert, Green. Bennett and Ballentyne. They're Wade's safety, in case of trouble like this. There are others. Wade has people he won't disclose."

"When they brought Mac into the ER," Hunter said, not wanting to talk about it with her, but seeing no other choice. "He told me I'd be going to Colorado after Wade, with you. I assumed he was delirious. You're not going to tell me you can predict the future."

"No," Shan shook her head. "Oh, I suppose we could guess like anyone else, but no one can predict the future. Too many variables. We have an insight into each other's emotions. Mac knew how we'd both react. It was an educated guess."

"You can tell where Wade is?"

"I can, in the right circumstances. It must fade with distance. He's getting weak. It's happened before, when I..." Shan eyed him speculatively for a moment. "When I went towards the coast, I lost them."

"The West Coast?"

"That's the one. Command has sent Scouts out for pre-Sweeps surveys. Another thing you haven't heard from me and don't know about. The point is, Wade is moving faster than we are. If I can't sense him, I can't find him."

Hunter shook his head. "We can't keep up with a car, Shan. You said he slept during the day."

"He only sleeps about four hours at a time. We can ride longer today, until after dark, and I might be able to sense what direction he's moving. I think it's east."

"If the road is clear and if the weather holds," he put an immediate restriction on moving after dark.

"Do you believe me, Hunter?"

"Until you get the chance to prove it and can't, I have to be skeptical, I guess." If he'd out and out said he did, they'd both know he was lying. It didn't take psychic abilities to figure that one out.

July 21 after dark

It was easy to convince Hunter to sleep that day and travel after dark. Logistically easier, now that they'd gained horses and a few supplies. The weather was another issue.

Her fever started hours later. She was cold, then hot, then dizzy. Stopping her horse, Shan dismounted and stood there, holding on to the saddle horn for balance. She couldn't recall why they'd stopped.

"What's up?" Hunter asked, dismounting next to her, ready to walk for a while. When he reached out to touch her, to see if she realized he was there at all, Shan recoiled, jerking away.

She stumbled under the horse's neck and sat down hard. "I suppose it was my brilliant idea to be out here in the dark," she said, confused.

"Christ," he mumbled, a hand to her forehead. "Ah, shit, Shannon. How long has this been going on?"

"What?"

"You're burning up." It wasn't a bit of a fever anymore.

"I started feeling crappy around dark. The fever, I didn't think I had one. I can't sense Wade anymore." Her speech was slow and slurred.

"That's the fever."

"How in the hell would you know?"

"You told me, when you're sick, it doesn't work right."

She'd forgotten. "Yeah, it doesn't. I told you that."

"You did," Hunter said, getting her on her feet. "We have to find a decent place to camp. A building, not a lean-to. Does it hurt to breathe?"

"No. I'm a little tired. We need to look for Wade."

"We're finished looking, for now." He gave her a foot up onto the horse, collected his reins, and pulled himself up behind her.

"We're still in Montana, aren't we? We've been riding around and around and around in circles."

"We're north of Cody. It's not far. That's where we're heading. Be pissed later. Right now, you're sick."

"And you're not a doctor," she finished for him.

"How did you figure out where we are?"

"Lucky guess. It's what I'd have done in your place."

Outstanding, Hunter thought to himself.

Hours later, Hunter navigated them to the Cody base. It took a short time to clear the building that would become their station. Shan slept on a dusty sofa where he deposited her, wrapped in a sleeping bag. It was colder than the day before, and he stoked up a fire, hoping the smoke wouldn't draw unwanted attention. Then he brought up supplies from storage, making sure to mark off what they were using on the inventory list. By the time he stabled the horses across the street in an old schoolyard Security had fenced off for that purpose, it was close to dark again.

"Hey," he said, sitting down. "Take these." He handed her a canteen of water to wash down the pills. "How do you feel?"

"Like I have the flu."

"The Flu or just a flu?"

"They both are pretty much the same," she said, curling back up in the sleeping bag.

"Great," Hunter said.

"Not worse," she told him. "Stop worrying so much."

"You're sick," he pointed out. "We don't have a hospital close."

"I heal fast."

"Stay put and try to rest while I look around. You have your Sig."

She didn't remember him being gone, but the next time she opened her eyes, he was sitting in front of the fire, eating. "Did you cover the windows?" Shan asked, a flashback to her childhood.

"This is the Cody base. They did all the maintenance while we traipsed around Colorado." He had his feet propped up on a box. "Hungry? I made some soup. Potatoes, onion, carrots, garlic, and chicken. Should be edible."

"That sounds good," she pushed herself up, propping against the arm of the sofa. He got her a cup of broth. She stared at the steam rising for a couple of minutes before trying it. "Did you find wild chickens?" she made a joke.

"No, but the frozen storage downstairs is short one chicken. I don't want to be digging into supplies too much. Plan on rabbit or grouse, something fresh tomorrow."

Shan finished, not making any more comments about his cooking because it was better than hers, even with the limited stock. He took the cup and stoked the fire on his way back from the kitchen.

"I got shot before," she told him, still groggy.

"I heard."

"Have you seen the helicopters?"

"During training, they took us out and showed us. It happened before I was in Security."

Shan stifled a laugh. "I'm sorry. I forgot you're the rookie." For whatever reason, it was amusing to her.

"When do I lose that title?" he wondered. He'd been an officer for two years now.

"When we get another rookie to harass."

"Chris Taylor."

"He's not assigned to a team yet. Then you'll be out of the woods."

"Fair enough, I suppose. Where did you get shot?" He couldn't recall any scars.

"In Sheridan," she said.

"Where on you were you hit?" he tried again. She was dopey from the sleeping pill he'd given her, along with antibiotics. Their supply of both was running low.

"Damned near the same place I am now," she said. "And here," she pulled up her shirt and peeled the waist of her jeans back, pointing. "Right above the hipbone. Nothing vital, but it hurt like hell. Pretty amazing I got hit twice."

"How did someone manage to shoot you twice?"

"The second helicopter caught me in the open, between checkpoints. I tried to evade, but they sort of had the advantage. That, plus they shot down an entire house. Then they got me." Shan wasn't the storyteller of the group.

"You played hide and seek with a military helicopter and lived to tell. And only got shot twice?" Hunter shook his head.

"They couldn't figure out how to work the armaments. Some idiot with an M-16 was leaning out the side, shooting at me. I shot back when I should've hidden."

"You're lucky they didn't know what they were doing."

"No shit. You sound like Wade sometimes."

"I've never sounded like Wade," Hunter said.

"You're a lot alike. That's why you two have a problem."

"You are why we have a problem."

"I'm a problem," Shan lamented, ready to fall asleep.

"I said something out-of-line, and he took it personal." Hunter wondered if she knew the story. He didn't think Team Three kept much from each other, not if the tale she told proved to be real.

"It was personal, though."

"What I said, I directed at Wade, not you, even if it doesn't sound that way now. You had to be there."

"I was. Depot North, last spring."

"It was a mistake, Shan."

"Apology accepted," she told him. "If it makes you feel better, remind me to give you a good slap later."

"That's a deal," he smiled, pulling the sleeping bag over to share. "I want you to sleep now."

"It's cold. Or is it me?"

"No, it's gotten cold."

"It's July."

"I was aware. Sleep now."

"There's something else I should tell you."

Hunter wondered what in the hell else she could spring on him. "Okay," he said.

"You said it yourself, that I heal fast. All of us do. Another one of those things we can't explain," Shan said. "I mean faster than you'd expect. You've seen. Then there's the fever. Kind of like the after effects. Once the fever burns off, I'll be all better. Mostly better, I suppose."

"How long does it last?"

"A couple of days," she shook her head. "Maybe longer. That's why I told you to stop worrying so much. Normal for us. The only thing I have to consider is dehydrating."

"You were going to run for Colorado alone, knowing how sick you'd get? Pretty stupid, Shannon." Hunter didn't mind telling her.

"I thought I'd catch Wade."

"We need to hide out here for a few days. Then we go home."

"When I'm better, I'll decide. If I can tell where Wade is, if I can sense him..." she started.

"Isn't the idea that he's running into an ambush a moot point? He has to have a plan," Hunter cut her off. "If he wanted you in Colorado, don't you think you'd be aware?" Assuming the whole psychic thing was real.

"Yeah," she said. "Ask me again later."

Hunter was pretty sure he'd go crazy when she fell asleep next to him. He didn't. He thought about what it was going to take to get her to go home.

Daybreak revealed the snow that had fallen overnight. Not significant in the valley, but enough to cover the ground. Higher up, more, and it would make the passes dangerous. It was still only July.

Chapter Eleven

Aug 5 Wyoming midday

"I get why you're messing around out here for no good reason," Hunter told her. They'd been traveling north, wandering through the remnants of roadside ruins longer than they should have. Caution, he understood. This wasn't caution. She was hiding out.

"Do you?" Shan asked, riding ahead of him. They dressed in bulky winter gear, disguising their identities, which was the intent. The fact she cut off most of her hair the day before they left Cody helped.

Snow had wiped the foliage from the trees, leaving them bare and the ground a muddy mess. It made traveling more treacherous. Nomads were moving as well, trying to find shelter from a winter that promised to be harsh.

"Stalling. Once we cross the dotted line, once we're back in Montana, you don't have a good excuse not to go home."

"So?"

"You're afraid to go," Hunter said.

She turned around in the saddle enough to glare daggers of ice at him. "So?"

"Bad news is bad news, unless you know something I don't." He stopped in mid-sentence as she swung her horse around.

"I've lost Wade out here. He's in Colorado and you damned well made sure I didn't follow him, didn't you?" She felt better, and that made way for the anger he'd been expecting since they left The Vista. It wasn't his fault, but he'd catch the flak.

"Mac made it an order, remember?"

Shan flinched. "Do you think I want to go back and hear I've lost Alex, too?" For that fraction of a second, she was being Shannon and not Capt. Allen.

He saw it, too, and understood. This wasn't about Security, or the 'Conda, or Team Three's secrets. Her face told the story. Dallas had said she was spoken for. Hunter wanted her to say if it was true or not. "We're out of choices."

She urged her horse on. "Just leave me alone."

"You can't hide out here in the badlands forever, Captain."

Shan digested that for a few. "I could try," she said. It was getting late in the season. They either had to go to Colorado and hope they beat the weather, or they had to go back. Home. Montana.

"We're going home." Hunter made the call.

"I can't go to Colorado now that the Nomads have had time to regroup. It could be something they expect and I'm not walking into another ambush. Wade will hide out on his own until spring. I'm safe in Montana." She fought the burning sensation in her eyes.

"You can't be certain about Mac," Hunter said.

"I can sense things," she snapped. "They revived him in the ambulance on the way to the hospital. And again when I got sick that first morning, this side of the divide."

"You don't know what happened after we left."

"Why do you think we're still out here? I don't want to go back. I don't want to find out."

"You heal fast. You told me that and I've seen it."

"We're not invincible. He..." She shut the images out of her mind. "I can't."

"Shan, no matter what, I'm here if you need me," he told her. "I see how you isolate yourself, and you're good at it. Try to remember, I'm not your enemy."

She nodded, silent again.

Aug 16 north of Anaconda, south of The Vista nightfall

They made good time the last day out of The Vista, considering they'd crossed snowstorms twice in the past week. It might not be official, but winter had begun. Shan was quiet, and Hunter let her be.

It was near dusk when they crested the Continental Divide, well inside the inner perimeter. A Scout and a Guardian could find their way close in the dark. For a few moments, they saw twinkling lights along the horizon.

"That's The Vista," Hunter said. "We'll be there by noon if we have to ride in on our own. If we pick up a Scout tonight, we can be in warm beds by morning."

"It's what, seven, seven-thirty?" The distant lights blinked out.

He nodded.

Shan dug the radio out of her pack. She'd pulled it out of their supplies earlier, but there had been no sign of anyone on the outer perimeter. It wasn't unusual this time of year, not when the weather was bad.

"Do you want me to make the call?" he asked.

She shook her head. "I've got it." Then, "Relay, callback. Is anyone on the air?" They waited a few minutes in case they trying to move to a better location. "We need to head west and pick up the interstate," Shan decided. "If they're out, they'll be all over us."

"Now that we're north of Butte, we should be clear." Hunter worried about outlanders, especially with the weather. They'd seen many bands of Nomads farther south. He'd been keeping track of where and how many. If anyone had spotted them, they hadn't cared enough to approach.

An hour later, they began picking up broken static. Hunter dismounted and excused himself. She didn't want an audience. That was obvious.

"Callback," Shan said, a knot in her throat making it difficult to speak. The one in her stomach had been there since they left Cody.

"Callback, caller, identify yourself."

She wasn't sure who, but he was clear and close. "This is Team Three."

"Call word?"

She turned off the voice modulator. "We've been gone weeks. I'll be damned if I know what the call word is. Capt. Lambert, Denny, is that you?"

There were a few moments of silence. "Shannon?"

"We're tired and cold, Den. Do you think you could send someone around to pick us up? We need a trailer and transport."

"Where are you? Who's with you?"

"We're south of The Vista, somewhere off I-90, past the I-15 exchange and east of Station One. Just me and Hunter."

"Hell, we can be there in a few minutes," he answered. "I have to relay to The Vista first. Get up on the blacktop so we can find you. This is some damn good news."

Hunter was behind her, watching. "Who's with you?" she asked anyway.

"Colin MacKenzie. The boy wants to be a Scout."

Her vision went blurry. "Den, what about Alex?"

He hesitated. "Shannon, do you want to do this now? I mean, there are ears on." Even with it being a Scout designated channel, other people in The Vista monitored it.

"Denny, just tell me," she said. Not knowing was far worse than she'd ever imagined.

"They made him a Commander, Shan. He's running the rotation shift out at Station One."

Wade's post, but it was the last thing on her mind. Mac was alive. Hell, he got promoted. Shan put her hand over her mouth and the flood of tears she'd held on to for so long came out. She didn't care if Hunter saw. Right then, it didn't matter. She crouched down next to her horse and let it go.

"Your mother is on duty, so she'll get the call," Lambert said. "That good with you?"

Hunter took the handset. "Capt. Allen is indisposed at the moment. Get it called in."

"Debriefing will take a couple of days, especially with Wade still MIA."

"Mac ordered me not to let her cross into Colorado."

"I've heard," Lambert said. "We had our own debriefing."

Good, Hunter thought. The idea he might have had to tangle with the Captain could make him unpopular.

"Is she all right?"

"She is now," Hunter told him.

"I knew she had a thing for Mac, hell, for years," Lambert said.

"You're right," he said. "We'll be on I-90 in a couple minutes."

"Standard protocol," Lambert said.

"Understood."

Shan rose and tried to dry her face on her parka sleeve. "Oh, damn, now I'm blubbering like an idiot."

"Do you need a shoulder to cry on?"

She laughed. "You've been waiting to ask me that for weeks." She hugged him, holding on for a long time.

"We've got to get up on the blacktop. Lambert said standard procedure."

"I hope so," she sniffed. "I may get fired tomorrow, but I'm still in Security tonight."

"You don't think you're over-reacting?" Hunter asked.

"It's possible. I do that sometimes. Let's go find out."

Lambert shined a spotlight on them while Colin MacKenzie stood in the dark, weapon in hand.

"Shan, dismount and walk towards me," he called out on the loudspeaker. Then, "Stop, turn around, face me again and lace your fingers on top of your head," he instructed, checking to make certain they were alone. Hunter was next, and he ended up kneeling in the snow, facing away, hands on his head.

Lambert came out to greet them, satisfied. "We're clear, Colin. Call it in." He shook Hunter's hand as he stood. "How are you doing?" he directed at Shan.

"Good. He should be a doctor, not a Guardian."

Hunter shrugged. "It wasn't so much me."

"I know." Lambert had a secret and couldn't wait to tell. "Command gave us the Cody Base. Council went in a hundred percent with them. It's happening."

Deirdre drew rotation shift, 6pm to 2am, two weekends in a row. A necessary evil, being Chief of Staff. This time, she brought her own deck of cards. Between her, three nurses, and a rookie officer, they could at least get a decent game of poker going. Ironically enough, they used pennies to bet with. The Vista had an almost endless supply of them and, other than some older ones being copper, they were pretty much useless.

An hour and a half later, the radio began beeping. It always made her heart jump into her throat when a call came in.

"This is Dispatch. We're bringing two officers in on a Code Fifteen."

Damn, Deirdre thought. She never remembered which codes were which. She swore they changed them to confuse people.

"What injuries are we getting?" the rookie asked.

"No injuries. Quarantine for debriefing. Team Five just picked up Lt. Hunter and Capt. Allen coming in on I-90."

Deirdre dropped her cards.

A crowd of people had gathered in the hospital lobby by the time Lambert drove them in. Dallas and Duncan showed up, both off duty when the call happened. Any idea of sneaking in during the cover of night was pointless after that.

Shan repeated her story to Lambert, the one she concocted with Hunter over the past week. "Wade doesn't want to be here right now. He's in Cody and he wants to be left alone so he can consider his options. He ordered us back because of that and the weather." She knew Hunter would look for answers of his own. So would Lambert, out of earshot of the rookie.

"You're sure he's all right?" Lambert asked.

"I am," she said. "Otherwise, I wouldn't be here now."

Colin, escorting Hunter, was walking ahead of them. "Do you think they're expecting us?"

Deirdre didn't wait for them to get to the lobby. "Your father spent three weeks convincing me you'd be home soon and the same three telling me you knew what you were doing out there."

"He's at least half right, Mom," Shan said, getting a powerful hug. "It was an impulsive thing to do."

"I'm glad you see that," Deirdre ushered them inside. It was noisy and jubilant, not usual for the ER. "I couldn't imagine that you'd be home before spring."

Michael came in right behind them and got a few words with Shan before Duncan waved for their attention. "You all are aware of the procedure for debriefing," he announced.

"Debriefed, debunked, and deloused," Hunter quoted a popular saying from Station Three. They quarantined most people coming from outside The Vista there until Command cleared them.

"Speak for yourself," Shan said and a ripple of laughter crossed the room. She was looking for one face in the crowd, not even certain they would have called him in from Station One.

Someone had.

Shan went to him. "Alex," she whispered, burying her face against his neck.

"Save it for later," he said in her ear. Everyone in the room applauded and several catcalls rang out.

Deirdre let the noise die down a bit before she broke it up. "All right, I have at least two officers getting physicals. I can arrange more if anyone else is due."

They dispersed, knowing the time to celebrate would happen soon enough. Duncan spoke to the pair and then excused himself to meet with Lydia Cameron. He'd heard their story, aware it was pure fabrication.

After a thorough going over, DeCino with Shan, and Kline getting Hunter, they were sent to private rooms on the second floor. Hunter took the time to kick off his boots before he was asleep in a proper bed.

Shannon stood in the stall, lukewarm water running over her. The hospital had its own generators, so she had dim light, not that she needed it to shower. The water was paradise. Tomorrow she'd be in her own room at Station Two. She wondered when Command would call for her and couldn't imagine them waiting long.

"I'm here," Mac said, leaning against the far wall.

She peered around the curtain. "I'll be right out."

"Don't rush."

"It's been a while since I've had a decent shower," she confessed. After a few more minutes of soaking, Shan turned off the water and wrapped herself in a robe. "What's that?" she asked, seeing he was holding something.

"A bottle of wine. I brought some dinner up too, in case you might be hungry." He went to her room and left it on the table before returning. "No lecturing me about the evils of alcohol."

"Maybe later," she told him.

"Later," he agreed.

"You told him to run us in circles?" Shan asked later, not ready to sleep.

He nodded, arms around her, a heavy quilt pulled up around them. The door to her room was locked.

"Why?" A simple question.

"I knew you were hurt, and it wouldn't stop Wade from going after them, or you after Wade. I was afraid you'd both get yourselves killed. So, I threw a monkey wrench called Hunter in your plans."

"What if the car hadn't quit?"

"You'd still have gotten sick. I counted on it. The safety of The Vista depended on what I did in those few minutes, and I was in no condition to be making decisions."

"I'd have been in Colorado by then." Shan rested her head on his shoulder, tracing the scar on his chest with her fingertips. Soon it would be fade away. The memory wouldn't. Someone from the hospital staff or Security was bound to notice Cmdr. MacKenzie's car in the south lot. She didn't care. Even if she would admit to nothing, she was beyond tired, but not ready to sleep.

"I told him to use whatever means necessary to stop the chain reaction you two seem to cause." Her and Wade.

"I talk mean, but I was in pretty sad shape. Between the fever and the nightmares... about The Junction..." She didn't want to think about it. "I felt your heart stop, Alex. Twice."

"Don't cry," he told her.

"Stop telling me that," she exhaled sharply. Then she cried for the second time in a few hours.

He held her. After a while, she got it out of her system.

She curled up with him, glad for the heavy blanket. The Vista was colder than Cody, even if it hadn't snowed yet. "Why Hunter?"

"He's not part of the 'Conda, and that made the choice for me. I needed Team Two here, just in case. What happened at The Junction, I don't remember. Council was throwing a command position at me, plus the Cody Base if I wanted it, the day after I woke up."

"I don't remember most of the two or three days after."

"What about the ambush?"

"Not getting shot, but everything else is too clear." He held her tighter. "I love you, Alex," she whispered.

He leaned over to kiss her. "Do you think I don't know that?"

"I had to say it."

"I love you, and I'll say it, anyway."

"What are we going to do?"

"We're going to Cody."

"I meant us."

"I can't say, not anymore. Everything changed that afternoon. We have to start over and hope we get things right this time."

Aug 17 8am Station Two

Team Three appropriated the second floor of the station to take care of business. That would take most of the day. Shannon started coordinating a schedule while Mac rounded up supplies for breakfast. A tiny kitchen sat in the back and someone was bound to get hungry. They expected to have company early and weren't wrong. Team Two – Green, Ballentyne, and Taylor arrived before the coffee finished brewing.

"What did you think you were doing?" Taylor lit into Shan. "Wade has a hierarchy set up for emergencies and you disregarded all of that. I'm his second. I was supposed to be out there, not you."

"And then what would you do?" she asked, uncertain of where their relationship stood, at least on a personal level. "How would you find him? If I couldn't, you sure as hell couldn't. It wasn't your decision to begin with. You're here to back us, not second guess us. The chain-of-command is Team Three, our seconds, and officers we pick for specific jobs. Don't think hitting on two of those gives you special privileges."

"It was uncalled for and damned dangerous."

"Thanks for the concern. I had no other choice. I'm Wade's partner, and you need to back off before we say things we'll regret tomorrow."

"Did you get any sleep?" Ballentyne asked, breaking them up. Shan and Taylor had been involved in long drawn out arguments before and they didn't have the time today. "You look like something the cat dragged in."

She rubbed her eyes, not about to give out the details of her night. "My lack of sleep isn't a concern at this point. There are genuine issues here. The first thing we need to be aware of is Hunter. We were in trouble, and I told him everything."

"Everything?" Green repeated. "As in, everything?"

"As in everything. I told him how I followed Wade. Then I told him why the 'Conda exists. No clue if he believes a word I said. We'll find out soon enough." Shan made no apologies.

"So we bring him in," Mac said. "Easy fix."

"We might reject him on the fact he used to run with the Caravans," Ballentyne joked. "That wouldn't be the worst excuse we've used." It was true, and he got a smile out of them.

"Not an option," Shan told him, glancing at Green. "The 'Conda doesn't get a say, not this time. He's my second. It's done. That, plus I suspect Dallas knows things, Gen En things. I got a clear impression of that the night we left. We need to meet with Team One and figure out who knows what and how."

"I'll get them in a room," Ballentyne said. "Keep a radio handy."

Shan acknowledged, "You deal with Dallas. I told Hunter I'd

prove to him I wasn't crazy, so that's my problem. He has a lot of questions. He'll want proof, and that's going to be an interesting trick all on its own."

"You can handle it," Mac said. "Show him something he hasn't seen yet."

Shan nodded.

"Agenda. Command will call Hunter and Shan soon, as in today, so they need to keep their options open. Team One is a priority. The 'Conda is on the short list as soon as we figure out what in the hell is next. Parents," Mac added. "See them the first time you have ten minutes free, Shan. Tell them what we're going to do."

"What's Command going to do?" Taylor asked.

"About the two of them? Your guess is as good as mine. Since she's my Scout, they didn't include me in the hearing." Mac wasn't too worried. "Whatever they do won't change our plans."

"What about Wade?" Green asked what they were all wondering.

"I've never seen him so..." she trailed off, at a loss for being able to express what he'd felt. More than anger, more than fear. "He was moving away, fast, and he was blocking me. It was intentional. He's never done that before." Shan wrinkled her nose, trying to sense him. She shook her head. "Wade has always said distance had nothing to do with that particular Gen En ability. I fade out, for a lack of better words, when we get some miles between us."

"How far?" Taylor asked.

"I'd guess two hundred miles, give or take."

"Do you know where he is?" Ballentyne asked. "We haven't been able to contact him in Cody."

"He's in Colorado. I know where. I just don't know why."

"Why he went there?" Green asked. "They hurt us. He was going to hurt them right back."

"We could regroup and not worry about them outnumbering us," Shan said. "He should have waited."

"So could they. Colorado's a big place. Be more specific."

"He's gone back near Lake George. Jacob Lowry's town."

"Does it have a name?"

"Skyline."

"That puts him damned close to the Nomads that have been fucking with us all season," Mac said.

"So he's still out to track them down," Green said, not a question. He knew better.

"Yes. This group is dangerous, more than what we usually run across, because they're organized," Shan told them the facts as she saw them. "They're in close to NORAD. I think they might have had something to do with the warhead at the Missouri Breaks."

"That's what you saw at The Junction," Taylor said.

"Yes." She wouldn't bring up other things. "We should be en route to Cody in a few days," Shan verified for them. "If we want to beat the weather, we have to go now. It's snowing."

"Cody?" Green asked.

"In Cody, when we were there."

"We don't want these Nomads coming back here in the spring. The idea is to draw them away. Cody, we can defend. The Vista…" Mac didn't want to consider that alternative. "They were testing us all summer. We failed. We're going to go back up Wade. Or he's going to back us up. We'll see in a few months how it plays out."

"Command is going to want answers," Green said.

"We tell them about the Nomads and give them the proof they want."

"Is there proof?" Ballentyne asked.

"The run-in Sweeps Team One had in Colorado, the mess in the jail, and the ambush at The Junction," Mac counted off the evidence. "All the same group of Nomads, all aimed at Team Three. That's pretty solid." He told them what he was going to tell Command.

"You were paying attention," Shan said.

"Don't give up Team Three. There are other people in The Vista aware of us. Our secret isn't such a secret. It's like meltdown," Mac said. "Everyone knows about it and pretends they don't. No, I don't think it's 'everyone', but you get what I mean. At some point, they might try to use it against us."

"What do we do?" Taylor asked.

"Deny everything. Speculation is just that, and there's no way to prove a damned thing," Mac said. "That's another good reason for Cody."

"Reservists will go right in to positions for the personnel we're taking," Green said. He handled the logistics of Stations One and Two. "We won't be leaving them short-handed."

"This is going to get messy. It's liable to be suggested we've fabricated the entire scenario to fit our agenda. If anyone wants to step away, do it now," Mac told them. "Command will cover us as far as they can, and that's a long way. We don't understand what's going on out in the world, and clearly, we need to."

"If you can't commit two to three years, say so," Shan added. "Skyline is an organized town, and it's going to take time establishing with them. You've seen what we put people through to vet them. There will be others, too."

"How are we going to get a Security group in?" Ballentyne asked.

"That's what she's responsible for–finding Wade. He can make initial contact, if he hasn't by the time we catch up with him," Mac continued. Wade was the least diplomatic of the team, but he was the one in Colorado. "That's putting us in their backyard, more or less, by the time that happens. We've got to be careful and make allies rather than enemies. After that," he shook his head. "Flip a coin."

Council Chambers 9am

The urge to fidget was overpowering, standing in front of several members of Command and Chairperson Haines, waiting for them to begin the inquiry. Shan waited, stoic. Next to her, Hunter didn't seem to have a problem with the waiting. He looked bored. She wanted to smack him. Duncan glanced up from the file he'd been reading. The other two Station Commanders let him do the talking, as they agreed earlier. Haines sat in as an observer, nothing out-of-the-ordinary. No quorum, it didn't have to be. A lecture. If any disciplinary action became necessary, it would be later, with a majority of officers only.

"This is on the record. I've been going over reports filed on July 15th," Duncan finally spoke. "Capt. Allen, you disregarded Maj. Dallas' request to return to the hospital on the night of the 14th, confiscated Car Eight, and took leave of The Vista without authorization. Do you deny any of these allegations?"

"No," she said. "We were in Blackout conditions, and I felt I was able enough to pursue Cmdr. Wade, believing he was still within or close to the perimeter."

"They didn't release you from the hospital."

"No. I left on my own."

"Did you have any sort of plan in mind?"

"Wade indicated he was following the Sweeps route. We stayed on the same roads until mechanical failure put us on foot."

"At that point, did it occur to you to return to The Vista?"

"We were still in contact. I thought... I thought he would come back with us if I could talk to him face to face."

"But that didn't work."

"No sir. We found him in Cody. Then I got sick."

Duncan nodded. "Lt. Hunter, as a medic, you could have ordered her back to the hospital at any time. You were aware of this?"

"Yes," Hunter said, keeping it short.

"Why didn't you?"

"Capt. Allen was mobile and coherent. The possibility of Cmdr. Wade driving into an ambush seemed to be her only concern. After that, we were in Cody. Once she recovered sufficiently, Wade told us to go home."

"Was it an order?"

"Yes."

"I'm holding you less responsible in this because Capt. Allen is the senior officer involved, and a member of Security Command," Duncan told him. "This is your verbal reprimand. You should have taken control of the situation as soon as you realized she was compromised. Keep that in mind, in the future."

"Yes, sir."

"You're dismissed."

"Thank you, sir." Hunter nodded and let himself out.

"Capt. Allen. I understand your concern for Cmdr. Wade. Again, you're well aware you should've waited for backup," Duncan told her. "It was irresponsible."

"You're not the first person to tell me that in the past few hours," Shan said.

"I imagine not. May I call you Shannon?"

"Yes, sir."

"I know how close team members are. Still, you must understand what you did was dangerous and unauthorized."

"I do, and I have no other excuse."

"Let's be honest. You believed Cmdr. MacKenzie had succumbed to his injuries."

She nodded, "Yes, sir."

"The Vista has tried to make a point of each governmental entity being responsible for discipline within itself. This holds true. Command has reviewed your actions and deemed them unauthorized. We'd like a written report of your activities within the week."

Shan hadn't expected Council to be out of the picture. "Unauthorized?"

"Young lady, you're one of the first few babies born here after the war. The high school, not to mention the Archives, keeps track of the first twelve Vista babies. You are one of those."

"I am."

"You understand what we went through to get here, to find this place and be able to survive after the war?" From the time they started school, the stories of how people founded The Vista were part of the curriculum. Some made it and some didn't, and that so many died that first winter. Only a handful of babies lived out of nearly a hundred.

"Everyone knows," she said.

"When our children do something rash and dangerous, we're remembering what happened to us. We remember. Even with meltdown, Shannon. We want to protect you. It's as difficult now as it was then. It's our choice, and now it's yours as well."

"I pledged to Security, so I could protect The Vista. That was my choice. So was the decision to follow Cmdr. Wade past the perimeters. Past the dotted line. For the same reason."

"Is that your statement on record?" Duncan asked.

"Yes."

"Very well. This is your verbal reprimand."

"Has my position in the team or Command changed?"

"No."

This was all settled before they got back to The Vista, she decided. Council had removed themselves from the situation, or Command had exercised its prerogative to disallow them, the more likely scenario. "The 'Conda has called for a Council meeting," Shan said.

"Yes," Duncan said. "I don't suppose you'd care to tell us what's on the agenda?"

She contemplated it for a moment. "We're going to ask for the Cody Base."

They all looked at Haines.

"You already have the Cody Base," Haines said, certain she'd heard.

"We need it now. Later is not an option. We discovered some facts that we were unaware of before the ambush at The Junction."

"Bring your facts to the Council."

9am Station Two

"You wanted to see me," Dallas said. He'd expected MacKenzie and Allen. It was Taylor and Ballentyne instead, and he wasn't completely surprised.

"We're here to talk about Team Three. You have certain suspicions." Taylor cut right to business.

Dallas rubbed his eyes. "Are you Security or the 'Conda?"

"Both today, or neither. I need you to talk to me before we decide. This is off the record."

"Twenty years ago is a more accurate description of what I know, but since the war, nothing is the same. Lt. Taylor, I'm uncertain if you're one. I've never been able to decide. You fit the criteria."

"For what?"

"What did they call it?" he asked out loud. "Biogenetic enhanced, or engineered? Something similar to that. Governments and corporations had a long and complicated name, and I don't remember. For years after the war, I had no reason to."

"I'm not," Taylor told him.

"How can you be certain?"

"Because someone who is told me so."

Dallas felt a chill run up his spine. It was true, then. The rumors, the media stories, the clandestine meetings no one would acknowledge later.

"What made you wonder?" Taylor asked.

"Team Three," Dallas said. "It wasn't obvious, not right off, but as I worked with them, I could see it. They're all..." Dallas hesitated at the word that came to mind.

"What?" Taylor prodded.

"Too focused, too coordinated."

"That's not what you meant."

"Security is what they've concentrated on, but they aren't confined to that. They're smart, too damned smart. You could drop them anywhere, in any situation even before the war, and I think they'd adapt. In Security, they can turn predatory. Feral. I've seen it. You have, too. Tell me I'm wrong."

"We aren't here to say you're wrong or right. We're here to find out what you know," Taylor said.

"Public information on the projects was limited, and little of it was accurate. Certain corporations attempted to adapt humans to space travel, intending to colonize other planets. Mars, Titan, and several Kepler planets were all being considered. There were missions planned, down to launch dates. None of that happened, of course." His information hadn't been what the public heard. After all this time, it still mattered.

It was Taylor's turn to be surprised. "I thought they were making soldiers."

"I can imagine it being a goal. They kept projects covert from company to company." An idea occurred to Dallas. "There are others."

"I'm not at liberty to say."

"Are you certain you aren't?" Dallas asked.

"I am, for reasons I can't discuss," he repeated. "What criteria?"

"It wasn't my field, and wasn't openly discussed. A few things I recall, but it's secondhand information. They chose the parents from think-tanks, from the top of specific professions, or those tested high in academic settings. No genetic abnormalities, no psychological issues, the usual things for astronauts. It was a cover, and a suitable cover. I've wondered about you, because you're smarter than you act, and ambitious as hell."

"I'm a lieutenant."

"You hide behind that. Anyone can see you're Wade's right hand."

Taylor disagreed, knowing it only appeared to be true. Shannon was. "Fair enough. All we have is information picked out of media reports from the last few years before the war. Enhanced humans wasn't a popular idea, especially with some groups. Our secrecy is for their safety and everyone's peace-of-mind."

"That's why the 'Conda exists," Dallas said.

"Not entirely. For now, I need to know where you stand."

"Regarding what?"

"A group of us are heading for Cody. We leave in three days."

"Are you asking me?"

"If you're interested, Mac is who you need to talk to. He's requesting Hunter go."

Dallas nodded. "I can't see myself doing this, even if Hunter does. There's a damned good chance you couldn't keep him away." He didn't mean only because of Shannon, but the fight they were going for. "I'm getting too old to be traipsing off cross-country." He had a family, wife and two teenagers, and he didn't want to be away as long as he suspected this trek would take.

"Then I need your silence. 'Conda things need to be left to them and Security things need to be left to Security. The two aren't always interchangeable. What Team Three does is just as well kept from as many as possible, civilian and otherwise."

"What are they going to do, out in Colorado?" Dallas asked.

"Stop any further issues before they reach home. For now, we need eyes and ears in The Vista."

"I can do that."

"Ballentyne is in charge of that aspect of our activities," Taylor told him.

"Keep us informed of what Council is plotting. They have an agenda. One they've kept hidden. If these things come to light, it's trouble for all of us. So, watch and listen. Be discreet." Ballentyne made it sound easy.

"What if someone is intent on going public? What if the shit hits the fan?" He'd long suspected the Council was keeping things to themselves. Their intent seemed to be The Vista remaining isolated.

Taylor had never understood why the saying was so popular. "Take cover," he said. "Don't worry about us."

"We'll go into details tomorrow. Pick a time," Ballentyne said.

"I hope you can handle what you're getting in to," Dallas told them, noting they'd neither confirmed nor denied his suspicions about Team Three.

"Right now?" Taylor said. "Not a clue."

Chapter Twelve

Aug 17 midday

"We're going to the shooting range now?" Shan asked as Mac turned the car west, heading towards the airport. "You promised me a home-cooked meal. This is subterfuge."

"We're still going to the cookout. Remember I told you, Security has secrets even you don't know about," Mac said. "We're going to see one first." The entire project had gone well, and she hadn't suspected what he'd been up to the past few summers.

"Fantastic," Shan said, not convinced.

"You go out to ghost cities, I get to do this."

"Why wasn't I included?" She knew the three of them separately were offered chances to go out on long distance recon, and that she was the only one who had taken the opportunity.

"The reason is simple. What we've been doing is dangerous, and I thought it would be better if you weren't part of it," he told her. "Like the whole Rock Creek thing. Wade's mantra. No one knows everything. Not even him. That's why we're in Command, so we have certain resources available. It's why he has Taylor following him all the time."

"Is Rock Creek locked down?"

"Like always. A secret cache we'd like to keep secret."

"Okay, define 'dangerous'."

"You'll see in a minute." He drove around the first hangar, going off road, and parked between buildings. They were invisible from the checkpoint. "Let's take a walk."

Shan followed him around the west side and waited as he unlocked the door. Few places in The Vista had to have a lock. Mac motioned for her to go inside. After one glance, she understood why the place was under lock and key.

"Airplanes?"

"After the shootout with the helicopters, we decided it might not be a bad idea to have some air support of our own." Mac shrugged. "We have these." Three pristine single engine airplanes sat on the cement floor. Small, quiet, and ready to go. "Another classic reason? You were the rookie. During the Blackout, after you got hurt, neither of us was sure you'd stay in Security."

"No helicopters?"

"No, sorry."

"Who pilots them?" The idea of flying made her uncomfortable.

"For one, me."

She stared at him for a few moments. He wasn't kidding.

"Does Taylor know about these?"

"No, but Green does. He's another pilot."

"How do we not hear them in The Vista?"

"We take them down to Sheridan and practice there. They aren't much louder than cars."

"Oh, sure," she teased, uncertain. "Airplanes. Where do you get parts?"

"The same place we get parts for the cars. Caravans bring us stuff, we fabricate other parts. We make airplanes go."

"No shit," Shan said. "That's the damnedest thing, Alex."

"That was the idea. It's a secret." He changed the subject. "We're heading to the Council meeting now to tell them we're packing to leave."

"I don't look forward to this. Haines told me he was calling our parents in."

"Why do you think they have a cookout planned this evening? It wasn't a coincidence. There's no choice, because we've already set things in motion. If we don't do something, The Vista could be a war zone by this time next year. We both can see it, and there's a damned good chance Wade did too, before we had a clue. First strike was theirs. With any luck, it will be the last."

"You think it will be that simple?" Shan asked.

"No, it won't be simple. The thing is, it's not impossible."

"Wade will be on this," she said.

"He already is. So you're aware, I'm asking Hunter to go with us to Cody."

"Any particular reason?"

"He works well with the team, and we can use that. You seem to get along with him, taking off cross-country twice. If you want to be alone, just say so." A joke, they both understood. "Wade has Taylor as his second. I have Green now. You made Hunter yours."

"It wasn't a conscious choice."

"Whatever your relationship is with him, it changes nothing between us. Do you trust him?"

"Yes."

"That's all I need. Let's get back to town. Council is going to throw everything and the kitchen sink at us. Are you ready?"

"Is there another choice?"

"Not really. The other thing I needed to tell you," Mac said. "We're only stopping in Cody. As weather permits, we're going on to Colorado. Maybe even if the weather doesn't permit."

"Jacob's town," Shan said. "Where Wade is."

"You're certain?"

"No, he wouldn't let me see," Shan told him. "If he's not there, he's close."

"We aren't giving the full story. Not friends, not family. Not Command unless they ask."

"Like always," she said. The fewer people in The Vista aware of their plans, the safer they'd be.

Town Hall 3pm

"You mean to go with or without the Council's approval?" Haines wanted to verify for everyone present what he was hearing. He'd indeed made good on his threat, inviting parents and various relatives of the officers. The meeting was closed to the public.

"We do," Mac spoke for the 'Conda. "With the incidents since Sweeps, we believe these Nomads could target the Vista. Command has our reports documenting the issues."

"You mean to leave us without proper defenses?" Richard Cameron started in.

"We've made certain that Vista Security will remain at full force even without the personnel we're taking." Mac had an answer for all their questions. If not, Shan and Green were there. "Command has given their approval. We'd appreciate yours."

"This isn't a Council matter," Haines said. "You decided."

"In good conscience, we can't sit here for the winter, not when we have this chance."

"The Cody Base is sustainable?"

"You were here in the beginning. Those people survived. They fought back. We'll do the same."

"What you forget," Haines said. "How many of us died trying. Be careful what you wish for, Cmdr. MacKenzie. You don't want to go through what we went through."

"We don't want The Vista to go through it again," Mac told them and it hit home. There was silence in the room.

"Understood," Haines said. "Now, what do you need you don't already have?"

"Your blessings," Mac said.

"Reluctantly granted."

"Capt. Allen," Hunter called, finding her outside Station Two. It was close to dinnertime. Cookouts in the town center were popular.

She waited for him. "What can I do for you, Lieutenant?"

"We have some unfinished business. Now is as good a time as any."

"You might be right." They were already running out of time. She used her radio on a personal channel. "Taylor, is Team Two around anywhere close to downtown?"

"Green is going out to the Ranchlands. You might catch him in town."

"I have things to discuss with Hunter, and I need a safety."

"What sort of things?"

"The things only three of us can discuss."

"If you're sure," Taylor said, sounding uncertain.

"It's not a choice. Join us or don't."

"Give me five minutes and we'll meet you there."

"That's way too easy, Shan," Hunter said.

"This is your idea. It won't be easy, but I won't lie to you."

"Who created the 'Conda?"

"Wade created the group when I was eleven. He thought hiding certain things would keep us safe." She didn't mind that he stood close and spoke softly. Later, there might be yelling.

"What's he doing out there, Shan?"

"We might discuss that." She waited as Taylor returned with Green.

"Do what you need," Taylor said, glad she waited until they were home.

"You have questions. Specific ones. Ask them now. I can't guarantee I'll be in the mood to answer them later," she told Hunter. She still had to go to her parents and answer the harshest questions.

"You're being Capt. Allen," Hunter said.

"Since I managed to not get fired, yes, I am. You've seen the lengths we've already gone to, in an effort to keep these secrets," Shan told him. "This, at least, is a security matter."

"A couple of weeks ago, you told me you were psychic." Hunter got to the point, wondering for a moment if it was another joke on the rookie.

"Yes."

"Prove it," he said.

"Just for the sake of sanity, I have a few things to say. I can't predict the future, I can't move things with my mind, I can't set things on fire at will, I can't do any of the weird shit you watch in those old movies." Shan suppressed the urge to smirk at Taylor and Green. They spent a lot of off-duty time watching them with Mac. "When I make the effort, I can sense the emotional state of others. That first impression is what I rely on. I'm right far more often than I'm wrong. In addition, and again, when I try, I can sense things that are happening nearby. Sometimes I see things that happened in the past, and they are random. That's a discussion for another day. None of these abilities are in my control."

"It's all of you, isn't it? Team Three?"

"I can only tell you about me," she confirmed. "Prove it?" she shrugged. "Easier said than done."

"Are you backing out on me?" Hunter asked, half joking and half challenging. He knew how to get her attention.

"Oh, please," she rolled her eyes. "Did you see the detonation on the Missouri Breaks?"

"No, I've told you that."

"Would you like to?"

"No," Hunter repeated.

"You asked me to prove it. I can let you see parts of my memory. It's a conscious effort, and one I can't always control. That's why I couldn't do it out in the middle of Wyoming. They know what to do if I can't stop," she indicated the pair sitting in the back of the room.

"What happens if you can't stop it?"

"I'm not up for finding out," she confessed. "The result of not having that control is unpredictable. In this situation, it's safe."

"I'm game," he told her. She offered her hand. He took it.

Nothing happened.

Then Hunter saw the flash, a nuclear detonation leaving a stark afterimage in his vision. He tried to blink it away and after a few moments, it began to fade. A domed cloud rose over the eastern horizon. It was near dark but the sky, suddenly full of color, reds and greens, with lightning and dust and smoke. He couldn't move, couldn't look away. The air grew quiet, so quiet he could hear his own heartbeat. It seemed like the entire world had fallen silent. Then he felt the push from the blast wave, and there was a deafening roar in his ears.

Shan broke contact.

Hunter stared, disoriented.

"Are you all right?" she asked.

He nodded.

"Sometimes I have control, sometimes I don't. That was precise, one of the easier ones I've accomplished."

After a moment, he asked, "What would the difference be?"

"The rest of my memory, me screaming like a banshee outside the library, the old one, because I was nine, and I knew what it was. Other less pleasant things, like seizures, blackouts, maybe worse."

"How did you do that?"

"I don't understand the mechanics. I let it happen, like I'm talking to you right now."

"How long have you been able to do whatever that is?"

"Since before the warhead. The first time I can remember, I was eight. We call it 'Gen En', and if it's an accurate term, I can't say."

"Genetically enhanced, or possible genetically engineered," Taylor added his color commentary. "Or neither."

Green had nothing to say, his opinion being that it was an unnecessary risk. He'd never voice it to her in front of Hunter or Taylor.

"If we are or not, I don't think we'll ever find out. The chance that someone is alive that could tell us is minimal," she told him.

"What about your parents?" Hunter asked. "They must have an idea."

"No," Taylor said. "From what we've been able to learn, most parents were never told. A few medical tests on a pregnant woman were nothing uncommon. The one person who might help, we aren't willing to involve."

"Who?" Hunter asked.

Shan rubbed her eyes. "Lydia Cameron."

"Oh, hell," he breathed. "She worked for the government."

"She did," Taylor confirmed. "The 'Conda won't involve her."

"Wade won't allow it, and I agree with him," Shan said.

"Deirdre is a doctor," Hunter said, the fact too obvious to let go.

She sighed and looked at Taylor. "Deirdre had nothing to do with it. She's not my biological mother."

"I thought..." he started.

"So do most people. That's the way it'll stay," Shan told him. "We've been cautious around her since we became aware. Wade knew, even then." Another conversation she'd be having soon.

"How many of you are there?"

"I'm not at liberty to discuss."

He spent a few moments digesting that.

"You're done. We're out," Taylor told her as he and Green left. "Call us if you need anything."

Shan waved acknowledgment and waited for them to shut the door behind them. "Wade's in Colorado. I can tell you where. Do you remember Jacob's town?"

"The one we never got to because we were overdue in Cody," he nodded.

"That's our aim until we find out it isn't."

"All right," Hunter said. "Why?" He didn't like secrets and these, well, these were above and beyond. "He's a Commander."

"Wade went on the offense because he thinks this all ties in to the problems we've been having all year. Now, he's taking cover."

"So we're going to back him up, whatever we find in Colorado?"

"That's my job. It remains to be seen who else is involved."

"When do we leave?" Hunter asked. He might only get once chance at questions, he was taking full advantage.

"Three days."

"What did Council say?"

"Council isn't involved in Command decisions. Haines said 'Good luck, you'll need it'. Command, I can't discuss."

"Someday you'll have to tell me about that."

"Someday," she agreed. "We have three days to get organized."

Aug 18

"You cut it really short," Deirdre said, messing with Shan's short hair. Or what was left of it. "I don't think you've ever had it this short. It looks cute."

"Cute?" Shan questioned, unsure if 'cute' was a good thing or not. "I got it trimmed up yesterday because when I chopped it off in Cody, I wasn't worried about how it looked."

Across the kitchen table from her, Kyle smirked, holding his week-old daughter, Kerrie. Deirdre had taken her for half an hour after they arrived, relinquishing her to Kyle when she started fussing to be fed. It was taking some getting used to having such a tiny human in the house, needing so much attention. Worse yet was knowing he wouldn't see her again for many months.

"Why did you cut it?" Deirdre went on.

Oh, great, Shan thought. "Hunter wouldn't let me wash it, so when it got gross, off it went. Snip, snip, done."

Deirdre eyed her.

"I was running a bit of a fever and it was snowing. He said no jumping in the creek."

"I've told you to jump in the creek plenty of times, and I got smacked for it," Kyle added his two cents.

"Hunter seems to have common sense. How did he get you to listen?" Deirdre asked.

"Ouch, Mom, I listen all the time."

"You should have been here, in the hospital."

"I'm fine now."

Deirdre peered out the front window. "Get another cup of coffee. Michael will be here any minute."

Shan helped herself. The coffee at the stations was usually hours old and stale.

"Refill me and I'll let you hold her." Kyle wasn't above baby bribery.

Shan obliged, taking her. "She's adorable. Must take after Tara."

"She looks like you," Deirdre said.

"True," Kyle agreed. Their unspoken understanding hadn't been so unspoken since the baby had been born. Michael and Deirdre were as much her grandparents as Kyle's parents and Tara's mother.

"That just means she looks like you," Shan pointed out to Kyle. They shared the same green eyes, the same smile.

"Yeah, like you said, she's adorable."

"You need help," Shan told him, shaking her head. Men.

"If you want to talk," Deirdre started, uncertain where to go with the conversation. There were so many things that had gone unsaid, for so many years. "We can."

"If you want to talk," Shan said. "Because you're my mother and that's that. Maggie is Kyle's mother. The rest, well, that's a twenty year old story I don't need to discuss. I know what I need to."

"How did you find out?" Deirdre asked.

"Things happen, rumors go around." Kyle shrugged. "Wade has access to files us peons don't, and he told us when he thought it was necessary."

Deirdre nodded. "I wish we had told you."

"Stop worrying about it," Shan said, handing the baby off to her.

"I worry about all of you taking off to God-knows-where when the weather is turning. The cold killed more people that winter than the marauders." They knew what winter she meant; the first one, starting right after the war.

"The flu didn't help," Shan figured.

"By November, the flu had run its course. We had four feet of snow sitting on the ground right here in The Vista. The temperature didn't get about freezing until the end of April." Some things she couldn't forget.

"We've planned this, we have the supplies, and everything you've been teaching us all our lives. Believe it or not, we were listening," Kyle told her.

She nodded, knowing they wouldn't change their minds. It had been too long. They'd been blackmailed into staying in the valley, and now that was over. "Just remember what you have here."

"Remember what we've talked about. The safe houses, the hidden ways out of the city. If there's big trouble, go. Those places have been stocked with supplies, too."

"What will Michael think of all this subterfuge?"

Shan snorted a laugh. "Subterfuge? That's a classic word for all of this."

"Michael is one of a few people that came up with the original idea, the first plans," Kyle told her. "He picked out the first cache, hell, he's been helping us supply them."

Deirdre was shocked, for the first time in a long time.

The group of six- and seven-year old kids dashed about the yard, rowdy, enjoying a warm day for the few minutes before they went home. They were Lydia's students four days a week. She watched over them, quietly relating a few things about her past to Shan. A first year Guardian trainee stood nearby, doing his time at the Annex before they assigned him to a team. Command reasoned, if they couldn't handle screaming kids for a few weeks, they couldn't handle a partner or a real Guardian patrol.

Shan blinked, thinking the entire conversation had gone off the deep end of reason, that she hadn't heard what Lydia was telling her. But she had, and nothing was going to change that.

"As long as you tell me my son is all right, I can spend the winter not worrying so much," Lydia said.

"He is, I swear it Lydia." She was uncertain how to approach the subject and asked, "If I took you to see Alex, would you repeat to him what you said to me?"

"Yes, I would. I won't forget what we're talking about, either. Everyone thinks I have brain damage. It's a lie. Now you see why I try not to think about the past."

Ten minutes earlier, Shan thought she knew their story, of how they came to The Vista after getting through the riots and barricades in Portland. Accurate, to a point, but their fight to survive started years earlier.

"I'll drive us over," Shan said, getting her parka. "He's staying with his parents until we leave."

"Good for him," Lydia told her. "He's going to believe me, isn't he?"

"Yes. I do. He will, too."

Lydia followed her out to the street. "Can I drive?"

Shan looked around. The trainee was busy keeping count of the kids while parents gathered. "Drive?"

"Geoffrey lets me drive all the time when he's taking me somewhere. That's not something you forget. Stick shift?"

"It is," Shan said. The roads were clear and empty. "Sure, you can drive." She was still trying to digest the revelation that 'Wade' wasn't his father's name, but a pseudonym created by his maternal grandmother. Lydia had gone to great lengths to protect him, before things fell apart, before he was born.

Mac was standing in the garage talking with his dad when they pulled into the yard. They fell silent, surprised by the appearance of their guests. "Lydia," he greeted, opening the car door, a questioning look at her passenger.

"Alex," she said, hugging him as she got out. "How are you doing? We worried about you."

"Pretty good. I get tired easy, but better every day."

"We need to talk," Shan told him.

"Come inside where it's warm," David invited them, holding the door.

They spent half an hour in the den. When they emerged, Lydia accepted an invitation to dinner. "Are you coming back later?" Mac asked Shan as the parents chatted.

"I'm expected at home, up until we leave. I mean," she tilted her head. "You understand."

He nodded, knowing they were all watching, subtly or not. "I'm in for the night. It wouldn't shock them if you stayed." Then he leaned forward and kissed her. It lasted longer than a friendly sort of kiss.

"Wade had to be aware," she said, breaking it off before she changed her mind.

"I agree. It needs to be a thing that never gets repeated. Find out who else knows. That's... no one should have to carry that around alone. Tell her."

Shan nodded. "She's not alone with it, not anymore. At least we have a clue about what we were supposed to be."

"A clue. Wade was right. The reasons behind it, not so much."

"That's the part I'll never understand," Shan told him.

"When you consider everything, they damned near pulled it off. If the flu hadn't mutated, the world would be a different place. Nothing we know would exist."

Chapter Thirteen

Aug 27 Wyoming nightfall

Fifty-four people and a hundred plus horses and mules followed old highways when there was no other choice. Overgrown access roads and game trails were preferable, being less obvious. Night brought some relief from the constant stress of being on guard, with the caravan stopping at caches dotted along the way south.

They weren't alone, catching sight of two groups of Nomads, both with fewer people; one moving southwest and the other westward. None of the travelers attempted contact, passing with only brief acknowledgment, a nod, a wave.

Several officers took careful notes on the people they saw. The decision would be Mac's, if they passed that information along or not.

"Is it everything you imagined?" Taylor asked, watching Shan unpack gear in the cabin she'd claimed. The overnight was in an actual campground, complete with cabins, fire pits, a handful of weather worn RVs, and an office building that was only missing windows.

Shan peered at him for a moment. "This isn't how I wanted to go to Cody."

"None of us wanted this, but here we are."

"We aren't ready." Shan stopped, correcting herself. "The rest of you aren't ready. I'm not pushing the idea with Mac that anyone other than the two of us is going on south. Plans change." She was aware he didn't like the idea. Taylor had voiced the opinions to her several times during the trek south. "You need to remember who is in command of this little expedition."

"I agreed on the terms to go to Cody."

"I'll make sure you stay in Cody if I think there's going to be a problem later. We're out here to eliminate a threat, not play the game 'Who's in Charge Now?'. Wade isn't with us. He won't be anytime soon. This is a security issue, not a personal one."

"Fair enough. After you find Wade, then what?"

"We figure out how to deal with the Nomads. That's why we're moving to Cody now. Not a secret."

"Is that your only aim? I know you've considered going on your own and seeing the world. All kidding aside. Taking off to who-knows-where, until you got over wondering what's out here. An impulsive idea that stuck, and now the team is in a position they could make it happen."

"After the Blackout, Mac was ready and Wade talked us out of it. There were other factors involved," she said. "Someone has to run Cody."

"Clearly. Who's staying here with you?" he asked as Green and Hunter made their way into the cabin.

"Mac is bunking in here. The last thing we need is a sick commander." Shan lit the kindling in the fireplace.

"How are you feeling, Captain?" Green asked.

"I had watch last night," she said, not mentioning the insomnia that had plagued her since July. He put a palm to her forehead, anyway. "Well?"

"The jury's still out," he told her.

"I'm not sick."

"That's your opinion," Hunter laughed.

"I second that," Green said.

"It's been six weeks since the ambush. I'm tired, I'm sore, and I'd be tired anyway and sore anyway from being on a horse so damned long," Shan told them. "Mac is exhausted and too stubborn to admit it. He might have a fever. One of you," she nodded at them. "Is staying here to check up on him overnight, if he likes it or not. So, who didn't draw a watch?"

"That would be me," Green said.

"Great. Taylor, what are you scheduled for?"

"Taylor One," he corrected. "Chris picked up the call sign of Taylor Two already. I've got nothing until midday."

"I'm doing some logistical stuff overnight," she told them. "We should be riding in to Cody a week from now. Then a whole new set of orders will happen."

"As soon as you contact Wade," Green said.

"Yes, and that's the catch. It's not as easy as everyone seems to think. No one moves out of Cody until then. We don't need to be riding into another ambush."

"Could someone sneak up on you twice?" Taylor asked.

"I don't know. We're going to find out."

"From what Mac said earlier," Hunter said. "We're pushing the last half of travel time, in case of weather, and other things."

"It's those other things that worry me," Taylor said.

"Same," Green agreed. To Hunter, "This is where you ask her if there's anything you should be aware of. Gen En things."

"Scary things that make people watch you from the corner of their eye rather than look at you," Shan said. It wasn't a common occurrence, but sometimes a new set of rumors circulated and trainees would chance hasty glances. Not just at her, any officer, any civilian, because talk was vague at best and wild stories were plentiful. She waited for Hunter to ask.

"Is there anything I need to know about?"

"Nothing in particular. Find me or Ballentyne if you need help. Otherwise, no concerns. I think you're late for your guard duty, though." After he'd gone, she turned to Green. "Thanks for giving him a push. He doesn't have a clue what to do about me."

"Hints are free. Professional advice is not. I'll discuss your bill later."

Taylor snorted.

Cody. It was closer to daybreak than midnight before they made their way to the empty city. Every Vistan felt a rush of relief. Weeks would pass before they had the compound set up the way they wanted. For a few days, though, some rest.

"No outside fires after dark, no weapon discharge unless it's unavoidable, no one goes off alone." Mac made a list for his officers. "Sweeps protocol. Debrief them and get teams on watch. Rotate every four hours." Shan and Green were in charge of operations management until they were settled in. Ballentyne was first up for some sleep. Mac was next because if he tried to get out of it, Shan would have something to say, in private. Probably in private.

"Got it," Shan said. "I'm going to send somebody out for fresh meat. Save the stored supplies while we can."

"Good idea," Green agreed.

"Sweeps protocol," Mac repeated. "Get someone from the hunting guild who's good with a bow."

"What else?" Shan asked.

"Don't take on a bunch of projects we don't need right off," Mac said. "Keep it simple."

"All I can do is try."

"I want you getting at least eight hours of sleep today or tonight. Then we can try for Wade."

"I've never slept eight hours in my life unless I was sick," she pointed out. "Let's say six."

"You're worried." Mac could see it.

"It's been weeks."

"So?"

"I don't know how he'll react, or how I will. We've never been apart this long."

"Wade has a plan."

"Of course," Shan said. "He has a backup plan for a backup plan for a backup plan. My concern is that he has backup. If he's gotten to Jacob's town, he's already set up some sort of protection for himself."

"His safety isn't the problem," Green said.

"I disagree that he's safe out here. That any of us are. They targeted Wade at The Junction. I can't forget that, and neither will he."

"We're the Nomads, out here."

"We need to be careful with the first impression we'll leave with people we meet."

"So, what is the issue?" Mac asked.

"How do we make contact if I can't get to Wade?"

Both men shrugged. "That's a good question," Mac agreed. "We don't need to have a bloody firefight against the people we want to ally with."

"My point," Shan said.

"We'll work on a secondary solution. With any luck, you'll be talking to Wade soon."

"We need to come up with something solid. I'll get Hunter and go find Jacob. Use him as a go-between."

"There's a plan." Mac said. "Let's get this place set up. We're behind schedule by about five years, and I don't want to be stuck here until spring."

Chapter Thirteen

Sep 3 Cody nightfall

"How long have you been in Security?" Hunter made conversation, intrigued by the mechanics of the group. The 'Conda wasn't what he expected, and two weeks in, he was impressed by their teamwork. He wasn't a member and didn't expect to be.

"Six years, the same as Wade. We were rookies together. Mac has a few months more," Ballentyne told him. "They take promotions and I'm comfortable where I am." He'd been a captain for over three years.

"What was Shan like, as a rookie?" He was taking a break after moving and repairing furniture most of the day. Each of the six housing units had a central room, being used as needed. Com center, operations center, supply area, sleeping quarters and now, a club had sprung up next to the cafeteria. Very little alcohol had gotten carried three hundred miles over the mountains, so Hunter's drink was a watered-down version. There were no plans or supplies for a still. They needed a place to relax, at any rate.

"Like she is now. She pushed boundaries, even with Wade and Command. Sometimes, she lost that fight," Ballentyne said.

"Lost?"

"They've demoted her twice. Lt. Allen, Capt. Allen, you never can tell. It's safer to call her Officer Allen."

Hunter had a good laugh. He'd seen hints of that wild streak. Thinking the run towards Colorado was out of character for her had been a mistake.

"Nothing serious. I don't remember what happened the first time, but the second was because she picked a fight with Richard Cameron in Council Chambers. They had to do something, and it didn't affect her position."

"No shit," Hunter chuckled. He'd been to meetings twice when she'd argued with Cameron. It seemed orchestrated to him rather than random, and it wasn't hard to imagine Cameron felt the same way. Council and Command were like that, uneasy allies. Not enemies, but adversaries on certain subjects.

"You've heard they took down a helicopter?" Ballentyne asked, not in a casual way. The story had grown in certain circles, but he'd been there.

"They, as in Team Three. I've heard bits and pieces."

Ballentyne nodded. "It was early in the day, and we had a good idea the Nomads were prowling around near Sheridan. There was a bunch of 'Conda Security people there because regular Security was posted in Anaconda and The Vista. Just in case things moved that way. Wade sent most of us to drive the main roads, and with a little luck, draw the helicopter out. We figured if it worked once, it might work again."

"After a few hours of nothing, they got to wondering where the helicopter had gone. Wade decided we should meet at the bottom of Robber's Roost and figure out the next move. You've seen the overlook by Sheridan?"

Hunter nodded, "Sure."

"Shan got there first, and the helicopter got there next. There used to be a line of houses in various stages of construction along the lower ridge. Large and expensive houses, with fifteen years of weather, and the only cover close enough."

"She said they shot down a house trying to get at her," Hunter remembered, thinking she'd been embellishing.

"That's pretty accurate. She returned fire until their sniper hit her. Then she retreated, but they knew where she was. They destroyed it. Shot it into splinters. That's when the armaments jammed up. Lucky for her, the sniper was using an M-16 with .22 loads."

"All this time," Ballentyne went on, "Wade, and Mac, and a dozen more of us are listening on the radio and trying to find high ground. Shan got hit again. It knocked her off the deck, and they lost sight of her. The helicopter strafed Wade at the bottom of the Roost.

He flipped his car in the gulch that runs up that main road. So his car is on fire. We don't know where she is, and they're both off the air."

"Damn." Hunter shook his head. It wasn't the story he'd been told.

"While the helicopter circled to make another run, Mac got to the first switchback on the Roost and waited. Still no radio contact. When they came around, Mac took a shot with the SAM. Big boom, end of helicopter number two. Shan and Wade spent a couple of weeks at Station Three recovering while Mac and Security clear out the rest of the Nomads on the ground."

"Shan makes quick work of that story. No details."

"The story doesn't get to the civilian population," Ballentyne said. "For any reason."

"Six officers died. That's no secret."

"A Nomad incursion at Sheridan. The mention of air support doesn't come up in the reports."

"They got damn lucky," Hunter said, trying to imagine working helicopters.

"Luck had its part," Ballentyne told him. "But you've seen them work as a team."

"Have we developed any defense against air attacks?"

"You'd have to ask Mac or Green for those details, but no, we don't have helicopters."

"She's different out here."

"Different from at home. The 'Conda is in charge, and they understand what Team Three is. She doesn't have to disguise everything she does."

"I get it."

"There's something I don't think you understand. All of us, whoever Team Three picks to go south - we're tagging along to get the team to their target."

"Meaning what?" Hunter asked.

"We're expendable. Mac won't say it, and Shannon sure as hell won't, but Wade made it clear a long time ago." Ballentyne didn't see a point of lying to him.

"This is one of Wade's contingencies."

"It is. Team Three is the only thing standing between The Vista and this group of Nomads."

"They knew about them before the ambush?"

"They plan for the worst-case."

"Since the bomb on the Missouri Breaks," Hunter said.

"We get them to Colorado so they can deal with this."

"I understand that." He remembered the carnage of the war, a dying world.

"For your information."

"Thanks for the warning. We do our job and keep our heads down."

"The best way to stay alive. What the hell is up with chickens?" Ballentyne asked. Twice Shan had stopped by with the express intent of telling them about wild chickens being spotted in the area.

"When she was sick, and we were here in Cody, I made her chicken broth. She asked me if there were wild chickens."

"Delirious."

"That's what she claims," Hunter said. "I told her to stick with the story."

"If you have any sense," Ballentyne said. "You'll make damned sure she knows how you feel about her. Especially now. Cody is everything Security has been working for the past decade. Both of you will get caught up in this and forget."

"Forget what?"

"Different or not, she needs to know what you're thinking. If you don't step up, someone else will, and I don't just mean Mac. You're not the only man here that would jump out a window for her."

Chapter Fourteen

Sep 5 Cody middle of the night

Shan couldn't sleep and took to pacing the main floor. The building was extensive enough to house half the personnel, but they scattered out between four of the six units prepped earlier by the Sweeps Teams. Someone had painted numbers on them, dubbing them 'pods'. Hers was Pod Two, across from Pod One, where Mac had taken up residence. The other pods set up similarly, providing a make-shift compound while they got organized. In time, they'd expand farther, but for now, everyone was close.

Chris Taylor drew the short straw for guard duty. She'd given him one of the couple dozen books hauled from The Vista to help him with boredom. Sometimes, more often than not, the watch was boring. The book was by Asimov, and it should entertain him for a few nights, at least. They had freeze-dried rations for a late dinner before she was off to pace. Chris would be relieved at 4am, and then she'd have someone else asking her why she was wandering the place, in the dark.

She settled in the main foyer, a large octagonal room where they staged most activities from. The electricity was working, but she wasn't interested in reading at the moment. Other matters cluttered her mind. Unable to sense Wade in the past three nights, it was driving her to distraction. The distraction fell to insomnia, making it even more of a challenge. She wanted to beat her head against a wall, not that it would help. At least she'd get a few minutes' sleep.

"Capt. Allen," Hunter greeted, having checked the roster and guessing where she was.

"Lt. Hunter," she acknowledged, feet propped up on the table and leaning back in her chair.

"Are you on duty?" he asked, taking note she wasn't wearing boots, but she was wearing a sidearm.

"No, I'm sleeping."

"You don't look asleep."

"I would trade three overnight shifts if I could get some sleep. Actual, real, REM sleep for more than an hour at a time. This is ridiculous."

"Only three?" he asked, turning on the light and taking a seat across the table from her.

"Five, ten, anything at this point."

"When was the last time you had a good night's sleep?"

"Before July," she offered, making it a jest, when, in fact, it was close to the truth.

He produced a worn deck of cards. "Want to play strip poker?"

"No, I don't. Deal." Shan sat up to get her cards.

"Seven-card stud, aces low, jokers wild."

Shan won the first two hands, lost one, won another, and lost the next three.

"Your deal," he said. "We're both naked now, except you still have your panties and socks."

She raised an eyebrow at him. "You're fantasizing now. I won, I still have clothes."

"You started out with more clothes. I won, four hands to three."

"I'm bored. It's time to walk the perimeter."

Chapter Fourteen

"Nice evasion. I'll go with you," he volunteered. "Are you planning on sneaking up on someone?" he indicated her footwear, or lack thereof.

"I don't want to keep anyone awake while I'm wandering up and down the halls. You don't need to follow me around, either," she told him. "I'm pretty sure you have things to do tomorrow. Today. Whatever."

"So do you. Why can't you sleep?"

"Because of all these projects." She sighed. "I haven't been able to sense Wade, either."

"There are weeks still."

"I used to have months. That's not the problem. Sensing him is one thing, talking while we're asleep is unrelated, and now both are gone." It was more, too. Shan stopped, not sure he understood what she meant, anyway.

"So what's different?" he asked.

"I've said it before. We guess at the implications of what we are. The ambush changed everything, including us."

"You still can't sense Wade." Hunter made it simple.

"No."

"Are you sure he's in Colorado?"

"Yes," Shan said. "The longer I think about it, the more I lean in to the idea he was blocking contact with me." They continued on down the hallway, passing the make-shift kitchen and storage room, heading for the lobby. "Then there's the issue of Mac."

"How is Mac interfering?"

"Setting up Cody like this is going to cause problems." She thought of Taylor, insisting Wade take over.

"You think they, what? Won't see eye-to-eye anymore?" Hunter asked. He couldn't imagine Team Three at odds with each other, not seriously.

"We always saw Wade being in charge here. He's not, he won't be. It belongs to Mac now. When Wade comes back..."

"If Wade comes back," he corrected.

"Mac won't step aside," she ignored the comment.

"Wade has a job waiting in The Vista," Hunter said.

"Wade is in Command. Station command is a critical position. It's been filled by now."

"They replaced him?"

"With Mac. It wasn't for show. They've replaced Mac, too. Scouts are easy." Shan felt relief to have him to talk with.

"That's not what I've heard," he said.

"Be serious."

"You got it."

"After this is all said and done, I can't say if Team Three will exist anymore. Mac will keep the Cody base. He's serious about it. As much as everyone thought it would be Wade, Mac has put as much time and effort into it. More now, because here we are."

"I wouldn't blame him. Neither will Wade."

"Wade. Even if he is off Security for a few months or a year, he can get the position back. That, and he's been leaning towards Council. It depends on which he prefers, but a Council seat could be an advantage for Cody."

"What about you?" Hunter asked.

"No idea," she told him. "I've never had to consider what came after Team Three." It was pretty clear the idea upset her.

"I should have minded my business," he apologized.

"It is your business now," Shan told him. "You know Wade has Taylor working with him, his backup of sorts."

"Sure. You call him Wade's second."

"Now you understand why. Our second is our backup. Mac has Green."

"And you got stuck with me."

She nodded.

"Fantastic," he said, meaning it. "We go home and get on with our lives." He caught that look, the indecision on her face. "Or not."

"The fact is, I don't know what I'll do after this."

"How can I help?"

"Cover me when the time comes."

"I will."

"About Mac," she told him. "I can't say where that's going, and I don't know where you and I are going. The last thing I'd do is lie to either of you."

"I can't compete with Mac."

"I never expected you to." It frustrated her, not being able to control the situation. Wade had warned her. "I want you to be my second at least through this mess in Colorado. Beyond that," she shrugged. "I can't make promises."

"You don't need to."

Sep 6 Cody daybreak

"Would you come across the compound and see me for a few minutes?" Mac asked Green on the radio.

"I'll be right over," Green replied, finishing his breakfast. He savored the coffee. It wasn't an emergency, or Mac wouldn't have asked.

Two inches of wet snow sat on the ground. Green noticed this as he stepped outside. It was falling out of an overcast sky. When he'd gone to bed, the stars were out. He stared up for a few moments before going to find Mac, leaving soggy footprints across the plaza.

"You might say, 'Hey, it's snowing'."

"I thought it merited closer observation," Mac said. "That and I needed to talk to you, anyway." The office area was coming along well, and they both stood, looking out the bay windows. Half of them would be boarded up as soon as someone had the time.

"What's on the agenda?"

"It's late, but we should hold a ceremony."

"War Day." Green knew, hell, they all did. Last week. They'd had more pressing matters, so they put it out of their minds. Mac was right, they needed to do something. Twenty years. "Any particular ideas?"

"Have everyone meet in the main hall after dinner. Shan's the historian; tell her she's our orator. Tell her something short is fine," Mac decided. "Or you can speak for us."

"My brother's the holy man, the shaman, he would. Me, not so much. I'll talk to Shan, or bribe her."

"Good idea. This will circle right back to me, because I'm in charge. At least she'll write up a decent speech. Next thing. Get the schedule and switch me off today's guard duty with anyone and make it up to them on the next round. I have a video feed to The Vista after dark."

"Got it," Green said. He'd take the job. "Is that all?"

"You might need to track her down. She took a couple of people out to do some scouting for me. The Com Officer will have her route on file."

Green understood. "I bet she had some fun things to say about the snow."

"This just started. With any luck, it'll burn off by midday." They both knew the more snow, the longer they were stuck in Cody. A handful of them had packed, ready to head south, waiting for a break. Shan out and out refused to leave a day and a half after they made Cody, even with Mac's assurance Ballentyne could run the place.

"Luck is a fickle thing," Green noted.

"A moment," Mac said, something else on his mind.

"Commander?"

"Just man-to-man."

Green nodded.

"Of all the people Wade trusts, I figure he left it to you, to keep Shannon safe if there was a tangible threat to The Vista. He's considered how impulsive she might be in certain situations. I can't think of anyone else he'd give that responsibility to."

"The first contingency, if The Vista came under attack. The second was if something happened to you."

Chapter Fourteen 223

Mac hadn't been aware. "If this goes bad, I want the same plan in effect."

"Understood."

"You volunteered me to give a speech about a war that happened before I was born?" Shan asked, finding Mac as he sat in the Com Center. It was a work in progress, and with the library and media rooms would occupy the entire ground floor of Pod One. Upstairs, a dozen Vistans, including Mac, had claimed rooms.

"You have a way with words."

She snorted an inappropriate comment. "Sure I do." Mac was, in fact, more articulate. He was also up to something and she didn't care to pry into his business at the moment.

"Remind everyone we're lucky to be here. I don't mean Cody. You write, I'll read. Join me for a while."

"Fantastic," Shan said, following him to his new quarters.

"We need to keep our focus. I can see us, letting it slip, getting soft. Especially with the weather setting in."

"You said the same thing when we got snowbound at Station Three two winters ago."

"That was for a month. This is permanent."

"When it comes down to it, Alex, you and I can make for Colorado. I don't see a problem, even with the snow and the mud and the rain. Remember Sweeps? A little time to sit back and take a breath won't hurt anyone."

"Who do you think would follow us?"

"Knowing why we're going? No one. If we go, give them an order to sit here and wait."

"You don't think Hunter would follow us? Follow you," he amended.

"No. I've made him my second, and he knows a lot of things someone not in the 'Conda shouldn't know. It started during Sweeps and there wasn't a damned thing I could do to stop it. You stole Green while I was off in Wyoming, and here we are."

"It wasn't on purpose," he offered. Mac leaned in and whispered to her, "Don't make plans, Shannon."

"For what?"

"Anything." He shed his array of weapons, getting comfortable for the afternoon. The radio was on a playlist of something slow and soft, not his usual preference. Another radio was a direct link to the com center.

"You mean us."

"I mean anything and everything. We're out of The Vista. This is the real world. What we know there isn't the same as what's true out here."

"You might be a little less vague."

"Life is complex. No one has time for regrets. I sure as hell don't want to be the cause of something you'd resent me for."

"That's less vague?"

"We're talking about Hunter and his influence on our lives."

"Ah. What's between you and me doesn't change or diminish if I feel something for someone else."

"That's what I said. You and I, we're good. Always." He kissed her.

"You said we were done with this," she whispered, distracted from other matters.

"I was mistaken," he told her. "Dance with me."

Shan deposited her sidearm on the bookcase shelf with the least amount of his scattered belongings before joining him. She wrapped her arms around his neck. Mac put his hands on her waist and they swayed with the music. After a few minutes, she rested her head on his shoulder.

"You don't have to play sappy love songs to get me to spend the night."

"It doesn't hurt." There was a guitar propped in the corner and he knew how to use it. He played for her often enough. She relaxed. "You're afraid," he whispered.

She nodded. "I am, Alex, and I don't like it."

"We'll get through this."

"What if we don't have a clue what we're going up against out here?"

"We don't. If you start second-guessing yourself, we'll be in trouble, Shan. We've trained for this sort of thing. We're ready. Like any other problem, we make a plan and we deal."

"Six months ago," she told him, "I wanted to find any excuse to get out of that valley. Now I wish we could go back and forget about all of this."

"If I thought we could, we would, Cody Base or not."

They gathered in the dining room without having to ask why. The guard shift came in, the com center team, too. Everyone. The electricity wasn't on yet, but the fireplace was. White candles lit the room, lined up on the tables, twenty more on the table moved to the front. It had stopped snowing outside, and it was quiet.

Mac let them settle in. There was no reason to hurry. "Twenty years have passed. The civilization our ancestors made, stopped, and the world changed that day. Humanity survived by luck, by persistence and struggle. We're here to remember that," he told them. "Because in remembering, we honor those who have gone before us, and then we move forward. It's what they would want, and what we must do. Everyone of us has their story, their lost loved ones. Now is the time to remember them. We know the names on the memorial outside City Hall. There are many more not listed, those lost in the years since. We honor them as well. Remember the past, look to the future. Tomorrow we move on."

Chapter Fifteen

Sep 6 Estes Park midday

"They're in Wyoming again," Vance said, flicking a cigarette butt on the pavement and grinding it to nothing with his boot heel. There would be more snow before dark. Some mornings, looking out at the scenery, he wondered why he hadn't stayed in Belize. Chances were, nothing was different there except perhaps the weather.

"You want me to head out and see what they're doing this time? Decide if this needs dealt with before it gets any closer." JT said, not needing clarification on who he meant. The younger man wore a heavy parka, hands stuffed in his pockets. He was ready to go home and be done with following shadows through the mountains. Home wasn't Colorado, nor were his loyalties tied to Vance.

"There are a lot of them this time. Dozens. You want to go up against that, knowing what we do?"

"All it would take is a little extra planning. There are only two problem children."

"That we know of. They're Altered and we aren't certain what their capabilities are, untrained or not."

"I go get the girl and the rest have no choice but to follow along." JT was taller than Vance, muscular, and two decades younger. He thought a couple of stray Altered weren't a problem as long as Vance didn't let them be. They'd dealt with a lot worse over the years. The Sixth being at the top of that list. Those clans were unpredictable, organized, and not even close to allies.

"You'll get yourself killed," Vance stated. He didn't look dangerous–average height, average build, brown hair he wore a little long, and hazel eyes enhanced by wire-rimmed glasses. The man was pushing fifty. He was also a fifth generation of The Altered, a label tacked on to the last of those with controlled enhancements. As more corporations went underground, it meant fewer restriction and more funding from anonymous sources. It all ended with the war.

"You want to wait for them to make a move?" JT couldn't sit through a meal, let alone wait months for things to fall into place. He was Vance's adviser the past four summers. He'd seen the dangers lurking out there. This was a lot closer than he felt comfortable with.

Vance had more patience. "When the time comes, you can go get her. We can, because I need them alive and cooperative. If you shoot their friends, they'll come in here and burn the place down."

He let it go unsaid. The Sixth attracted other Altered, a simple fact. It might be their plan, to do what Vance said.

"We need her. We need Wade. Once we get them, things are going to be interesting."

"Where do we do this?"

Vance contemplated that. "We'll make sure she comes here first. We need to meet them on our terms. That's where Wade comes in."

"Are we trusting him now?"

"Once they make contact, he can bring her in and save us a lot of defensive planning. They haven't had outside influences, a bit of luck on our side. Those 'problem children' are still more dangerous than your soldiers."

JT scoffed, "You're over-estimating them."

"No," Vance corrected him. "I've underestimated them and it's past time I stopped. They've developed skills I never could. They're the first post-war Altered and I can only guess what they're like. Shannon has a good idea about things. She'll figure out what we want fast. We're going to be careful, or she's going to see us as enemies and you'll find out why I'm concerned. I'll have to call Cooper in to deal with things his way."

"Like I said, let me go take care of it."

"You want to eliminate one of the handful of people on the continent that can take on Rafe?" He couldn't count on The Sixth to step up because he wasn't their problem, not yet. "You want to assassinate a teenage girl? If I wanted that, I'd send Cooper now."

"I didn't say that. I've seen what Altereds can do when they set their mind to it. If they're as lethal as you say, why haven't you dealt with them before now?"

"I've had no reason to. Montana is a long way away."

"Take my advice. Call Cooper. Do things the hard way. You're the reason Rafe stays where he is."

"What you need to understand is that they won't be easy targets. Rafe hasn't been able to kill them, and he's tried. Do you still think you have a chance?"

Cody Sep 7 sometime after midnight

Green, Ballentyne, Chris and Kyle Taylor started a poker game late. It was going to be a long night. The power had gone out in Pod One twice since Mac dismissed them, and the security watch was on edge. They locked up and dug out some old movies while two other officers walked the floors, hoping the power stayed on. If not, they had cards and candles.

After the power came back on the second time, Shan wandered

downstairs. She had on socks but no boots. Blue jeans. Her hair was down and the shirt she wore was sizes too large. No body armor. "Hey," she said, drowsy.

"Join us for a movie," Chris invited, trying not to stare. He was sixteen, he couldn't help it.

Shan shook her head. "Not tonight. Damon, I need to talk to you."

"Sure," Green said. He followed her down the hall for privacy. "What can I do for you?"

"Funny you should ask. You're the pharmacist here."

"It's weird I got the job." Everyone knew he had been spending as much time taking classes at the Ranchlands hospital as on his Guardian rotation.

"I need something for pain. Nothing specific or severe."

"You all right?" he asked.

"It's not for me. We pushed ourselves to get here ahead of the snow. Mac's feeling it. That's why he's not sleeping, and now he's running a fever."

"I've got antibiotics, too." He invited her to his room.

"It started a few hours ago and I don't think it will get worse. If I can get him to sleep, he'll be fine in a day or two," Shan told him.

"He's hurting, then so are you," Green said.

"His injuries were a lot more extensive than mine." She had the vivid image in her mind still. Forever.

"If you need it, speak up. You aren't sleeping."

"Different reason, but thanks. I don't want both of us down at the same time, anyway. It's not a concern."

"Is raw cannabis all right? I want to keep the pills for emergencies."

She nodded, "Sure."

"If you don't sleep soon, if you don't get in contact with Wade, I'm going to recommend it, as your medic," he warned her.

"I understand. Thanks."

Green followed her back to the foyer. He watched as she disappeared onto the second floor. Chris was looking, too, a natural reaction to a pretty girl.

"Oh, come on," Kyle said. "She's my sister, for crying out loud."

"Your what?" Chris asked.

Sep 7 daybreak

"We've got Nomads east of the city," Ballentyne said as he burst through the main doors of Pod One. "My handset is dead. I need someone to get to the com center and get us on alert right now." He'd been on patrol, alone, thinking no one was moving because of the snow.

"Got it," Mitch Elliott announced, running.

Kyle Taylor came down the stairs with Shan right behind him. They'd been talking on the landing.

"Nomads," Ballentyne repeated.

"Yeah, I heard. You're in charge," she told him.

"Where's Mac?"

"Asleep, and I don't want to wake him unless this is a problem." She had the last word on that subject. "This isn't a problem yet."

"Drugged?"

"Asleep," she repeated.

"Bad timing," Taylor said.

"He's on the verge of being sick." She'd spent most of the night with him. "We can handle Nomads. How many are there?"

"I'm going to go find out," Ballentyne told her. "Team Two on recon." He showed her where they were on the old fold out travel map tacked to the wall. "Lock it down, wait for word. Send a team to the roof to monitor the interstate."

Taylor retrieved Uzis from a weapons locker. There was gear stored in the lobby repurposed as a dayroom. It took them less than a minute to get suited up with all their tactical gear.

Chapter Fifteen

"I should go," Shan said while they dressed.

"You're in charge until Mac is, or until I get back," Ballentyne told her.

"Are you taking me off this because I'm female?"

"You know me better than that," he told her as she followed them onto the plaza.

"I do. I'm a Scout."

"So is Taylor, and I'm well aware of your qualifications. I'm doing this because I can, and because we need you in Colorado with Wade." He stopped on the walkway. "Are you going to pull Command rank on me?"

Shan crossed her arms. "No, I'm not."

"Good," Ballentyne said sharply. "Now I'll tell you why. Since the ambush at The Junction, you've gotten more and more fixated on thinking everyone out here is after you, after Team Three. They aren't, Shannon. You need to realize that, the sooner the better for all of us."

"You've discussed this with Mac."

"No, not a discussion, I've told him the same thing. I can step back and see it. You can't, you're caught in the middle. Right now, you need to trust me to do my job, and go do yours. Get to the com room and get this place locked down."

"Understood," she said. "What do you need?"

"Green's bringing the horses around. Wait for me to report in. Get everyone account for, keep an eye on the roads. You know the routine. Watch your back," Ballentyne said.

On cue, Green was there with two more horses, dressed in camos because it was his usual attire to begin with. Big shotgun, medium handgun. Warpaint. It was a psychological thing he did it during Sweeps, and when they traveled where they might see others.

"What the hell?" Hunter asked. Half a dozen officers from Pod Two were responding to the alert.

"Nomads," Shan said. Green leaned down to say something, and she nodded. "Go," she told Team Two.

"Where's Mac?"

"Not available. We're on lockdown until further notice. Pod Two is Parr's. Get with him. I've got the com center and I'll be issuing orders in about a minute." Shan retreated, getting an Uzi for herself on the way.

Chris sat in the west corner, opposite the single door, watching Shannon. She paced, then stared out the windows in the foyer facing the plaza. An Uzi was on the counter next to the array of equipment his brother had set up, but she was packing a 10mm Kimber she'd acquired. Seven other Vistans had retreated upstairs for the lockdown, having nothing to do but wait. They were in radio silence. She was in charge of the Cody Base.

"Are you all right?" he asked. "I mean, is there anything I should know about?"

She shook her head, leaving the window to join him. "I'm not doing anything to worry about. Just basic stuff."

"I meant, are you watching the team or something?"

"No."

Curious as hell, and afraid to ask for details, he nodded. Noel, arriving at the com center from walking the inside perimeter of the Pod, stopped any chance of it being discussed. He took a seat in front of the radios and propped his feet up on the counter.

"Are we supposed to be doing something?" Chris asked.

"Waiting," she said.

"We're supposed to sit here while she paces the floor, cleans her boot gun, then fiddles with the radio," Noel quipped. He'd seen it before.

"I can fiddle with the radio first," Shan offered.

"Your choice. We're just relief."

Sitting on the edge of the counter, Shan crossed her arms, striking up a familiar conversation. "You both are aware of the purpose of the 'Conda."

"Do you mean the edicts we swore an oath to uphold?" Noel asked. "Or the ones Wade took us aside to talk about later. The unwritten ones."

"The unwritten ones," Shan confirmed. Chris looked surprised. "Did you imagine you were the only one he spoke to in private?" she asked him.

"No, I was just under the impression..." He looked at Noel. "He's Pacifica, too. I didn't think he'd hear everything."

"No one knows everything," Shan said, a force of habit.

"Outside Team Three." Chris looked for her to verify.

"I can't say if that's true or not. Each of us is different and we have unique abilities. At least, as far as we can tell. When Wade and I run across ghosts together, we don't sense the same things."

"I didn't know about that," Chris said.

"One time. The point being, Team Three is going to Colorado for a specific reason. If you go with us, your job is to get us there and keep out of the way." She regarded the younger Taylor. "You won't be going on. Mac has already said as much. Don't take it personally."

"I won't," he said. "I get it."

"It's my job to see that you both understand this. You can't discuss it with anyone, ever. Not girlfriends, not parents. Chris, you can't talk about it with Kyle. Noel can't talk about it with Pacifica. That's the oath you took, and it supersedes all others. The only case where you can discuss this would be with Command."

"They know about it, about you?" Chris had no clue what would be offensive to call it and what wouldn't. Or if he could even say it.

Shan rubbed her eyes. It was another one of those gray areas, and there were so many. "I can say, what we are isn't an issue. We're in no danger from them having that knowledge."

"But you are from others? In danger?" Noel asked.

"Before the war, there were specific groups that pushed the idea we shouldn't exist. There's a good chance some of that sentiment is still around."

"What does that mean?" Chris asked.

"They didn't consider us human and wanted us exterminated. What do you think scared Wade into creating the 'Conda?"

Both men absorbed that bit of information.

"Are you afraid people in The Vista believe this?" Noel asked.

"We can't take a chance. You see why."

"Is Pacifica one of your concerns?"

She shook her head. "Not for that reason, no. Security and Pacifica have different views on how to deal with outsiders. I wish we could trust everyone that wanders through Montana, but here we are now, proving that we can't."

"What do you need from us?"

"Trust our judgment. Remember, Cody is here as an addition to the security of The Vista. This venture to Colorado is a distraction, nothing more. If you have questions, don't sit on them. Ask."

"I can do that."

"Yeah," Chris nodded. "Me too, I'm in."

"Stay in the com center for a few because I have to go explain to Mac why I committed mutiny and stole his command while he was asleep," she told them, hopping off the counter. As an afterthought, she added, "That was a joke. He's awake. I'm going to tell him why we're on lockdown. Relax a little. Team Two is as capable as any of us to deal with a few Nomads."

"It's daylight," Mac said, sitting up and rubbing his eyes.

"That's observant. How are you feeling?" Shan asked, touching his forehead. "Your fever broke."

"I guess. What time is it?"

"A little before ten."

"You going to join me?" he asked, patting the heavy quilt he was buried under.

"You are feeling better, but not now. We're on lockdown." She sat next to him.

"Why?"

"Nomads following the interstate. Team Two is taking care of it."

"You should've woken me."

"So you could tell Ballentyne to take Team Two out and look? If they'd ridden through town, I would have. He dared me to pull rank on him."

"And you didn't, or he'd be the one reporting this."

"I got lectured and sent to my room. Or your room, I suppose."

"Three of my four senior officers are out screwing around in the snow." He shook his head.

"Yes," Shan confirmed. "I'm in charge until you get up and get moving."

"Fantastic. Am I in any condition to be running things?" He looked around for his clothes.

"Where's your sidearm?" Shan asked. "It's been ten hours or better since you had any drugs."

Leaning over, he found the holstered Remington 1911 .45 hanging from the bedpost and showed it to her.

"You're fine," Shan said. "Is that big enough?"

"You tell me," he said, winking. "Besides, someone stole my Kimber, and I needed a decent replacement."

"You can have it back any time you want."

Mac shrugged. "Not an issue except that it's a damned big gun."

She shook her head. "Not an issue. I like big guns. Come on downstairs and we can get a game of cards or something going." Impulsively, she kissed him, jumping up and heading out. "I've got a room full of rookies. Don't keep me waiting."

He didn't.

After a while, boredom took over. Noel pushed back in his chair, staring at the ceiling, holding a book he'd lost interest in. Mac had taken up a similar position, but with his tattered cowboy hat pulled over his face. Shan was curled up on the floor in the corner behind the desks, using her parka as a pillow, wide awake, waiting. Chris sat next to the radio, walking the perimeter at the bottom of the hour, and catching an occasional question about their status from someone upstairs.

"What time is it?" Mac asked as Chris came back from his rounds. They had hourly contact with the other Pods.

"Ten to twelve."

Noel groaned and murmured, "Is that all?"

"Do you know where they're headed?" Mac asked none of them in particular.

"I do," Shan said.

"If they're not back by nightfall, you'll get Hunter and go find them." Mac didn't leave it open for discussion. They fell silent again.

Shan asked, "What time is it now?"

"Almost one," Noel answered.

She stood, grabbing up her parka. "This is insane. Cmdr. MacKenzie, I'm requesting permission to gear up and go scout for our team. Because I'm a Scout. That's what I do."

Mac sat up, pushing his hat back. "Remember what I said about three of my four senior officers being out? It won't be all four of you. We're waiting until dark to do anything."

"Fantastic," she said, hands on hips. "I'm going to walk the perimeter. And then I'm going to walk the perimeter." Shan wandered off, shaking her head. "A little later, I guess I'm going to walk the perimeter."

Noel grimaced, raising his eyebrows. "I'm glad she's not pissed at me."

"She knows I'm right."

Chris remembered how she'd reacted to the attack at Depot North in the spring. "She won't run from a fight."

"I wish she would, now and then," Mac said.

"You could make it an order."

"The team doesn't work that way. It's not in our nature. We have rank, sure, but it's for the convenience of others. Our decisions are mutual unless Command is involved."

"She didn't argue, though."

"She knows I'm right, and we already set a timeline for taking action. We have at least three observers upstairs, plus Team Two. Nothing is happening that we can't wait to hear about."

"Both of you are getting restless. Everyone can see it."

"We need to get to Colorado damned soon. We need to find Wade." With that, he got up, following Shan down the corridor.

"I'm not sneaking out," she said.

"I didn't think you were." He watched as she zipped her parka and grabbed more gear, a helmet, and binoculars. "Rooftop surveillance."

"If that's okay with you."

"As long as you keep your head down. I want you to do me a favor. If I read something wrong, tell me. Even if we're in a roomful of people," he gestured towards the com center.

"Bold of you to think I'd be able to tell the difference. If I sense things different from you, I'll say so. I don't think there's a right way or a wrong way, to be honest."

Chapter Sixteen

Sep 7 early evening Cody

"What happened out there?" Hunter asked, finding an out-of-the-way place to stand. A group of people were milling around the room, waiting. Someone had set up a projector television and picked out a couple of movies for the evening.

"Nomads," she said. "We tracked them west. They weren't hostile, so it was a good practice alert. I'm going to schedule more training. Mac will debrief everyone in the morning. At least we'll have a routine, something to do in the meantime." Shan always kept to the back, near a door, a force of habit. It was an old western movie, but at least it wasn't the same one she'd listened to the night before. She was there for the company.

"Aren't you the one that refused to get back on the road?"

"I am. People make mistakes when they're tired. We don't need mistakes."

He wondered how often any of them admitted to such a thing. "What are you doing later?"

"Waiting for you." She was dressed casually, off the schedule for a few days. Jeans and a blue flannel shirt, boots, and no camos. Sidearm. "I need your help."

"Now?"

"Tonight, later, for a few hours."

"Outstanding. For what?" He had an idea, but he asked anyway.

"Trying to get ready to head south."

Wade. "You found him?" Hunter wasn't certain if it was a good thing.

"He's not lost, and no, I haven't contacted him. I'm doing things a little different tonight, and I need you there. You volunteered for this when you agreed to be my second. With the way things are," she shook her head, letting the thought go. "I don't expect anything, but I can't take the chance."

"You've had problems?"

"Like everything else about the Gen En, it's unpredictable. We've talked before. You know what to do. Bring a deck of cards," Shan told him. "I usually sleep during the day. All this travel has messed my cycle up beyond repair."

"Great. Want to play strip poker?"

Taylor gave them both crusty looks from the other side of the doorway. "Take it to your room," he said, annoyed.

"That was the plan," Hunter answered right back. "Stop eavesdropping."

"Knock it off," Shan told them.

"Who's on duty?" Taylor asked Shan.

"Ballentyne. Mac is somewhere in the building, too."

"So," Hunter summed up. "The chain of command is Mac, Mick, Shan?"

"Dear gawd," she shook her head. Both men were close to the same height and build, but Wade had seen to it Taylor had extensive hand-to-hand training. She didn't know if Hunter could hold his own or not, and she didn't plan on finding out.

"Green, Taylor," Taylor said, making a point.

"So you're fifth in command? Does that come with rank?" Hunter asked, feigning seriousness.

"Fuck you, rookie," Taylor said jovially.

"Are we really going to fight with each other?" she asked.

"No," they both said.

"I'm not having this discussion again," Shan told Taylor.

"I don't want to hear about what you do on your own time. Keep your rookie in line, second or not."

Hunter was ready to invite him outside to continue, but he'd heard about the Allen and Taylor fights. Heated arguments that, according to rumor, left them not talking to each other on more than one occasion, at least on a personal level.

Shan saved him the effort by stepping out into the hallway. "Do you think it's a lot of fun for me, with you being Wade's second?" she asked as Taylor followed her.

"It's not like Wade and I have the same sort of relationship you two have," he scowled.

"You don't have any idea what our relationship is."

"And I don't want to. That's the point of having your own room."

"The point of him hanging around is so I don't get into something I can't deal with on my own. Of everyone, you should understand that."

"And here we are, stuck with a bunch of rookies, waiting on the weather. For how long, Shan? How long should we wait?"

"Until Mac and I decide it's time. You knew what we were getting in to, coming out here. Stop nitpicking at my second."

"Why didn't you follow him to Colorado?"

"I'm not playing Twenty Questions with you. It's done."

"We're doing this wrong."

"If you have any brilliant ideas, Kyle, we're open to suggestions."

"I got nothing new," he admitted.

"Me either. So step back."

"Do I have another choice?" he asked, knowing better. When it came down to team dynamics, they shared a symmetry, a balance, and rarely at odds over a decision. Seconds were only that - second opinions, second choices. Sometimes, it irked the hell out of him.

"No. We'll find Wade. Things are different here, but that's what we wanted. Now we've got it. You get to decide if you want to be here, or The Vista." She went back to the dayroom, leaving Taylor with that thought.

A few minutes into the movie, she retreated upstairs, Hunter in tow. It was quiet despite the crowd, and she'd lost interest in being social for the evening. His room was at the end of the hall.

He lit an oil lamp, more reliable at this point, and waited.

"You have questions. Ask," she said.

"I do. Who was your second before me?" He had his suspicions, but he'd also learned jumping to conclusions wasn't the best idea.

"Now you've been eavesdropping." Shan stripped off her holster and hung it on the coat hook.

"You were louder than you think."

"Fair enough. Green was."

"What happened?" He'd figured Green, Taylor a close next guess.

"Mac sort of stole him when we were here the first time. It wasn't planned or anything, but it worked out pretty well." She sat on the sofa, kicking off her boots, then curled up with a blanket. Hunter moved to the floor next to her.

"Taylor seems damned protective of you. I mean, everyone in Security watches out for everyone else, but he goes out of his way." Hunter had seen that right off.

"That's complicated." Shan couldn't think of how else to describe it. "And it's not protective, not as far as I can tell. It's more like a competition."

"Explain it to me. We have the time."

"I told you Deirdre isn't my biological mother. She's not Kyle's mother, and neither is Jaycee Taylor." Running her fingers through his hair, her thoughts strayed elsewhere.

"What?" he asked, confused.

"That's what I said," Shan remembered. "Kyle isn't three days younger than me, he's three minutes younger than me."

"Twins?" he asked after a few moments. The similarities were there. That bit of information gave him a new perspective. He'd said it in jest, and it came back to being true.

"We are. He's known for years. I found out a few weeks ago. Like I said, complicated."

"That's an understatement," he agreed. "Is he like you, is he Gen En?"

"No."

"Are you sure?"

"Positive."

"Complicated," he repeated. "You weren't joking. Why didn't you know sooner?"

"We all grew up together, and I mean in the same house, so it was natural to consider them as brothers."

"But not Mac."

"Yeah, not Mac. I think I've always known and just let it be because the adults said nothing. They had their reasons."

"What reasons?"

"I've never asked."

He nodded. "I don't know if I would, either."

"I need to find Wade, the sooner the better," she said. "Taylor is pissing along because he's a second and doesn't get to say what we do or don't. Mac is impulsive. I'm damned sure getting the idea we're going to Colorado soon. We need to be aware of what's going on, because I'm not riding into another ambush."

"So go to sleep," he told her.

"I'll get right on that." She stared at the ceiling. "What am I supposed to do?"

"I can rest easier when you're close. You relax, I relax."

"I have cards." He smiled to himself.

"We may need them. Or I'll send you out for a brick to knock me over the head with. Whichever."

After a few minutes, he pulled a book out from under the sofa and started reading by lamplight.

"I brought that from The Vista," Shan pointed out.

"I got it from Chris."

"There are a few others when you finish. Plus, someone found the library downtown with entire sections of undamaged material. We should go raid the place soon."

"It's a date," Hunter told her. "I thought you were trying to sleep."

"I am." After a few minutes, she sat up and stretched out the other way.

"Sleep," Hunter repeated. When she didn't have something smart to say, he moved onto the sofa next to her. Eyes half-closed, he was certain she was asleep. Or something close. "Shan?"

"Not now," she whispered. She fidgeted around, settling in to get comfortable, leaning on his shoulder. "We're on the road."

~Wade?~ she asked, disoriented at first. He was driving Car Ten, on the interstate south of The Vista. It was hot out, their windows down. A breach of protocol, but it wasn't an actual memory. ~I can't sense you, you're too far away.~

~Distance has nothing to do with that ability,~ he told her.

~For you.~

~True, but you need focus.~

~I can't.~

~Practice.~

~Damn it, Wade, I've been trying.~

~Getting frustrated won't make it easier,~ he warned. ~Where are you?~

~Cody. Again. It's as far as we got in July.~

~I wish you'd waited until spring.~

Shan flashed to anger. ~Maybe you should have stuck around and told me that. You're an officer. Act like it.~

~Why do you think I'm out here? I'm not supposed to tell you, this is on a Command directive.~

She contemplated that for a few. It was an order, after the fact. They both were aware. ~Where are you?~

~Colorado.~

~Well, that's helpful.~ Shan remembered what she wanted to tell him the most. ~About Alex.~ She could feel his sudden rush of emotions, sharp and bright. ~He's here with me.~

He had no immediate response. His anger faded, changed.

~He's in charge of Cody. They gave us the base, and here we are. Council didn't get any say.~

~I didn't know.~

~I've been trying to tell you for weeks. You were blocking me, and you have no idea how angry I am.~

Again, he kept his thoughts to himself. ~Is The Vista secure?~

She wasn't as subtle. ~For now. We're coming to Colorado. Be ready.~

~Use the Sweeps route. I'm close.~ He realized if they were already in Cody, there was no talking them out of it.

~Estes Park, not Jacob's town.~

~Yes. There are other Gen Ens here. Try not to start a war with them. I don't trust them, not yet. Keep that in mind. We'll rendezvous soon.~ Wade had reservations, but he was out of options, at least for the time being.

~Mac is getting cabin fever and we haven't been here that long. Snow or not, we'll be moving south within the week. How much is on the ground?~

~None right now. You?~

~Close to a foot. How do you want me to handle this?~ she asked.

~Get with Mac and pick a team. The fewer the better, less than ten. You know who works well with us. Don't bring me rookies.~

Shan understood what he meant. ~Chris Taylor is the rookie now. Hunter sort of got promoted. He's my second.~ Shan was pretty sure he swore. ~You saw it happening, back in April, and you tried to stop it.~

~Green was a better choice. Once you're here, we can discuss that and make solid plans.~

~Why don't you trust them? The people you're with?~

~They're afraid of us. I think they should be. We won't include them in any activities unless we have to. Like things at home, there are issues to be aware of. Get here and we'll figure it out.~

~Will we be in contact now?~

~I hope so. Focus, Capt. Allen, it's all in your focus.~

When Shan woke, it was hours later, and not long before daybreak. They were curled up on the sofa, buried beneath a blanket.

"Hey," he said as she tried to slip away.

"I was going to get out of here without waking you."

"I wasn't asleep."

Neither of them were in a hurry to go. "You're comfortable."

"Thanks for pointing that out," Hunter told her.

"I don't mean being crammed up on the couch together. I mean, I can sleep when you're close. I'm not comfortable like that with most people."

"Can I ask you something?"

"You can ask."

"I know, I know, you're under no obligation to answer. Since I'm in on this, tell me about your abilities. Tell me the things you wouldn't before."

"I've never lied to you," she said.

"You've never given me any details. What's it like?"

"We attribute a lot of minor things to the Gen En process." She thought of something easy to explain. "Are you familiar with synesthesia?"

"Where one sense overlaps onto another."

"Some of our abilities are similar, as far as we can determine. The most obvious thing, when I meet a person, I know if they're Gen En or not. The reaction is subconscious."

"You said the other Gen Ens aren't aware."

"If they know, they're far better at hiding it than we are." She suspected it was possible.

"Am I?"

"Gen En? You're not."

Satisfied with that, he said, "Go on."

"Other sensations happen on their own. I can sense strong emotions in others, but it's a conscious effort. Like getting up and walking across the room, or holding your breath. Sometimes, I see things from the past. We call the reaction 'ghosts'. That happens at random and I can ignore it. Like I said, there are a lot of incidental sensations. I'm only relating my about my experiences, in case anyone asks."

"Meaning Taylor?"

"Anyone. 'Conda members know, without details most of the time. It's obvious who is part of the inner circle. What's between you and me stays that way."

"Even from your partners?"

"I can't imagine they'd ask, but that would be your call, taking into consideration the circumstances."

"What about talking to each other when you're sleeping?"

"Wade and I have been able to do that since we were kids. I don't remember how we figured out we were both having the same dream. Then we decided it wasn't a dream. It doesn't happen as often as you'd think."

Hunter chuckled. "I never imagined something like that could happen, not in a million years."

"The consensus is, it was a residual effect no one accounted for."

"An accident?"

"We've found no reference to it in any pre-war media. That's another story, though. So, yes, we think the effects were accidents, at least in the beginning."

"If you can sense others, could others can sense you?"

"I expect that's true. It's one reason we have seconds. I've told Wade you're my mine. He's in the south, not far off the Sweeps route. That's where we're going."

"You found him. You need to tell Mac."

"In the morning I will. A few hours won't alter the schedule for today. He wasn't lost."

"The rest of the ride south is going to be tricky."

"It's like all the scenarios we run the trainees through. Getting into a fight is easy. Surviving is the difficult part."

Sep 10 mid morning Cody

Mac summoned them early, but not too early. He needed them awake and focused. Parr, Green, Ballentyne, and Shan. They'd become his inner circle over the past few weeks. Quinlen as well, but he was on watch. It was time for the next stage of their trek.

"I'm not as good at planning these excursions as you might think."

"You got us here," Green said, passing a thermos around.

"The next step, I'm getting us to Casper. We're keeping close to the Sweeps route, until we get to Colorado, weather permitting. At that point, we'll have another meeting."

"What cities are we looking at?" Ballentyne asked.

"Laramie, and Estes Park. There are no more caches this far out. Jacob's town is marked on your maps as a reference. I doubt we'll get that far. The first is likely an empty city, the other is our goal." Mac understood limits of their options once they crossed the border. "I haven't been glossing this over and I don't plan to start now," he said.

"Everyone knows why we're going. We mean to target the Nomad leading the offenses against us. You're aware, when this is over, Command may not see things the way we do. They could have hard questions, too, ones we'll have to answer."

"What are our contingencies if they try to throw exiles at us?" Parr asked first. "Because Cody is under the laws of The Vista."

"The caches are property of the 'Conda. We developed them, we supplied them, we'll man them over the next few years. Hell, if Casper is good, we might set up a depot there." Mac had his own ideas on expanding their reach. "The point is, it remains to be determined what laws apply to Cody. Council will fight us on this. Command has assured me the issue will resolve in our favor."

"We break from The Vista?" Ballentyne asked.

"No. We remove ourselves from their jurisdiction. Our own council, our own laws."

"Or we lie," Parr suggested. It wasn't the first time that option had come up.

"Ten people keeping a secret. Not a simple thing to do." Shan didn't consider it viable.

"The 'Conda has been keeping our secret," Mac said. "They are more than ten."

"After talking to Dallas, I have to wonder how many people know about our little 'secret'," Ballentyne said. "It's a damn difficult thing to do. Wade requested as few people as are viable. We all understand why a smaller group is essential," he went on. "Other than keeping secrets."

"Let Wade make the call," Parr suggested. "He's the one with the inside to Council."

"We'll figure it out," Mac said. "When we get to that bridge. I've picked my team. Anyone can decline the invitation and it will have no influence on positions in Security or the 'Conda." He didn't believe any of them would. "Once we connect with Wade, we'll reconsider our objective. At that point, there might only be three of us continuing on."

"That seems risky. Can three of you do this?" Green asked, still uncertain whose second he was supposed to be.

"Yes," Mac said. "One of us has already met him." They all looked at Shan. "What can you tell us?"

"Not a lot. He calls himself Rafe, and they brought him in to Station One on July 2nd with a group of Nomads out of quarantine at Station Three." She drummed her fingers on the table. "He seemed defensive, but hell, we'd locked him up for weeks."

"There was nothing that caused you concern?" Ballentyne asked.

"Something felt off. I'd escorted the caravan in because their regular driver wrecked going out there, and I blamed that. Later, I sat in on his interrogation and talked to him. Nothing stood out from any other routine debriefing."

"What does that mean?" Parr asked.

"Despite what you might hear," Green said. "She can't read everyone."

"A simple explanation, and in this case, true," she added.

"You're certain he's responsible for the attack at The Junction?" Ballentyne asked.

"Without a doubt. I had him in my sights, but he was out of range. During the ambush," she shifted in her chair, then stood and started pacing, lost in thought. "I sensed a flood of things. One I've been able to decipher, to see apart from the other images, that he had a hand in setting off the bomb on the Missouri Breaks."

"Son of a bitch," Ballentyne exhaled. "Military? Again, like with the helicopters?"

"If I was to guess, I'd say yes."

"He's dangerous, no doubt," Mac said. "That's why we're going to Colorado."

She held up her hand in the light filtering through the window, feeling it as if it were a breeze. Green motioned for them to be quiet. Shan could hear someone running a generator across the plaza, sensed the horses at the stables stomping restlessly for their breakfast.

"What's out there?" Green asked her.

"I wish I had a clear idea," she answered. "Something is still off. It feels like someone standing in the shadows, just out of sight." Shan turned back to the room.

"Wade?" Parr asked.

"No. He claims I have to learn to focus. I'm not sure what in the hell I've been doing the past few weeks, but it wasn't tracking him."

"A lucky guess?" Green asked. He didn't believe in lucky guesses.

"The fact I knew how he'd react, where he'd go. Call it a guess."

"How do we rendezvous with him?" Parr asked.

"He'll see to arrangements, since there are other active Gen Ens involved. Not ideal conditions for any of us, but we can work with it," Mac said. "We could use the allies."

"Three sets of eyes are better than one, and distance inhibits me," Shan said.

"Might that change?" Ballentyne asked.

"I think our abilities will evolve out here. I think Wade's already have."

"Adapt and survive," Green said.

"While I agree, I won't lie. The idea scares me."

"Get packed," Mac told them. "It's time we do what we're trained to do, and stop sitting around waiting. Bring up concerns now."

"Who else is going?" Green asked.

"Not you," Mac told Ballentyne. "I need you running things here. We'll discuss that soon, on our own. Green, Parr, pack. Noel, Taylor, and Quinlen. Hunter. Notify them. Tell them to be ready to move before first light on the twelfth."

"Got it," Ballentyne said, knowing that trust didn't come easy.

"That's five snipers, two close-quarters shooters, and three medics," Green told them. "Six snipers and one kill team if you count Wade. I see a plan forming."

"I hope so," Mac told him. "Eat, sleep, practice, get ready to go. Unless we get snow, the date is set."

Chapter Seventeen

Sep 18 mid morning Casper

"Looks like the entire place is sealed up," Green reported back as they regrouped off the road, in the treeline, hidden from a casual observer. They'd been canvassing the area since before daybreak, working through the northwest edge of the city.

"Surprising how many are," Hunter said. He'd spent years in the caravans, picking places like this clean of everything they might use in The Vista.

It was a mall, as good as anywhere to camp for a few days, better than most. Dozens of stores stocked with all types of items, if Nomads weren't in the city and Scavengers hadn't ransacked the place. So far, the prospects were good. Perishables deteriorated long ago, but it warranted a closer inspection. At least, in Hunter's opinion. Their progress, slow and cautious, only found evidence of long abandoned camps scattered along the interstate.

"Do we need a vote?" Mac asked.

"Shouldn't we be moving while the weather's good?" Parr asked.

"This time of year it doesn't matter," Green said. "We see clear and beautiful one day, three feet of snow the next."

"I could use a break," Shan added.

"I have to agree with her. Stay," Taylor said, for his own reasons. Noel and Quinlen nodded. Parr just shrugged.

"You know how to find a way in?" Mac asked Hunter.

"The usual ways. If all else fails and we can't break in a door or truck bay, we get up on that second level and go through a skylight."

"You're in charge of getting us in," Mac told him. "As quiet as you can. Pick someone to help you. Shan has previous commitments."

"Got it." He headed off, motioning for Noel to join him.

"What previous commitments do I have?"

"In a minute," Mac said. "Quinlen, bring back game. There seems to be plenty of mule deer in the area. We can roast fresh meat right out here by the loading dock. Once we get those doors open, we'll have cover and plenty of room so we can move around. Get off each other's nerves for a few days."

"Taylor, get a watch set up, Sweeps protocol, six-hour shifts. Consider this a gateway city. No one does anything alone, no one goes off without telling someone else." Mac was already mapping out plans for Colorado.

"Should we set up a radio base and relay to Cody?" Taylor asked.

"Yes," Mac said. "As soon as you can, get on it. Shan, I want you to catch the details I might miss. In the next forty-eight, we need to get Wade updated on our progress." He dismounted, crouching beside his horse, looking over the city. He hadn't seen the ghosts Shan warned him about, not yet. The place looked like a potential base camp for future journeys, and he hoped it wouldn't happen here.

"Green, see about the basics - water, electricity, a backup heat source. Look around and let me know what our options are. Parr, when we get inside, find a place to stable the horses," Mac finished. "Start unpacking our gear and getting organized when you run out of other things to do. At least, something that looks organized."

"Let's do this," Taylor said. They broke up in groups, glad for the change in routine. It would only get more difficult now, the farther south they traveled, and the closer winter crept towards them.

"That smells good," Noel said, walking in with Shan. They'd set up inside the truck bays, the building secure. It was after dark, and a mule deer quarter was roasting over the fire. The city appeared empty of people. It was occupied by an abundance of wildlife.

"It does," she agreed. Freeze-dried and dehydrated rations lacked taste. The roasting meat filled the night air with an aroma that promised a memorable meal. "With my luck, I'll be on watch first."

"No. Taylor said you were off the rotation."

"That can't be good."

"You're right," he laughed, knowing she wasn't wrong.

Mac met them near the bonfire where everyone was congregating. "I think we'll be good here. We might consider setting up a cache, as long as the city stays clear."

"It doesn't look like anyone other than passing travelers has been here in..." she shook her head. "Twenty years?"

"Could be," Mac agreed. "You wonder if The Vista is the biggest city left on the planet. Maybe this is the answer."

"Scary idea," Taylor said. "Let's say we're the biggest place in North America."

"There's no way to guess," Shan dismissed the idea. "Not until we get out and look for ourselves. I don't mean Sweeps."

"What do you mean?" Hunter asked.

"It's about time we learn what else is out here. Who else is out here. We don't have any idea, because we've been hiding out in the valley, stagnating, and it's not by accident."

"That's what Sweeps are for."

"Sweeps are a distraction," she said.

"Why else would Command be sending Scouts out on their own?" Green asked.

"Those that are in Command," Taylor added a simple fact, "shouldn't be discussing it."

"How in the hell does Green know, then?" Quinlen asked.

"Who do you think I took with me?" Shan said.

"Team Two?" Parr figured.

"Just him," she nodded towards Green. Ballentyne was central in an agenda Shan wasn't part of. The idea didn't concern her.

"When was this?" Hunter asked.

"Last summer," Green said. "Middle of July. Officially, we were rotated out to Station Three."

"For something not discussed outside Command," Taylor said. "We know a lot of details about it, now don't we?"

"No, not really. I decide what's appropriate to discuss unless it's a sealed file. This isn't. I have no reason to hide it here," Shan said. "Because who is going to run back and report it?"

"True enough, although I have to wonder how much it means," Mac added his thoughts. "Council doesn't control Sweeps routes. Both of our legislative branches are hiding something. I'm not the only one saying so."

"Why doesn't Command step up, then?" Parr asked.

"They have," Taylor said. "And Shan just told you how."

"So what's out there?" Hunter asked.

"Indications are, the farther south we go, the more people there will be," Shan said. "Might be," she corrected.

"What does that mean—there's no one north? North of what?" Parr asked.

"An observation. The weather is harsher than before, colder, more treacherous. People will migrate south where it's not deadly cold. Simple deduction."

"You haven't seen people?"

"I have. They formed Security way back when because The Vista is right on the interstate. Poor planning, but under the circumstances, I suppose there wasn't a choice." She took a seat on an old metal bench, waiting for dinner to finish roasting.

"The villages I've seen are small, and they're off the main roadways."

"How small?" Hunter wondered. "And where?"

"Two places in eastern Washington, less than three hundred people each. That's a rough guess. There were a dozen encampments of thirty or forty people apiece, in the same area. We were only in contact with one camp. They had little to say to us, and we were being discrete. Another Scout went south, towards the Dakotas."

"That would be me," Taylor said.

"Did you go alone?" Noel asked him.

"I did," Taylor said.

"I got permission to take someone with me, and he had the same option. It wasn't because of my sex, or because Wade had any say in the matter. He didn't, by the way," she said. "Taylor wasn't aware of my venture out until we were both home. He saw more people than we did, the point I was trying to make."

"The place was close to a thousand people, just across the dotted line, in South Dakota," Taylor told them. "From their movement over a handful of days, I'd say there is at least one more village close by."

"So, more people south and east," Noel said.

"Not necessarily," Quinlen added. "Factor in the nuclear strikes and mark off metropolitan areas."

"That takes care of the east and west coasts," Hunter said.

"I remember," Parr said. He, Hunter, and Quinlen, all close to the same age, and had close to the same memories of the war. They fell silent, not being on a pleasant subject.

"Red Zones exist. For the question all of us have considered, no, it wasn't just North America. It was a worldwide event. We're uncertain how extensive, but the lack of communications that exists to this day speaks volumes. Since there are people here, we can assume there are people in other places. A long philosophical discussion for when we're home. For now, get some food, get some rest. First watch is Quinlen," Mac told them. They all kept to the bay, eating at leisure and crawling into sleeping bags as they got tired. Hunter and Green had the second watch. Daylight and third shift found Mac and Shan sitting on the upstairs balcony, watching the sunrise.

"What are we doing today?" Shan asked, swinging her legs like she was a child in a too-large chair. She had no fear of heights.

"We're moving on into the mall. We can relax, recharge." Mac wanted a few days off the road. They all needed it.

"Nothing specific? You're feeling okay?"

He shook his head. "Taylor is testing the radio. That's as far as my plans reach."

"Fantastic. I'm picking up some fresh supplies. New clothes. Hell, I'll bet there are at least three sporting goods stores in here." Shan was always in the market for new gear.

He stood and offered her a hand up. "I'll buy you breakfast," he told her.

"It's a date," Shan smiled back at him.

"I have a question."

"You don't have to get permission to ask me anything."

"What would have happened if you'd caught up with Wade?"

A scenario she'd considered before. "It was early enough in the year, maybe we would've finished this already. We'd be somewhere in Colorado now. And can you imagine me stuck with Hunter and Wade all winter?" She laughed.

"You think all three of you'd survive until the weather broke?"

"All we could do is try. I wish we had the chance." Shan sighed. "If those two not liking each other was my only problem."

Green waited for them to finish, pacing the main floor for the past half hour.

"I want you to realize you might be letting your emotions influence you judgment," Mac said, leading the way down.

"I hope so," Shan replied to the accusation.

"That's a dangerous thing to do."

"Oh, excuse me. You've never let your emotions take over?" She put her hands on her hips. Both men suppressed grins, Mac better than Green.

"Not that I can recall."

"Let me refresh your memory. You got on the radio with the... people in the helicopter, and challenged them to a shootout because you didn't know where I was. Where either of us were."

"You did what?" Green asked. Stories got old after a few years. This was new to him, even though he'd been there.

Mac rubbed his eyes, and the grin broke out. "That's mere rumor and speculation."

"Bullshit," Shan said. "Wade told me. His radio was still working, Cmdr. MacKenzie. You called them out. They had a helicopter. You had a SAM."

"No shit," Green said.

"I had a plan to draw them away from you and Wade. It worked."

"Emotions had nothing to do with it," she snorted.

"It's not a good habit to get into. Keep in mind, we're going to great lengths for this venture into the world. We're still a team and you're still the junior officer of that team," Mac wasn't joking now.

"I understand," she said. "Are we staying in today?"

"We are. I don't want anyone going out alone, but the mall is secure," Mac said. "In case you didn't see it, there's a book store on the lower level, down by the south entrance."

"You know where to find me, then," she said. Green was there for a reason and Shan left them to their plotting.

She had run shotgun for caravans before. The inside of an untouched mall was another thing. Stores in The Vista were small and space conscience. This place was massive. Eventually, she found a map of the building, a five foot long wall decoration near what she marked as the main entrance. Shan pried it off the wall in one piece and dragged it back to the bay.

"They hermetically sealed most of these stores for shopper's convenience," she told Taylor, propping the map up where they had stacked their supplies. "It was a standard practice." The sign said so, at any rate.

"This will be helpful," Taylor said. "Mac's out with Green."

"Still?" She'd been wandering for a good couple hours, picking up four books. A series. Books were heavy, but good trade material, so only four.

"It's all clandestine. Or not. I think they're messing with the radio antenna. I told them they'd get better propagation after dark. You know how he is."

"Mac? Sure. He has to try it for himself. Where's everyone else? Who's making supper?"

"Off raiding stores. You should find one and pull out your camping gear. Privacy at a premium. I've got mess duty, so be prepared." Taylor had already claimed a spot in an electronics store. "Go digging around in here, see a glimpse of what life was like before."

"Good plan," she said. "I'm checking here next," Shan pointed at the map. "Consider it claimed."

Taylor laughed. They'd all been sleeping on the same frozen ground. It was a bed boutique.

Sep 22 daybreak

"I need to see you before breakfast." Mac said on the radio channel he designated for Shan, aware Hunter was staying in the storefront with her. Overnight watch had presented a new obstacle for them, one he hadn't considered until a few hours ago.

"No problem," she answered, sounding like she'd been asleep.

"There is," he told her. "Not an emergency. Stop by when you're awake."

Four minutes later, Shan appeared in the cove he'd claimed in the back of a sporting goods outlet. "In The Vista, we'd be under quarantine."

"Who's sick?" she asked.

"Green started running a fever overnight. I've got him set up on the other side of the walkway. He's tired, but he'll be fine. Hunter is our secondary medic." Mac offered her a cup of not quite coffee.

"How are we for medicine?" She took the cup, sipping. Bitter, as always, but a stimulant.

"Good, for now. We'll be out if everyone gets ill."

"We need to warn everyone, so we can get hold of this."

"I cross-trained as a medic, I know," Mac agreed. "Chances are, more of us will be down within the week, if it's a contagious thing. Who's had watch with Green since we got here?"

"You and Noel each have once, and I have three times."

"Damn it," he said, afraid of that. If they both were sick, it could create more issues. "He's not your second anymore."

"I'm not the one making up the schedule."

"If it's the actual flu, we've all had some version of it. There has to be an immunity."

"No idea. I get delirious from a high fever." It wreaked havoc on their abilities, for whatever reason, and would make it impossible for her to contact Wade.

Mac nodded, "I remember. The other thing we have to consider - if we're down for any prolonged time, this run south is over. We can't fight the snow, not along the divide, not in November. We'll be here until February, at least."

"Snowbound in the Rockies," Shan said. "All the Nomads and Scavengers, too."

"You're probably right."

"Do you want me to call them?" she asked. Noel was shuffling around in the makeshift kitchen on the other side of the store. Parr and Quinlen were in early off their watch for food, an hour before breakfast.

"We might as well do this."

Shan let herself into the radio room. Taylor had moved upstairs right off, saying they needed someone on a high point. The reason was as good as any. "This is a recall," she announced, noting a voice modulator was installed, so they'd all sound the same. "Come on over to the staging area. Alert Six," she added to confirm no emergency.

Again, it took minutes for them to congregate. "Where's Green?" Hunter asked her, knowing he wouldn't get preferential treatment. She didn't have the chance to respond. Mac came over and everyone waited.

"Green is down with a fever," Mac told them. "Not a serious issue, but since we are only eight and we've all had contact with each other, an actual quarantine is pointless. That means plans are on hold. We'll be here a week, maybe longer. In the meantime, I'll be sending you out in pairs to survey the area, one pair at a time, once a day. We don't want to bring attention to ourselves if other people are close. If this gets drawn out or the weather turns, there's a chance we'll go back to Cody. Find something to do or ask me for an assignment. We're well set here, so use the time as you want. Short rotations, Sweeps protocol. Questions?"

"What if you and Shan get sick at the same time?" Taylor asked. He saw the obvious problems.

"You run shifts as you can, and take notes of anything we say," Mac said.

"Why notes?" Noel asked.

"A fever makes us more susceptible to things. Gen En things we are usually unaware of," Shan told them. "It also hinders our regular abilities, Gen En ones, I mean."

"If we can't get back on the road in a reasonable time frame, or if there's substantial snow, we get to start all this over in a few months," Mac said.

"We knew that was a risk before we left The Vista," Hunter said. "She'll be able to tell Wade what's happening. Can we expect any help from that end?"

"Good point," Mac said. "Shan, find out."

"Don't count on that. Wade is hesitant about his current company," she said.

"I can radio relay after dusk," Taylor said. "Decide what you want me to tell Cody, and what you want them to tell The Vista."

"I talk to Wade, you talk to Ballentyne," Shan told Mac before he could give her the job.

"Fair enough."

"That sign she dragged down here says there's a pharmacy on the second floor. Would anything be of use to us?" Parr asked.

"No drugs, not after two decades," Hunter said. "Other supplies, to be sure."

"Go find out if there's anything you can use." Mac gave him something to do. "Who has stable duty?"

"Jeez," Shan rolled her eyes. "Green was supposed to help me." The horses occupied the farthest dock, but it still needed mucking out and fed.

"I got it," Quinlen volunteered.

"Do a quick scout of the area while you're over there."

"Anything in particular?" she asked.

"No, just look." Mac shook his head. "You dreamed about helicopters last night. Make sure the sky is clear."

Shan was glad for the speed he seemed to adapt. "So did you, and it woke you up."

"In the meantime, back at the ranch," Quinlen let them know they were wandering off the topic of the morning.

"If any of you feel ill, fever, sudden headache, any of the usual symptoms, come in, get here and Hunter or I will decide what to do with you next. Hunter, stay close. Shan, you too, for a minute of your time." He had a couple of things to discuss with Taylor.

They dispersed. "You're looking a little raw around the edges," Hunter told her while they waited for Mac.

Shan grimaced, wrinkling her nose. "I'm not contagious."

"I'm the medic. Maybe I should decide that."

She moved next to him and whispered, "I can tell you, no one else here is going to get what I've got."

It took him a few seconds to understand. "Oh, hell, Shan. I didn't know."

"That's because some men don't understand a simple cycle, and it happens every damned month. Good grief."

"I'm sorry," he offered.

"I didn't mean you. It was a generalization. Don't be sorry. Be glad it's not the flu."

Mac found his way upstairs later, after everyone settled in. "You've been with Wade since before Shan needed a second," he started a conversation with Taylor. The pair didn't have a truce. It was more of a ceasefire, for now.

"It's not a conscious choice when they pick someone. Was she pissed you stole Green?" Taylor wondered, no way he'd ask her. She'd made it pretty clear her relationships were none of his business.

"Not really."

Taylor snorted a comment.

"We've started doing the thing, where we talk to each other while we sleep. She's been able to talk to me for years," he corrected. "Now, sometimes, it's a two-way thing. They've both mentioned random memories can show up." Mac still didn't know how to get control of that aspect, but then, she claimed she didn't, either.

"Their abilities might not be the same as yours."

"The thing is, I don't want my memories popping up for her to see. Parts of my life I don't want her to know about," Mac told him, quite aware of the differences in their abilities.

"You mean Cassandra."

"That's a big one, yes, and other events. You're aware of the exiles. Command has a specific set of rules, and people, to deal with that problem." He was one of those people.

"Mac, even if she wasn't Gen En, do you think she wouldn't have a clue? She's been in Security years now. Things get said, and you see how damned fast she picks up on those sorts of things." Taylor hadn't. Wade told him about both.

"Does she know?" A simple question.

"She knows what happens with certain exiles. Most people in Security have a clue about that protocol. I doubt if they have given her specifics unless she asked. No reason to. Another one of those things best left unsaid."

"What about Cassandra?" The biggest mistake of his life, and there was no fixing or changing it.

Taylor rubbed his eyes. Mac recognized the move as something Shan did when she was trying to figure out how big of a lie to tell. "Don't do that, don't sugarcoat it. I can tell if you do."

"Of course you can. She knows."

Mac shook his head. "Damn."

"She's known since before she joined Security. It doesn't matter to her," Taylor said.

"It does matter," Mac disagreed. "To her, to me, and it's something that will never be resolved. You can bet it's why Wade thought of genetics and that her and I shouldn't..." He stopped, realizing he was talking to her brother.

"Yeah. Mix genetics. Have children," Taylor finished. "You're right. Just because Wade says so doesn't mean it's true. His mother used to be the biologist. That's not a thing any of us understand past the basics."

"This time, I agree with him. I don't think Shan does."

"I'm aware, but are you willing to take the chance? Because it's not like she'd disappear off the face of the planet," Taylor told him, knowing how harsh he sounded.

The woman, calling herself Cassandra, had come in with a group of Nomads. Mac, a sixteen-year-old rookie; she was twenty-two and mysterious, something new and exciting in his routine life. Weeks after they cleared quarantine, she'd gotten pregnant. The group disappeared one night in the autumn, before the snow started. It wasn't the first time people had moved on, and Command wrote it off, despite Mac's involvement. Security wouldn't search for them, and he couldn't do a thing.

"Maybe you should talk to her."

"After this is over."

"No secrets," Taylor told him. "There is no way to keep secrets in Security."

Oct 1 midday

"You wanted me?" Shan asked Hunter, finding him in the back of the store they'd been calling home. He was sitting on the floor, cleaning a rifle, the big one he always carried broke down in a scabbard slung on the left side of his saddle. A Barrett .50 caliber, if she remembered correctly, and she did.

He raised an eyebrow, wondering if it was a loaded question.

Shan glared at him for a moment. "Oh, honestly."

Putting the rifle aside, he got up and closed the door. "I've given the 'all clear' for everyone. We're going to be on the road in thirty-six hours."

She was ready. "And?"

"And this may be the last chance I can get you alone before we're back home in The Vista. We need to talk." Hunter kept his voice low.

Shan took half a step back. "Two seconds." She got her radio. "Hey, K."

"Go ahead," Taylor answered.

"If you need me, call me on the radio. I'm going to be out for a few."

"Anything I should know about?"

"Getting a view from the sky-walk."

"Got you," he said.

"Sky-walk?" Hunter asked.

"The only place we can expect no eyes or ears."

A few minutes later, they emerged on the deck. It had been an outdoor cafe once upon a time. Hunter and Quinlen had determined the east facing section was sound the third day they occupied the building.

"So talk," Shan said.

He peered off across the valley. "I should've done something about this a long time ago."

"About what?"

"About you, about us," Hunter told her, nodding. "I wish," he corrected, "I wish I had taken the hint when we were in Colorado."

She looked puzzled.

"When we were at Jacob's. You gave me the 'go' and I ignored it. Mistake number one."

"What's mistake number two?"

"Thinking I still have a snowball's chance in hell with you."

"Why are you so convinced you don't?"

He smiled. She might not see the problem, but she considered him a friend. "After Sweeps, sure I did. After The Junction, I lost that chance."

"You have me all figured out."

"For weeks, you thought you'd lost Mac. When you found out you hadn't, you changed. Your relationship with him changed."

"What do you want me to say, Hunter?" she asked. He was aware her relationship with Mac was changing still.

"Nothing, I want you to listen." He wrapped an arm around her shoulders. "Later, when this is over, I don't want us to be strangers. Let's not be people that just work at the same place. I'm not asking you to move in with me, but someday, I might. My point is, if you ever need me, all you have to do is ask. I mean that."

She nodded.

"Will I be your second when we're finished in Colorado?"

"I'm not certain," she confessed.

"Doesn't matter. What I said, I meant."

They watched the empty valley for a while until the wind started. Shan hoped it didn't mean snow. Hunter hoped it did.

After Dark

"If anyone has a problem or concerns, I need to know about it now," Mac told them as they sat down to supper. Dehydrated rations would be back on the menu soon. They had a variety of those, and fresh game wasn't a problem. The war had been a boon to the wildlife population.

"We'll be out of radio contact with Cody, maybe until this is over," Taylor said. "I don't see it as a bad thing."

"I agree," Green chimed in.

Shan rubbed her eyes. Mac was drinking something alcoholic with his meal. "Everyone should remember that," she told them. "When we go stealth. If we do. I mean Team Three."

"What's the plan?" Quinlen asked.

"Wade is arranging for us to meet with Vance and his people in as neutral a way as we can." There was no trust. It didn't need to be said.

"There is the possibility I'll send the rest of you back to Cody, or here, after we rendezvous with Wade," Mac said. "The three of us work better as a team, alone. We haven't made that a secret. It's all speculation until we have a clear idea what we're dealing with."

"Won't that be Wade's call?" Taylor asked.

"No," Mac said. "I'm in charge here."

Taylor shrugged. "Do I pack the radio equipment?"

"Pointless. Whatever story we take back to The Vista, we'll

decide on later. Pack essentials, nothing else. We need to move quick and quiet."

"How many organized groups are we dealing with in Colorado?" Green asked.

"Two," Mac said at the same time Shan said, "Three."

Mac looked at her, a silent question.

"We've always suspected we were being watched," she told them. "At least two groups are directly involved, likely three, and because I don't have a damned good idea about it. One, Vance's group, has Gen Ens. I don't know if they are the same ones I was aware of before. The others we'll find out about soon enough."

"Being watched? In The Vista?" Green repeated. He already knew the details and was aware of how furious Taylor would be if he found out. So, he asked a lot of questions. The others needed to hear the answers, anyway.

"Since before the nuke on the Missouri Breaks," Mac said.

"I can't sense their intentions. I can't tell anything specific about them yet, only that they are there. Here. I thought there were two, but I'm uncertain now." Shan knew less about it than Wade, and he could explain it later. She was angry at him and that wouldn't change until they had words.

"Close?"

She shook her head. "Yes. If there are two or three..."

"There are more. Our view is narrow."

"Have you sensed them since we left The Vista?" Green asked.

"Until we got here, no. I don't mean Casper, but about a day before we got here."

"Good," Taylor said. "Hope we get lucky and they're going to step away from this."

"I've never had a sign of who they are or what their interest is," Shan repeated. "We'll worry about anyone else when the time comes. Concentrate on the task at hand."

"Regroup," Hunter said. "Make up a new story to tell."

"How many times in the past has that happened?" Parr wondered.

"Does it matter?" Shan asked. "Do you wonder if our parents told us the truth about everything? Because they haven't and it's not because they don't remember. It's because they think it's for the best. Same situation here."

"You still pissed off about the whole 'brother' thing?" Taylor asked, laughing. He got a few chuckles from the rest of them. Mac wasn't so amused. Council had as many secrets as Command. It was dangerous, and why they were in the position they were in.

"I could be," she said, taking the hint to relax a little. Taylor saw Mac was drinking. "Later, I meant. The Vista is safe. Do we want to go back and tell them how dangerous the world is? Sure, there are other Gen Ens. I think most are like the others in The Vista, and they'll never realize they're different. That's the way it should be."

"As long as it's not a threat," Green said. "How would we be able to tell?"

"We watch," Mac said. "We keep driving circles around The Vista. Keep running Sweeps, and we get out of Cody and establish contact with those places out here in the world. We keep doing what we've been doing."

"You don't think this could happen again?" Taylor asked. "The targeting of Security, of your team?"

"I hope this is an isolated incident."

"Team Three was the target."

"Which of us is the most visible? Team Three. Someone with a point to prove, someone with a grudge. We'll have a better idea about it after we get to Wade."

"He has a point," Shan agreed. "We get an occasional Nomad who imagines he's going to run across us and prove how tough he is. Or somebody hoping to find a profit in an established city. We deal like always."

"What happens when one of our inactive citizens gets together with another one and then Gen En babies? It's bound to happen," Taylor broached a subject Wade had forbidden.

Shan looked to Mac. He nodded, "Go ahead."

"It's not that simple, and also unlikely to happen in The Vista," she told them.

"How can you be certain?" Quinlen pressed.

"Let's just say I am."

Taylor sat back in his chair, an idea forming, one he'd had before. "Because they're all male."

"The ones I'm aware of are."

"You can't be a fluke," Hunter said.

"No, I'm not."

"Maybe you can't sense them," Taylor said.

"That's a distinct possibility," Shan agreed. "The problem with our ideas about all this is that it's been too linear. Gen Ens were embryos tampered with in laboratories. This is true, to a point. Some of those are now decades older than us."

"Meaning, Gen Ens have reproduced and passed traits along to their children for at least two or three generations," Mac added.

"Also true. Most inherited traits seem to be recessive. Keep in mind, my opinions are conjecture. Council saw to it they purged our media sources. A few things, books, newspapers, occasional electronic devices, brought in with caravans have given us a little more information. What we don't know is vast."

"Right now, our purpose is to find Wade," Mac said, pushing the conversation back to their immediate issues.

"We have one definite target," Parr said.

"Potential target," Mac said. "In the field, anyone's call. If these Nomads go aggressive, you've been trained how to handle them. If either of us gives the word the same thing. They've already showed their intent. We get Wade. After that depends on their actions."

The meal was a silent affair, each of them mulling the next few days over in their own thoughts. It remained unspoken that not all of them might be going home.

Green stood in the doorway to the bay, arms crossed, leaning on the wall, talking to Shan. He looked serious, and the conversation, intimate. It had been going on since supper. They'd deposited their equipment on the floor, packing for departure.

"What is it, Lt.?" Mac approached Hunter, who was busy quietly repacking.

"I'm not the rookie anymore?" he asked, taking an inventory of his gear. Three duffel bags and he had room for one.

"Hell no," Mac said, as if it were obvious.

He nodded towards the pair. Jealousy had crept into his thoughts, and that pissed him off. Hunter didn't feel that way towards Mac because there was no point. This was different. "I thought I was her second."

"You are."

"It doesn't look that way to me."

"Green and Shan are closer than either of them shows," Mac told him. "This isn't something new. He was her second for close to four years."

"He was her second. That's all?"

Mac shook his head. "I doubt it, but not my business."

"And it's none of mine."

"She isn't concerned about her social life. She's trying to figure out how to get us into and out of Colorado, alive."

"I know," Hunter gave him.

"The thing about Shannon, she doesn't connect with someone right off. There needs to be a sense of trust, and that takes time." It seemed an important thing to say. "She has developed an attachment to you."

"Why are you telling me?"

"Because it adds one more complication. The last thing we need is you messing with her head."

"I hate to break it to you, but I've stepped out of her personal life," Hunter said. "For now."

Mac nodded. They both knew it was a fair warning.

"Alex," she called across the room. "Are you ready for this?"

"Probably not," Mac answered, knowing they'd been up to something all evening.

"Both of you," she told them. "Time to find out what we're supposed to do tomorrow."

"How do we manage that?" Hunter asked.

"I'll show you," she promised, leading them to the room Green had been occupying.

Mac got suspicious at the array of alcohol lined up on the counter. Hunter waited, and Green gave her a shot glass. Dark rum. She drank it, eyes watering. "Smooth," she managed. "Pick your poison, Alex."

"If this is a test..." he started.

"A generation ago, they used drugs to control the abilities of our predecessors. We know this from media we've pieced together. It works. Now we're going to talk to Wade and figure out how we find him, avoid bloodshed, and keep the peace."

"Scotch?" Green asked. Mac nodded and took the glass. Shan had a refill.

"Is this the best way to do this?" Hunter asked.

"The only way I've been able to get Wade when I'm awake," Shan confessed. "I don't have the focus or control like he does. Have another," she told Mac. He did. "Don't mistake this for a safe way to communicate and don't mistake this for permission to drink."

"Be careful," Green cautioned as she waited for another. "Some variables aren't pleasant."

"I know," she said, leaving her glass to sit for a few minutes. The prospect of a massive hangover wasn't her ideal morning, but there wasn't an option.

"What variables?" Hunter asked. "Because I don't even understand why I'm here."

"You're my second," Shan said, catching the glance that passed between him and Mac. "And because I said so. You're responsible for making sure I can find my room later and don't do anything stupid in the meantime. The variables, vary." She grinned, pleased with herself.

"Fantastic."

"Exactly," she said, going ahead with her third shot. "If I barf, let's all pretend I didn't."

"As convenient as you think it is, getting shit-faced is overrated," Mac told her. "You end up doing things. Stupid things that you might remember."

If she had a fear, that was the thing – Mac not being in control. "Why do you keep doing it if it's so overrated?"

"There are times it seems like a good idea," he told her, having another shot.

Green shook his head, cautioning Hunter not to get involved. Shan sat on the couch, deciding to say nothing rather than respond. She stared at the ceiling, humming.

"Want another?" Green asked.

"Not yet," she said. Then, "Boston."

"New York," Green came back.

"I hear Boston," she repeated.

"How do you 'hear' Boston?" Hunter asked.

"Rock band, mid 1970s I think. Wade listens to them all the time."

"Not here," Green told her.

"A safety. Can you hear it, Alex?"

"No."

"Sit down, get comfortable," she told him. "If you fall asleep first, I'll see to it you wake up naked in the snow."

"Ouch," Hunter said.

"Scary thing is, she's not kidding," Green added.

Mac took a seat, stretching out and propping his feet up. "Now what?"

"Have a drink," she said, taking another from Hunter. "At some point, you'll recognize a difference, a change in your perception. That's what we're looking for." She downed the rum, shuddering as the liquid hit her stomach. "Too much. I might chuck it all back up for real, and then we get to do this again in a couple hours."

"Lean back, take deep breaths," Hunter said.

"If they draw this out too long, it won't happen," Green told him.

"If they get alcohol poisoning, it won't happen."

"I'm fine," Shan said, pushing back on the sofa, an arm thrown over her eyes.

"Everyone could shut up now," Mac announced, taking her cue and closing his eyes. It might help. Hell, anything might help.

Shan started giggling. "We could, if we really wanted to." She clamped a hand over her mouth, eyes watering. "Focus," she said through her fingers. "You've got no damn focus."

"No more for you," Hunter said, crossing his arms and expecting an instant argument. Instead, she went from giggling to full out laughter.

"Should have waited on the last one," Green observed. "We might have screwed up the entire process."

"Oh, for fuck's sake," Mac used one of his father's favorite sayings.

"Relax," she said, getting back to the situation at hand, wiping her face dry on her sleeve. "As soon as I can see Wade, we'll be good to go. So, I need you to focus. All of you."

Green put a foot up on a chair, leaning forward to rest. He started tapping his boot heel against the frame. Shan winked at him, recognizing it as a ploy to get Mac's attention.

"A storm front is moving through," she said, voice low. "Can you sense it? Windy as hell, in Estes Park."

"I can feel something," Mac answered. "Don't much like it."

"What do you see?"

"Mountains. What else would I see?" He paused. "Elk, bedding down in the snow, downtown. There's a lake, too. I don't recognize the buildings."

"I got this," Shan said, knowing she could hold Mac's attention, for a short time anyway. It would have to be enough.

A bit later, she did indeed have to throw up. Hunter held her hair back, and when she was done, he tossed a blanket over her where she'd curled up on the floor next to her bed. He made sure the solar heater was on before he joined Green on watch. Mac slept undisturbed on the sofa where they'd left him.

Chapter Eighteen

Oct 3 north of Estes Park midday

The rider decided pointing a rifle at her was a good idea.
Shannon didn't think he was serious about using it. Even if he was, shooting at a moving target from horseback involved less skill and a lot more luck. "Go," she told Taylor, turning her horse to take a parallel path in the opposite direction. They were maskless, obvious, and ready to do whatever they needed.

"That's the girl," a dark-haired Nomad shouted to the one with the rifle, the older one most likely Vance.

"What was your first clue?" he asked, reining his horse around hard, anticipating a pursuit.

Shan let her horse pivot, hand dropping to her hip. The younger man shook his head "You're my priority," he said, drawing a .45 and aiming down the slope as she got hold of her sidearm. He was serious. "Don't do it," he told her. "Drop the gun."

"Come take it," she said.

"She's baiting you," the first warned. "Shoot her horse."

"No," Shan snapped.

"Toss the gun and dismount," the younger one demanded.

She urged the horse on, sending it bolting for the trees. They wouldn't take the chance of shooting it from under her, not cliff side in the shale. With the sun high in the sky, the ground was a treacherous mess.

"Running east," the younger one reported to whoever they had waiting.

"Follow her," the first barked orders, turning his horse to head across the gully.

That would put him in front of her fast and limit her options. It was a simple matter, to keep them guessing by doubling back, and it worked well until Shan's horse hit a wide patch of loose rock and half-melted ice. They started sliding. The animal panicked, struggling to regain footing. For an instant, Shan flashed to Noel's close call in a landslide during Sweeps. She tried to get the animal to head towards the crest, but he was fighting her. A heartbeat before they slammed into a pine tree, Shan got her leg up out of the way. Off balance, she caught a branch instead and then the horse went down, rolling.

Unseated, she grappled to get hold of anything solid to stop her downhill descent. In a few moments, the flailing horse scrambled to his feet at the bottom of the gully. It might as well have been miles away. Shan pushed herself up against a boulder, vision spinning. For the first time in weeks, she didn't notice the cold. As the searing pain in her shoulder leveled off, she realized both her saddle guns lay in the snow somewhere uphill.

"My name is Vance," the first Nomad told her. He was crouched in a resting position thirty feet away, reins in one hand and a gun in the other.

She sat cross-legged, leaning forward so he couldn't tell if she had a weapon or not.

"Did the horse roll over you, Capt. Allen?"

"Please repeat the question," she murmured, trying to get her bearings, trying to buy everyone a little more time.

Chapter Eighteen

"Our people are out there, ready to kill each other. Do you want to play games with me?" Soft-spoken, intense. Gen En of a sort she hadn't encountered before.

"You don't know who we are or why we're here."

"Wade came here to track down Rafe. You're here for the same reason. I've made it my job to see to it you don't screw up. I know what you are."

She peered at him. "So what makes you think we're only here for Rafe?"

For a split second, she caught Vance off-guard. They both had ulterior motives, and now he knew hers. "You've targeted all of us."

"Do not call for help," she said, wondering who he meant, showing him the 10mm in her lap and letting that sink in for a few moments. "I'm here to talk to you, one on one. We don't want loose ends. We don't want to do this again." She hadn't been certain before. "I can see you there, in Montana, ten years ago. You and Rafe." There were others, too.

"Then you know what happened. I tried to stop him, and then I tried to kill him. I succeeded as far as detonating the warhead as it cleared the silo. It took a dozen of my people."

"Who was the target? Where was that missile going?"

"We had no way of knowing that," he told her. "Pre-programmed before the war."

Shan couldn't tell if he was lying or not. His memory of it didn't seem confused, but she couldn't get a clear sense of the event, at any rate. "Why didn't you warn us? You've had years," she accused, suppressing the memory.

"As long as you stayed in Montana, you were safe," Vance said. "Coming south this spring was your mistake. Camping on his doorstep, another."

She considered he was right about what triggered the events of the summer. The pain in her shoulder was steady, and it was snowing again. "Do you have a plan, or is that up to us, too?"

"I need you and Wade to finish it, but you need me so you'll have a clue about what you're up against. Until now, you haven't," Vance made his case.

She had little time to make her assessment of Vance. The others would come across the ridge at any moment. "Will he go back north, after us, if we decide not to act now?"

"He will. He'll use anything he can against you."

"You have your answer, then. We're going after Rafe. You can help us or get out of the way," Shan told him, standing. He followed her lead, keeping his gun down. The rider coming from the same direction she'd ridden wasn't one of his people. Indigenous, wearing red and black war paint on his face. He picked up her scattered weaponry and waited, a shotgun in his lap.

"We need to get our people together to figure this out in a civilized manner," Vance said.

"Be here tomorrow, with Wade," she told him. "When I decide it's safe, you'll see us." Green offered her an arm, and she pulled up behind him, grabbing her horse's reins.

Vance watched them ride off, giving no orders to follow. He wasn't surprised. They were smart, like he'd predicted. As dangerous as they were naïve, too. Tomorrow would be interesting, so long as they didn't start shooting each other.

They crossed the ridge, disappearing into the tree line. Green kept changing direction, moving at a pace just past safe. It was still their aim to keep Vance's attention until it got dark. At daybreak, they'd rejoin their group.

"We're clear," Shan said in his ear, one arm wrapped around him tight. "Slow down. This trotting is killing me."

Green let the animal slow to a brisk walk. "You're hurt."

"I made a perfect one-point landing on my shoulder."

"You need to take better care of yourself."

She knew a joke when she heard it, but there was a subtle question. "I might have broken it. I couldn't very well let Vance see I hurt myself by jumping off a horse."

"We'll stop soon and I'll have a look at it."

"Did everyone get to their regroup points?"

"Oh, yeah," Green said. "I think I scared the hell out of them when I turned around and came towards them. There had to be orders not to confront us."

"Vance is calling them all back by now."

"What did he say?"

"He said The Vista wouldn't be safe, ever." She wasn't okay with the revelation, even after suspecting as much all along. Hearing him say so made it real.

"That answers all of your questions."

"Not even close."

Oct 4 daybreak

They sat across the long-abandoned parking lot, watching each other, waiting for someone to make the first move. If the risks didn't outweigh the benefits, they might become allies. It all remained to be seen and hinged on what Team Three decided.

His life was about to be dictated by The Altered, and this time, they were Wildblood. Vance understood more than anyone else, being intricately tied to their mutual foe. If he was to have any part of their offensive, there needed to be a clear way out. Rafe was unforgiving, and their current treaty was tenuous. Vance couldn't afford another misstep.

Today, his escort was Cooper. JT was trigger-happy around The Altered, too biased to be objective and he'd gone south, gone home, to avoid the situation. Cooper didn't have as many preconceived ideas about what was happening, but he wasn't ignorant either. He'd do what Vance said and save the questions for later.

Wade hadn't told his team to come in, or to relax, or anything else. What happened was going to happen at their direction, not his. He was on the sidelines, his motives many and ulterior.

Shan dismounted and came towards them on foot, no hesitation, no tactical gear, no fear. A pair of camouflaged men followed her, and all three were armed.

Vance followed her lead. He didn't want his people to run up against them. It would be a bloodbath.

It might anyway. As Shannon approached, Taylor drew his sidearm. Vance saw big trouble staring down the weapon.

"Taylor," Wade called, moving into view.

Cooper drew and aimed at Shannon, the second time in a day. The chain reaction was Hunter drawing on Cooper, and the rest of both groups were unsure what to do but arming themselves, anyway.

Mac sat in the tree line, a bead on Vance, wanting to pick off the dark-haired man with a gun on Shan, but trusting her judgment. Their target was Vance.

"This is how wars start. Stand down," Vance ordered his people.

"Stand down, Taylor," Wade repeated. He and Shan were the only ones without weapons in hand.

"I can't swear you're not under duress. Until that happens, I have to take my orders from someone else."

Wade glanced at Cooper. "Stand down." If he moved to engage, Wade would take him out before anyone realized what was happening. He'd run for cover, because all hell would break loose.

"I can't do that either," Cooper said. Vance was a target, just as sure as Rafe. He'd seen it for years. When the two weren't plotting to take over the Front Range, they were plotting to kill each other.

"Shannon, where's Mac?" Wade gave her their safety.

"Sitting out there with a big gun. Just in case." Shan got on her mic. "Come on down and join the party. This is going to get ugly before it gets pretty."

Cooper stopped targeting her, but didn't holster his weapon.

They had one sniper, there could be others. Maybe he'd been right all this time, and Vance had gotten soft over the years.

"Cooper, relax," Vance told him.

"We're here for the same reason," Wade said.

"We've been avoiding each other for so long, we don't know what to do now," Shan said.

"Then we call it even and sit down to talk," Vance said.

They waited for Mac, being the actual leader of the group. "Mac, this is Vance," Wade introduced.

~Cmdr. MacKenzie, in case you forgot,~ Shan corrected privately, anger back to simmering.

"We need a minute," Wade said, excusing himself and his Scout, motioning for her to follow. "Whatever it is, it can wait," he said as they walked away.

"I don't have the time to discuss everything that's wrong. Mac is running the things you were supposed to. It's not fair to him, or to you. We don't belong here. Fix it."

"I'm trying, but I need your help, and his. Play along, you know how."

"I'm nowhere near finished."

"You can throw things at me later. Right now, we have to diffuse the situation. Vance brings Cooper in to deal with problems. We are the problem. This can be fixed, here and now, but I need cooperation from my team. You won't do anything rash, will you?" Wade asked, understanding her frustration.

"I've been doing rash things for three and a half months," she offered. "Things I should've never had to do, and things that might come back to bite me later." Anger wasn't her entire emotional state. It was running in overdrive now that she could confirm he was safe, or at least safe for the time being.

"You're mad at me. You have every right to be."

"I am. You left me there to deal with everything."

"You were capable," he began.

"No," she snapped. "You thought Alex was gone. So did I. What in the hell was I supposed to do in The Vista, alone?"

He hesitated. "If we lost Mac, I had contingencies in place. You wouldn't have been in The Vista at that point."

She fell silent for a few moments. "I hate your damned plans. If you're going to include me in them, you'd better tell me. We're a team."

"If something happened to Mac, you wouldn't be thinking right, not for a long time. I wanted Green to get you to the cache in Idaho and regroup from there."

"What cache in Idaho?" She'd known her former second was up to something that night, but later, it wasn't a concern. Later, she forgot about the sensation. Too many things happened too fast for her to pinpoint any one.

"We have them in Idaho, Alberta and Washington, besides the ones you know," he told her. "I started supplying them as soon as I got into Security. They were in place long before then, so we put them to use," he told her. They both understood why. The specter of someone watching.

"What do you want us to do?"

"We hole up in Estes Park with Vance and his people and try to figure out a reasonable end to this," Wade told her.

"Reasonable," she repeated. "None of this has been 'reasonable'. I don't expect it to start now."

"Neither do I. We're going to find out what Vance expects, and learn what we can about the world. Play along until it's time to change the plan."

She nodded. "One of his other people, goes by the name of Caulder. Is he here?"

"Vance has him underfoot in the summer, calls him JT," Wade said. "He sent him back for whatever reason they want to makeup. He has issues with us."

"To where?"

"South," Wade said, uncertain where he called home. "Why? Is he Gen En?"

"No, but I can see him. Joseph Terrance Caulder, born in Alabama in 2032. Two older brothers and one younger sister," Shan recited.

"How did you find that out?"

"I know his brother. So do you, but not by Caulder."

"Hunter?" Wade said, considering it for a few moments.

"Yes."

"Are you going to tell him?"

"When I get the chance."

"A little déjà vu happening here. Remember how that turned out for us?"

"We're not safe here."

"No, we aren't."

Chapter Nineteen

Dec 1 Estes Park mid morning

"Do it again," Mac told him, unimpressed with the grouping of bolts on the far left. Two of ten had missed the life-sized target. They'd been practicing with crossbows, and he didn't think Taylor was putting as much effort into it as he could.

"Sonofabitch." Taylor stalked off across thirty-five yards to retrieve the bolts. He came back, jamming a bolt into the groove. "This is a waste of my time."

"Do you want me to call Quinlen in to give another lesson?" Mac asked. "Because I can do that. Or we can fuck off for another two months waiting for something that might never happen. Either way, here we are."

"And throwing sticks at targets is going to do what?"

"Keep us busy, like all the other things we're doing that mean little. So, do it again."

They'd occupied an old field house near their quarters for training as soon as Vance allowed, after a brief confinement. The Vistans were stir crazy by then. They were worse now.

"You do it," Taylor challenged, handing off the weapon.

Mac aimed and fired, hitting the target a fraction to the right of the center. Then he did it again, the bolt lining up next to the first. "Two years with the hunting guild."

"I'm a sniper. I should be able to do this, damn it," Taylor spat. "Give me a rifle and we solve the problem."

"It's not a problem, not yet. You'll learn this, like all of us, in case we need stealth," Mac told him, handing him the crossbow. "Almost everyone here is a sniper. Practice."

"We aren't even going to be there," Taylor shot back. "Why keep training us when we're bystanders?"

"Because I said," Mac told him. "We haven't set plans. You might get dropped in the middle of a mess. We're not going to have a lot of warning when it's time. So practice and stop acting like you're doing us a favor by doing your job."

"Pointless," Taylor fired, missed, and dropped the crossbow. "Fucking pointless."

Shannon wandered in, not finding a single Vistan on the plaza. Some mornings, they had breakfast there. It was clear out and it was cold, a heavy frost rather than snow. The lack of snow here surprised her.

Mac and Taylor were sitting in the bleachers, the one section that was rolled out, deep in conversation. Taylor was nursing a bloody nose and Mac was wearing a brand new black eye.

"What's up?" Shan asked out of sheer morbid curiosity, already having a good idea. It wouldn't be the first time the pair had exchanged words, or fists.

"Practice," Taylor said, holding his nose. "I can't hit shit," he waved at the targets across the building.

"I see," she said, thinking that the condition of Mac's face disagreed with his statement. "Lt. Taylor. Kyle. If Team Three chooses not to rush back to The Vista when we clean up the Nomads mess we're dealing with, who is in line for promotions? Think about that before you answer."

"All of us. Maybe not the rookies." He shrugged. "Rookies, too. I'd say Green and Ballentyne. They might even get an invitation to Command."

"Ballentyne won't take the position," Shan said. "They offer him a promotion every year. It's a courtesy. Green is part of the Ranchlands Patrol and won't go to Command, either. I meant you. Do what Mac says. It's important, if you think so or not."

"You've been setting up scenarios."

"Several. You have a part in most. Don't ask, just do."

He felt a little foolish, but not enough to admit it.

"Has Green been through here?"

Taylor cleared his throat.

"He's not your second, Shan," Mac told her.

"I need a partner for the afternoon, and no one is around to volunteer."

"Because you had a spat doesn't mean Hunter's not your second," Taylor echoed.

"We haven't had a 'spat'. I go out at daybreak for a look around and you've all disappeared. I figured you were here, talking about me."

"Your choice," Mac told her. "Wade was at the annex offices with Vance a little while ago. Hunter had the watch until midnight. He's liable to be looking for a meal about now. Everyone else is in the city somewhere." They got to go, half the group at a time, for day trips.

"Vance gave me clearance to ride the loop," she announced. "So I am, company or not." The path led out to an overlook. It was a pleasant view of the valley and a great strategic point.

"You and Wade won't go out together anyway," Taylor said. "Other options are pretty limited." Team Three members were quartered in separate areas, self-imposed, for their safety.

"Thanks for the primer on all the new rules for the winter," she scowled. Vance wouldn't have given her permission to go if he hadn't already gotten a report from his own watch. The Vistans were guests, with a few limitations. Neither side was willing to test those limits yet. She could see it coming.

"Be careful," Mac said. "It's too damned quiet here, and I wonder why every day."

"Vance said it's always quiet in the winter," Shan remembered an earlier conversation. "I'll go track Hunter down. I need some time out of here, or else. My cabin fever is a nasty thing. Try not to punch each other anymore today."

"Not a problem," Taylor told her.

"Whatever you hear," she added, "Try not to worry."

"Why?" Taylor asked, suspicious. Neither of them answered. "Great. More secrets."

"Team Three business," Mac said. "Command business. Things I don't even want to consider."

"But you do," Taylor said.

"Not as much as you. Capt. Allen is going to do some recon on her own, on orders."

"You're all bat-shit crazy," Taylor said. "Team Three, not Command."

"Pretend we aren't the same," Mac told him. "Pretend you didn't know that before any of this started."

He didn't have a thing to say.

"Warn Wade for me," she told them.

Taylor shook his head, picking up the crossbow. "That's fucking fantastic. Leave me that job."

"What are we doing out here?" Hunter asked, trailing a few paces behind her, leading his horse up the snow-covered incline. "It's kind of chilly out today."

"It's colder here than The Vista," Shan agreed, wrapped in layers of thermals and insulated snow camos. She'd known no other weather. The brief summers brought violent storms and little relief.

"Is that why we're out? To see how cold it is?"

"Sure. I'll let you in on a secret, though." She stopped, letting him catch up. Their breath was white in the thin air. "I don't like it here."

"Oh, hon, that's not a secret," he laughed.

She ignored his sarcasm. "None of this is real. We're just seeing what Vance wants us to see."

"And that's not such a secret, either."

"All this subterfuge is because of Rafe. My problem is, I don't understand." Shan smiled at him. They hadn't spoken in days, and she missed that. It wasn't for any reason other than Team Three's business occupying her time. "I feel like Vance is scratching the surface. He's not telling us what's happening here."

"What are you going to do?"

"Yeah, about that. My first instinct is to run. I can't say that to anyone else because Wade bases a lot of his decisions on my first instinct." They stopped, reaching the summit of the trail. There was a picnic area farther along the ridge, and an aspen grove running north. Everything was still covered in a fine layer of frost.

"With good reason," Hunter said. "You're pretty accurate. If we run now, to where?"

"I wish I had an idea. Somewhere not here." She stared out across the overlook for a few moments. "You're not 'Conda, and you're sure as hell not part of Wade's inner circle."

"What's your point?"

"You don't know about the…" She almost said 'ghosts,' but they weren't ghosts. They were alive, and they were here. "The other Gen Ens we've been aware of. The ones that have been watching Wade and I as long as either of us can remember."

"No, I don't."

"Because it hasn't been necessary. Like most things we do, knowing makes you a target by association." She was blunt, as usual.

"Why is this an issue all of a sudden?"

"Why do you think we're here?"

"Here, as in Colorado?" Hunter saw that look on her face. "You mean out here, now? Damn it, Shannon, what are you trying to do? Is Mac aware of this? Or Wade?"

"Not in detail."

"Where are they? How many?" He didn't dare to chance looking around.

"I can't tell. Wade never let me contact them before."

"This, this is crazy," Hunter told her, ready to call for help.

"That's the same thing Taylor said."

"He knows, and he didn't stop you?"

"In case you hadn't noticed, Taylor doesn't get to tell me what to do. I'm not here on a whim. It's an order," she said.

"From who?" Hunter asked, knowing. "Command sent you out here alone?"

"I'm not alone."

"I'm not good with this," Hunter told her. "Not even a little. This isn't just dangerous, it's stupid."

"It's planned. You need to relax. I know my job."

"No," he shook his head. "This is chaos."

A covey of quails scattered from the stand of trees, catching her attention. A heartbeat later, Shan was going for her sidearm, reaction slowed by bulky gloves. Hunter tried to draw, but a blinding flash caught him, caught them both, putting a stop to any gun play that might have happened. The flash bang was visual and sonic, and they both went down. The horses bolted.

Shan stumbled around, going to one knee. There was a lot of shouting from voices she didn't recognize. By the time she drew the Kimber and blinked the afterimage away, it was over. Four hooded figures were pointing weapons at her. Hunter was down, uninjured, three more targeting him. Seven to two odds wasn't something she'd gamble on, not with her distorted equilibrium making the ground spin.

Struggling to her feet, Shan held the gun up, keeping her other hand visible. One of them snatched the weapon from her and searched her for more.

"Hey," Hunter protested and got the same treatment in response.

"Say nothing," Shan told him.

The intruder found her boot gun and the knife on her belt. "Vance wouldn't let Wade out here, on the off-chance we'd cross paths. When you showed up, that changed everything," he spoke quietly.

"Stop it," she said like an order, as they zip tied Hunter's hands. The one speaking to her gestured, and the others went about the business of containing him in a more civilized manner.

"Shannon," he said, making it clear he knew who they were. "Between you or Wade, you were my first choice."

"Why?"

"Wade plays the diplomat. He's not. Neither are you, but you wouldn't be out here if Vance was a concern. That means you're more open to make concessions."

"Who are you? I don't talk to strangers."

He pulled the hood off, revealing short, black spiked hair and brilliant blue eyes. He was young, like her. Shan contained her shock at how much he looked like Rafe. "Capt. Allen, we are The Sixth. Perhaps Vance has mentioned us."

They got dark hoods over their heads. Shoved onto horses. From the motion, they were moving downhill. East or south. She heard muffled talking from the other riders, but Hunter remained quiet. She was glad about that. After more than an hour of riding in silence and a repeated change of the direction, they stopped and Shan dismounted, waiting. It was colder, getting dark, and if they didn't report back to Vance's compound soon, the Vistans would go on alert. No one would search for them, however, not at night. Tomorrow, if Wade deemed it necessary. He wouldn't.

Someone took her arm and led her along a dirt path. They climbed stairs and twice a hand on her head kept her from smacking into something. They went down a few steps and through a doorway that clanged shut with a metallic sound. After a few more steps, he pulled her hood off.

They were inside a massive building, well lit by electric lights, and new. Or at least, it appeared to be.

"Where's Hunter?" she asked.

"He's being brought in through another entrance to keep you confused and disoriented."

"What do I call you?" She got a better look at him.

He considered it for a moment. "Call me Kaden."

"Not your real name."

"No, of course not," he agreed. They reached the bottom of yet another set of stairs. "I brought you here to talk. If you're going to be Vance's assassin, you have a right to know the things he won't mention. Do you understand?"

"He's incapable of dealing with his own problems."

Kaden laughed. "That's more accurate than you realize. Also, because he's afraid of you. He's more afraid of us, but that's the way it is, the way it's always been."

"Why?" she asked as he cut the zip tie binding her hands.

"Vance claims we're not quite human. He might be right, but what's the point? We are what we are."

"And you're The Sixth," Shan repeated, rubbing her wrists. "The sixth generation of genetic experiments."

"No, we aren't. It's not an accurate representation. While we are genetically enhanced, after the first five, there were no more 'generations'. It was a numbering system, nothing else."

"What am I?" she asked anyway.

He smiled again, perfect white teeth. Disarming, even charming, in other circumstances. "Considering your background, if there was the opportunity to classify you on paper, they would call you a fourteenth. After the twelfth because old superstitions hold on."

"The thirteenth?"

"Also, the last of us enhanced by technological means. Governments spent a lot of time tacking labels on things they didn't understand or wanted to manipulate. We are both."

Two men escorted Hunter in, ending the conversation. "Are you all right?" he asked as they cut him loose.

"I'm fine."

"What now?" They didn't have a hell of a lot of choices. He was ready to go out fighting, but she was standing there and he wouldn't.

"Now it's time for dinner," Kaden told them. "That little venture took longer than I expected. You're considered my guests here. Tero will show you to your rooms."

"One room," Hunter told him.

"One room," Kaden said. "Someone will be around in half an hour to bring you to the cafe, assuming you'd like to eat."

"We would," Hunter answered again.

"If you need anything, tell him and he'll make the arrangements."

"The Kimber," Shan spoke up. She was absorbing every sensation about this place, knowing she might have to make more of those rash decisions on what others would consider a whim.

"It doesn't belong to you," Kaden replied.

"It suits me."

"You'll have it," he said. "But until I escort you back to Estes Park, I'm keeping your weapons. You understand."

She nodded.

"Half an hour," he repeated.

Tero showed them into the room and left them to their own devices. Shan didn't check to see if they locked the door. She did lean on it for a moment, collecting her thoughts.

"Are you all right?" Hunter repeated, looking for a more substantial answer this time.

"I am," she nodded, shedding her outerwear and going about investigating the room. It was lavish and large compared to her room at Station Two. False windows draped with jewel tone curtains, the lush maroon carpeting looked new. The bed, large and covered in heavy, sewn quilts. A stocked bar, complete with a mahogany counter Shan suspected was antique. A doorway in the back led to a spacious bathroom with a granite walk-in shower.

Hunter had a barrage of questions. "Are these the Gen Ens watching you? Does Wade know? How much trouble are we in?"

"Wade knows I took off with you." She doubted Kaden understood the friction between them. "Trouble? We'll find out soon enough. If Vance has been straight lying to us, Mac and Wade and the entire team could be in more trouble than we are." She walked around the room, inspecting every corner. "I found them the usual way. Kaden was out here, waiting. Watching. His intent isn't clear to me, but I have no sense of hesitation like I do with Vance. We're guests, not prisoners."

"And that's how you feel in Estes Park."

"Yes."

"A few hours ago, you were telling me Vance was hiding things from us. We've found out what. Whom."

"I knew they existed. Vance avoids discussing them. That's why we were here."

"Great. What do we do now?"

"Have supper?" she said, sitting on the edge of the bed to test it. "I don't think Kaden has any nefarious plans for us. It doesn't feel that way. If he wanted to kill us, why drag us here?"

"To find out about The Vista," Hunter said.

"What could we have that would interest them, other than Wade and I?" She didn't agree with the idea, not yet. "As far as technology, they walk all over us. You saw the size of this place. I swear, it's underground."

He looked around, studying the ceiling. "Maybe."

"Pretty sure. It's leftover from before the war, but they've repurposed it to their needs."

"I'm no civil engineer."

"Me either."

"What does he want with you?"

"To discuss all the things no one else will," Shan said. "At least, I hope. We'll find out."

"What in the hell is The Sixth?"

"Who, Hunter, who are The Sixth. Our hosts. I still think this complex is at least partially underground," she said. "The walls are warm. Some sort of geothermal source, maybe." These were details she'd want to share later.

"The Sixth," he repeated.

Shan wrinkled her nose and squinted at him. "A rogue variation of Gen Ens. The one thing Vance seems to be afraid of."

"Afraid of who?"

"Rafe and The Sixth."

"Oh, holy hell, this is Rafe's compound?" Hunter was ready to go again. Still. He hadn't been able to protect her earlier, and it pissed him off. It scared him more.

"No," Shan said. "Not hardly. Rafe is in Manitou Springs and that's more than a hundred miles from here. This might have been a military post of some sort. Vance said there are facilities all up and down the Front Range, and that various factions have occupied and renovated some of them."

"For what?"

"Defensive position, I imagine. I'd like to find out for myself. According to files I've dug up in the archives, in Vance's library, they were different. More experimental. The corporations lost control of most early on. It forced them to end large percentages."

"They murdered children?"

"My question too. I asked Vance."

"And what was his answer?"

"He said they 'disposed of dangerous experiments'."

"You're not someone's fucking science experiment," Hunter spat out, angry.

"Neither were they."

"Why were they called dangerous?"

"Hunter, you're asking the wrong person. Vance wouldn't elaborate. He either doesn't know or won't tell us. Wade has tried to get details from him, but nothing so far."

A soft knock on the door, and a girl of about ten stuck her head in. "If you'll follow me, I'll show you to the dining area." She had dark hair hidden under a gray scarf, but her eyes were the same bright blue as Kaden's. They followed her, taking a flight of stairs down, across an empty plaza and through a short entryway to an adjoining area, this one well lit and quite occupied. At a quick estimate, Shan figured there were thirty-five people having their evening meal. Some of them wore weapons, some didn't, and none of them seem concerned about their guests. The girl led them to the rear seating section. Less traffic and more privacy.

"Maia, did you introduce yourself?" Kaden asked, motioning them in. He wore smooth black leather pants, boots, and a gray suede shirt, leaving Shan and Hunter feeling under-dressed in their camos. It wasn't exactly a formal setting, anyway. Half a dozen tables scattered in a more leisurely fashion here, decorated by colorful candles and fresh flowers.

"I'm Maia," the girl said, intrigued by the newcomers.

"Hunter."

"Shannon."

"There's a Shannon in my classes," Maia offered. "But he's a boy."

Shan smiled.

"Go see if your brothers are back," Kaden told her and she was gone in a flash, back the way they'd came. "Almost a teenager. Don't let her demeanor fool you. She's not even a little shy."

"I understand," Hunter said.

"You like speaking for her. Instead of her."

"When she has something to say, you'll know."

"Fair enough. Have a seat. We'll eat soon." Kaden took a chair facing out, watching the crowd. More of his earlier entourage had taken up nearby tables, passing plates.

"Are they here to make sure we don't cause trouble?" Shan asked.

"You aren't here for trouble."

"I'd like to believe that."

"Drinks?" Kaden asked, watching them taking stock of their surroundings.

"Sure," Shan said. "Wine, sweet white, if you have it."

"Ice wine?"

"Better yet," she said.

"Beer," Hunter said. "Any sort."

"You're trying to get a feel about how large an operation we have here, how diverse our supplies are," Kaden said. "I'll tell you what I can. Like I've said, we're here to talk. It's about time, don't you agree?"

"I do," Shan said. "Past time, but my opinion doesn't always count." A boy who could have been Maia's twin brought a bowl of cut up fruit for an appetizer. "Is everyone here a Sixth?"

Kaden laughed. "Oh, no, that would be like thinking everyone in The Vista was Gen En of some sort because I met you first. Besides that, Shannon, you know better, don't you?"

She smiled and nodded.

"A lot of you have similar features," Hunter said.

"Blue eyes seem to be dominant, don't they?"

"Dyed," Shan said. "You want to look alike. People here dye their hair dark and dress similar. Is it to confuse Vance?"

"Vance, Rafe, whoever."

"But you look like him, like Rafe. I've sat across a table from both of you."

"You've met him," Kaden said, even more intrigued. "I wasn't certain he'd gone north this summer."

"He came after us. Why do you think we're here?" Hunter asked.

"You're here for her," Kaden gave a nod towards Shan. "The reason we resemble each other–Shannon is right. We use it to our advantage where we can. It makes it difficult for our enemies to distinguish one of us from another. As for the other, the same corporation modified Rafe and I, it's possible we share DNA. So I've been told."

Hunter stared, first at her, then Kaden. "You and Rafe?" he repeated.

Kaden nodded.

Shan thought she'd misunderstood him. "He's Gen En?" she asked, furrowing her brow, trying to sense something that hadn't been there before. Nothing still.

"Rafe is Gen En, an Altered, and he is a Sixth. I grew up in his clan," Kaden said.

She shook her head, mind racing.

"Vance didn't tell you," Kaden said. "The one bit of information you needed most, he omitted."

"I should've seen it. I understood what you are, what Vance is, before we met."

"Some of us can sense other Altereds. You and I both fall into that category. A few individuals are invisible, even to us. Vance has assumed you know what Rafe is, or he is withholding that information from you on purpose. With him, I never can tell how he's going to react."

Shan felt a headache coming on. "That explains a lot of things I couldn't place before."

"I can't imagine Vance has given you anything. You're not his allies, you're a weapon to be used against a former comrade that's outlived his usefulness. The problem is, Rafe is smarter than Vance. I don't know which is more cold-blooded."

The meal was grilled steak, beef, and an array of vegetables arranged on a bed of grain. They ate, listening to music from overhead speakers and watching children play on the plaza. Shan picked at her food, distracted. No more of a horticulturist than she was a civil engineer, there were varieties of produce she hadn't seen before. A lot of things seemed unfamiliar.

"So." Hunter took the lead. She had finished a bottle of ice wine on her own, and he wasn't certain how coherent she'd be. Too quiet, and that was bad any way he considered it. "What do you want?"

"The short version. For years, since their original band of survivors parted ways, Rafe and Vance have been testing each other. They've put the entire region at war. In the meantime, we've established safe zones and trading posts from central Wyoming to New Mexico, Colorado to Nebraska and the Dakotas. It was far from easy, and we're still working on expanding. Their feud is interfering with everything we've accomplished." Kaden had considered what to tell them. "We want an end to this."

"Who do you speak for?" Shan asked.

"I represent more than one interest, and they prefer to remain anonymous for now."

"That's helpful," she noted, wishing she had more wine.

"Not at all, but safer."

"Why us?" Hunter asked. "Why her?"

"Because she's one of the few people capable. I don't mean only Shannon. Wade, too. The best bet would be all three of them. There's a third."

"Is there?" Shan asked, defensive.

He regarded her. "Yes. Just because I can't see him doesn't mean he's not there. Like Rafe."

"Rafe knew that, too," she pointed out, the memory of The Junction a bright spark jumping into her thoughts.

Kaden cocked his head, picking up on the sensation. "When was this?"

Hunter crossed his arms, shaking his head. He was getting used to being on the outside of these sorts of conversations.

"Middle of July." Shan offered no details.

"You should've waited until spring to stage this little coup."

"We're not giving him more time to regroup."

"It's not only time that you're running up against. Drop a visual like you just gave me, on him, and he's going to be in your mind and you'll wish you never left Montana."

"I'm not afraid of him."

"Yes, you are, and you should be. You were afraid of him before I told you what he is. He meant to kill the three of you. Rafe's not someone to let a mistake like that go."

"He's not walking away from this," Shan said, eyes narrowing, adrenaline running. "We're here to eliminate him. Vance knows, and now you do. It doesn't matter how, and it doesn't matter who thinks they need to get in the way."

"I don't quite believe that either, Shannon. I'll explain why." Kaden pushed back in his seat, glancing around the cafe. "The vast majority of 'our kind' grew up in clinical and controlled environments."

She nodded, hearing something about her origins for the first time. It had her full attention.

"You and I, Wade and a handful of my Sixth, those of us around our age, we're the first actual generation of The Altered to be raised like other children. Parents, families, playtime, friends. You get the idea. It wasn't like that for the others."

"Thousands," she guessed.

"I don't know actual numbers. It's tens of thousands at a low estimate, possibly into the millions before the war. The point is, we're different. We have emotions and morals they never introduce to our counterpoints. When Rafe decided you were a problem, it was a calculated risk to eliminate you, the thing they trained him for. Over time, he's developed some darker emotions about humans, too. The fact you survived is going to gnaw at him until he corrects his error."

"How does that make me a liar?"

"You have those emotions, that moral compass, and it won't let you kill people you perceive as innocent."

"And you think that's true, without a doubt?"

"We've been watching you. Not always me, but I'm certain you were aware of it."

Staring at him, she tried to pick out a lie. There was none. "If it comes down to it, we'd do what we need to save our home."

"You'd try to protect The Vista at any cost," Kaden told her. "I believe that, but you're not indiscriminate. That's the difference. The thing to remember is, you aren't alone here, and you don't get to make those decisions alone. We have laws, and people to enforce them."

"Yet they've done nothing about Rafe," Hunter said.

"It's not for the lack of trying. Killing isn't a simple thing. And again, we have laws to consider, like you do. Most Altered aren't aware they're different. All the better for them. We didn't get that choice, but we do what we have to."

"Everyone makes that decision, every day."

"True. Some of us are given far more difficult decisions."

"You can see other Gen Ens," Shan said, bored with listening to them being philosophical. "When did you realize? How long have you known?"

"Always, like you. At least I was aware of what I was sensing."

"Wade told me."

"I'm glad you weren't alone. Neither was I."

"What do you know about Rafe? Tell me the things Vance won't."

"Rafe is a pariah, even by the standards of The Sixth. I'm sure Vance will tell horror stories, and there will be some truth to them. Vance isn't our ally, however. He's been the opposite. Rafe, he sees someone who has coherent use of their abilities, someone he perceives as a future threat. He feels the need for chaos and death. You've seen that."

Shan tipped her head.

"Any alliances Rafe agrees to are short-lived. He's cold-blooded, and worse, he's intelligent. When he finds your worst fears, those are the things he'll use against you."

"So we can expect him to target The Vista."

"He's already tested our defenses," Hunter said.

"We won't interfere when you go after him. Later, let's say next season, if there's contact between your people and mine, there will need to be concessions. We have those established boundaries, trade routes and outposts to protect."

"We aren't welcome here," Hunter interpreted.

"Your ambassadors will be safe to come and go, but negotiations are required," Kaden confirmed.

"Wade's been begging the Council to let us get out in the world." Shan had seen them deny the requests for years.

"They refused?"

"They've insisted there was nothing to see. I have to wonder if they didn't set our Sweeps routes up to avoid population."

"Command wouldn't do that," Hunter told her.

"Not only current, but previous officers have files sealed away. Things I'm not qualified to view."

"Council would have a hand in it?"

Shan grimaced. More information than she wasn't willing to share.

"Send your delegates," Kaden repeated. "Keep your soldiers at home."

"Are you going to help us?" she asked.

"If it were up to me. It's not."

"You want them to kill Rafe because he's interfering with your commerce?" Hunter wanted to get it right. "But you won't help. Against a Gen En you know."

"You don't see the entire picture. He helped establish this chain of outposts. He knows who we are and where we are. There are thousands of people under our protection. Rafe threatens all of that. He also has influence, and that puts some of us at more risk than others."

"You're afraid you're next," Hunter said.

"You were part of his clan," Shan repeated what he'd already said.

"We're the breakaway faction, as far as he's concerned," Kaden said. "For the reasons I've expressed. The time is coming where he'll want this place back or burned to the ground. Right after he clears out Estes Park. That puts my Altered in a precarious position, and thousands of innocent people in the crossfire. The less attention we bring, the longer the peace will last. It won't be forever."

"What I call Gen En are The Altered?"

"Yes."

"How do we get at him?" Shan asked, having clarified they were the same.

"Make yourself blind to him."

"How?"

Kaden shook his head. "That's for you to figure out. I can't tell you how to control your abilities."

"Tell me about The Sixth, then."

Kaden looked at Hunter.

"He's here to keep me in line," Shan told him. She sensed Kaden could tell her all about The Altered, and that he wouldn't. Not now.

"I'm her bodyguard," Hunter stated, enjoying his beer, pretending to ignore the conversation.

"If you'd rather he not be here, I'm still his senior officer."

"Does that bother you, having a little girl boss you around?" Kaden directed at Hunter.

"Not even a bit." Hunter didn't blink. He was watching several couples dancing out on the main floor, past the cafe. Others were playing with the younger children. The urge was there, to ask her for a dance.

Kaden considered his options. "You're going to tell him what I tell you, anyway."

"If he needs to know." Shan had no problem with what Hunter was aware of.

"Fine, then, a brief, if you will, on the history of the twenty-first century. The Sixth was created to survive the end of the world, or at least the end of civilization, as it used to be. Events didn't fall into place the way they'd schemed, and the result was a limited nuclear exchange that mutated seasonal viruses, and those were the wildfire. The rest is what we've been left with. But it turns out, the world goes on fine, even without so many people." Kaden sat back, gauging their reactions. "Of course, it's far more complicated than that. Events I'm not allowed to disclose."

Shan didn't respond. Hunter shook his head, running a hand over his face, disturbed by the revelation. "Is there proof?" he asked, not wanting to believe humanity was so barbaric.

"She knew," Kaden pointed out.

"Not long ago, someone told me the story. I hoped it wasn't true, but knew it was," she said.

"We were supposed to be their soldiers, their scholars, their breeding stock," Kaden continued. "They thought their wealth and power would buy them anything they imagined, that it would save them. A handful of years before War Day, they began discovering they couldn't control us. It led to countermeasures during and after the war. They never understood what they'd done."

"Do you mean The Sixth, or all of the Gen En?" Hunter asked.

"All of us. The Sixth, even more so. Vance is far from what we are. Ask him."

"I will," Shan said.

"You're here to remove the biggest obstacle preventing us from making the Front Range livable. I won't interfere with that. Again, it's not up to me. It's up to Shannon and Wade. They have to get close. Rafe can't be aware of what they're doing, and since she's already met him, that poses quite the dilemma."

"It's impossible," Hunter said.

"Not hardly. It's going to take focus and precision."

"Focus, great," Shan said. "It took me weeks to find Wade because my focus sucks."

"You were injured, too," Hunter reminded her.

"No excuse."

"I have something I want you to try," Kaden said, excusing

himself. "I'll be right back. Maia will be around if you need anything."

"What sort of something?" Hunter wondered after he left.

Shan shrugged. The girl appeared, offering a fresh bottle of wine. "No, thank you. Can I get water?" The colder the better, Shan thought, a headache starting.

"Of course," she said. When she returned, she was carrying a pitcher of water, with chunks of ice. "It's cold," Maia pointed out. "I wasn't calling you a boy," she explained as Kaden returned. "You're very beautiful. You should let your hair grow out more."

"Thank you," Shan smiled. "I cut it when I was sick."

"Sick?"

"I got hurt. I'm better now."

"Are you a Sixth?" the girl asked.

Shan looked at Kaden for an answer. "She's a fourteenth," he said.

Maia giggled, knowing the story. She took Hunter's empty beer mug, leaving three shot glasses in its place, and departed.

"Cute kid," Hunter said. "Related?"

"No, but she follows me around when I'm here," Kaden said. He held up an old, discolored bottle. "This won't hurt you. It's not much more than distilled alcohol."

"What's the 'not much more'?" Hunter asked.

"You're her bodyguard," Kaden said. "You can have the first shot. I won't say what because I'm not a chemist. Absinthe and something added, especially for The Altered. It hasn't killed me. It won't hurt you either." He poured three shots.

Hunter picked his glass up. "Last chance to say no."

Shan took hers and all three drank. "Oh, that's nasty stuff," she coughed, eyes watering.

"You don't hold your booze so well if I remember," Hunter said.

"Well enough."

"Expect nothing spectacular," Kaden told her. "You might notice a change in your senses, you might not. Hours, not more than a day or two. It's not dangerous."

"Can we go back to Estes Park tomorrow?" she asked.

"You're not my prisoner."

"Interesting choice of words," Hunter added.

"If Wade thinks Vance, or any of his people, or anyone, is in our way, he'll react," Shan said.

"You mean retaliate," Kaden said, more a statement than a question.

"I do."

"You're what might be called his handler."

"I'm his partner, and I'm his friend."

"You keep him under control. There are times you've been pushed to challenge him because his boundaries aren't yours."

"I'm not at liberty to discuss the dynamics of my team," she said, not liking the cold sensation she felt as the conversation turned. "What I said is nothing you weren't already aware of."

"Fair warning, then. We all have someone to answer to, and Vance has allies. Listen carefully, when he makes threats."

"Feel better now?" Hunter asked, sitting on the edge of the bed.

"Yeah," Shan told him, arm thrown over her eyes, sprawled out, not moving. "It wasn't the shot, but all the wine."

"Couldn't have helped."

"I'm aware."

"Serves you right, though. Are you going to be sick?"

"No, and I don't need a lecture," she said, sitting up. "I give lectures about the evils of too much alcohol, I don't get them. What time is it?"

"Four, five in the morning."

"Huh. It's my birthday."

Hunter had forgotten, being kidnapped and all. "How does it feel to not be a teenager anymore?"

"I think I have a hangover."

"You did that on purpose."

"I had to manage what Wade might sense. If he knew we got snatched up like that, I can't predict how he'd react. You've never seen him... He's quiet until he's not. They can joke all they want."

"And you're what? Calm and collected?"

"Most of the time," she said. "Plus, I let all of this happen."

"I figured. That doesn't mean I approve, but it wasn't my decision." His trust had become tempered with seeing first-hand how resourceful they were, as individuals, and together.

"Don't think I'd walk you into a situation that wasn't planned out. Or myself. This was no more dangerous than a regular Scout run. Less, considering they want something from us, as much as Kaden avoided saying it."

"Are they allies?"

"Right now, they're neutral. You heard him say he doesn't have a choice. Whoever is in charge isn't getting involved." She looked sideways at him. "It's up to them to decide how Vista Security interacts in the future."

"What are we doing today?"

"I get to be in Command. If we can't trust Vance, we need to figure out what our next move is."

"You can't trust Vance."

"I never claimed I did. This all moved past being a simple Nomad incursion the moment Kaden told us Rafe is Gen En, an Altered, and Vance didn't. We're being used. Now I'm certain, and in a few hours, so will my team."

Shan picked at her breakfast, still woozy. Sometimes, she forgot to eat at all. Hunter didn't. He ate; hash brown potatoes, three eggs over easy, toasted wheat bread, zucchini in a butter and herb sauce, thick strips of bacon. The coffee was real coffee. She wasn't certain she liked it. Maia was their company and commented she'd already had breakfast.

"You're here to keep an eye on us," Shan said.

"Someone has to," the girl replied. "It feels kind of like spying on people. I don't like spying on people, but sometimes you have to."

"They sent a ten-year-old to watch us?" Hunter asked. "What if we were hostile?"

"I'm twelve," Maia said. "Plus, if you were bad, they'd have sent my brother and you wouldn't want to mess with him."

"How old do you think I was when I started hanging out in Dispatch and learning the routines?" Shan asked. "When I learned to drive a stick shift?"

"Her age?"

"I've been in school for almost a year," Maia told them. She didn't specify for what.

"Her age," Shan nodded.

"We teach them young," Kaden said, joining them on the now-empty plaza. "Because if we don't, how would they be able to defend themselves?"

"Exactly," Shannon agreed.

"A few moments of her time," he said. Hunter nodded and went off to be entertained by Maia. "I want you to do something when you get back to Estes Park," Kaden told her. "You need to tell him," he indicated Hunter. "About his family. It won't matter much in this venture against Rafe, but it will matter to him."

"How did you know?"

"The same way you and Wade did. You and I aren't that different."

"That's not what I see," Shan said.

"The only difference, I was taught about my abilities, trained to control them. You've never known for certain, never had someone who could show you. The fact you are learning on your own terrifies the people who want to control us." He returned her sidearm. "They're still out here, you know."

She nodded, storing that bit of information away for later.

"Tell Hunter, do it soon. Don't trust Vance, don't trust that he will help you against Rafe, even if it seems that way."

"Now what?"

"Now you go back. If you're ready," he said, offering them hoods. "You remember the routine."

Chapter Twenty

Estes Park Dec 2

They both stood in the upstairs media room designated as the Vistans' gathering place. Green was with them, stoic, armed. Shan wondered how he managed that, to get hold of a sidearm as Vance confiscated theirs. She didn't ask. If anything happened while they were gone...

She'd know about it by now. Hunter was sweating it, though.

"Remember where we are," Green warned, tapping his ear. Guards close by.

"I suppose there's a plausible explanation why you went off the map in the middle of hostile territory, in the middle of winter, with no word? Wanting to be alone is no excuse to put any of us in danger," Wade spoke as he strode in to the room. Taylor was with him. Two of Vance's men stopped right outside the door.

"Me or her?" Hunter asked.

"You first."

"I'm the senior officer," she interrupted, annoyed.

Hunter realized it was another one of those safeties the team had developed. There were plenty of places to be alone in the half-empty city. He shut up.

"Get rid of them." Wade told Green, meaning Vance's guards. "Round up the others," he told Taylor. "I still want to hear from you first, in a minute," he repeated, quieter. Green shut the door behind him as they went out.

"We didn't stand a snowball's chance in hell," Hunter said when Wade indicated it was safe to speak. "They knew how to disable her."

"Are either of you hurt?"

"No."

"Hangover," Shan said. "Not from the flash bomb. It was a sonic device. I was down damned near before I realized they were there. If they wanted us dead, we would be."

"Sonofabitch," Green muttered, returning.

"They would send you out there." Wade rubbed his eyes. "I thought you'd be more careful about it."

"I'm not here to be careful. What would the point be if I scared them off?"

"What would be the point if you got yourself killed?" Hunter asked.

"What did we stumble into?" Wade asked.

"We're in the middle of a border feud," Hunter said. "They started establishing outposts right after the war, and then they split into factions. Those factions are fighting over who gets what."

"We got involved by crossing into disputed territory during Sweeps," Shan clarified.

"We caused a break between Vance and Rafe just by being here?" Wade asked.

Shan wasn't sure where to begin. "Not exactly. This started years ago. Rafe hunts Gen Ens," she said. "He sees them as a threat. Because he's Gen En."

He fell silent for a moment. "Are you certain?"

"Without a doubt," she said. "I thought I should tell you in person." Shan could imagine him losing his composure.

"Say so, if Vance lies to me. I want answers, and I'm going to ask him."

"Ask me what?" Vance wondered, bringing his own guards along, Cooper in the lead. They all carried weapons today, not that it scared Green. He let them in anyway.

"It would have been good to know Rafe is Gen En," Wade said. "Since we're the ones going up against him."

"You're not joking," Vance said after a moment.

"Kind of vital information to withhold." Shan had to speak up, as angry as Wade.

"You saw me eight hundred miles away and you couldn't see him when he put a bullet in you? How is this my fault?" Vance spat out. "You're unschooled and you want to take on Rafe? The best military minds in the country trained him."

"And look where it's gotten us all," Wade came back, not raising his voice, not yet. The rest of the Vistans filed into the room with more of Vance's men.

"I never said who shot me," Shan said.

Vance paused again, seeing the mistake. Lying to them would be another. "No, but he did."

"Is he here?" Wade asked.

Shan glanced at Hunter first, then Green, hoping they understood how precarious their fates were at that moment.

"Rafe hasn't been in the city for years."

"You've been in contact with him," Wade said. "Why?"

"We have business dealings. That hasn't changed."

"It's why you're so eager for us to eliminate him."

"I've made that clear."

Wade nodded, satisfied for the moment, not hardly finished.

"Did they say who they are?" Vance asked Shan. "The Sixth. Which faction?"

If Wade hadn't wanted her to talk to Vance, he'd have said so. "They didn't mention names."

"What emblem did they wear?"

"I saw nothing like that," she shrugged.

"This close," Vance said, rubbing his temple. "There are only a couple of groups right here. Yates causes the most trouble. He had close ties to Rafe, back in the day. Who's in charge now?"

"I spoke to someone calling himself Kaden. He didn't seem in charge, and I didn't get a tour of the place."

"If 'Kaden' is Yates," Cooper sneered. "We don't have to guess. He wants to take it all and leave us begging for help."

"Isn't that what you did to him?" Shan asked, getting the impression from Cooper himself.

"They're dangerous and can't be trusted," Vance repeated his stance. "We've all seen the proof with Rafe." He was ignoring her, knowing it wouldn't stop the question.

"Is that what happened?" Wade repeated for her.

"Not quite," Vance said. "You'd have to have been there."

Wade didn't believe him.

"The Sixth were aware and uncontrollable. Attempts were made to eliminate them before things got out of hand. It's not personal, it's self preservation."

"Bullshit," Hunter called him on it. "Kaden is her age. Explain that."

Vance fell silent for a moment. "When they took to calling us a particular 'generation', it had nothing to do with actual generations. It's the level of genetic manipulation. The first five were straightforward. The Sixth, there wasn't a lot of documentation on them. No one could quite pinpoint which corporation started with them or why they were different."

"So Yates has someone else in charge," Cooper said. "It doesn't mean he's a Sixth."

"You claimed they were obsolete," Wade said to no one in particular because they all had the same story. Rehearsed.

"There were no safeties, no control once they began seeing aberrations," Vance admitted.

"What has that got to do with the problems here and Rafe wanting..." Mac got it. "The Vista." They were a barrier. He shut up. He was supposed to be the silent partner.

"Nothing other than Rafe is a Sixth, and he is far more dangerous than you've imagined, even with what he's already done. It's been a stalemate since the war," Vance said. "If he had The Vista backing him, the scales would tip. You have people and resources he doesn't. If Rafe occupies any place, Estes Park, The Vista, any of the bigger outposts, we'll be on the downhill slide. Wade and Shannon were unknown factors. He wasn't willing to risk dealing with you out in Montana."

"Until this spring," Wade said. "We got too close."

"What do they want?" Vance asked.

Wade gestured for her to speak up.

"They want to ally with The Vista," she told them.

Cooper shook his head, and Vance had nothing to say.

"They don't want a war," she said.

"He told you this?" Vance asked.

"Yes."

"And you believe him?" Cooper asked, his disdain obvious.

"He could've killed us. We'd never have seen it coming. Who's Yates?" Shan asked.

"If we're going to continue this talk about The Altered, I'd like to do it with them," Vance said. "Not everyone from Montana."

"Not all your sentries," Wade added his own conditions.

"Cooper stays."

"Hunter stays."

Vance considered it. "I'd prefer to do this in my office, but this is acceptable."

The uninvited filed out, going to the first floor lobby to stare at each other.

"Yates was military, Special Forces of some sort. He set up a couple of defensive positions in Colorado, right after the war," Vance continued. "We were south of here then, Rafe and I and Moore. The four of us and a handful of others established what are the trade routes and outposts now."

"All Gen En?" Wade asked.

"Yates was the only one in the core group who wasn't. He was cautious about all of us, knowing what we were and where most military organizations stood on our mere existence. Smart, too, well-trained, but not ready for the things getting thrown at us. He took it personally, when Rafe started targeting the other Altered. He and Moore broke from the group and headed north. They knew they weren't safe, but they did it anyway."

"Was?" Shan asked.

"It's debatable if Yates is even alive. Moore has gone off the map, but the last I'd heard, he was out along the trade routes, keeping the competition away."

"How did Rafe find us?" Wade asked.

"The two of you were like a neon sign to him," Vance told them. "Twelve years ago."

"The warhead. It was a warning. What's stopping him from trying it again?"

"It was an accident. The launch systems to the missiles have lost power and they're dead in the silos. Besides, he has a purpose for The Vista."

"I hope you're right," Wade said.

"How do we make it so he can't see us?" Shan asked. "If I can't see him, there must be a way."

"I can't tell you how," Vance said.

~Can't, or won't,~ Shan added her thoughts to Wade.

~Agreed. Someone is directing The Altered in charge of the trade routes, and we don't know who. It's not Vance,~ Wade said to her.

~It's not Rafe.~

"Kaden said it was all in the focus," Hunter remembered.

"I won't have an audience around while we figure it out. What we know stays with us," Wade said.

"No one is outside the compound anymore unless they're in the city," Vance told them.

"That's my call," Wade said. "Or Mac's. Not yours. Unless you're revoking our status as guests., and then we'll be on our way south."

"You want to handle this all on your own," Vance said. "A dangerous gamble."

"You'd prefer us out of the way, just like Rafe would."

"You're unprepared."

"We're not the children Rafe thinks we are. That you think we are. We're going to do what you and your army haven't been able to in ten years. Help us or not."

"You're going to go out there and die trying," Cooper said.

~Don't,~ Wade warned Shan, feeling her anger.

"Tell me what you need," Vance said. "Don't expect me to make this public or obvious. You fail, I pay the consequences." He took his leave, not at all pleased with the events of the day.

"When did Vance decide we weren't to be trusted?" Hunter asked.

"When they found us in Montana, twelve years ago," Wade said.

As the rest returned, Shan said what she'd thought for months. "Some day soon, one of us is going to have to end Cooper. I hope I get the chance."

"No you don't," Wade said. Another conversation he needed to have, in private.

"What do we do now?" Hunter still wondered how much trouble he was in. He'd helped her disobey orders from Wade and Mac, but carry out orders from Command. He felt a long-overdue headache starting up the back of his neck, into his shoulders.

"The same thing we've been planning since July," Wade told him. "You should get something to eat and catch a few hours of sleep."

Hunter made conversation as they headed to the cafeteria. "I never can guess what you two are talking about."

"Oh, he's pissed," Shan said. "Just not at you."

"At the entire situation."

"He's trying to figure out which is worse – having Rafe as an enemy, or Vance as an ally."

"Which is it?"

"At least we know where we stand with Rafe," she said. Neither choice was acceptable. "We should have gone south as soon as we recovered Wade. It's too late now."

Chapter Twenty-One

Dec 2 after dark

As soon as she got to their room, Shan started stripping off gear and heavy clothes, dropping them in various places, waiting, because Hunter lagged back, speaking with Parr for a few minutes.

"We need to talk."

"Every time you say that, I worry," he pointed out, closing the door.

"I've meant to do this, damned near every day. 'When the time is right'." Shan smiled to herself. "The time is never right. I guess I understand a little better how Wade felt."

"About what?"

"I was angry at him for not telling me about Taylor sooner. It wasn't all his fault, but he caught hell."

"What am I going to catch hell for?"

"Not you. We have been suspicious since we made contact. It's one of those things that happens." She stopped in front of the fireplace, watching the flames, and he stood next to her. "I won't let this go on for ten years. Too many complications, and it's important."

"I don't suppose I understand what you're talking about," he told her.

"No, you don't. You've heard Wade and Vance refer to JT He'd be Vance's second, a job he shares with Cooper, from what I can tell."

"He got sent south, to Jacob's town. Poor attitude about us. About Team Three," Hunter nodded. "I don't think he was the only one. And?"

She guessed just saying it was the best way to go, if a little uncouth. "Hunter," she started, and stalled. "Oh, hell."

"Shan, seriously."

"I can't put it any other way. JT is your brother."

Hunter thought about it for a long time, the only sound in the room coming from the crackling fire. She let him be.

"Without a doubt?"

"Without a doubt," she said. "I sensed something unusual as we got close. I waited until I asked Wade in person, and he agreed. We've confirmed who he is with local sources."

"The rest of my family?"

Shan had done the research. "At first, I considered Jacob's town, but that wasn't right. It's a way point. They're at a place called Angelfire." She handed him a file she'd gotten from Vance's private library. "I also have permission for you to take leave and go out with the next caravan, after we deal with Rafe. I need you here until then."

He nodded, staring at the folder. "You could've waited to tell me."

"Yeah," she agreed. "Except you need to know now. For the past twenty years. I can read emotions, Hunter, remember? Hide it from everyone else all you like."

"I'm going to go read this," he said.

"I'll see you in the morning."

Chapter Twenty-One

Shan kicked the blanket off, struggling, disoriented in the dark. Something had intruded, abrupt and harsh, like a nightmare only worse. Memory. Hunter had a light on seconds later.

"I can't breathe," she rasped, pale, gasping.

Hunter checked her vitals, forcing calm, abruptly aware how little he knew. "Try to relax," he talked to her. Asthma was rare, and he couldn't pinpoint a problem. "You are breathing, Shan."

She shook her head, pushing herself to sitting. "Can't."

Hunter grabbed her radio and keyed it, uncertain what else to do. "Green," he said. "Shan, now."

It triggered her memory.

"She's aspirating out into the mask," someone was shouting. Shan couldn't see anything. "Roll her on to her side, her lung is collapsing."

"Where's Green?" another voice called, one she recognized as Mac.

"Wade's hurt. He's trapped in his car and it's burning."

"The helicopter is down," Mac yelled. "Call a Code Thirteen, damn it, before we lose the whole team."

Shan tried to shake off the memory. She tugged up her shirt, running her fingers along her ribs. "Can you tell if my ribs have been broken?" she managed, still not catching her breath.

Hunter checked. "Right here," he said, stopping on her eighth rib. "There's a dimple and a ridge."

"You've listened. Do I have both lungs?"

"Yes," he said, wondering where Green was. A moment later, Hunter knew as he rushed in. "She says she can't breathe, but there's nothing wrong with her I can find."

"She's asleep," Green said, knowing at a glance. "Or something like asleep."

"What?"

"Slap her, wake her up before she hurts herself or one of us for real."

Hunter slapped her, not anywhere as hard as he was capable of.

Shan's eyes rolled for a moment. She blinked.

"How do I tell if she's awake?"

Green leaned over, gazing at her. "If she's asleep, her pupils stay fixed."

"I'm awake," she said, teeth chattering, suddenly cold. Hunter pulled the blanket around her.

"What in the hell happened?" Green asked.

"She couldn't breathe."

"Why?" He checked her pulse.

"Collapsed lung," she repeated what she recalled. "Someone said it. I felt it. I've never been..." She touched her ribs again. "How did I get shot and don't remember it?"

Green straightened up. "It's not my place to explain."

"What?" she asked, still disoriented.

He got on his own radio. "Wade. Shan has some questions about that problem we had at Sheridan."

Knowing double-speak when she heard it, she went defensive. She got angry a moment later. "What can't I remember, and why not?"

Hunter wondered the same thing.

"He'll be here," Green said. "Are you all right?"

"I'm fine. Except the whole memory thing. Were you there?"

"I was," he admitted.

"And?"

"I can't say. Orders. 'Conda orders."

"You've got to be kidding." Not being an actual member, there was no pulling rank on him. She got up to get dressed, not bothering to chase them out.

Chapter Twenty-One

"I wish she'd come out of her shell and not be quite so shy," Hunter observed, looking away to be polite.

"Yeah," Green agreed, keeping his gaze on the doorway across the room. "It's a horrible problem of hers."

A few moments later, Wade came through the door. "Both of you stop thinking about my Scout being naked."

"Not our fault," Green offered his best excuse.

"Oh, for crying out loud," Shan said. "I'm dressed now."

"What happened?" Wade asked them for the second time in a few hours.

"She said she couldn't breathe. Apparently, she wasn't awake." Hunter gave his version.

"Flashback, no idea what triggered it," Green said.

"Sheridan?" Wade asked.

"Yes," Green told him.

"We need to talk alone," Wade said in a low tone. "I can't swear this building is secure today, just because it was yesterday. We're going to hike over to the stables and visit the horses, make sure they're being fed and groomed. In case anyone asks, I had insomnia and was looking for company. Let Mac know, let Vance think whatever he wants." He meant to be misleading.

"On it," Green said.

"You got hold of the situation fast," Wade spoke to Hunter. "Fast is imperative. Good call."

Hunter acknowledged with a nod, "Understood."

"We'll be back for breakfast."

"What don't I remember?" Shan asked as they sat in the loft over the tack room, waiting for the sun to come up. They'd brought a thermos of coffee and a radio.

"Some details of what happened at Sheridan," he said. "At least, not accurate ones."

"I got that." She paused, a lot of stray thoughts in her mind. "Is that why I have nightmares?"

"I imagine it could be one reason."

"Are you going to tell me the truth?"

"If you want me to."

"I'd like to hear," she decided, putting her gloves on. The weather was cold, it was going to stay cold.

"You were out, drugged, and I replaced your actual memory with one less traumatic. Less traumatic for me, maybe. I don't know why. I wasn't even certain it was possible."

"An experiment?"

"More of an accident."

"Did I flat line?"

"No, nothing that bad. You took one in the ribs, not the shoulder. Why?"

"Mac, at The Junction. I mean, I felt it."

Wade hadn't known.

"Was your car on fire?"

He smiled a bit to himself. The story had grown. "No. Sections of the helicopter came down fifty feet up the road. From the Roost, it looked like me. There was steam from the water spilling out of the radiator, too, and a brush fire from debris."

Shan mulled it over. "How did you do it? My memory, I mean."

"Simple visualization. I'll show you. I can't tell you how."

"Have you messed with my memory since then? Kyle, and now this. I hate being lied to."

"I never set out to lie to you. Kyle, that wasn't my lie, Shannon. The memory was. I didn't think it would last and after all this time, I didn't see how to make you understand." Wade offered her a refill on her coffee. She accepted. "No, I've never done it since."

"When you told Vance we'd take care of if ourselves, this is what you had in mind."

"Worth trying, at least. With Mac here, all the better. We'll find out if this can work. If not, we need to back off and reassess. Maybe retreat to Cody. Keep Mac a secret, at least. They can't see him and we'll keep it that way."

She rubbed her eyes. "I think Kaden had a hand in this."

"Possible," Wade conceded. "We could use allies here. I don't know if Vance will be when Kaden is involved. I need your insight."

"Vance isn't an ally, he doesn't plan to be."

"I'd rather have allies than enemies."

"Kaden said to send ambassadors, not soldiers. We are neither."

"True. If we figure this out, we might have to rely on Vance watching our backs." Wade didn't like it, but it was time to see where they stood.

"The rest of our team is here. Zero trust in Vance. Bring them in or send them home."

"We're going to be out there, alone. I don't mean as a team, I mean alone." Wade had been planning for five months. "I'm going to brief everyone soon."

"You're a glutton for punishment," Shan told him. "I still hate your plans."

"This one won't be any different," he promised.

Jan 6 Estes Park The Vistans compound

Parr wandered in to the cafeteria ahead of Hunter, coming in from watch. With patrols from the city, they still had their own watch. Everyone had fallen into a routine, uncertain what they were waiting for.

The lights weren't on in the kitchen. There was a note, and weaponry of a sort, on the table.

Hunter read it out loud. "Wait for the other Vistans to join you. This is a test. Team Three will conduct the test. Full stop until everyone else is present."

In a few minutes, they had all gathered for breakfast, part of the routine. So was boredom.

"Team Three is your aim," he continued, reading to them. "Take a gun and ammo. You are now armed. So are we. We sealed the floor for this exercise. Defend yourselves. Ready, set, go."

The men snatched up the ping-pong guns and white plastic balls fast. "Hallway," Green said, being the senior officer.

Parr looked, and seeing no one, dodged out and went low. "Clear," he called. The others joined him.

"We should split up," Taylor said. "There are five of us and three of them."

"And they're going to kick our collective asses," Noel said, having observed them during war games.

"They can try," Green said. "Taylor and I have both trained with them."

"That's nice for you," Quinlen said. "I think we should split up, too."

"Fine," Green said, knowing it wouldn't make much of a difference. "Work in a pattern from north to south, west to east," he directed, pointing. "Meet back in the cafeteria. Keep in mind, they've probably split up too. Go down fighting."

"Ping-pong balls?" Hunter asked.

"Because rubber bullets hurt like hell," Taylor said. "Trust me." They scattered.

"How long are we going to let them run around the dorm?" Mac asked, the three of them sitting behind the half wall that divided the kitchen from the dining area.

"A few minutes," Wade said. "An hour. It depends."

Shan grinned. They'd come in early and had breakfast. None of the others had checked the kitchen first. Weeks of sitting were making them all antsy and careless.

"It's going to be soon, isn't it?" Mac asked.

Wade nodded. "Depending on the weather, for one thing." The snow was minimal, and if it warmed up even a few days, travel wouldn't be a problem. He wouldn't wait those few days. If the forecast was good, they'd move, as long as nothing else changed.

"February is colder," Shan said.

"This will be over by February," Wade said. "We could be on our way home."

"I could handle that," Mac decided. All three of them had been training in close quarters and hand-to-hand. Green had been running the rest of them through a tough regimen as well.

"If they stick to their plan," Wade said, meaning their game of tag. "One or maybe two will come through that door in about five minutes." He nodded towards the service door behind them. "You want to take care of them?" he asked Shan.

"Sure."

"We're going to go opposite directions in the main hallway and, with a little luck, catch them in the dayroom or heading back here. Rendezvous in the north corridor in, say, fifteen."

Shan turned off the lights that were on and turned on half the ones in the kitchen section, moving off to the south end, well hidden behind a freezer unit. She crouched down in the shadows and waited. It was eight minutes before the door opened and another minute before someone eased into the kitchen, ping-pong gun loaded and ready.

It was Taylor. He slipped in with a purpose. As he swung around to look left, Shan sprang up, silent. She put a hand on his shoulder and the toy gun against his spine as she whispered, "You're dead, Lt. Taylor."

"Sonofabitch," he exhaled. "I looked. Where were you?"

"Behind the freezer."

"That space is about four inches wide," he pointed out.

"It's about three feet wide," Shan said. "Sit down. We'll finish this in a few."

"Don't sound so sure," Taylor told her, sitting on the floor.

She felt the door move as much as she saw it and swung around in time for Green to slap the plastic gun from her hand as she did the same thing to him. They stood there, disarmed.

"Put up your hands and defend yourself," she told him, doing just that.

"I'm your combat instructor," he reminded her, going into a defensive stance anyway.

"And I'm armed," Mac said, coming up behind him. "And you're dead."

"Well, that figures," Green lamented, sitting down next to Taylor. "Too damned quiet. It's not natural."

Shan retrieved her gun. "No, it's not," she agreed, smiling at them. Few people could sneak up on Green. She wasn't one.

"Parr and Quinlen were heading north. I plan on doing to them what I just did to Green," Mac told her. "Go get your second." He retreated the way he'd come, grinning. Shan headed out the same set of doors their opponents had a few minutes earlier.

Hearing someone cutting across one of the interior rooms, she ran, just enough to be heard if they were paying attention. Parr tried to catch her, but she was gone before he got there.

"They use her as bait and sneak up behind you," Parr told Hunter as they passed. "Wade got Noel at the end of the hall."

Shan doubled back and ended up in the outer hallway again, tucking her toy gun into the waist of her jeans at the small of her back. Hunter caught up with her a few seconds later. "Lost my gun when I hit that last door," she lied.

Hunter was checking to see if the rest of Team Three was indeed trying to sneak up on him. "I don't trust you," he pointed out. "I didn't see any ping-pong balls lying around."

"Are you going to shoot me, Hunter?" she raised her eyebrows, showing her hands were empty.

Her shirt was unbuttoned a couple of buttons more than usual. He thought it was a good look for her. He tapped the plastic gun against her arm. "You have the gun," he told her. Shan smiled, running her fingers across his shoulder just enough to...

Chapter Twenty-One

Reach back and retrieve her gun unnoticed. "Lt. Hunter, you are dead," she said, putting her gun against his rib cage. "Do you know why?"

"Because I'm stupid. Because I let you distract me," he corrected. "I knew better."

"Take a seat," she directed. "Men are predictable, but that only works once. It's not a fair test. You didn't call it, I win."

He nodded, sitting. "I hope Quinlen shoots you."

"Fat chance," she noted, heading towards the cafeteria.

Five minutes later, Wade called everyone back via the intercom to have breakfast. "Wargames are over. Team Three has whooped you all. Hunter survived the longest. Come eat now. I'm treating you to an amazing breakfast that someone else prepped."

Mac and Shannon were absent.

"If nothing changes here," Wade told them while they finished. "It's a 'go' in four days. Starting tomorrow morning, Team Three will be with Vance in the final planning stages. Read nothing in to that. Vista Security is still in charge of this operation. Vance is still not an ally."

"This is still Estes Park," Green said.

"Vance needs us more than we need him at this point. It may not hold true later. I have briefed you in specialty teams and one-on-one about your assignments, and we'll do it all over again before we leave. Pack what you need, take care of anything else."

Taylor was the first up.

"Your job is important," Wade told him, cleaning his Glock as they sat in the lounge. They had an open view of the front doors, of who came and went. The back, locked, was seldom in use. "Make sure the rest of the team are doing their assigned jobs. Keep Mac clear. We lose Mac, and the entire plan is pointless."

"Who's watching your back?" Taylor asked, not liking the idea. It seemed more reckless than usual. There was nothing to compare it with, however.

"When the trigger happens, when Shan and I regain our memory, we'll watch out for each other."

"It's the time before you get your memory back I'm worried about. The things that could go wrong, you can't plan for that."

"No, we can't. I'm counting on Rafe being smart. He's going to want to know what we know about The Vista, Vance, and a lot of other things. We have to make ourselves more valuable to him alive."

"He only needs one of you alive."

"We are The Altered, and he can't predict anything about us, even knowing that. Keeping both of us alive doubles the chance of breaking one or the other. It won't go on that long."

"There's the idea he might try to convince you to join him."

"He might."

"I'm more concerned that Vance won't hold up his end."

"There aren't a lot of options. We're here and Rafe hasn't been giving him any breathing room for a long time now. All he has to do is deal with the Nomads from Manitou. He does that now."

"Is this something you want Shan doing?"

"I'll be right there with her. There's no one that can do this but her and I," Wade said. "As long as everyone remembers what their job is. Keep them organized, keep them on focus."

"We won't slack off now."

"Since you're our radio operator, I want you to relay to Cody tonight or tomorrow night. No details, but give them the timetable we're working with. Don't let Ballentyne talk you in to giving up things he doesn't need."

"The less they know."

"All the better."

Chapter Twenty-One

"Get her in and find cover," Wade told Green. "You're my close-quarters shooter. You have your orders about what to do once we identify Rafe."

"Kill anyone I don't recognize. Cover the two of you," Green said, being professional and emotionless.

Wade knew better. "When the alarm sounds, civilians could be in the immediate area. Handle it however you see fit, but you're aware of our concerns about bystanders."

"Avoid civilian casualties."

"Find and scout the airfield when we recon. Vance says it's on the north side. Save the story that you know nothing about airplanes. Denial. Not just a river in Egypt. I've been aware since the project started. If you need to steal one, do it. As I understand, the single engine ones have the range to get you to Cody."

"They should," Green agreed.

"That's your call, again. If I can't, your job is to get Capt. Allen and gather the other team members. Any means, like the contingencies we've planned out before," Wade said.

"Understood."

"Parr is the senior officer of the sniper team," Noel said, repeating what he'd heard.

"Parr, Hunter, you," Wade said. "I need snipers on high ground. You'll confirm where once you arrive. Do what Taylor tells you, do what Parr tells you." He looked sideways at Hunter. They'd have private words. "Hunter, too. Don't shoot Green. He'll be in close, sneaking around. Identify your target before you pull the trigger. Basic training, you know that. Radio contact may be sketchy."

"You didn't want rookies here." Noel knew it was true.

"Yet, you're here."

He was skeptical.

"I'd leave you behind if I didn't think you could handle the assignment," Wade said. "That goes for every single Vistan we picked to make this trip. We've prepped as much as we can. It's time to go."

"Quinlen is large-arms now?" Parr asked.

"Mac has been training him for weeks. I wish we had longer. We don't." Wade dismissed them, waited a few moments until they left. "Hunter. If you have a complaint, now is the time."

"So you can leave me here?"

"An option," Wade confessed. "Not likely. I need a sniper, not you trying to babysit Shan. She's going to be inside Rafe's compound and it won't be safe for her, not for a second. I'll be there, too." He explained in more detail because Hunter was smart enough to shut up and listen.

"When the event happens that's our trigger, it'll take Rafe about a second to understand what we've done. We need to be that precise. If he's standing next to one of us, or both of us, his first option is to kill us. It's an easy way out. Taylor is going to attempt to wait until there are eyes on us. It might not be possible."

"That means you have about a second to kill him."

"Another good reason for snipers and large arms fire. A firefight might give us more time." Wade paced, considering. "Rafe assumes she's weaker because she's female. We've both seen it."

"You're going to use that," Hunter said.

"Yes. The thing is, even after we trigger, and Rafe knows we set him up, he still can't see Mac."

"You want to distract Rafe so Mac can sneak up on him. He could still decide to kill you."

"Not a good strategic move," Wade said. "He'd opt to keep us alive, at least for a time."

"So he can torture you for information to take Vista Security down," Hunter said, not at all convinced.

"You don't think Team Three can handle this Nomad? Because we're like him, and that makes him just another Nomad."

"When you put it like that," Hunter said. "It's all the other Nomads."

"Why do you think damned near everyone here is a sniper?"

"Something Parr said this morning." Hunter had one more thing on his mind.

"Go ahead."

"He said you use her as bait. You did this morning. At Sheridan, looking for the helicopter. That's what you're doing now, isn't it?"

Wade didn't have to answer. "You're dismissed, Lt."

"Is this a good idea right now?" Mac asked.

Shan was busy stripping off his holster and shirt after joining him on the daybed in a corner of his quarters. "A little distraction would be nice, yes?" She wore jeans and a tee shirt. No shoes or socks, no gun, no knives he could see, and no camisole. "Besides, where do you think everyone else is?"

"They've gone in to town," Mac said. "Ah, sure. Distraction would be nice," he agreed. "What about Hunter?"

"I didn't ask him, and he went with the others. No big deal." Shan sat up for a moment. "You're my first choice, Alex. Hunter. I don't know where he stands. Now he's decided he doesn't want to compete with you."

He laughed.

She put her hands on her hips. "How is it funny?"

"You've never gotten turned down, have you?"

"This is what you want to talk about?"

"No," he said. "But it's true." Grabbing her leg, he swiveled around and rolled her beneath him, kissing her. "Don't take it personal."

"How should I take it?"

"Shannon, shut up," Mac whispered. "The night's going to be gone too fast. Let's not talk about anything."

"Am I on your list of people to eliminate?" Vance asked, deciding it was time to clear the air.

"No," Wade said. "I'd like Estes Park as an ally."

"They call you and MacKenzie 'commander'. I assume you have a certain amount of influence with whatever military system you have in place. Will I be dealing with them, a civilian government branch, or both?"

"That's not a decision I'd make, or influence."

They walked through the plaza. The sky was clear, temperatures hovering near freezing. Snow wasn't in the forecast, and plans hadn't changed. Cooper and Taylor stayed close by, silently measuring each other up.

"You'd like to include The Sixth you've contacted as allies."

"I would. Can you see it happening?"

"It's not impossible. The Front Range needs to unify its towns and villages, and the marauders would move on. North would be a problem for you. As it is now, there's plenty of room for various groups to set up and live off the work of the smaller, isolate places."

"Something to negotiate another day," Wade said. His interest in helping Vance gain control over trade routes was close to zero.

"Once we get the signal, my people will move in, round up the stragglers, and cover your retreat. With no leadership, those left in Manitou will scatter. A concern for a few weeks, more in the summer, but it's nothing we haven't dealt with."

"He won't have someone to take charge in his place?"

"No," Vance said. "Since the incident in Montana, he's gotten more paranoid by the year. When you showed up this spring, it set him on a rampage. You're damned lucky there weren't civilian casualties. To answer your question, if anyone started being ambitious, especially another Gen En, Rafe got eliminated them."

"Rafe isn't the way he is by accident," Vance went on. "It's how they trained him. As much as the companies claimed otherwise, they wanted soldiers, and they made them. The problem with creating a sociopath is that they don't get along with other sociopaths, or anyone else."

"Being a soldier doesn't make you a sociopath."

"No, of course not, but in this case, it's a fact. I should tell you a story about Rafe, one he told me himself and others confirmed over the time I was with him."

Wade waited for him to continue.

"This was June, just before everything unraveled. Rafe had been working out of Texas for several years and had very little supervision by then. He understood what was happening, and why they sent him there," Vance told him. "The facility Rafe targeted was between Kansas City and Wichita, an intermediate training facility. Twenty-one Altered lived there. The only solace I've had was that he killed them before he set off the internal purge and torched the place to the ground. There were a couple dozen civilian contractors, too. He's efficient at the tasks assigned."

"Expect no compassion," Wade said.

"He doesn't know the word. The Sixth are the same."

"I don't know them," Wade said. "Until they give me a reason not to trust them, that's the way it is. I gave you the same advantage. Rafe should have stayed out of Montana. So should you."

"Don't let him get away or you'll spend the rest of your life looking over your shoulder."

Chapter Twenty-Two

Daytime

Blue sky through bare tree branches. Scattered high clouds. After a few minutes of staring, she realized what 'blue sky' and 'tree branches' meant. Also, that she was lying on the cold ground, a horse grazing a few yards away.

She sat up, testing each of her limbs, then cautiously stood to gauge her surroundings. It appeared she'd fallen off her horse, but she couldn't imagine why. No sign of anyone else.

High mountains lie in all directions, with snow on the tallest peaks. An inventory of her saddlebag gave her a little bearing, but no memory other than the obvious. One thing she was certain of - she didn't want to be there. There was nothing around her, or in her memory. Something was very wrong.

Once she determined what direction she'd been traveling, she pulled herself onto the horse and got moving, away from whatever was causing her to run. If she remembered something, anything, she'd feel less helpless. She couldn't think of a name to call herself, the horse, or where she was going. Maybe, she hoped, the afternoon would be more revealing.

Half a mile down the trail, a wave of vertigo hit her, and she recognized the sensation. This time, she managed to get off the horse before she passed out.

"I need to understand what happened," Rafe spoke, not needing to raise his voice. A dozen men followed him, listening to every word. Two were consultants. The rest were there for a single purpose — kill anyone he said to.

"They're faking it," Murray said. It was a simple solution, and simple was usually the right answer. As one of Rafe's advisors, it was his job to keep him current on events in the city, in Manitou, no matter how minor. This wasn't minor. He'd come in from the northern outpost with the news of intruders. The militia was on alert, but with snow falling, nothing was moving in the mountains. Even the wildlife had settled in.

"No," Rafe said. "If they were, I'd be able to sense some residual memory, see some reaction. There's nothing. As The Altered, they are uneducated, clueless. Something else is at play."

"Wade is keeping you from seeing them."

"He's the first one I noticed years ago. I'm not even certain this is him. It's feasible that they were sent out as a distraction while he tries to find a way in here. They might be unaware of their abilities, but they are far from harmless. When I walked into one of their police stations, I spoke with her at length about my reasons for passing through Montana. There was no recognition then or when I shot her and her partner last summer. They managed to kill two of my men."

"Would the Warlords send them here?"

Rafe didn't bother to respond to such an accusation.

"What if they had a spat?" Dark sarcasm. "Went at each other and this is the result."

"They might have turned on each other. Our kind has a tendency to do that," Rafe said, considering how that might have played out, in the snow and the dark, lost along the Front Range.

"Can you do something like that?" Murray asked. "Erase someone's memory?"

He ignored the question. It was irrelevant.

He took the hint, falling silent.

"Put them in a room together, see what happens," Trent, the other advisor, spoke up.

Rafe stopped for a moment, intrigued. "What do you think they'd do?"

"They'd go defensive, they'd fight," Trent said. "One would think you planted the other there. See which survives."

"Do you want me to throw a gun in the middle of the floor and let them brawl for it?" Rafe asked, a question loaded with disdain.

"If they're like the others, they'd fight," Murray agreed.

"You can't overlook that she's female," Trent scoffed. "That's unusual. Hell, she's the first one I've seen."

"It's unusual, yes," Rafe said. "But not unprecedented."

"Wade might notice that," Trent said.

"Physical appearance was the first thing they learned to manipulate when they started this little experiment in human engineering. As visually oriented as humans are, you don't think they'd let any of us be unpleasing to the eye, especially not the females," Rafe said.

"Not everyone is as degenerate as you," Murray told Trent.

"They could sit down and consider why they're here." Rafe did and had been for the past three hours since his patrols had discovered them. They'd been almost a hundred miles from each other. Brief questioning had revealed only that they had no memories.

"What do you want to do?" Trent asked.

"Let them sit," Rafe said. "Give them a chance for whatever this is to wear off." It could be a temporary effect or a drug-induced condition. "For now, I'm with Allen. Trent, you have instructions on

Wade. No sleep. Don't damage him. No internal injuries, no broken bones. Superficial only. Is that clear?"

"Keep him awake. Use the line of questions you've given me. No serious injuries."

"Are my directions clear?" Rafe repeated.

"Yes. Clear." Trent changed the subject. "Did The Sixth have a hand in this?"

"No," Rafe said.

"Why not?" Murray asked.

"Yates isn't there with them anymore. Not in Colorado, maybe not alive. That would put them in chaos and the last thing they'd do is make a move on me now. This is the Montana group, spurred on by Vance. The Warlords wouldn't dare."

"Then why are they still alive?" Trent asked.

"Because I want to know." Rafe didn't have a plan, but by morning he would.

"What?" Murray asked what they both wondered.

"Everything they know."

She sat in an old wooden chair, arms crossed, watching the sentries as intently as they were watching her. It unnerved them rather quickly, in her opinion. They didn't move from their positions near the door. They wouldn't make eye contact, either, but she sensed their confidence eroding away. With no sleep, her own nerves edged towards frayed. She didn't intend to let them see that, not that they could. Human, but not like her.

There was no way to tell how much time passed. She'd evaded them out in the wilderness until after nightfall. Falling from her horse left her bruised and sore; hungry, cold still. The only thing that was certain, if she fell asleep, she'd die.

He strode in, and for an instant, they all stared, the guards holding their breath. Tall, undetermined age, black hair, sharp features, and blue eyes, cold eyes. "Out," he spoke, and they retreated without a word. She sensed their relief as the door shut behind them.

Dragging another flimsy wooden chair from the table, he sat in front of her, silent, scrutinizing. She returned the look, holding her resolve.

Long minutes passed before he shifted, the shadow of a smile crossing his face. "The guards," he gave a brief nod towards the closed door. "You felt their uneasiness. I sense the same reaction from you."

She continued to watch him, fighting fatigue, digging fingernails into her palm.

"Your silence means nothing. We can sit here until daybreak. In time, you'll tell me."

"Tell you what? I have a few hours of today," she said.

"I'm certain there's a reason for your current condition. First, I'll tell you something. Your name is Shannon, and I've known you most of your life."

"It's not polite that you know my name, and I don't know yours."

"Rafe."

"We're acquaintances," she said, understanding it wasn't true even as she spoke, even if he told her it was.

"We've met."

"Met? Under what circumstances?"

"I won't divulge those details." She was more centered, more resolved, than he'd expected. "We're not friends. In fact, we're the opposite, even though you can't remember why at this moment. If the circumstances were right, we could become a great asset to each other. The catch is, it's up to you, not me."

Shannon took note he was wearing a sidearm. None of the guards had been, and that struck her as odd. They'd taken her handguns and knives, a healthy fear obvious. He didn't share that fear. "Why am I here?"

"In this room? I wanted to observe you without distraction. Determine if you can recover any memory. I want information, unfiltered and unbiased by outside influences."

Chapter Twenty-Two

She shook her head. "I told you, I remember nothing. Because you say a thing doesn't mean it's true, either."

"There are ways to push through memory loss, depending on the reasons for it." He stood.

She regarded him.

"Pain is one of those ways," he told her, emotionless.

"Fantastic," Shannon said, her tone as blank as his. "Other options?"

"Drugs I don't have access to. Time that neither of us has."

She felt an edge of uncertainty cut into her thoughts. "So you're going to what, torture me, and hope it brings back my memory?"

He got closer, close enough to make her want to fidget. "Not yet."

"I don't understand."

"You weren't the only lost wanderer we picked up out of the mountains yesterday," Rafe told her, stepping back. "Follow me."

She did, thinking it was the best course of action at this point. It was a short walk down the hall, and her legs seemed steadier than before. A good thing, in case she got the chance to run.

Two more sentries stood at each end, and they carried military rifles of some variety. Boarded up windows. Rafe took her by the arm as they moved to the last door on the left, into a larger version of the room they'd come from. Same faded walls, gray floor and dim light.

Four men occupied the room. Two of them had been beating a third while the last watched. They stopped, leaving him slumped in a chair as Rafe appeared.

He guided her to another chair, and she sat. The man next to her was bloody, conscious, and if she'd ever seen him before, she didn't have a clue.

"Do you recognize him?" Rafe asked.

He shook his head as she looked him over. "Don't answer anything."

"Shut up," one guard growled.

Rafe stared hard at the man. He backed out of the way without another word. "Do not interfere with their interactions again." Rafe continued, speaking to his prisoners, "One of you will answer me. I can promise that. You're far from the first strays I've dealt with. You can draw out your memory, if you want to badly enough." He gestured, and the guards resumed beating her counterpart.

"Threatening me won't get you what you want," she sneered, temper flaring.

He back-handed her, careful not to draw blood but with enough force to snap her head back and make her vision spin. "Let's try this again. Shannon, this is Wade. Am I correct?"

She glared at him, anger rather than fear.

Rafe slapped her again, open-palmed this time.

"You hit like a child," the man being beaten said, spitting blood on the floor. "Untie my hands and let's do this right."

"I don't need you jumping to defend me," Shan told him.

"Say that again after they bring out the cattle prod."

Rafe took a baton from a guard, swinging it until they both saw, understanding his intent. It wasn't a casual threat He moved, striking out at who he believed was Wade. His collarbone snapped, and he pitched forward onto the floor, struggling to get up for a moment before he passed out. "I can kill him," Rafe told her. "I can take days. It's up to you what happens next."

"What do you want from me?"

"I told you. When you remember, you'll know, and I'll know. Then we talk."

"This is a test, and I don't have the answers."

"We'll see," Rafe told her, gesturing for them to put him back in the chair. "I've had enough trouble with you. I'm done letting it go."

She had nothing to say.

"How about I have my sentry heat a blade? We don't want him to die, not today, not tomorrow. But an eye, he could lose an eye." One of his men took out a long, serrated blade, glinting light off it onto her face.

"Why in the hell would I tell you anything?"

"Because you're next," Rafe said. "After I take one of his eyes, I'm

Chapter Twenty-Two 341

going to take one of yours. When you can't scream anymore, you'll tell me anything I want."

Shan sprang up and the nearest guard grabbed her. Tried to grab her. She was faster and pivoted, putting an elbow in his solar plexus, spinning and kicking him in the face as another came at her. Attempting to slap the knife away from him didn't work, and he swung at her. Shan caught his arm, staying from in front of the weapon and kicked him twice in the gut. As he went down, she looked to see who else was close enough to strike out at.

Rafe was pointing his sidearm at her. "Are you finished?" he asked.

She stopped, dropping the knife she'd taken.

Rafe holstered the gun and held up the baton. Then he moved, a blur, striking her above the knee. Shan hit the floor, no chance to react, white-hot pain searing through her entire left side. She couldn't move or speak, curled up, tears running down her face and dripping onto the concrete.

He crouched next to her. "That's what I've been looking for. That's what we've tried to get him to do all night. Defend himself. Prove you are what I think you are," Rafe whispered to her, waiting for his men to get up. "You've bought yourself another day. I'll let you in on a little secret, too. Whichever one of you that remembers first wins. The other one gets a bullet in the brain."

When she came around, the room was dark. They were alone, lying on the concrete floor, and the man Rafe called Wade was unconscious. It took her a few minutes to get to her feet and look around, with the pain in her leg constant, but almost bearable. She surveyed their prison, checking every corner, every shadow, hoping to find a way out, aware of how unlikely it was. A fireplace sat on an inside wall, gray and dead, the room on the uncomfortable side of cold. There was a single window and a pair of doors, the window and outside door boarded up from the other side. It was past nightfall. Empty shelves, an empty table, two chairs. As she peered out the gap between two-by-fours nailed across the window, he groaned and swore.

"We're on the second floor. It's been snowing and looks like about a foot on the stairs," she told him. "A sentry too, from the tracks outside. Two guards are walking the hall every few minutes. Both doors are locked. There's an alarm on both, too. It's dark out."

He sat up with a groan. "Thanks for the weather report."

"You're hurt," she said. Her leg throbbed from the knee into her hip, but it was easing, as long as she didn't put her full weight on it. Not broken, at any rate. He was in obvious pain.

"Collarbone," he said. "Nothing to worry about now. Maybe a couple ribs, too."

"That's not good," she frowned.

"He baited you."

"You were almost one eye away from being a blind man," she came back, annoyed he'd seen it. "I'm not going to sit here and wait for them to come back and start again."

"Explain to me how you did that," he said, using a chair as support. "Beating two grown men."

She considered it for a few moments. "Damned if I know."

"He said his name is Rafe. Does that mean anything to you?"

"No. You?"

"Not a thing. He said I'm Wade and you're Shannon, as if it meant something revealing to me. He wasn't certain."

"He is certain who I am. We've met, but he wouldn't say how or why."

"Both of us are considering the other is lying. There's no working our way around that. First opportunity, we get out of here. We go our separate ways, but we go. They'll be expecting us to do something. How bad is your leg?"

"Nothing to worry about," she repeated what he'd said.

"We need to run."

"Then I'll run," she said. "Rafe said he plans to kill one of us soon. I don't think he intends to let either of us leave here. I have no clue where we are, or where we're supposed to be. The odds aren't good with any option."

"I think, anywhere is better than here. I'd rather deal with the elements than let Rafe get what he's looking for out of me," Wade said.

"What does he want?"

"You tell me."

"Stand by," Mac spoke on the radio to Taylor for what felt like the thousandth time. Every five minutes for the past twenty-two hours, save a brief rest when Parr had taken watch, he'd said the same thing.

The ground blind Mac occupied was overlooking the west end of the main thruway of the garrison. Parr and Quinlen were waiting somewhere farther up the mountain, in strategic positions. Noel at the east end, Hunter in the south, and Green was on the move and in radio silence.

"Got it," Taylor returned. "Weather check." Same answer.

"It's not snowing," Mac told him, end of the conversation. The blind wasn't quite tall enough for him to stand in, and there was no room to move. He wandered outside to stretch. It was cold, warmer since the sun had come up, but cold enough, it worried him. Every detail was a concern. Working around the storm had been tricky.

"Stand by, moving Team Six. Team Six, forward position and wait for further orders," he said, restless. In reality, only Quinlen was moving, getting ready to start a chain reaction that would put the entire valley on alert. Recon showed less than forty people in the camp, and an airstrip at the top of a ridge a mile north of him. Mac had made certain Green scouted it for himself before he moved on.

Two buildings that looked rebuilt, including barred windows, sat in the middle of the occupied zone. He was watching one, Noel the other. If nothing was happening, they'd make something happen. It appeared there were only a few people that might be civilians, a handful of women the night before, and no children. Mac pegged it as a military outpost. Taylor agreed. The actual town of several hundred was miles to the east, and not a concern.

Then Hunter said, "I've got movement northeast of me."

Mac had gotten comfortable but was up, peering through binoculars a moment later. "I want all eyes on," he told them. "Visual confirmation. Team Six, are you in place?"

"Affirmative," Quinlen answered.

"There are several people moving from the three-story brick," Noel reported. "I can't get a clear view. They're walking west on the main road." He was closer and couldn't take the chance of moving.

"I've got them on visual," Hunter said. Three of the group headed north onto a side street, while four continued on. "The group of four moving west are not any of our targets."

"Three heading towards me are not any of our targets," Mac said. He swore to himself. After a few more minutes, he told them, "Stand by." Then he swore some more. Come hell or high water, at midday he'd order Quinlen to fire grenades into the camp. Unless, of course, they verified targets before.

"Two coming out, north side three story," Noel said. "Not any of our targets."

"I've got a group, ten or more," Parr reported at the same time Mac saw movement at the east end.

"I cannot identify all of them," Noel said. "No ID."

"No ID," Parr confirmed.

Mac held his breath for a moment, heartbeat pounding in his ears.

"I've got Wade," Hunter said.

"Green, you're up," Mac told him. "Everyone move to their secondary positions."

"Verified visual on Wade," Noel called in as they moved in

different directions. "Wade is with the group milling around west of me. There are four hostiles with him, all armed."

"Allen?" Mac asked. Thinking he could stay objective had been a mistake. He needed to know.

"Maybe," Noel replied.

"She just came out of the same building with two more hostiles," Hunter said. "Confirmed visual on Wade and Allen."

"Confirmed visual on Wade and Allen," Noel repeated. "They don't appear to be restrained. Six hostiles present, seven more in the immediate area. All targets and hostiles are wearing winter camos."

"Taylor," Mac called him on the radio, not relieved but ready. It was time. "We have them both. Do it now." Then he headed for his secondary position.

The air-raid alarm at NORAD wailed to life for the first time in twenty years. Taylor let it run. They were fourteen miles away. He was in a secure position, and in charge.

"Quinlen," he ordered. "Fire at will."

Everyone in the camp stopped and peered skyward as the unknown noise grew into a siren echoing across the narrow valley.

"What in the hell?" one guard expressed all of their concerns.

Shannon reeled, unsteady. For an instant, she thought she might pass out, but she remembered all the things that were important for her to remember right then. All the things that would keep her alive. Dropping to one knee, she wound up to go.

Wade blinked, and moved. He slammed into the nearest guard, broken bones and all. It was Trent, and he didn't have the chance to put up a fight. West of them, a boarded-up storefront exploded, sending fiery debris in all directions.

As Wade tackled the man closest to him, Shan lunged forward, twisting away from the guard restraining her. She snatched a sidearm from his partner, who hadn't even started to react, and double-tapped both in one fluid motion.

"Down!" Wade barked, turning on the last three as she dropped. From somewhere above them, sniper fire took out two, and Wade got the third. He swung around to aim at Trent. The dazed man offered little resistance. They grabbed dropped weapons to arm themselves, Wade dragging Trent to a side street, Shan covering his back. The siren faded to an eerie silence.

"Now what?" she panted, shaking from the sudden influx of memory.

"We stick to the plan. You remember the plan?"

She nodded.

"You do what you're here for," Wade repeated, voice low. Rafe's people would be out in force, looking for them. They'd left the dead in the street and couldn't count on their snipers anymore. He handcuffed Trent, handing her a pair of confiscated blades. He kept a single one.

"Got it," she said, surveying their surroundings to line it up with the map she'd memorized.

"Don't take unnecessary risks."

A firefight broke out in the next block and they moved in opposite directions, Wade pushing Trent along and Shan heading back the way they'd come. She wanted to go towards the fighting, but she stuck to her goal, following a wide alleyway past the building where they spent the night. Moving in the knee-deep snow made progress slower than she liked, gunfire urging her on.

Then someone started shooting at her from the street. Return fire gave her enough cover to get around the next house, sliding to a stop and sitting down in the snow that had drifted along the building.

"Clear, at least for a minute," Parr told her. "I only got one of them. Are you hurt?"

"No," she said. "How are we doing otherwise?"

"Everything is on schedule," he said. "We need to find out where Rafe is and get ready to bail out of this backwater."

"I'm working on that," she agreed, standing to test her leg.

"We're on radio silence until we're not."

"Got it."

Chapter Twenty-Two

He knew it wasn't like her to have so little to say. "We're clear. Let's go."

Shan followed him, cutting across the main street. He directed her inside one of the abandoned houses, making sure no one was following. Green and Noel pointed AK-47s at them as they came through the door. "Clear," Noel said, turning his attention back to the street.

"Here. Body armor." Green gave her an equipment pack. "Wear it." She slipped it on and re-zipped her parka. "You need something bigger than a .45 to take out an entire camp of Nomads," he said, passing her an Uzi and extra ammo.

"Thanks," she said, slinging the weapon and pocketing the clips. "What's your status?"

"We're blocking the street to keep the area clear," Parr said. "Until we get new orders. Are we getting new orders?"

"Not from me. Taylor's in charge until..." Shan shrugged. "Hell, don't ask me. We should put him in charge and go on vacation. Somewhere warm, and not here." Not that she couldn't remember everyone's orders, she hadn't been told. Neither had Wade. The one person who set the final plans wasn't there right now. He was sneaking around near the airstrip. Mac knew, and he wasn't telling.

"Take it easy," Green said, seeing she was on edge. "Take a breath."

"I'm fine," she told him. "Heading for the armory."

"Both of you?" he questioned. "I don't like either of you being in the primary target zone, let alone both of you. There's no way to guarantee you'll be clear later."

"It's the only chance we have to draw him out," she said. "Keep moving, keep them guessing. This is almost over."

"There's a dead guy out back by the alley. We need to move," Parr said.

It took a few minutes to clear the next house. Boarded up for years, or decades, there was more dust than snow in this one. Green stopped her as the other two moved to the front to watch the street.

"Are you all right?"

She shook her head. "No. That was fucked up."

"Waking up with no memory? I imagine."

"And scary."

He nodded, letting her talk.

"Scary and fucked up," she repeated. "I never ever want to do that again."

Green wrapped an arm around her shoulders for a few moments. She was shaking. "You got this," he whispered.

"I do," she agreed. "Or at least, I will. We will."

There was gunfire, close. "That's not us," Noel called. "Not Quinlen. The Nomads are sweeping the main street."

"They can't decide where we are," Green said. "They're trying to flush us out."

"I've got to get east, now that I can shoot back," Shan said.

"Be careful," Green said.

"If I can," she answered. "Wade gave orders to watch over me. Disregard. Make sure Mac is clear. Make sure he gets up the mountain."

"We're you supposed to tell me that now, as part of our timetable?"

"Yes. That's all I've got, and I don't know what it correlates to. I hope you do."

He couldn't tell her he did.

A swarm of Nomads converged on the dead-end street, and all of them were pointing weapons at her. Shan looked for a quick escape, knowing they were under orders to bring her back alive.

"Stop," the nearest yelled, waving the AK at her as if she hadn't seen it already.

She did, holding up the .45. They relieved her of her guns, and she silently swore when they found both knives. Boot sheathes weren't all that concealed.

"We've got her," he reported on a handset.

"Bring her to the Quartermaster's," Rafe told him. "If she tries to escape again, shoot her and I don't mean in the knee."

Shan didn't fight or flee.

"Welcome back," Rafe told her in a tone that made her blood turn to ice. "I expected you to try something ill-advised, and you didn't disappoint. Tell me, did you put a lot of thought into it, or just spur of the moment? If that was your best, I'm disappointed." He held a bloody knife. It was a threat. "Bringing in what, a dozen people to take me?"

"Once we took the armory, everything else would be easy," she said, defiant.

"Now you remember. What was your trigger? The siren or something completely subtle, like a fucking avalanche?"

"I'm still missing blocks of memory. Your guess is as good as mine."

"Interesting," Rafe observed, circling her. "How many people and how many Altered?"

"What is 'altered'?"

"The Altered. What you and I and Wade are. Not human, not quite. Laboratory created beings meant for things better than this. The arrogance and ignorance of humans has led us here. Despite that, you want to protect them."

"I won't help you."

"Of course you will," he said, as if it were obvious. "You told me the armory was a target."

"There are a dozen men standing in the street," she pointed out, voice ratcheting up a notch. "You already knew."

"Did Vance mention I can see other Altered, or did he let you come in here blind?" He sheathed the blade after wiping it clean. "I think, the latter, because that's how he works. Pretends he's helping while he sets you up for a fall."

"I'm done talking."

"I can still hurt you, Shannon. You can block out pain, at least for a time. How tough are you? We're going to find out." He grabbed the collar of her parka and jerked her along beside him to an interior room.

There was a reason no more grenades had been going off. Quinlen lay on the floor, unconscious. There was blood, not a lot, but enough.

"Human," Rafe pointed at the motionless Guardian. "Not very talkative, either. Usually they are." He shrugged, gauging her reaction. "Let's see how the next one does." He took a set of old metal handcuffs off a rusted table, clamping one end around her right wrist and the other to a re-bar U protruding from the wall. The table held a variety of edged weapons. It was out of her reach.

Murray dragged in the next prisoner. Hunter. They left him on the floor next to Quinlen.

Shan didn't react, didn't blink. She waited, surveying the room. Three doors, a staircase up and a pair of tall windows with open shutters. She tried not to consider it, but they were far from the first of Rafe's enemies to be brought to this room. There was an underlying sensation, something like a foul odor, and it invaded all her senses.

Rafe showed her the cattle prod, letting her get a good look at it before he hit Hunter with a jolt to the back. It brought him around, fighting to get away. He passed out after a few seconds, still again. Quinlen's reaction to the sudden shock was to regain consciousness, screaming.

He turned. "So you're aware," and hit her in the same place he'd struck with the baton.

Someone threw cold water on her. Shan came up trying to fight, still handcuffed to the wall. She hadn't lost consciousness, but close enough to put her on the floor. Quinlen had stopped screaming.

"This can go on for days. How many Altered?" Rafe continued.

"One," she growled at him. "A hundred."

"One?" he laughed. "There's you and Wade, at least. That is Wade, yes?"

"I thought you could see other Altered."

"Now that he has his memory back, I'll recognize him. I knew you by eyesight because we've met."

"In July," Shan said.

"Not for the first time. If this is Wade, and it is, he's figured out how to avoid that ability of mine. I'll have to ask him where he learned the trick. It wasn't an accident, but it was recent."

She looked disinterested.

Rafe took the knife out. "He needs to join us."

Wade stopped, pale. Dehydrated, broken bones, no sleep, none of that caused the wave of nausea. He put a hand on the wall to steady himself.

"What?" Noel asked, hefting an AK-47.

"We need to step it up. He's torturing them."

Noel didn't ask who.

Shannon dry-heaved until she couldn't anymore and then sat there, eyes closed, shaking.

"You're going to watch," the Nomad standing closest to her spat, dragging her up by a handful of hair. She jabbed at him with her left hand, breaking his nose, and kicked him hard in the stomach. Her aim was off. He went down. "You bitch, I'll cut you until you bleed to death," he wheezed.

"Not 'bitch', one of The Altered," Rafe reminded him, all of them. No sympathy. "That's what happens when you get within striking distance. I warned you. No one retaliates, no one touches her." He brought the cattle prod around and jolted her, just for a moment. Shan's knees buckled. "Except me. It's much more intense when the other subject is like us," he told her. "You'll experience that as soon as they catch up with Wade."

"I won't feel a thing," she answered weakly.

Rafe looked amused. An explosion somewhere off the main road rocked the building, the rafters creaking and dust falling like a curtain. "That's not a grenade. Your friends have mortars, perhaps." He regarded her for a few moments. "I'm moving this to the armory and sealing it up," he told Murray. "More room, more secure. Bring her along once I radio you. Kill the men first." He motioned for the sentry whose nose she'd broken to accompany him out.

Four others stayed behind with Murray. She waited, watching the door close, giving Rafe a few moments. "Do you think I'm so dangerous it takes five of you to walk me across the street?"

"Yes," Murray said. "I do. He doesn't, but Wade is still out there."

"Let me go," Shan put to him. "And when this is over, I'll give you the city. I have no use for it." She saw the words catch his attention. The others looked skeptical. All had a dangerous fear of Rafe, that much was clear.

"What about them?" he meant the men on the floor. Hunter and Quinlen.

"I don't remember them. Hell, I might not have ever met them before," she said, knowing Hunter was listening. What he didn't hear, the cautious footsteps outside, and he was about to do something brash.

"You don't have the city. I'll do what I was told."

"No, wait," Shan barked, more for Hunter than Murray, giving a sideways glance towards the rear door.

The Nomads flew into action, raising weapons, and Murray drew his sidearm. Shan ducked for cover. Nothing happened. She started laughing, using her free hand to cover her mouth.

Murray pointed the gun at her and strode forward, intending to hit her, orders or not. "You're fucking crazy," he said, drawing back. He never got to follow through.

Vistans burst from upstairs, and one of the side doors leading from the cellar. They opened fire, short and accurate bursts. She clamped her hands over her ears, eye squeezed shut, the sound deafening in the small room. When it stopped and she looked again, the Nomads were dead and a pair of Vistans were clearing the rest of the floor.

"Can you walk?" Green asked, helping her up and examining the cuffs. Parr was checking on Hunter and his partner.

"No choice," she said. "Key?"

Green produced his own. "Standard on most of these old metal ones. Are you hurt?"

"Not so much. How are we doing?"

"I can't tell. Focus, Shan."

She nodded, putting an arm around his neck to steady herself as he unlocked the cuffs.

Hunter struggled up off the floor, helping Parr.

"He needs a doctor," Shan whispered to Green, glancing at Quinlen. He acknowledged.

"We need to go," Parr said, handing her a .380. "Stop losing so many guns."

Shan smiled and nodded. "I'll work on that. Clips?"

"None."

She retrieved Murray's .45 from beneath the table, where it had fallen. "Take point, Capt. Green. Can you take the rear?" she asked Hunter.

"Got it," he said. "Thanks for the warning."

"I couldn't just sit there and let you put yourself in the line of fire."

Outside, they crept around the back. "I'm supposed to evac you out in the Cessna, drop in to NORAD to pick up your brother and head for Estes Park. Or Cody. Whichever place I determine," Green told her. That meant Cody.

"When we get Rafe."

"When Cmdr. Wade or Cmdr. MacKenzie says so," he made his orders clear.

"As it stands," she whispered to them as they made their way west. "We should be ready to take the armory. By that I mean chuck ordnance in there and incinerate the place. We have the recon we came here for."

"We're set to meet with other team members at a couple of checkpoints and watch their backs while they engage." Green knew where. They couldn't ease up yet. It was late afternoon, and they'd start losing light soon. He got them to their rendezvous point.

They'd dug into an old storefront and set up barricades out of the furnishings. There were a pair of M-249 machine guns set up and aimed at the street through a slat.

"That's subtle," Shan noted.

"I'm past being subtle today," Green told her. Shan looked like a ghost. Hunter was the walking wounded, but he'd at least gotten Quinlen stabilized and both stitched up. Green knew she'd gone in on purpose, and she could handle it. The pair of Guardians getting caught wasn't part of the plan. Mac wasn't aware, and he wouldn't be until after it was over.

"Sit down and rest for a few," he told her. She did.

"Now you're listening to people?" Hunter asked, sitting on the floor next to her.

"He's medical."

"So am I, and you told me to jump off a cliff the night we took off out of The Vista."

"That was different."

"How so?"

"We don't have another choice now," she said.

"Are you hurt?"

"I felt everything, the cattle prod, the blades, the beatings. So, yes and no."

"Can't you block out things like that?" Hunter understood little about her abilities, but he was sure she'd said that more than once.

"I can," she told him. "That would have defeated the purpose of getting and occupying Rafe's attention. He thinks we want the armory, the city. He doesn't realize we're here to kill him."

"Wade sent you in as bait," he said, anger flaring. "I fucking knew it."

"I volunteered, Hunter. Remember that later, when you lie on a report about what happened."

"There had to be some other way."

"What?" she asked.

He shook his head. Even if he thought of another way, she listened to Wade before anyone else.

"Understand that I don't remember these things the way you might think. After, it's like watching one of your old movies, not that it happened to me. It didn't."

"They're overrunning our primary," Green interrupted, listening on his headset. "We have to go now. Parr, stay with your partner."

"The fuck you say," Quinlen said, struggling to his feet. "Let's finish this."

Chapter Twenty-Three

Jan 9 afternoon Manitou Springs

Their primary staging area was forty-one hundred feet from the armory, due west, high in a tree line. Clear line-of-sight but hidden, or so they'd thought. Somewhere across the valley, a video monitor had picked up the Vistans' movement. A dozen Nomads made their way up the mountainside, and the flaw became obvious.

Green's group made slower progress than any of them wanted, with drifting snow impeding even the uninjured. They were all feeling the effects of fatigue, cold, and various injuries. Quinlen was keeping pace.

Close gunfire sent them scrambling for cover. Shannon found herself staring up at the cold gray sky again and she couldn't move, blink, or even call for help.

She hadn't moved, either. Hunter grabbed her, pushing her off the trail. It took him a few seconds to realize she didn't see him. Her gaze was fixed, unfocused. Knowing she couldn't have fallen asleep, he slapped her.

Green glanced over to see what was happening. Shan curled

Chapter Twenty-Three

forward, putting out a hand to keep from falling face-first into the snow. Something not good, he decided. They were two miles from the Cessna.

She gasped, looking around for a moment, and snatching the headset Hunter wore. "Wade's down, Wade's down, Wade's down." Looking at Hunter, she shook her head, dizzy and nauseous. "It's bad. We have to go right now."

"Go," Green told Parr and Quinlen, ushering them on ahead. "Capt. Allen, do you want to head for the airfield?" The word to evac might happen at any moment.

Shan shook her head, getting back to her feet. "Wild horses," she told him.

Hunter had a questioning look as she took the lead.

"Wild horses," Green repeated. "Couldn't drag her away."

Hunter followed her. It was his job, and he'd have been right there, even if it wasn't. She went in, both guns drawn. They'd gotten another M-249 set up on its bi-pod before the Nomads found them. It was the smaller of the armaments they'd carried for a hundred and fifty miles. Wade and Noel were both down. "Cover," Hunter warned, seeing intruders. She dove forward, rolling, the heavy snow stopping her sooner than she anticipated. Hunter was firing back, standing in the open like he had good sense.

It only took her a heartbeat to understand Noel was beyond help. Focus, she reminded herself.

"Shan," Green yelled. "Move it."

"Shannon," Hunter echoed, rounds popping in the snow close to both of them. She scrambled for Wade. "Cover her," he called out, trying to do the same. If there was a sniper–and it looked that way to him–she'd be the target.

Wade was alive. He'd taken at least one hit, high in the chest, under the edge of his body armor. Green caught up with them and she moved back, letting him try to stabilize Wade. He was bleeding profusely, a bright spray in the snow, breath labored.

"Get on the radio with him," Wade rasped, fighting to stay

conscious. "Confirm his position." He'd been attempting to when the Nomads found them.

She took the handset, trying to figure out of something to say.

"Focus," Hunter snapped at her, afraid she'd go catatonic like she had at The Junction. Then they'd all be dead.

"Shan," Wade managed. "Vance said Rafe has stockpiles. Nukes."

"Here?" she asked.

"Try to find out if and where. See his lies, or see the truth. You've done this before. Make sure he's in the armory. If he's not, you know what you have to do."

She nodded, ducking inside the blind, glad he'd kept that bit of information to himself until now. "I was told you have warheads here," she spoke to Rafe. Recalling the sensation of Mac's heartbeat stopping, Shan was aware Rafe would sense it. She was counting on it.

"Of all the things you could say right now, that's not something I considered," Rafe answered.

"When I was nine, you detonated a Minutemen ICBM almost in my backyard. How did you override the guidance system?"

"If I explained it to you, I doubt you'd understand the logistics. A simple version, an ability the Wildblood don't possess - I visualized the launch code."

"Kaden told me a lot more about you than Vance." It caught his attention; she felt his surprise. She also sensed Rafe wasn't afraid of her, didn't consider either of them an actual threat, but an inconvenience. Kaden elicited an unusual response.

"Too bad about Wade," he said. "I could have used him, his abilities. What are you going to do now? Your options seem rather limited."

"Not your concern."

"I can call my men back, change their orders. I need eyes in Vance's operation. Just say the word. You can't trust The Sixth, little girl. They're unpredictable, undisciplined, the Wildblood, and they are dangerous."

That word again. Wildblood. He meant her, he meant Wade. "You're a Sixth."

"You can't trust The Sixth."

"Tell me about the missiles."

"Let's see if this means anything to you. The government got forty-some launched during the last day of the war, which was also the first day of the war," Rafe told her. "Most were intercepted and destroyed before they could detonate. It was less than one percent of what they had. I started stockpiling everything within the year, all over the western areas of the continent. What do you think, Shannon?"

"I think I'd like to kill you."

"Persistent, I'll give you that. Do you want me to tell you something that will make you lie awake at night?"

"No."

"I'm not alone out here. Neither are you."

"Where are you?" she asked.

"I'm safe. You never will be."

Armory, she sensed, getting a crystal clear image from Rafe. "Cmdr. MacKenzie. Now," she said on the second handset, keying them both. "That is Wade with me," she verified. "You didn't 'get him'. We wanted you to think you did. We are Vista Security, and everything we've done in the past thirty hours was to make you believe you won. Do you know what 'checkmate' means?"

The TOW anti-tank missile fired from a position opposite them, across the valley. Mac launched the second moments later as the first struck, sending a brilliant fireball into the darkening sky. The second penetrated the bunker. Most of the explosion was contained, tearing through interior areas, incinerating everything. When it reached the armory, the multiple detonations ripped away the face of the mountain, causing dozens of avalanches on nearby slopes.

Shan emerged to stare at the destruction. The missile launch had scattered the remaining Nomads.

"Geiger Counter?" she asked.

"No unusual radiation spike," Mac reported. "I'll check again before we go."

"Now you can ask where Mac is," Green told Hunter. "Shan. Shannon."

She looked at them, blinking like she'd just woke.

"We have to evac now," Green told her. "We've got two critical." There were still, covered forms in the snow as well.

"Parr took fire covering us. He's gone, Noel is gone," Hunter told her.

"We can't leave them here, like this," she said. Later, in private, she would mourn.

"I'll bring some men back and give them a proper burial," Green promised her. "Right now, we need to get Wade and Quinlen to the plane and a hospital. I can't deal with a chest wound and blood loss out here."

She was out of adrenaline, running on automatic. The men made a travois from the blind while Shan dismantled the machine gun and stashed it. Some Nomads had left their horses behind. Two miles didn't seem so bad after that.

It was dark before they got those two miles behind them. Green tranked Shan the moment he got her to sit down.

"Why in the hell did you do that?" Hunter questioned, buckling her into a back seat of the Cessna.

"Wade is critical. I wanted her out, drugged, because it will keep her clear. I don't know what it would do to her if I lose him when they are in contact, or whatever you want to call it."

Hunter nodded, understanding. "You ever fly at night?"

"Yeah, in the summer, around Sheridan, where I've flown hundreds of hours." Green pulled no punches. "Make sure you're secured back there. We're going to be cutting it close on the fuel."

Chapter Twenty-Four

Jan 15 morning Estes Park

"Have you been sitting there for days?" Wade murmured, groggy, painkillers wearing off.

"We've been running shifts," Shan told him, curled up in an overstuffed chair, resting her head on an arm, wrapped in a blanket so only her face was visible. "I drew the short straw and get to be here to have a scintillating conversation with you when you're half asleep."

"You're the one half asleep."

"True. I'm not even sure what day it is."

"Me either. I talked with Mac and Taylor earlier. It was still dark, so maybe today."

"You all conspired to not include me."

"Conspired to let us heal. Are you discharged?"

"I got cut loose three days ago."

"What are you doing here, then?"

"Watching you sleep." She sat up, looking like she'd been doing the same. It was still her job to keep him safe, and where they were wasn't safe. "The alternative is to go to our quarters and be bored there."

"I've got a few things to occupy your time. What do you have to do to get a decent meal?"

"I leave an order. They gave up trying to send me away, and bring me whatever I ask for," Shan admitted, moving to the edge of the bed, holding on to him for a long time.

"Mac insisted on not waking you. We both know your aversion to hospitals." He got back to the topic at hand. She favored her left leg. He'd been listening to her walk down the hall to his room several times a day, even if he hadn't been conscious.

"Did he tell you about the mess we made?"

"He gave me a list of damages and said you'd fill me in. We did what we came here to do, but it cost us." They both contemplated that for a while, knowing it could have been any of them. "How are you doing?" he asked, sitting up slow.

"Better. Five days is a pretty damned good recovery time, for the record. I mean you, not me. I'd go back to my room and stay in bed for another week, for real, if we didn't have certain issues." She smiled, but there was that look. "Mac picked Taylor up out of NORAD because Green brought you and Quinlen right here. We have two airplanes, courtesy of Rafe. They were tactically acquired."

"Did you think you'd get rid of me that easy?"

"For a few minutes, I wasn't worried. Then we started losing people."

"I'm sorry it had to be you giving orders. It should have been me."

"Any of us, but there I was. It was surreal."

"I understand what you mean." And he did, more than what a simple statement could express.

Mac knocked on the door and let himself in. "I didn't expect you to be here so early," he told Shan, getting a cup of coffee from a carafe he'd brought last visit and taking a seat.

"Stir crazy," she admitted, ecstatic that they were together. For a brief time, it was all that mattered.

Chapter Twenty-Four

"She hasn't left," Wade said. "Make sure she gets to our quarters and sleeps in a proper bed tonight. With our guards posted."

Mac nodded. "Consider it done." They were being discreet again, so Vance didn't pick up on Mac or his actual status.

"There will be an extensive debriefing," Wade went on. "We have to get our stories to verify each others, but have enough variants we don't sound rehearsed. Manitou Springs never happened. Simple explanations that don't leave us open to questions. Council and Command get the same reports. We'll work out the details later."

"No one is going to tell them the number of Nomads we crossed. Cody Security has its own secrets," Mac agreed, already thinking about those details.

"You're supposed to be in Cody, and I'm AWOL. Command is going to see it that way. We've told Council to stuff their rules. They'll look for a way to retaliate. We give them fewer chances of digging a hole to throw us in." Wade had dealt with them before. He would again.

"They understand we figured out they lied us to," Mac said. "You think they'll just let it go?"

"What choice do they have?" Shan asked.

"They can't take Cody from us," Wade said. "Command is going to go a long way in making these issues go away. When this is done," he shook his head. "They'll still go after someone, even if it's keeping up appearances. We won't let it be junior officers."

"Your position is vital; mine isn't," Shan said. "My rank means nothing. Let me step up."

"Us," Mac corrected. "She's right. Vista Security titles mean nothing in Cody. Council wanted to break up the team almost from the beginning, and Command has been..."

"Wary," Shan said.

"You have to wonder why, don't you?" Wade said, putting the idea out. They knew, they always had.

"Not anymore."

"Command backs us for a reason. They put us in our positions for a reason," Shan said. "Past and present, some of them are like us."

"Makes sense," Mac said.

"If the situation arises, I'll name names."

"Not now," Mac said. "Because we all have suspicions, and we're all probably right."

"What are we going to do now that we're out here in the world?" Shan asked them.

"Mac is going back to Cody. I've got no problem with the base being his. We need to find if someone is leaking information back to The Vista," Wade said. "And why we didn't know about it sooner."

"I'm getting a refueling station set up in Casper. That will make travel time from here to Cody six hours in clear weather." Mac told his plans for air travel. "Seven pilots in the 'Conda and another eleven civilian ones. No idea how many are training."

"How far is The Vista from Cody?" she asked.

"By air, in the right weather, four or five hours."

"So, in ten hours, we could be home?"

Mac nodded.

"When are we going to go back and stand in front of Command and Council?" Shan asked, knowing they had to.

"Yeah," Mac said. "Put some closure to this."

"When they insist," Wade said.

"I can handle that. After the past few days, I can handle that," Shan said.

"We," Mac repeated. "Try to remember that. You're never alone."

"Because of Vance, but more, because of The Sixth, some of us are staying here. Shan has a connection with Kaden and we can use it. We have to find out what's going on. When I say 'we', I mean Team Three or Cody Security. We can't say anything to them, but we can find what else they've hidden from us."

"Who are you going to enlist for that?"

"Green and Ballentyne are perfect. They're untouchable. A few of our 'Conda officers might back out when we tell them we're

Chapter Twenty-Four

moving operations to Cody and Casper. Not a problem. We'll get established, even if it takes more time."

"What about Hunter?" Mac asked.

"I told him about his family in Angelfire. He's going to ask whichever one of you wants to be in charge for permission to go south this spring," Shan said. "In case he doesn't get the chance, I told him he had permission."

"Has he asked you to go with him?"

She shook her head. "No. He won't, I told him not to. There are a lot of reasons." The obvious reason was sitting there, getting ready to have breakfast. She knew how she felt about Mac, and that their relationship had to have limits. Hunter might be a part of her future. Time would tell.

"I plan on a debriefing with all of us tomorrow. One thing we need to make clear: zero trust in Vance." Wade wanted to share his plans.

"Tomorrow is a little ambitious."

Wade understood what she meant. "It is."

"Nightmares."

"I can take the edge off, take the memories you don't want."

It was how they'd bluffed Rafe, by blocking each other's memories, not knowing if it would work. "I'll think about it. I can do the same for you. If Kaden hadn't drawn out that bit of memory you'd messed with, I don't know how we'd have gotten to Rafe."

"We already had the idea," Wade said. "Whatever you decide. Anytime."

"I need the memories of all this. What are we going to do in Colorado for a year?" she asked. It seemed like a long time.

"Find out about the trade routes and clans disrupting them. Do a Sweeps run." He threw a few ideas around.

"A Sweeps run to where?" Mac asked.

Wade smiled. "I understand Texas has quite a few established villages. A starting place."

"Texas. We need to consult Kaden before we step foot anywhere," Shan said.

"Be careful who you trust."

"I didn't say I trusted him."

"You're both right, though," Mac offered. "Rumor has it we're not welcome in Texas."

"Rumors," Shan said. "Start with Texas and keep our options open."

"Ask that question you've been holding on to," Wade directed at Mac.

"Do you think Rafe is dead?"

"He started blocking me about half a second before the first missile hit. Now, I've got nothing," Shan said. "Rafe is dead. I don't enjoy guessing, but he was in the armory. No doubt. There's a difference between actual memory and forced perspective. I'd see it, if there was a deception."

"You'd sense if he fake it."

"That's what I said."

"When Green goes back, a team will go with him, clear out any stragglers, and check the armory. Mac will get a sense, too." Wade wanted to go, but it wasn't possible yet.

"We'll go in a few days, or in a week. We'll take our time," Mac said. "The three of us. Stay overnight and scout the area. We need to do this."

"Yeah," Shan agreed.

Wade did, too. "Good idea," he said. "Shan, you get to tell Vance we're going out there. He's learned it's pointless to argue with you."

"I'd rather you get someone else to do it, but I've learned it's pointless to argue with you."

"No, you haven't," Mac grinned. She never had, she never would.

"At some point, we need to discuss this 'wildblood' designation," Wade brought it up. "We all heard Rafe. Another thing Vance failed to mention. Be discreet, get in the media center, see if there's any mention. I don't want to confront him."

"When Rafe said it, he meant us," Shan said. "Kaden knows, and he'll tell us his version."

"Again, caution. Everyone, including us, has ulterior motives."

"I believed when this was over, we wouldn't be a team anymore," Shan confessed the thing that bothered her. "Was I wrong?"

It was Wade's call, his decision.

"You were wrong."

~end of Book 1~

For More

For more -

The Wildblood Series

Backlash: Prequel to The Wildblood

Trilogy 1

The Vista: Book 1 of The Wildblood
Renegades: Book 2 of The Wildblood
Bloodlines: Book 3 of The Wildblood

novellas

Outliers: Team Two
Outliers: Texas

More to come!

In case you missed it -

Backlash: Prequel to The Wildblood
Introducing Team Three

Facing an unknown adversary that threatens to wreak havoc across what little humanity remains, they must rely on their unusual abilities, and hope they're strong enough to stop the chaos.

The first to join Security, **Mac** is the outsider despite knowing he's as different as his partners. All three are Gen En, genetically enhanced, and he understands it's not a safe thing to be.

Wade is their unofficial leader. Few people outside the team have his trust, making him seem difficult and distant. He's protecting everyone by hiding what they are.

As the Scout, **Shannon** keeps watch on the long-abandoned roadways. This gives her time to consider what might exist beyond Montana. More curious than afraid, she wants to see for herself.

Together, they are unstoppable. Their enemies are gathering.

And next -

Renegades: Book 2 of The Wildblood

Uncontrollable. Unpredictable. Dangerous. The Wildblood.
Now, Team Three know what they are.

Renegades takes up with Team Three out among clans of the Altered, and cities where civilization has held ground.
One of the most pressing obstacles turns out to be their own governing council, a threat as real and treacherous as the Nomads of

the outlands. Unwilling to confront those issues, they scatter along The Front Range of the Rocky Mountains to establish who are allies, and who are not.

It's only a matter of time before the team is forced to face the consequences of their actions, and of a war none of them remember.

What would you do to protect your home?

Bloodlines: Book 3 of The Wildblood

Learning the truth about the Altered, and the legacy of The Vista, is the first priority of Team Three. It may earn them exile from their home. They know this. **Failure is not an option.**

Loyalty has its price. So does revenge. Someone has to pay.

Also by S. A. Hoag

On another world, in another time, there is -

Tau Scorpii: The Myth of SolTerra

Left to live or die on their own, scattered Terran clans struggle against the elements, other species, and each other. They don't know how or why they're on Sedna, but they are. It's about to get even more difficult to survive. The weather is changing, and no one knows what's next. A group of warriors must make peace with each other while looking for clues to their past. The alternative is extinction.

About the Author

S. A. Hoag is an author, artist, amateur astronomer ("I just look at the stars, I can't tell you their names."), hockey fan, and accidental desert-dweller. Born in the middle of the Rocky Mountains of Colorado, she has lived in a number of cities, in a number of states, and is off on another adventure when not writing or painting. Science Fiction has always been her first interest in reading and writing. Many other genres sneak into the novels and that's all right with her.

www.topazo8.com